Dear Reader,

It's that time of year again! Happy holidays to you all—and a very special thanks to those of you who have joined Silhouette Books at Christmas for the past seven years.

Silhouette's Christmas collection is a wonderful tradition that many people share. Authors provide the "main course" of the banquet, but countless others provide the trimmings—editors, artists, designers, marketers, typesetters, proofreaders, printers—the list could go on and on. So to our guests, let me say: sit down, get comfortable and prepare to enjoy this holiday feast!

Begin by letting four-year-old Joni Madison work her magic on you, as well as on the surly, taciturn man she and her single mother meet. In "Joni's Magic" talented Mary Lynn Baxter has created a truly touching tale of Christmas enchantment.

Then, let Sondra Stanford's "Hearts of Hope" fill *your* heart with hope. This is a delightful tale of a lonely elementary schoolteacher who decides to brighten her home with a giant Christmas tree. When her student's handsome dad helps trim the tree to fit, love tucks itself into their lives, too.

And who can resist Santa Claus? You'll enjoy meeting Timothy Holt, a shy marketing consultant, who is able to woo his lady love far more effectively wrapped in a Santa suit in Marie Ferrarella's charming fable "The Night Santa Claus Returned."

Finally, Jeanne Stephens's "Basket of Love" proves that love can come when you least expect it. Working together to bring the holiday spirit to those less fortunate than themselves, two people touched by tragedy find the healing power of giving and the miracle of love in this moving story.

May love and the joy of giving find a place in your life, as well, this season.

All the best,

Isabel Swift
Editorial Director

D0034352

Silhouette CHRISTMAS

Stories
1992

Mary Lynn Baxter
Sondra Stanford
Marie Ferrarella
Jeanne Stephens

Silhouette® Books

Published by Silhouette Books New York

America's Publisher of Contemporary Romance

SILHOUETTE BOOKS
300 East 42nd St., New York, N.Y. 10017

Silhouette Christmas Stories 1992
Copyright © 1992 by Silhouette Books

JONI'S MAGIC
Copyright © 1992 by Mary Lynn Baxter

HEARTS OF HOPE
Copyright © 1992 by Sondra Stanford

THE NIGHT SANTA CLAUS RETURNED
Copyright © 1992 by Marie Rydzynski-Ferrarella

BASKET OF LOVE
Copyright © 1992 by Jeanne Stephens

ISBN: 0-373-48236-1

First Silhouette Books printing November 1992

CONTENTS

JONI'S MAGIC

Mary Lynn Baxter

Recipes from Mary Lynn Baxter:

APRICOT SNACKS

Dried apricots
Cream cheese
Pecan halves

Spread dab of cream cheese on dried apricot and top with pecan half. Chill in the refrigerator and serve.

YUMMY HOT CORN CASSEROLE

6.9 oz box Chicken Rice-A-Roni (Prepared according to directions)
10.5 oz can cream of celery soup
11 oz can Green Giant Mexicorn (Use 22 oz if more is desired)
8 oz jar Kraft jalapeno Cheez Whiz

Mix all ingredients, place in a 2½ quart casserole and bake at 350°F. about 30 minutes.
Alternate: To minimize spicy taste, use Kraft Cheez Whiz without the jalapeno peppers.

Chapter One

Lacy Madison smiled as she stared at the stacks of brightly jacketed books on the check-in counter. Her idea to set up a hardback rental section had proved a huge success. The shop's entire business was increasing daily, and she couldn't be happier, especially as Christmas Day was fast approaching.

Humming to the tune of "It's Beginning To Look Like Christmas," Lacy reached for the top book, a nonfiction bestseller, one she hoped to read soon. She stole a moment and indulged herself, leaning against the counter and thumbing through the pages.

She was nearly at the end when she came across the envelope. Frowning, she examined it. It was an American Express bill that had been opened, but the owner's name wasn't visible. She extracted the contents, then watched as a folded piece of stationery fluttered toward the floor.

"Oops," Lacy muttered, trying to trap the pink sheet between her fingers.

When she failed, she bent, picked it up and scanned the contents. Color shot into her cheeks. The letter was personal—written to a new customer in her shop. Lacy had never met the mysterious Boothe Larson, but Sue, her part-time help had. Sue had labeled him a "hunk," only to add quickly that he was surly and close-mouthed.

Lacy could identify with wanting to keep quiet. After two years, she was still trying to put distance between herself and her painful past. She'd thought she had had the best of everything years earlier when she'd married a bright, young executive, even though she hadn't known him long.

Maybe she'd been looking for something new, something challenging in her life. She had gone through four years of college and still hadn't known what she wanted to do. She'd worked as a legal secretary in a large corporation, but had hated it. Artistic by nature, Lacy liked working with her hands. But her parents, before their untimely death in an auto accident, thought that foolish, drilling into her that the only way to make it in this world was to have a steady job that paid well.

Lacy saw her marriage as that new challenge she craved. For the first few years, she was happy. But then her husband didn't get the promotion at work he thought he deserved and began drinking. He turned mean. Lacy's life and that of their daughter soon became unbearable.

Desperate to leave town and start a new life, Lacy answered a request by an old friend of her mother's with whom Lacy had kept in touch. The woman wanted someone to manage and eventually buy her bookshop in a small resort town. Lacy hadn't hesitated.

And she hadn't been disappointed. Camden, Arkansas, had proved to be heaven on earth. The town was the center of a rustic resort area in the wild and beautiful Ozark Mountains. The entire region was an artist's dream. Magnificent pine and hardwood trees shaded streams with enough black bass and bream to whet any angler's dream. And fishermen with families meant money.

Once she was settled, Lacy had put her artistic talent to use and learned to work with glass, transforming it into lamps. Small odd-shaped lamps, cut and molded by her loving hands became her specialty.

Now Lacy was determined to sell those lamps to various department stores in order to earn enough money to purchase the shop. She paused in her thoughts and with burgeoning pride took in her surroundings. The shop, rich with her own touch, was both quaint and adorable. Antique bookcases and secretaries held her hard- and soft-cover books. Interspersed among them were the lamps that would eventually garner the money needed to meet her goal.

"Mommy!"

Her daughter's lilting voice drew Lacy sharply back to the moment at hand. She shook her head, then realized she still clutched the envelope in her hand. She eased it into her pocket. "In here, darling."

Although she had been up for hours, Lacy had left Joni asleep in their upstairs apartment. Lacy glanced at her watch and saw that it was nine o'clock. With the shop due to open at ten, she'd be hard-pressed to get all the books checked in.

Joni rounded the corner, dressed adorably in a red jogging suit that Lacy had laid on the foot of the bed. The top had a Santa's head painted on the front.

Lacy smiled and opened her arms. "Hi, sweetie." Joni ran to her, flung her arms around Lacy's neck and hugged her. Lacy returned the hug. "Did you sleep okay?"

"Uh-huh," Joni said, beginning to fidget.

"How about some cereal?" Lacy smoothed her daughter's riotous curls, which Joni hadn't bothered to comb.

"Then can I have an Oreo?"

"Absolutely not, young lady. By the way, did you brush your teeth?"

"Uh-huh."

"Good."

"Maybe I can have a cookie later?"

Lacy tweaked Joni's nose. "Maybe."

Her four-year-old daughter was bright, precocious and a constant challenge to Lacy. But Lacy loved rising to that challenge, determined her child would turn out to be a responsible and productive citizen.

The task wasn't easy, though. Sometimes she lay awake at night, the responsibility pressing on her heart like lead. If only she had someone to share her burden—a man to love. But she didn't—and that was that.

Joni pulled on her hand, demanding attention. "How long till Santa comes?"

"Three weeks, darling," Lacy answered automatically. She'd bet her daughter had asked that question a thousand times since Thanksgiving had ended and the Christmas decorations appeared in the stores.

"I dreamed about Santa, Mommy."

"Suppose you tell me about it," Lacy said, taking her daughter's hand and heading to the rear of the shop where a staircase led to the living quarters.

For Lacy, the attached living quarters had been a blessing in disguise. She had decorated the small space with a hodgepodge of furniture—some wicker, some antiques. It had charm all its own, with an abundance of live plants, two skylights and flowered cushions on the chairs.

"I'm ready to hear about your dream," Lacy said once Joni was seated at the kitchen table and had eaten several bites of her cereal.

Joni laid down her spoon and said in an excited whisper, "I dreamed that Santa came down the chimney."

"Mmm, that's nice." Lacy's tone was as serious as her daughter's features. "But is that all?"

Joni giggled. "No. He burned his buns, Mommy."

"Joni!" Lacy lifted her eyes toward the ceiling and prayed for divine guidance. "Wherever did you come up with that?"

The child shrugged her shoulders at the same time footsteps were heard on the stairs.

Lacy's brows came together in a frown. "Sue?"

"None other," Sue Petty said as she crossed the threshold.

Lacy eased back in her chair and breathed a sigh of relief. "For a minute I thought maybe I'd opened up. I'm so out of it, I wouldn't have put it past me."

"Hi, Sue," Joni put in.

"Hi, yourself, pumpkin."

"Know what? I dreamed that Santa came down the chimney and burned his buns."

Sue blinked for a minute, as if trying to digest what Joni had said. Then she looked at Lacy and burst out laughing.

Lacy spread her hands helplessly. "What can I say?"

"Nothing," Sue responded. "I know how you feel. I have one at home who's just as mouthy."

Lacy thanked her lucky stars every day for Sue. Not only was the plump, dark-haired, dark-eyed young woman a born salesclerk, she was also a friend. Sue had come by the shop the first day Lacy opened and asked if she needed any help. Lacy had hired her on the spot. What made their relationship even better was that Sue had a child a year older than Joni. When Lacy needed her to, Sue looked after Joni.

"Want some coffee?" Lacy asked.

"No, I'm going to go ahead and open up."

"Ah, sit down," Lacy urged. "It's early yet."

Smiling, Sue sat down as Lacy poured her a cup of coffee, then handed it to her.

"Can you handle it a while by yourself this morning?" Lacy asked.

"No problem."

"I need to run into Harrison and buy Joni a pair of shoes."

Joni clapped her hands. "Oh, goody. Maybe I'll see Santa."

"Maybe," Lacy said, removing Joni's cereal dish and taking it to the sink. When she turned back around, Joni was pushing away from the table. "Run and brush your teeth, then bring the comb and we'll do your hair."

The child skipped to the door, then swung around, her eyes wide and serious. "Mommy, Daddy won't be here for Christmas, will he?"

Lacy heard Sue draw in a quick breath while her own heart faltered. "No, honey, he won't." Even to her own ears, her voice sounded raw. "You know that."

Joni hung her head, only to quickly lift it toward Sue, a smile on her lips. "Can Melody come to my house and get her present?"

"Of course, she can," Sue said, flashing Joni an indulgent grin. "Then you can come to our house and get yours."

Joni's face brightened.

Lacy swallowed the lump in her throat. "Mmm, that sounds like fun. But for now, run on and do what I told you."

"She's a mess," Sue said the minute the child disappeared.

Lacy sighed. "More than you'll ever know."

"She misses her daddy."

"Yes, she does," Lacy responded in a small voice.

"Is there a chance you'll get back together...?"

Lacy lifted tear-filled eyes. "No."

A silence fell between them. Sue cleared her throat, and said, "You've never said and I've never asked, but as a friend who cares deeply for both of you, I'd like to know what happened with your ex."

Lacy braced herself against the cabinet and fought off a shiver.

"Look... forget I asked."

"No, it's okay. I... want you to know. Following a long and messy divorce, I had just started to put our lives back together when my ex kidnapped Joni and whisked her out of state. She... was two years old."

"Oh, God, how awful."

"Well, as you can imagine, I nearly lost my mind."

"What did you do?"

"I used my savings and hired a private detective. He eventually located them. Joni's daddy was arrested on the spot and later sentenced to prison." Lacy's voice was barely audible now. "As soon as I could, I packed and came here." She avoided Sue's probing gaze. "The... rest you know."

Sue looked as if she wanted to say more, but didn't. Instead she sipped her coffee, then after a moment said, "Not all men are like your ex-husband, you know."

Lacy took a deep breath and forced a smile, determined to lighten the mood. "Probably not, only I'm too chicken to do any sampling."

Sue chuckled. "You know what they say, all work and no play makes Jane a dull girl."

"That's me."

"Pooh. You have lots to offer a man. Billy wants you to go out with a friend of his from work."

"Tell that sweet husband of yours thanks, but no thanks."

"Granted, he's no Boothe Larson," Sue said, ignoring Lacy's comment. "Nevertheless, he ain't bad."

Lacy unwittingly dipped into her pocket where she curled her fingers around the envelope. She must remember to mail it to him. "Speaking of our new customer, how many times has he been in the shop?"

"Only twice that I know of."

"I can't imagine why he came at all."

Sue pursed her lips. "Loneliness, I reckon. Word around town has it that he was at one time a forest ranger who fought fires. And now for whatever reason, he lives like a recluse because he hates people." Sue made a face. "I can testify to the latter. When I checked his book out, he watched with a scowl on his face that reminded me of an old bear with a sore paw."

Lacy laughed. "I wish I could've seen that."

"No, you don't."

Lacy laughed again.

Sue shot her a look.

"Mommy, what's so funny?" Joni stood in the doorway.

"Nothing, honey." Lacy curbed her laughter. "Just grown-up talk."

Thirty minutes later Lacy sat behind the wheel of her Honda.

"Damn," she muttered, having realized she still had the American Express bill stuffed in her pocket.

Joni sucked in her breath and covered her mouth. "Oh . . . you said a naughty word, Mommy."

"You're right, I did and I'm sorry."

"I'm ready to go see Santa."

Ignoring an impatient Joni beside her, Lacy tapped her nails on the steering wheel while her mind raced. Since she hadn't mailed the envelope, why not return it in person? What could it hurt? Nothing. Anyway, it was a lovely morning for a drive, she further rationalized.

Joni kicked the back of her legs against the seat. "Mommy, let's go."

Lacy cranked the engine and ground her teeth. After all, curiosity killed the cat.

Chapter Two

Spike eyed his master and wagged his tail.

"I know, boy," Boothe Larson said, "you're hungry. Well, you'll just have to be patient a little longer. I'm about to wrap things up here."

Spike whined, then inched toward Boothe on his belly.

Boothe ignored the black Labrador retriever and continued to pound the log with the ax. Despite the morning chill, he was stripped to the waist, sweaty and dirty. And alone. But he didn't mind. He preferred it that way.

He paused, leaned on the ax and gazed about. He'd take the outdoors anytime. City living wasn't for him, and not because he'd chosen to withdraw himself from the entire human race, either. He hated the hustle and bustle synonymous with large cities. This isolated cabin was where he chose to be; it was his safe haven.

He knew the townsfolk thought him odd, but he didn't give a tinker's damn. He wanted only to be left alone to nurse his despair with self-directed anger.

Had it been just a year since his close friend was killed in the fire and himself injured, leaving him with a permanent limp and scars on his soul he couldn't get rid of. In that year, Boothe knew he'd aged. He dreaded gazing in the mirror each morning. Though just thirty-five, he looked and felt ten years older.

But then he'd never been young or carefree. Reared in a home surrounded by violence, he had distanced himself from others. It had been his only means of survival. He didn't know where his mother was—and couldn't care less. Worse, he didn't even know *who* his father was.

Boothe had thought that when he'd gone to work as a forest ranger, he'd found his calling in life. Then tragedy had struck: a burning tree had gotten out of hand. Though he'd lunged toward his friend and partner to push him out of harm's way, he hadn't been quick enough. The tree had fallen on them both. Boothe had come through with only a shattered leg. His friend had lain dead.

Following months in the hospital, the woman he'd planned to marry decided she didn't want to live with a cripple who might be permanently disabled and unable to make her a comfortable living. Angry and disillusioned, Boothe had packed his bags and headed for his hideaway cabin in the Ozarks.

Spike thumped his tail. Grimacing, Boothe pulled his thoughts away from the painful past and slammed the ax into the wood. "One more, then I'll feed you."

Sweat poured down his face as he bent over and reached for another piece of wood. He hadn't even straightened when he heard a car door slam. What the hell?

He pushed himself to full height, cursed, then whipped around. He didn't want company, despite the fact that the intruder was an exquisite brown-haired child who held the hand of an equally lovely red-haired woman with creamy skin and enormous eyes the color of Texas bluebonnets.

"Whoa," he said under his breath. Women no longer interested him. And no eyes, no matter how extraordinary, were going to make him play that game again.

Still, he leaned on his ax and waited.

Instinct warned Lacy that this man resented her presence. She'd made a mistake coming here; once again her impulsiveness had backfired. Nonetheless, she clung to Joni's hand and approached him.

"Mommy, that hurts," Joni whined, trying to disengage her fingers.

Lacy relaxed her hold, but she didn't turn loose. She had spied the big, black dog next to his master, standing posed to strike.

"Look at the big doggie, Mommy."

"I'm looking," Lacy said absently, her entire concentration on Boothe Larson.

When she and Joni came to a halt a safe distance back, Lacy saw his expression tighten and his eyes narrow. Yet his hostility didn't stop her from staring at him or her thoughts going wild.

He *was* Hollywood handsome, she discovered in surprise. Not that she hadn't believed Sue when she'd said as much. She had. But *handsome* was relative, after all.

His prominent cheekbones bore no compromise. Nor was there any leniency in his thin-lipped mouth or softness in the unyielding jaw. This man was hard through and through.

Although Lacy judged his height to be under six feet, he looked bigger due to his muscular shoulders and latticed stomach, both glaringly obvious since he didn't bother to reach for the shirt that hung on an upright log. The hair on his torso glistened with sweat that reminded her of drops of morning dew.

She swallowed before switching back to his face. Suddenly her mind-set changed. She decided he *wasn't* handsome; his features were much too hard and rigid. Even the unusual gray-blue color of his eyes couldn't temper the emptiness and pain she saw there, neither of which he bothered to hide.

Another of the walking wounded, Lacy thought, searching for something to say that would fill the embarrassing silence, a silence that exacerbated her clamoring thoughts.

Her daughter had no such inhibitions.

"My mommy's name is Lacy, and mine's Joni. What's yours?"

Boothe's gaze lowered to the child, but no smile softened his lips. They remained tempered steel. His voice, however, lacked that hard edge.

"Boothe Larson."

Joni gazed up at Lacy, then back at Boothe, her tiny nose wrinkled. "That's a funny name."

"Joni!" Color flooded Lacy's face, and she could have cheerfully throttled her daughter. She opened her mouth to reprimand Joni, only to hesitate.

A smile flirted with the edges of Boothe's lips, catching her off guard. Just the slight adjustment in his features was stunning. Suddenly he appeared human.

Lacy looked on as he squatted so that his face was almost even with the child's. "You think that's a funny name, huh?"

As if basking in the attention she was receiving, Joni turned loose of Lacy's hand and stepped closer to Booth. "Uh-huh."

"It's 'Yes, sir,'" Lacy prompted gently.

"Yes, sir," Joni repeated with a grin. Her perfect set of baby teeth sparkled in the sunlight.

"I think it's a funny name, too," Boothe said.

Joni giggled. "You do?"

"Boothe is a family name, or so I was told."

Such scorn underscored those words that Lacy almost flinched. But Joni was oblivious to it as she pointed to the dog and asked, "What's the doggie's name?"

"Spike."

Spike lay beside Boothe, and when he heard his name, he thumped his tail and yawned.

Joni giggled again. "Will he let me pat him?"

"No, honey," Lacy put in, tugging at Joni's arm.

Joni turned her attention back to Boothe, her head cocked to one side as if in deep thought. "Do you have a little girl?"

"Joni, that isn't any of your bus—"

Boothe cut Lacy off. "No, Joni, I don't."

"Well, do you have a little boy?"

"Nope, sure don't."

Joni was silent for a minute. "I don't got a daddy, either."

A silence fell, so deep that even the sounds of nature couldn't penetrate it.

Lacy didn't know which she wanted the most, to hug her child against her heart or put a muzzle on her mouth. She did neither. She stood reed straight while the color once again surged into her face.

But Boothe wasn't watching her. His eyes were on the child. "That's too bad. Little girls need daddies."

"I used to have a daddy."

Lacy sucked in a sharp breath.

"That so," Boothe said.

"But my mommy and daddy got a divorce. Do you know what that is?"

"Hush, Joni," Lacy said desperately, "that's enough."

Boothe cleared his throat and stood, his gaze fixed on Lacy. This time Lacy did flinch. What little warmth there had been in his features was gone now. His eyes were cold, and his lips were twisted into a bitter line.

"I guess you're wondering why we're here," Lacy said inanely, fighting to ward off the worst chill she'd ever felt. Yet she wasn't afraid. Why was that? she wondered.

"The thought definitely crossed my mind," Boothe said in answer to her question.

Lacy ignored his brusque sarcasm and said, "By the way, I'm Lacy Madison. I own Books 'N Things in town."

His hair was dark, with threads of silver weaved throughout. She knew that when he put on a shirt, the length would create a ragged edge around his collar. He ran an impatient hand through its thickness, giving it a tousled look and waited, as if expecting her to say something profound.

"I came to return this." Lacy reached into her pocket and drew out the envelope.

Deep lines dented his forehead. "What's that?"

"An American Express bill."

He was clearly puzzled.

"Yours, actually."

"Mine?"

She held it out to him. He folded it against the palm of his hand, a hand that she knew would be callused from manual labor. Then in a flash, she wondered what that hand would feel like caressing a woman's body....

Her breath caught. How could she think such thoughts about a complete stranger? Maybe her brain had short-circuited. Either that or she had been with-out a man too long.

"Where did you get this?"

Lacy jerked herself upright. "I found it in the book you returned."

"I see."

Lacy licked her cotton-dry lips. "There's a letter in-side." The instant she offered the explanation, she wished she hadn't. The envelope's contents was none of her business, but she couldn't help herself; she was cu-rious. The woman who wrote the note had apparently meant something to him. She had stopped just short of begging him to give her another chance.

Boothe's fingers noisily probed the envelope and when he saw the pink sheet, his features froze once again. "Thanks," he said roughly.

Lacy knew it galled him to say the word, especially since she knew he could see the curiosity that burned in her eyes.

Boothe stuffed the envelope into his pocket, then lifted the ax, his way of saying the conversation was at an end.

Lacy shivered at the same time she heard a cry.

"Mommy!"

With her heart lodged in her throat, Lacy swung around at the same time as Boothe. But both were powerless to stop the black dog's excited lunge toward the charging child.

"Oh, my God!" Lacy cried, and watched in horror as the huge dog jumped up and slapped Joni in the chest with its paws.

The force was such that the child toppled backward, her head striking a piece of wood.

Lacy screamed into the deafening silence.

Chapter Three

Stark, paralyzing panic rendered Lacy motionless. She couldn't think, nor could she move.

"Mommy."

Joni's pitiful whimper, followed by silence, proved to be the catalyst that moved Lacy. Later, though, she didn't remember forcing her leadlike limbs into a dead run toward her child. Even at that, Boothe beat her by a split second. Their knees hit the ground simultaneously beside Joni.

"Joni, baby, Mommy's right here." Lacy ran her hands over every inch of the child's body. Only after she touched something wet did she see the blood. Panic turned into sheer terror. "Oh, no...oh, no," she muttered, her eyes darting to Boothe.

"Let's get her inside," he said gruffly.

Lacy fought back tears as Boothe, despite his bad leg, scooped the dazed child into his arms and strode the short distance to his cabin. With a gentleness that seemed totally contradictory to this man's iron strength, he laid Joni on the couch.

"Is—is she unconscious?" Lacy managed to ask as she knelt and eased Joni onto her side in order to check the wound. Blood was seeping from a gash at the back of her head, near the base of her neck.

"Joni, can you hear me?" Boothe asked. His fingers worked along with Lacy's to clear the hair away from the cut. Once that was done, Lacy looked on as he probed the flesh around it.

"Mommy," Joni whimpered.

Tears pricked Lacy's eyes while relief weakened her legs. She must have whimpered herself because Boothe shot her a concerned look.

"You're not going to do something stupid like pass out, are you?"

Though his rude comment was exactly what she needed to jerk her back in control, Lacy nonetheless would have liked to have slapped his face. "No," she said in the coldest tone she could muster, then turned her attention back to Joni.

"Good, because she's going to be all right. I'll get some hot water and bandages. Stay put."

Stay put. Lacy fumed as she held her daughter's tiny hand in hers. He made her sound like his damn dog. Again she had the urge to smack him. But not now. Later, maybe. At the moment, Joni was all she could think about.

"Mommy, my head hurts."

"I know, darling, but it's going to feel better real soon. We're going to put some medicine on it. Okay?"

"Okay," Joni sobbed.

Boothe eased down beside Lacy once again and with an agility that she never would have associated with his big hands, he washed the wound, which was not nearly as bad as first thought, then bandaged it.

When the bandage was in place, Lacy realized just how close Boothe was to her. She could see the tiny lines around his eyes, smell the sweat that lingered. But most of all, she could feel the muscular hardness of his still-bare arms and shoulders as they brushed against hers.

She shivered suddenly, then edged away. His eyes darkened, and his lips stretched into a tighter line as if he could read her thoughts, thoughts that said she found the idea of being close to him repulsive. But that wasn't the reason for her withdrawal. She *didn't* find him repulsive, and that was what upset her.

Boothe stood. Lacy peered up at him and smiled a genuine smile, hoping to diffuse his anger. "Thanks for taking charge," she said.

His reply was terse. "Spike did the damage."

Lacy didn't offer a comeback. Instead, she eased onto the couch, lifted Joni into her arms and cuddled her close.

"Mommy."

"Mommy's here," Lacy whispered.

The child sighed and curled closer, her eyelids fluttering shut.

Once Joni was sound asleep, apparently over her fright, Lacy tried to bring her own scattered emotions under control. She couldn't; her heartbeat refused to settle. She massaged her temples with her fingertips, feeling the tiredness spread. Boothe's brooding silence didn't help any, either.

He stood by the window across the room and stared outside. She studied his left profile, which appeared carved out of stone. Stifling a sigh, she turned away and looked around the room. The cabin's rustic interior was quite cozy and immaculate, she noted with shock. High-beamed ceilings towered over a row of windows, a rock fireplace, leather furniture and a huge, brightly patterned area rug.

But what caught her attention and held it was a cluster of wood carvings that covered a bay windowsill opposite Boothe.

Finally, Lacy couldn't stand the silence another minute. "I understand you're a forest ranger."

He swung around, steely eyed with a set face. "I guess the town's biddies have to have something to gossip about. Might as well be me."

Their gazes held in a measuring silence.

"Is that how you got your injury?" she pressed, for the life of her not knowing why. Maybe it was because he aroused emotions in her that she didn't understand.

"Yes."

She was aware of his mounting fury and knew it was time to halt the conversation. But she couldn't. "Those wood carvings, did you make them?"

His face shuttered. "Yes," he said again.

Her long dark lashes swept down and veiled her frustration. Joni stirred, and for a moment Lacy rocked her child in her arms. She felt his eyes watch her every move.

"I . . . we need to go."

"Right," Boothe responded, "only not home."

Lacy frowned. "Why not?"

"I think Joni ought to be checked by a doctor. She's sleeping much too soundly to suit me."

Panic flared anew inside Lacy. "You . . . don't—"

"No, I don't. Still, I think she should be checked. I'll change my clothes and drive you."

Lacy opened her mouth to say something, only to snap it shut again.

Lacy stretched her tired muscles, then yawned. Still, she couldn't seem to wipe the haze away from her eyes. She blinked and the room came into focus. It hit her then where she was—in a hard chair in the corner of a hospital room. Her gaze darted to the bed where Joni lay asleep. For part of the night, Lacy had slept in the roll-away bed next to Joni. But it had been so uncomfortable, she had opted for the chair, which she'd found even more uncomfortable.

Lacy sagged weakly against the chair's hard back. Joni was fine; that was all that was important. Soft-spoken Dr. Moore had said so after giving her a thorough check.

"The little lady's none the worse for the accident," he'd told Lacy with a gentle smile.

"Thank God," Lacy had said, then looked at Boothe.

Boothe's eyes, however, had been on the doctor. "No stitches."

"The butterfly bandage will do the trick. But as a precaution, I'd like to keep her overnight."

Lacy's eyes widened. "But...I thought you said—"

"Now, Lacy, calm down," Dr. Moore said. "I did say she appears to be fine. But again, I want her observed."

"I think that's a good idea," Boothe said.

Lacy drew a quivering breath. "All...right. Of course, I want to do what's best for Joni."

"Let's see about that room, then, shall we?" Boothe said, taking charge.

Not long afterward, Joni had a room and was tucked in bed by Lacy and a nurse, while Boothe stood aside and looked on. When the nurse had gone, leaving them alone, neither seemed to know what to say.

"What...about my car?" Lacy had finally asked.

"Don't worry, I'll take care of it."

Another silence.

"Er...thanks again for everything," Lacy said, forcing herself to meet his eyes.

His gaze was on her mouth. A flush of scarlet dyed her cheeks. He jerked away, his expression grim. "I gotta go."

Only when she later spoke to Sue on the phone, had Lacy managed to pull herself together. Sue assured her that she would handle the store and even bring Lacy a toothbrush if she wanted her to.

Lacy laughed and said no, that she'd survive till morning.

Now, with the sunlight beginning to spill through the blinds, Lacy fought off thoughts of last evening and tiptoed to the bed. After leaning over and kissing Joni's rosy cheek, she decided she could leave her daughter long enough to get a cup of coffee in the waiting room across the hall.

The instant she crossed the threshold, she pulled up short. Boothe was sprawled in a chair, sound asleep.

She inched closer. When she was within touching distance, she paused. Her pulse quickened. He was one fine-looking specimen. She immediately clamped down on her foolish and impulsive thoughts, which was no easy feat. By nature, Lacy was impulsive and trusting. But since she'd been burned so badly, she had vowed to temper that side of her personality.

Love the second time around, if it ever came, would be a slow process. And certainly not with someone like this embittered man. Yet, he was a multi-faceted individual, she decided. The way he had barked at her, then gently handled Joni proved that.

Lacy gazed at his capable hands and thought again how they would feel touching her. Flushing, she tried to turn away. But she couldn't stop staring at him or control the ache that settled in a deep and familiar part of her.

His eyes opened. "Lacy?"

Shaken to the core at being caught red-handed, she opened her mouth and again found she couldn't say anything.

Boothe shifted to his feet without taking his eyes off her. Something powerful leapt between them.

A harsh breath visibly jarred his chest before he tore his eyes off her and said, "Is Joni all right?"

Lacy clamped down on her lower lip to stop its trembling. "Er...she's fine. In fact, the doctor's due any minute to release her."

"I'll wait and take you home."

The tension in the car, if anything, was more palpable. Lacy was aware of every move Boothe made as he handled the Cherokee expertly. Joni, feeling good and seated between them, was too busy basking in the attention she had received to notice anything amiss. In fact, since they had left the hospital, she'd chattered almost nonstop.

"Mommy, do I have to go to bed when I get home?" she asked.

"No, not unless you want to."

"I don't. I want to go home with Boo."

Boo! Lacy didn't know whether to laugh or cry as she sought Boothe's reaction to the shortened version of his name.

A reluctant smile crossed his lips.

Lacy almost gasped aloud. Again the change in his features was startling. She dropped her gaze to Joni. "Hey, what's the baby-talk business all of a sudden, huh?" she asked, desperate to assuage the uneasiness that surged through her.

Joni grinned, then switched her attention to Boothe and asked, ''Where's the doggie?''

''At my place,'' Boothe said, clearing his throat.

''What's he doing?''

''Well, let's see . . .'' Boothe paused and rubbed the thickening bristle on his chin. ''I'll bet he's outside on the porch, whining for me to come home.''

''Is he mad at me?''

''No. Are you mad at him?''

Joni apparently had to think about that for a second. ''No,'' she finally said in her most grown-up voice.

Lacy smiled to herself, fascinated with yet another side of this man. She'd been right. There definitely was more to Boothe Larson than the indifferent front he had demonstrated on their first meeting. His patience with Joni matched her own.

''But you know what?'' Joni added.

Without taking his eyes off the road, Boothe said, ''No, suppose you tell me.''

Joni scooted to the edge of the seat and placed her hands on both sides of her hips, all the while staring at Boothe. ''If he hurts me again, I'm gonna spank his butt.''

''Joni!'' Lacy cried, aghast. ''I can see right now, young lady, that we're going to have to have a talk.''

Joni's bottom lip protruded.

This time Boothe's lips more than twitched; they burgeoned into a full smile. To Lacy's relief, he turned his head and didn't allow Joni to see it. But she saw it. . . .

Boothe maneuvered the vehicle into the driveway of the shop. Once Lacy unlocked the door, Joni raced inside, leaving Lacy alone with Boothe.

''Thanks again . . . for everything.''

"Don't mention it."

"Would . . . you like to stay for breakfast?"

His jaw set tightly. "No," he said curtly.

Anger reared its ugly head and Lacy spoke before she thought. "Well, excuse me for thinking you were human after all."

She saw the fury mount in his face and his eyes become slits. Then he pivoted on his heels and walked to the Cherokee without so much as a backward glance.

Chapter Four

The following morning Boothe and their verbal skirmish were still very much on Lacy's mind. *Forget him!* she admonished herself. For all she cared, he could wallow in his misery. He'd made it quite plain that he didn't want to socialize with her or anyone else. A self-centered bore was what he was.

Lacy sighed impatiently, then trudged to the window and peered outside. A heavy snow blanketed the ground, and more was predicted, putting her in a holiday spirit. Growing up in Texas, she'd had little experience with snow. Now she looked forward to it. The sky was filled with snow clouds.

Gray-blue clouds . . . the color of his eyes.

Jeez, she was obsessed with a man who couldn't care less about her. She had to stop thinking about him, but no amount of self-flagellation could get him off her mind. The loneliness he wore like a shield tugged at her. Maybe it was because she could identify with it. She loved her child, but a four-year-old couldn't take the place of a man.

What had made him so hard and antisocial? She would probably never know. She turned away from the window with a jerk. Indulging herself like this was sheer folly.

She would fix a quick lunch and then go to work. It was Sunday, and she planned to spend the afternoon making lamps while Sue operated the front. But first lunch.

Twenty minutes later, the chicken-and-mushroom casserole bubbled in the oven. Joni sat at the table coloring in a picture of a dinosaur.

"Mommy," she said, "this is hard. Will you help?"

"Not right now, hon. In a minute, after I finish the salad."

The doorbell to the outside entrance rang.

Joni scrambled out of her chair. "I'll get it."

Later, Lacy couldn't say why she had followed her daughter. When Joni jerked open the door, Lacy's jaw dropped.

Boothe leaned against the pillar on the porch, holding a teddy bear.

"Hi, Boo," Joni exclaimed, her eyes on the stuffed animal.

"Hi, kiddo," Boothe said, but he didn't look at the child. His eyes were on Lacy. And again something powerful stirred between them.

"May I come in?" he asked awkwardly.

Lacy was still grappling with the idea that he was here and, for a moment, couldn't find her voice. "Of course," she said at length. She heard the tremor in her voice and hated it.

"Is that teddy for me?" Joni asked.

Boothe extended his hand. "You bet."

They made their way into the living room, where Boothe sat down on the couch. He looked wonderful dressed in jeans, blue shirt and boots. As usual, his hair was tousled as if he'd just shoved his hands through the coarse strands.

"Looky, Mommy, looky what Boo brought me."

"That's nice, honey." Was the gift his way of apologizing for his churlishness yesterday? "What do you say?"

Without warning, Joni crawled into Boothe's lap, looped her arms around his neck and kissed him on the cheek. "Thank you, Boo."

Lacy heard his sharp intake of breath, and her heart almost stopped beating. Please, don't let him reject her, she prayed, watching the color recede from his face.

Though clearly flustered at this show of affection, he tweaked the child on the chin and said, "You're welcome. When I saw it in the store window, I said to myself 'Joni should have this.'"

The child's eyes sparkled, and Lacy knew she was about to hug him again when he eased her off his lap and stood. "Well . . . guess I'd better shove off."

"Would you like to stay for lunch?" Lacy blurted out, only to wish she'd kept her mouth shut; his rejection the last time she'd issued a similar invitation still smarted.

Joni grabbed his hand. "Come on, Boo. You and Teddy can sit by me."

"I don't—"

"Oh, please," Joni pleaded.

Lacy watched in suspense as a myriad of emotions flickered across his face. Then he took a breath so faintly, she felt it more than heard it.

"You sure you don't mind?" he asked at last.

Lacy's insides uncoiled. "I asked, didn't I?"

A reluctant smile spread across his lips. "Something sure as hell smells good."

"Then you'll stay?"

The simple question fell into the charged silence.

"I'll stay."

Now it was Lacy who was flustered. What would they talk about? What if he didn't like her cooking? Get a hold of yourself, she ordered silently. It didn't matter what he thought—about anything.

But darn it, it did matter.

Joni grabbed his hands and led Boothe toward the table. Once they were seated and Lacy had their plates heaped with food, the child faced Boothe and said, "Have you made your Santa wish list yet?"

"Nope, can't say that I have."

"After lunch, you want me to help you make one?"

Boothe looked at Lacy, his gaze sharp and searching. She felt his eyes slide over her entire body. Again she experienced that little ache she was trying so hard to ignore.

His lips quirked, and though he spoke to the child, he never took his gaze off Lacy. "Sure, I'm game. I guess Santa ought to hear from me, too."

Warmth surged through Lacy, and she knew suddenly that everything was going to be all right.

"Oh, Lacy, that's absolutely exquisite."

Sue's gushing compliment brought a smile to Lacy's pinched features as she held the tiny glass lamp up to the light for closer inspection. "You really think so?"

Sue frowned. "Hey, what is this? If it's one thing you have confidence in, it's your work."

"I know," Lacy said with a sigh. "It's just that I—" She broke off and turned away from Sue's close scrutiny. "Oh, never mind."

"What's with you lately?" Sue asked with the bluntness that only a close friend could get away with.

Lacy put down the lamp, and hoping to avoid the question, she purposely counted the new lamps on the table.

"I'm waiting," Sue said, tapping her foot.

Lacy forced a grin. "Don't mind me, okay. I guess I'm just a victim of this Christmas frenzy. It's getting to me."

Sue flapped her hand through the air. "I don't believe that for a second, but I'll let it go for now."

Lacy hated not confiding in her friend, but she couldn't. Sue was right, though, she was not herself. Continued thoughts of Boothe had her nerves on edge.

Three days had passed since he'd stayed for lunch. And though he hadn't tarried long after the meal was over and his Santa list completed—a smile crossed her lips at the memory—she hadn't been able to stop thinking about him. Yet contrary to that, she wasn't comfortable with the emotions he evoked in her, because they weren't reciprocated.

"Mommy, where are you?"

Glad of the respite from her troubling thoughts, Lacy said, "We're in the workroom, honey."

Joni raced in, all smiles. "What you doin'?"

"I'm working. Want to help?"

"Yeah," Sue said, "I could use an extra pair of hands out front."

Joni shook her head. "Mommy, I wanna play with Boo's doggie."

"I don't think that's a good idea." The words were rushed.

Joni thrust out her lower lip. "But I want to."

"I'm glad you're not afraid of the dog—that proves you're a big girl. But Mommy's busy right now. We have a lot of Christmas orders to fill."

"But—"

"I'm with you, Joni," Sue said. "I think that's a swell idea."

Lacy blinked. "You do?"

"Yep. You've been working too hard. A few hours of sunshine will do you good."

"Can we, Mommy?" Joni pressed. "Can we?"

Lacy gnawed at the inside of her cheek, her thoughts in a whirl. She was tempted, even though she knew it would be a stupid thing to do. Boothe would think so, too, she knew. He would resent another invasion of his privacy. Anyway, if he'd wanted to see her and Joni, he knew where to find *them*.

Yet Sue was right, the day was beautiful and there were those wood carvings. She hadn't forgotten them and would give her eyeteeth to sell them in her store. They would make ideal Christmas gifts, and she had the perfect place to display them. . . .

"Oh, all right," she said, turning to Joni, "you win. Run get your coat."

Sue gave her a curious look, which Lacy made a point to ignore. But Sue's knowing chuckle followed her all the way out the door.

Boothe paused a second and wiped the sweat off his brow. He intended to rebuild the seat on this wagon today or die trying. When he'd started the project, he'd known it would be a dilly.

He stood back and surveyed his handiwork thus far and was pleased with the results. He'd found the old wagon in the barn shortly after he'd bought the place. But it wasn't until several days ago—following his visit to Lacy's—that he decided to restore it, knowing it would take time and every ounce of energy he possessed.

Even so, physical labor hadn't killed thoughts of Lacy.

He had somehow taken for granted that his privacy was forever sacred. He hadn't bothered to fence his property because there was already an impenetrable fence around himself. He hadn't thought anyone would dare cross the forbidden line—unless he chose to let them. That was before Lacy, who in a matter of days had swiftly knocked a hole in that fence, leaving him vulnerable and exposed.

Now as he grabbed his hammer and beat another nail into the board across the back of the wagon, he ached to touch her. He reached for another nail and cursed himself. He felt like a well-oiled machine whose parts had suddenly gone berserk.

And there was the child with her dainty features, cap of curls and angelic smile. How could he forget her? She'd snuck up on his blind side as well, found a soft spot in his heart and wormed her way into it.

Their relationship had to come to an end. He had nothing to offer Lacy or her daughter. Besides, he wasn't interested in a ready-made family. All he was interested in was returning to his job as soon as he got his bum leg in working order again. No woman in her right mind would want to live with a man who risked his life and limbs on a daily basis, especially not one with a child.

Anyway, who said Lacy was interested in him? He sensed she had her own problems. She'd suffered, too. He didn't know how or why, but he'd bet it had something to do with Joni's daddy. The pain continually lurked behind those lovely blue eyes—not for the world to see. Only misfits like himself, who had also been to hell and back, were able to pick up on the pain.

He was just horny; that was his whole problem. Maybe he ought to... Forget it! He wanted Lacy and no one else. But he damn sure couldn't have her, so that was that.

He reached for another nail. He heard it then—a car door slam—and knew without turning around who his visitors were.

"Oh, hell," he exploded, hoping that if he ignored them, they'd go away. But they didn't

He whipped his head up and around. Mother and daughter walked hesitantly toward him. He felt his stomach shrink to a knot.

Lacy looked exquisite. She *was* exquisite. No, that wasn't the word. Edible. That was it. She looked good enough to eat in a pair of tight-fitting jeans and a turquoise sweatshirt that, despite its thickness, failed to disguise her fully defined breasts. Little pink rosebuds, that's what her nipples would be like.... God, but he wanted to touch her. No! He only wanted to be left alone.

He nearly tripped over himself hurrying to meet them.

Chapter Five

Boothe and Lacy met halfway between the barn and the house. Joni lagged behind, in search of the dog.

Lacy concentrated her gaze on Boothe, wetting her lips. "I . . . er . . . hope we're not disturbing you."

Her upturned face held him captive, especially her mouth. And even though it was set with firmness, it still looked soft and inviting.

He cursed silently, trying to regain his perspective. But his heart refused to settle, and his lungs actually ached from labored breathing.

"Spikey. Here Spikey." Joni's shrill voice shattered the moment.

"Joni wants to see the dog," Lacy said in a slightly strangled tone, sounding embarrassed.

Boothe turned to face her again and forced a calm into his voice he was far from feeling. "That's probably a good idea."

"No, it isn't," she said bluntly. "It was a lousy idea." She faced Joni, who was squatted, waiting for the dog to appear. "Come on, honey, let's go."

Against his gut instinct, Boothe said, "Please . . . don't go."

"Are you sure?"

Their eyes held briefly before he dragged his gaze away. "No," he muttered brusquely, "I'm not sure about anything."

"Here doggie, here doggie," Joni called again. "Spikey, where are you, you bad doggie?"

Boothe could have hugged Joni. Her sweet voice loosened the tight thread of tension in the air. His mouth twisted into a reluctant half smile. "He's been in the woods all morning."

Joni ran to Lacy's side and peered at Boothe. "Is your doggie mad at me?"

"Nah." Boothe placed two fingers between his lips and let out a loud whistle.

Immediately, the dog bounded out of the woods and didn't stop until he was at his master's side, panting loudly while eyeing the child.

Joni giggled, reached out her hand, then drew it back.

"Maybe you should just talk to him," Lacy said, concern lowering her voice.

"He won't hurt her," Boothe said, taking the child's hand and placing it gently on the Lab's head.

The dog raised its head and licked the tiny palm.

Joni squealed in delight. "Looky, Mommy, he likes me."

"That's wonderful. Now, tell Spike bye. We have to go."

"I bet Spike would like to play fetch with you, Joni."

"Oh, Mommy, can we stay?"

Lacy's face had a curiously naked look on it. "You don't have to do this."

Boothe's insides clenched like a big fist, yet he heard himself say, "I know." Then to Joni, "Come on, kid, let's get a stick."

A few minutes later, after Joni had thrown the stick to the dog several times, she said, "It's your turn, Mommy."

The dog's panting was louder than ever. Spike sat beside Boothe, resting.

Lacy laughed and shook her head. "Not me, honey."

"Chicken," Boothe taunted, his lips curving in a daring smile.

Her eyes flashed. "Hand me that stick."

Boothe held it out and she grabbed it.

He had to give her credit; she had spunk. His gaze went back and forth between those pouting lips and those sparkling, blue eyes. She reminded him of a wild mare that needed taming. What he'd give to do just that....

"Go get it, boy!" Lacy raised her arm and took a huge step forward, only to suddenly lose her balance. "Oh!" she cried.

Boothe lunged forward and grabbed her. But because they were both in motion, they toppled backward, the snow bearing the brunt of their bodies.

Somehow, Boothe managed to land on bottom and buffer Lacy, who fell squarely on top of him. For a moment both were so stunned, they couldn't utter a word. Through eyelashes dusted with the frigid powder, Boothe squinted at her.

They matched each other breath for breath. Close by, a bird chirped while a puff of wind rattled the tops of the ice-laden trees.

Boothe felt his body turn rigid, though he didn't move. He couldn't. The feel of her against him racked his body with sensations that set him on fire. He ached to touch that sweet dent in her neck with his tongue....

Her face and lips were twisted but not from the cold or from anger as he'd first thought, but with laughter.

He felt his own laughter building inside when Joni plopped down in the snow beside them, her features bathed in answering laughter. "Mommy, you're clumsy."

Lacy strove to right herself, as did Boothe. They made it a point not to look at each other.

"It's time we got back to the shop," Lacy said in a paper-thin voice. "Tell Spike bye, Joni."

Instead of turning toward the car, the child clasped Boothe's hand, looked at him and said, "Will you come to my Christmas play at school?"

"Oh, Joni, I don't think Boothe would be interested."

Lacy's breathy tone and uneasy gaze left no doubt that she was not in favor of her daughter's invitation. She looked so miserable, it seemed unfair to stare.

Boothe winked at Joni. "I think I can work that into my schedule. When is it?"

"Two days from now," Joni responded.

For the second time since he'd met her, Lacy seemed at a loss for words, which was fine with him. Frankly, he didn't know what to say, either, feeling a fool thirty times over for allowing his emotions to get the better of him.

Lacy was a threat to his peace of mind and much more. He'd do well to remember that.

It was only after she and Joni were in the car and the engine was purring that she said, "Mind if I ask you something?"

"Depends on what it is."

"You—you know those wood carvings..." She paused, and her breath crested on a sigh. "I'd love to sell them in my shop."

He concealed his outrage with difficulty. "Forget it. They're not for sale. Now or ever."

"Well, excuse me," she said, stabbing him with an icy glare that matched his own.

Before he could make a comeback, she shoved the car in gear and sped off. He didn't know how long he stood there cursing her. And himself.

For the next two days, Lacy was so busy in the shop selling books and lamps for Christmas gifts, as well as decorating the house, that she was able to keep thoughts of Boothe away.

But now, as she finished dressing on the evening of Joni's play, she couldn't seem to stop him from intruding, mainly because she was too tired to fight.

Damn him. Just when she thought she was close to figuring out exactly what his game was, he shoved the knife between her ribs. Anger had rolled off him in waves. Well, it would be a cold day in hell before she mentioned his precious carvings again. For all she cared, the bone-headed jerk could rot in that wilderness.

She wouldn't lay herself open to his rudeness again, no matter how good his body had felt against her, reminding her how long it had been since she'd been touched by a man's hands.

Lacy cast a wild look around the room, then walked out, counting on leaving her memories behind. Anyway, she and Joni were going to be late.

"Hurry, Joni," she said, turning into the kitchen to switch off the coffeepot.

Joni bounded into the room. "I'm hurrying, Mommy."

Lacy gave her daughter an indulgent smile, thinking how angelic, how precious she looked in her angel costume. Then she chuckled. Precious, yes. Angelic, no.

"What's funny, Mommy?"

"Nothing, honey. We need to be walking out the door this minute."

"But I'm not ready," Joni whined.

"Joni!"

"I can't find my purse."

Lacy prayed for patience while she scanned the premise for her own purse. Just as she spotted it, the doorbell rang.

"Great," Lacy muttered, wondering why she'd even bothered to get out of bed that morning. Talk about Murphy's Law...

"I'll get it, Mommy!"

"Oh, no, you won't," Lacy countered. "You'll find your purse."

Ignoring her daughter's mumbled protest, Lacy hurried to the front door and yanked it open. Boothe, looking like a million dollars in a blazer and slacks, stared back at her. She felt her jaw go slack despite her efforts to maintain control.

"I gather I wasn't expected." Dark amusement toyed with his mouth, but his eyes were unreadable even as they probed hers.

"Uh...no, no, you weren't." Her voice came out a tight whisper.

"Is it okay if I come in?"

Her legs weren't working right, but somehow she stepped aside.

Boothe crossed in front of her and didn't pause until he reached the archway between the living room and kitchen. As she followed him, both her mind and body churned. He smelled as good as he looked....

"Hi, Boo," Joni said, tearing around the corner like a tiny missile and launching herself at him.

His lips curved into a smile. "My, but don't you look pretty."

"Mommy said you weren't coming to my play."

Boothe's eyes rested on Lacy, a taunting smirk on his lips. "Oh, she did, did she? Well," he added on a drawl, "that's too bad, because I planned to come all along."

"Oh, goody," Joni said, slipping her tiny hand into his big one.

Lacy was barely breathing, but she met his gaze without flinching.

Suddenly Joni dropped Boothe's hand and jumped up and down. "Mommy, you're under the mistletoe. That means you're 'posed to kiss Boo."

Silence, deep and complete, fell over the room.

Lacy was aware that Joni was studying the various Christmas traditions at four-year-old kindergarten, but that did nothing to lessen her shock or embarrassment.

"Hurry, Mommy," Joni urged from what sounded far-off to Lacy. "We have to go."

A small, involuntary whimper escaped her lips. Surely this wasn't happening. Surely, in just a few seconds, she'd wake up and find that she was dreaming.

Lacy lifted her head, and when she did, Boothe's face, so close to her own, filled her vision. Before she could recover, his lips closed over hers. She was so dumbstruck, she couldn't do anything. Then her lips parted and collided with his tongue. Her knees almost buckled under her.

She sank her fingernails hard into his shoulders and clung as his greedy mouth, hot and demanding, feasted on hers.

Then just as quickly as the kiss had begun, it ended. Boothe coughed.

Lacy swallowed against the dryness in her throat while panic flared inside her, yet she couldn't stop herself from looking at Boothe. Through veiled lashes, she tested his reaction. He appeared unaffected, but she knew better. The dew of sweat on his forehead gave lie to that ruse.

"We'd better go now," Joni said in her most grown-up voice.

Without looking at each other, Lacy and Boothe turned and followed the child out the door.

Chapter Six

"Ouch!"

"Sorry, darling," Lacy said to her squirming daughter, "but you're going to have to hold still."

Joni had just awakened from her nap and Lacy was forced to comb her hair quickly since Sue was due to pick the child up shortly. Sue had promised her daughter, Melody, pizza for lunch and had invited other friends to go, as well.

"Okeydokey. All done." Lacy leaned back and surveyed her handiwork. Joni's curls were long enough now that she could pull the front ones back and secure them with a barrette, which enhanced her doll-like features and her big, brown eyes.

"Do I look pretty, Mommy?"

Lacy hugged her. "You look beautiful."

Joni wiggled out of her embrace, bounced toward the door, then stopped and whirled. "Mommy, when are you gonna put up the tree?"

Lacy sighed. "Soon. I promise. But I've...we've been so busy at the shop, there just hasn't been time. Maybe we'll look for one tomorrow evening, okay?"

"Okay." Joni was quiet for a moment. "Can Boo help us?"

"I doubt that he would want to," Lacy said lightly, trying to ignore the flip-flop her stomach did at the mention of Boothe.

A tiny frown knitted Joni's brow. "Bet he would."

"Well, we'll see," Lacy said at the same time the bell on the shop door chimed. Joni dashed off to see if it was Sue.

Saved by the bell, Lacy thought with relief. She wasn't at all happy with Joni's deepening attachment to Boothe. In the end she knew the child would be hurt by Boothe's rejection of them both. Lacy knew it was just a matter of time till that happened. But what about herself? She was worse than her daughter. Despite the fact that he made her mad, he fascinated her, and she couldn't stop thinking about him, about that *kiss*.

"Mommy, Sue and Melody are here."

Lacy shook off her disconcerting thoughts and made her way out of the office and into the shop.

"Are you sure it's all right if I take the afternoon off?" Sue asked in an anxious tone.

"Of course. You deserve it—you've been working like a dog for weeks." Lacy grinned and made a shooing gesture with her hands. "Out the door. Pam and I can handle it."

Lacy had hired Pam Riley, a young high school student, for the Christmas rush. She had turned out to be a jewel. "Anyway, it's Sunday," Lacy added. "We close early."

Sue smiled. "Whatever you say—you're the boss."

The next few hours passed in a blur. Pam operated the front, charming each tourist that came through the door so that each left with at least one purchase, if not several. Each time Pam came to the back to get a lamp from stock, a giddy feeling surged through Lacy. This Christmas was going to be the best ever, which meant she could put a healthy lump sum down on the business.

Her book sales weren't shabby, either, she reminded herself as she spent the afternoon checking in several boxes of books, and arranging them attractively on the racks. To her delight, several of the hot bestsellers were grabbed before she could display them.

By the time five o'clock rolled around, Lacy didn't know whether she was more excited or more exhausted. Still, she hadn't done as much work on the lamps as she had hoped. She'd planned to finish three special orders this afternoon, then make some for the shop. Any moment now Joni would be home, demanding her time and attention.

"Lacy?"

She looked up. "Is it time for you to go?"

"Yes, only there's a man at the door who says he'd like to see you."

Lacy frowned. "Who is it?"

"Said his name's Boothe Larson."

Tiny tremors shook her. What did Boothe want? It didn't matter. She'd treat him with the coolness he deserved.

"Lacy?"

"Er...send him back, then lock the door behind you." She forced a smile. "Thanks for today. You did great."

Once Pam had disappeared, Lacy concentrated on gathering her scattered senses, but time was against her. Within seconds Boothe appeared in the doorway and the glimpse of him shook her with pure delight.

He seemed to sense her positive reaction, because his aloof expression turned to surprise, and then he smiled. Lacy was reminded of the sun peeping through a dark cloud.

His eyes captured hers and for a moment an unguarded spark of desire passed between them.

Then he glanced away and the spell was broken. "Smells like Christmas in here," he said, the smile still flirting with his lips, though his voice sounded slightly strained.

"Maybe that's because it is," she responded, dismayed by the hoarse quality she heard in her own voice. All he had to do was walk through the door and her insides turned to jelly.

He turned and faced the shop. "Did you do all this? The decorations, I mean?"

What do you want? Lacy clamored silently. But when she spoke, the turmoil within didn't show. "Yes—with Sue's help, of course."

"Sue?"

"My part-time help."

"Was that Sue who just left?"

Lacy shook her head, their inane conversation playing with her psyche. "No, that's my Christmas help, Pam. Joni's with Sue and her daughter—eating pizza."

"Ah, I was just about to ask about my little friend."

"Well, now you know," Lacy said, only to feel her stomach muscles knot. It was nerves, and it took all her effort not to shout at him to get to the point of this visit.

He was just too big, too intimidating for her peace of mind. And he looked too darn good, dressed in a pair of worn jeans and blue wool shirt that complemented his eyes and the threads of silver in his hair. It was open at the collar, revealing the hair on his chest. She felt her palms sweat.

"I like your shop," he said.

Lacy felt herself relax a little. "Christmas is my favorite time of the year. I love to make a big deal of it."

"It shows."

And it did. Besides the beautiful Christmas tree with red velvet bows and satin balls covering it, baskets of holly and brightly colored ornaments were scattered among the books and lamps.

He sniffed deeply. "Is that wassail I smell?"

"No, it's potpourri. The smell of Christmas, actually. It's simmering in potpourri pots."

"It smells good enough to drink."

She laughed uneasily. "I'm afraid it might be lethal."

"I'm afraid you might be right."

She broke into a soft wispy laugh.

"No mistletoe, though, I see."

That comment threw her stomach onto a falling elevator. "No, no mistletoe."

She heard his quick, indrawn breath as his gaze fastened on her lips.

The memory that lay between them rose unbidden to the forefront of their minds. They both remembered the sucking pull of his mouth. They looked away—anywhere but at each other.

"Show me how you make the lamps."

Lacy whipped her head back around. A white line surrounded his lips, and she knew he was as shaken as she was.

Turning, she almost ran to her work area. She was aware that he stopped beside her, but she avoided his eyes.

"If I show you how I make my lamps, will you show me how you do your wood carvings?" She ventured a look at him.

"Maybe," he said gruffly.

"That's not good enough."

"Oh, all right."

She hid a smile as she lifted a small sheet of colored glass off the shelf in front of her. "The glass comes in all colors from the factory. Using a pattern, I cut different sizes and shapes."

"Ah, then you adhere the glass to the preformed shades."

"Right. I wrap the edges of the glass with copper foil, solder the pieces together and cover the topside of the mold, followed by the underside." She placed the glass back on the shelf. "That's it in a nutshell."

Boothe crossed his arms and leaned against the counter. "That takes a helluva lot of talent."

"More hard work than talent, I'm afraid."

"How much do they sell for?"

"Depends on the size and detail of the glass. None are priced under fifty dollars. But some are two hundred." She lifted a tiny mushroom-shaped one. "This particular one is two hundred and fifty."

"It's dainty, like you," he said thickly, only to then grimace as if he could have cheerfully bitten his tongue rather than have said those words.

The front door rattled, and Lacy jumped.

"Joni's back," she stated, skirting past him.

Seconds later, she came back into the workroom with Joni skipping beside her, grinning.

"Hi, Boo," Joni said. "Did you come to see me?"

"That I did. I thought maybe you and your mother might like to go to my place, pick out a tree and chop it down."

A heavy sigh came from Lacy. So that's what this visit was all about. Would she ever understand this man? She feared not, and that in itself kept her on edge.

"Wow! Can we, Mommy? Can we?"

"Oh, honey, I don't—" Lacy broke off as her eyes unwittingly sought Boothe's.

He didn't say a word, but the muscles along his cheek and jaw stood out in sharp ridges, and she caught another glimpse of pain in his eyes. Or had she imagined it?

It was too late, anyway. She couldn't have turned him down herself. "I'll get my coat."

"Well, what do you think?" Boothe asked. "Will it pass muster?"

Joni cocked her head and peered at Boothe, obviously puzzled. "What's 'muster,' Boo?"

Boothe kept a straight face while Lacy grinned. "I was asking if it's pretty," Boothe explained patiently.

Joni stared at the perfectly shaped cedar. "It's the bestest and the prettiest tree I ever had."

"Me, too." Lacy strove to keep her tone even, but failed. Not only was the perfectly shaped tree dazzling in its beauty, laden with dozens of twinkling lights and decorations, but the afternoon had been dazzling, as well.

When they got to Boothe's place, they had gone immediately to the woods, to a place where Boothe had already sighted several possible Christmas trees. He had made a big deal of letting Joni choose the one she wanted.

Afterward, he had handed her a small ax and told her to start chopping. She had squealed with excitement. Following that first swing of the ax, Boothe had knelt beside Joni and together, they had felled the tree.

Lacy had looked on in silence, her throat so tight, she couldn't say a word.

The magic hadn't stopped there. They had arrived back at the house where they munched on popcorn, sipped hot chocolate and decorated the tree. Through it all, Lacy had been aware of Boothe with every breath she took. She'd been so aware that she'd taken extra precautions to make sure their hands didn't touch as they placed ornaments on the tree. Still, she basked in the feel of his eyes on her.

Now, as they stood back and surveyed their handiwork, they couldn't be prouder. Yet there was one more thing left to do.

"Are you ready, kiddo?" Boothe asked.

Watching the big man hold the fragile child ever so gently high in his arms brought unwanted tears to Lacy's eyes. If only... Forget it! she told herself fiercely. He wasn't interested in taking on the responsibility of a ready-made family. Yet she'd seen him look at Joni; there had been a longing, a flash of pain that had somehow made him vulnerable. Or maybe it had been her imagination because she *wanted* him to want them.

Once the angel was in place, Joni twined her arms around Boothe's neck and gave him a hug. "Isn't she pretty?"

He tweaked her on the nose. "Yeah, she is, only she's not as pretty as you."

Suddenly Lacy experienced that same feeling that she'd had in the woods. She couldn't say a word, nor could she move. Something sweet filled her heart.

Boothe eased a squirming Joni to the floor, which forced Lacy to get herself back on track. She held out her hand to her daughter. "It's time you were in bed, young lady."

"Oh, Mommy—"

"None of that whining. It's been a long day."

Joni rubbed her eyes, then strutted up to Boothe. "Will you come and tuck me in?"

Unable to second guess Boothe's response, a gasp rippled through Lacy.

If Boothe heard it, he ignored it, having eyes only for Joni, who was now nestled between his legs. "You bet, that is if it's all right with your mother."

"Oh, she doesn't care. I 'member one time my daddy read me a story."

Silence riveted the room.

Over Joni's head, Lacy's eyes met Boothe's. Her mouth was dry. Her legs were wobbly.

"What if I read you one?" Boothe finally asked, though his voice sounded taut. "Would you like that?"

"Uh-huh." Joni grinned. "*Rudolph* is my favorite."

Careful not to look at Boothe for fear he would read her raw emotions, Lacy clasped Joni's hand. "Come on. When you're ready for bed, we'll call Boothe."

Boothe strode back into the room fifteen minutes later.

Lacy stared wide-eyed at him as he crossed the threshold and eased down on the couch beside her. "Is she asleep?"

"Yep, after the first page."

Lacy smiled. "She had quite a day."

"We all did."

"I don't know about you, but I'm exhausted."

Boothe feigned surprise. "You, the workaholic? I don't believe it."

Lacy gave him a pointed look. "Well, believe it. Keeping up with Joni requires immense stamina."

"Yeah, she is a little package of dynamite."

"I—I want to thank you for this afternoon. You've made this Christmas extraspecial for Joni and I appreciate it."

"What about you?"

"What—what about me?"

"Have I made it special for you, too?" His voice sounded ragged, as if he had a cold.

A disconcerting roar commenced in Lacy's head. "Yes," she said in a tiny voice.

"I rarely remember ever having a Christmas tree, much less presents under it."

His voice was matter-of-fact, but he had an air of secret pain about him that broke her heart. A picture of him at Joni's age, at Christmastime—without parents, without love—flashed in Lacy's mind. She blinked back hot tears and said with a sunny smile, "Perhaps this Christmas will be different."

"Think so, huh?" he said, his eyes on her lips.

Then he shifted his gaze and their eyes met, fervently. They both glanced away.

Lacy stood and headed toward the kitchen. "I'll get us some more hot chocolate."

"Where's Joni's daddy?"

Lacy stopped cold in her tracks and swung around. "He...was in prison."

"Was? Where is he now?"

"Dead."

Chapter Seven

Her words fell heavily into the mounting silence.

"Sit down...please," Boothe said. His voice sounded as if he'd swallowed a piece of glass. "The hot chocolate can wait."

Not certain her legs would hold her up much longer anyway, Lacy sank back onto the couch. Boothe's eyes demanded an explanation she was loathe to give. She hated dredging up old wounds and reinfecting them. Yet for some crazy reason, she knew she'd tell him, as if he had the right to know her deep, dark secrets. But then when it came to him, her willpower was nonexistent.

"How did he die?" A pulse beat at his temple.

"In prison...in a riot."

He muttered an expletive.

Tears were perilously close. Lacy turned away. She didn't want him to see the tears.

"If you don't want to talk about it..."

She tried to smile, but her chin wobbled.

He cursed again. "Sometimes I can be an insensitive jackass."

Lacy's smile strengthened, then disappeared altogether. "We all have our moments."

Neither spoke for the longest time.

"Look, I think I oughta go," he said brusquely, then placed his palms on his thighs, as if ready to spring from the couch.

She began explaining in a monotone. "There—there was a prison riot. Somehow Dan got caught between two gangs and was stabbed."

Boothe's features registered shock, but before he could say anything, she bolted from the couch and said in a rush, "I'll be right back. I'm going to check on Joni and get us some more chocolate."

Once she reached the kitchen, Lacy leaned against the counter for support. Her hands were icy. Somehow she managed to make the chocolate, though she kept looking over her shoulder, thinking Boothe would follow her. He didn't. With the two cups on a tray, she made her way to Joni's room. The child was sleeping soundly. She looked so sweet . . . so precious. . . . Only when the lump in her throat got too big to swallow around did Lacy turn and leave.

She entered the living room, and warm air hit her in the face. Boothe had stroked the embers in the fireplace and sat watching the mesmerizing flames as if deep in thought.

"Mmm, that feels good," she said, suddenly feeling awkward and slightly unclean. Discussing her ex-husband's violent death always brought on that feeling. She'd tried to stifle it but she hadn't been able to. It clung to her like an offensive odor.

Boothe took the cup from her extended hand with a silent nod of thanks. For a minute they sipped the hot liquid, the muted darkness pulsing around them.

"Does Joni know?"

Lacy leaned over and put her cup on the coffee table. "She knows he's . . . in heaven."

"But not how he died."

"She's too young to handle something like that."

"Did you love him?"

Lacy shot him a glance. "Strange that you should ask that. No one else ever has."

Boothe shrugged, then waited.

"I thought I did. But then he started having trouble at work, and after that, he changed."

"Did he ever mistreat Joni?"

His voice had dropped a notch, and it sounded forced, as though the question had been dug out of him. He cared for the child; she was certain of it now. Somehow that gave her the strength to continue.

"No, not even after the divorce or when he took her across the state line."

"You mean he kidnapped her?"

"Yes," Lacy said simply, then went on to tell him about how she'd hired a detective to track them down.

When she finished, his features were grim. "I know I shouldn't speak ill of the dead, but maybe he got exactly what he deserved."

"Well, I definitely thought he deserved prison, but the other—" She broke off with a shiver. "When . . . I was told he was dead, it broke my heart."

She saw Boothe clench his jaw, but she continued, "Not because I still loved him, but because of the waste. He had so much potential. Anyway, I got a chance to start over, so I took it." She smiled through her tears. "And as they say, the rest is history."

"So now you have what you want?"

"Almost," she said pensively, staring into the flames. "When I own the shop free and clear, maybe I can say that."

"That's important to you, huh?"

"Yes, because it means roots, stability for Joni and me. And that's what's important, especially after our upheaval. Hopefully Joni won't bear any scars."

Boothe didn't respond. Instead he finished off his chocolate in two long sips.

"What about you?" Lacy asked after he sat his cup down. "What do you want?"

"To get back to my job," he said tersely.

"Are you afraid that won't happen?"

"Damn straight I am. You can't fight a fire with a bum leg."

"What do the doctors say?"

He snorted. "They don't know."

"They must say something," she pressed.

"Yeah, time—just give it time."

He got up suddenly, crossed to the fire and stoked it. When he faced her again, the shield was back over his eyes. *Oh, no, you don't,* she thought fiercely. Besides, she burned to know what had made him withdraw from the human race. She'd bet his injury wasn't the only reason.

"Well . . ." she said, kicking off her shoes and curling her feet under her.

He frowned. "Well, what?"

"You know what, but I'll humor you anyway."

A faint smile edged his mouth.

"It's your turn to come clean, to air out all the family skeletons."

He snorted again, then rejoined her on the sofa. "There's none to air, none that I know of, that is."

"Everyone has a family."

"Not me. My mother ditched me when I was too young to know it. My daddy—well, who the hell knows. My mother sure didn't."

Lacy stared at him, horrified.

"Not a very pretty story, is it?"

"No...no, it isn't," she whispered, shaken to the core by what he'd told her.

"But I learned the hard way to change the things you can, and what you can't, to let it go."

"How did you injure your leg?"

He told her.

"I'm sorry about your friend."

"Yeah, me, too."

"There was a woman involved, too, wasn't there?"

"How did you know?" There was a rawness in his voice that he couldn't quite hide.

She shrugged. "Instinct, I guess."

"When I got hurt, she split." He laughed without humor. "The thought of being tied to a cripple who couldn't make her a living scared the hell out of her."

"You can't judge all women by her."

"Could've fooled me."

His words winded her. "I'm sorry you feel that way."

"Ah, hell, I didn't mean that. I—" He stopped as if he couldn't go on.

Suddenly there seemed to be nothing left to say. Their eyes met and clung. The flush on Lacy's cheeks deepened. It was the way he was looking at her that did it, as though he could gobble her up. An ache developed deep inside her, and she ran her tongue over her parched lips.

"Lacy." His voice cracked.

"What?"

"Don't," he said roughly.

She swallowed. "Don't what?"

"You know."

"No, I don't." This time the words were barely audible.

"Your tongue. The way—you keep trailing it across your lips."

"Oh."

Their eyes continued to hold. Neither moved or spoke. The antique clock on the wall hummed, then chimed out the hour. Wind whistled against the windowpanes. They didn't so much as flinch.

"Lacy?"

Her heart rate was so high and the ache between her legs so intense, she wasn't capable of responding. She wanted him so much that she was in pain. Yet if she gave in to those feelings, she feared instinctively what would lie ahead. She desperately wanted to head off catastrophe, to prevent her and Boothe from being swept to destruction. She couldn't. She could only stare at him with tear-rimmed eyes and trembling lips.

Groaning, he reached for her. She landed against his chest. His lips took hers, completely, possessively.

Fire filled her veins as she threaded her hands through his hair to bind him closer, to fuel her rage and the fire settling between her thighs.

He pulled back; his eyes pleaded. "I want more."

"Me, too."

"I want all of you."

They stood then and, in the firelight, shed their clothes, pitching them aside.

Boothe's gaze roamed her body and for once there was no coldness in his eyes, no aloofness. The heat that radiated from them seemed to burn her skin, but she lacked the will to move. She no longer thought of what the consequences would be; she no longer cared. Lacy only knew that she might not survive if she couldn't have him.

"You're beautiful," he whispered. "Your breasts—they're perfect."

Her eyes followed his. Her breasts shone like white porcelain in the firelight, except for her nipples. They were rose hued and budding hard.

She flushed. He smiled, then touched one with the tip of a callused finger. She flinched, not from pain, but from the burgeoning throb between her legs.

"Where?" he asked.

She didn't pretend to misunderstand. "In there."

Without taking his eyes off her, Boothe reached for her hand and led her into the bedroom. The firelight provided them with ample light.

He sat on the foot of the bed and drew her toward him. His gaze continued to pay homage to her breasts, the flat planes of her stomach, the enticing curls at the center of her.

He raised his head and, without meeting her gaze, parted his legs so as to fit her body between them, putting his lips level with her breasts. He covered one entire nipple with his mouth, then flicked his tongue across it.

"Oh, Boothe," she whispered, clinging to him.

Only after her breasts glistened with moisture did he plead, "Touch me."

"Yes, oh, yes." She wrapped her hand around his hardness and caressed it.

He groaned. His eyes glazed. After a moment, he seized her hand. "I . . . can't take any more." But instead of shifting so as to get inside her, he moved his hand and gloved her warmth and exerted gentle pressure.

Lacy squirmed under his tutelage and quickly lost touch with reality. Soon his finger found its mark, and she cried out just as his mouth locked on hers.

Finally he pulled away and fell back on the bed, taking her with him. She rested atop him, flesh against flesh.

"You're like a soft, fragrant flower—your hair, your skin...." He licked the dewy skin of her shoulder.

She moved slightly, enabling her to surround his hardness once again.

He stiffened, then moaned and grasped her buttocks so that he penetrated enough to weld them together while he turned her on her back. With a cry, she sank her fingers into the base of his neck and guided his mouth to a pulsating nipple even as he thrust deep into her.

She lifted her hips and answered his thrust with a greediness that matched his. Only after their cries rented the air did they breathe.

Lacy awakened near daybreak. She moved slowly and realized how tender her joints were—and remembered what happened.

She twisted her head. Boothe was on his side, sound asleep. So she hadn't dreamed his lovemaking, after all. But what did it mean? she asked herself wildly.

Was it just sex? Yes, of course, it was. Her battered heart settled. That had to be the case. They were both victims of their own bodies—two misfits, lonely entities who needed physical release. To attach any lasting significance to the act would be sheer folly and only bring more pain raining down on her.

Only it was too late. She had done what she promised herself she wouldn't do—she had fallen in love with him, impulsively and thoroughly. This time, her heart told her, it was the real thing and would last forever. This man, whose loneliness masked a kind and generous heart, had tapped emotions deep inside her that no one ever had, certainly not her ex-husband.

That didn't make her feel better, though. Nor did it solve anything. She still faced pain and disillusionment.

He awakened suddenly and sat on the side of the bed. She stared at his muscled back, and it was all she could do not to lean over and trail kisses up and down his spine. Touching him had become synonymous with breathing.

As if he could read her thoughts, he turned around. His eyes were dark with passion. "If I touch you again," he said in a whispery voice, "I won't be able to stop. And I wouldn't want Joni to wake up—"

"I know."

"I'm not sorry this . . . happened."

She lowered her eyes.

"Lacy, look at me."

Her head came up, and she licked her colorless lips. He groaned, but remained unmoving. "I'm not sorry, either," she said at last.

He got to his feet, then took the spread from the bed and covered himself with it. "I'll see you later, okay?"

Lacy remained rigid until the bedroom door closed behind him, then she fell back against the pillow, clutched the sheet to her trembling lips and let the tears flow.

Chapter Eight

Boothe held the rough cut of the wood carving at arm's length and surveyed his handiwork. Not too bad, he thought, lifting the knife and taking another tiny nick out of the bird's beak. Once that was done, he sat the carving back on the worktable and flexed his back. His muscles were stretched to the breaking point. He'd been hard at work since early morning, and the bird was one of three animals he'd done in only two days.

He'd had to keep busy in order not to think. However, work hadn't eased Lacy's image from his brain.

He kept telling himself he was nuts to have let his guard slip and made love to her. Nothing had changed; he still didn't have anything to offer Lacy. The fact that he'd let his heart overrule his head merely added fuel to an already raging fire.

Now that he had sampled the delights of her body, his hard-won discipline lay in shambles. The need for her crawled through his gut, created an unbearable ache in his crotch, an ache he thought he'd forgotten. Her beauty, her laughter, her cries pulled at him like a physical force.

His breath suddenly hitched in his lungs. "Damn," he muttered, and wiped the perspiration off his brow with his fingertips.

He wanted to see her. And Joni. It had been two days since they'd made love, since he'd slipped out of her house like a thief. But he hadn't gone near her, nor had he picked up the phone and called. At first he'd tried to pretend it hadn't happened, that he hadn't been that stupid. Then he vowed it wouldn't happen again.

He knew better than that, too. In spite of all his intentions, and whether he liked it or not, his life had assumed a new purpose, a new meaning. Lacy had brought something special into his dreary existence.

Yet unanswered questions haunted him, questions he couldn't block from his mind. Should he chance another relationship? What were Lacy's true feelings? Did she care for him—really care?

When his leg began to throb, he eased into an old wooden chair and leaned his head against the wall. Eyes closed, he tried to forget her, then was startled by the persistent ring of the phone. Unable to ignore it, he got up and made his way to the cabin, his thoughts in more turmoil than ever.

"Oh, Lacy, it's the prettiest thing I've ever seen."

Lacy's face glowed with satisfaction as she scrutinized the delicate lamp a customer held. "You're right, Maxie, it is beautiful," she said, only to then laugh. "Nothing like bragging about my own work."

"Trust me, my dear, you're entitled." Maxie watched as Lacy put the lamp into a box. "Just wait till my sister in Seattle sees this. I'll bet she'll have a conniption and have to buy herself another."

"That'll be wonderful," Lacy replied.

"Well, thanks again, and Merry Christmas."

"Merry Christmas to you, too, and be careful traveling."

Once the woman was gone, Lacy took a deep breath and slipped one foot out of its shoe, then the other. Her feet were killing her. She should've known better than to wear heels, but she'd felt the urge to dress up today, having chosen a turquoise velour jumpsuit in hopes of boosting her spirits.

Why didn't he call? How could he not know how much she wanted to see him? He'd told her he wasn't sorry they had made love. If that was true, then, dammit, why didn't he call? He couldn't be any more rattled and unsure about what had happened than she was. In the light of day, she had thought she'd see things differently, that maybe she hadn't fallen in love, after all. She knew better. A woman didn't get that suffocating feeling in her chest or the twist in her gut if she wasn't in love.

"My, but it's quiet in here."

Exhausted by the confusion of her thoughts, Lacy smiled brightly at Sue, who had come out of the workroom. "I know, and isn't it nice."

Sue arched an eyebrow at that. "Why, Lacy Madison, I can't believe you said that, not when you need every penny you can get your hands on."

"You're right, only my feet hurt," Lacy wailed.

Sue laughed, then grew pensive. "You look mighty nice. Is something happening I don't know about?"

"No."

"Mmm."

Lacy threw Sue a look. "What's that 'mmm' mean?"

"Well, Joni said she had a new friend."

An alarm went off in Lacy's head. "Oh," she said carefully.

"Yeah, she even told me his name."

"Okay, Susie. Out with it. Say what's on your mind."

Sue grinned. "I figured if he's Joni's friend, he's bound to be yours, too."

"Remind me to put that muzzle on my daughter's mouth when she gets home from the party."

"So you're not going to reveal any secrets, huh?"

"That's right," Lacy responded with saccharine sweetness.

The phone rang.

Sue rolled her eyes. "Ah, saved by the proverbial bell."

Lacy stuck her tongue out as she lifted the receiver. She listened for a minute, then grabbed her stomach and gasped aloud. Seconds later, she dropped the receiver back onto the hook.

"Lacy, what's wrong?"

Lacy thought she might strangle on the hot bile that rose to the back of her throat. She coughed, and only then was she able to talk, though her teeth chattered, garbling her speech. "It's . . . Joni."

"What about Joni?" Sue demanded.

"She's missing."

Sue blinked. "Missing? I don't understand."

Lacy's composure shattered. "Oh, God," she cried. "What am I doing standing here? I've got to go."

Sue didn't ask any more questions. "I'll close the shop and go with you."

Boothe! She needed Boothe. He'd help her. He'd know what to do. "No . . . you stay here. I'll call Boothe."

Lacy felt Boothe's eyes on her as she sat beside him in his speeding Cherokee. But she kept her gaze straight ahead, her back rigid while her insides were clenched like a big fist.

"Try to relax, okay?"

"I can't," she said through stiff, colorless lips.

And she couldn't. Lord knows, she'd tried. But she was poleaxed with fear. When Marion, the hostess of the party, had dropped the bombshell that Joni had disappeared, Lacy had thought someone was playing a dirty joke on her. Then she'd heard Marion's sobs and knew it was no joke.

For months following the kidnapping, Lacy had refused to let Joni out of her sight. Only since she'd come to this small town had Lacy felt safe enough to let her guard down, to relinquish that tight control.

Now the nightmare was happening all over again and she couldn't stand it. Unthinkable images and possibilities popped into her mind, exacerbating her torture. Still, she tried to make rational sense of it all. Joni's sudden disappearance couldn't have anything to do with her ex-husband. He was dead; he couldn't hurt them ever again.

Yet she wanted to scream as agony twisted and turned inside her. Instead, she breathed deeply and glanced at Boothe. Only his calming presence kept her from falling apart.

The instant she'd told him she needed him, he'd said without hesitation, "I'm on my way."

She'd waited outside the shop, and when he'd pulled up in front, she'd jumped inside the Cherokee. They had been traveling only ten minutes but to Lacy it seemed like an eternity. Her baby! Despair overwhelmed her. Oh, God, please let her be all right.

"Lacy."

"What?" she said in a muffled tone.

"Tell me what the lady said."

She faced him. "There's not much to tell. All I heard was that Joni was nowhere to be found."

"What kind of party was it?"

Lacy's teeth banged together.

"Take a deep breath," Boothe ordered.

She did.

"Now that's better," he said, and repeated his question.

"It's a birthday and Christmas party combined. And to think I almost didn't let her go."

"Why?"

"Because I couldn't go with her. But she'd cried when I said she couldn't attend, and since I knew Marion, I gave in."

Anger had stripped his face of expression. "How could she turn up missing? Where the bloody hell were the adults?"

"I don't know." Lacy's words were spiced with fear, and she couldn't stop shivering.

"Hey, take it easy. We'll find her."

"How can you be so sure? What if—"

"Don't," he said sharply. "Let's see what we're faced with. Don't borrow trouble. She'll be all right."

He sounded so sure; she wanted to believe him. She *had* to believe him.

A short time later, Boothe brought the Cherokee to an abrupt halt in front of the house. Both he and Lacy spilled out at the same time. A frantic Marion Holt stood waiting for them.

"Oh, Lacy, I'm so sorry...so sorry."

"Just tell me what happened!" Lacy cried, stopping short of grabbing the hysterical woman and shaking her till her teeth rattled.

Lacy's words had the desired effect. Marion calmed immediately. "We...they...the kids...were playing hide-and-seek." She paused and sniffled.

"Go on," Lacy said.

"And everyone was found...except Joni. We...can't imagine where she got off to."

Boothe muttered a curse.

The blood drained from Lacy's face, but somehow she managed to ask, "How many chaperons are there?"

"Two—and they're out searching now."

"Come on," Boothe said, "show us where Joni was last seen. We don't have much time to waste." He peered at the sky. "Another snow is predicted for tonight, and from the looks of things, it's not going to wait."

Lacy's eyes followed his, then she felt her stomach plummet to her knees. As if he sensed her predicament, Boothe reached for her hand. They were halfway across the snow-covered yard when a figure appeared around the corner of the house, arms waving.

They stopped in their tracks.

"I've found her," a woman called. "She's fallen into a ravine."

All three adults broke into a run. Breathing hard, they stopped within touching distance of the woman.

"Where?" Lacy asked in a shrill voice.

"Over there."

"Oh, God." Lacy all but thrust the woman aside as she scrambled toward her child. All the while she prayed that those horrible images she'd conjured up would prove false. Joni with broken limbs, facial lacerations, even paralysis.

"I think she's all right," the woman was saying, "at least as far as I can tell."

"Let's get busy," Boothe snapped, taking charge.

They heard Joni before they actually saw her. The pitiful whimper, "Mom-mee," floated up the embankment. In that moment, Lacy felt pain so severe, she feared she would black out. But she didn't. Her strength came from Joni. Her child needed her. She mustn't let her down.

The woman who guided them stood back while Lacy and Boothe knelt at the top of the ravine and looked down. Despite the dim light of the cloud-covered sun, they could see Joni. She sat huddled at the bottom, her chapped cheeks saturated with tears.

"Mommy!"

"I'm here, darling. Are you all right?"

"I fell."

Lacy fought back the tears. "I know. Tell Mommy if you're hurt."

"Mommy!" Joni cried again.

Lacy cast frantic eyes to Boothe.

"Hiya, kiddo," Boothe said in an unruffled tone.

His voice dried Joni's sobs. She held up her tiny arms. "Boo, come get me."

"I'm on my way, sweetheart. You just hold tight, okay?"

Lacy noticed Boothe's features were pinched as tightly as hers. "Are you sure you can…I mean…" She broke off when she saw the look of grim determination in his eyes. Rescuing Joni was something he had to do, and she had to let him. But, dear Lord, she was scared for both Joni and Boothe.

"Be careful, Boothe," Lacy pleaded, her eyes grave as she took in the steepness of the slope. The snow covering was sealed in ice.

Boothe nodded before grabbing the nearest bush. Using its branches as leverage, he began a slow trek downward. Lacy looked on anxiously, feeling numb and slightly ill. What if he hurt himself? She raised a hand to her mouth to keep from voicing her fears.

Though his eyebrows were drawn together and his face pinched, he didn't hesitate. He made his way slowly and was halfway there when his bad leg suddenly gave way, buckling under him.

Lacy smothered a scream.

Boothe cursed vehemently as he struggled to regain his balance.

"Are—are you all right?"

"Yes," he said with terse hoarseness.

Lacy sensed his frustration and anger at his inability to function. Her heart went out to him, but she dared not let him know that.

"It's my bad leg," he bit out.

His face was gray and his eyes were sunken in his face. More than that, he couldn't move. He was trapped by his own inadequacy.

Panic rushed through Lacy, but she ignored it. "Stay put. I'm coming."

Boothe cursed again.

Lacy took a deep breath, then followed Boothe's path down the embankment. By the time she reached Boothe, he had sunk into the snow, his face twisted in pain.

"Let me get Joni, then I'll help you."

He shook his head in tight, angry movements. "Forget me. Just get her, if you can."

The next few minutes passed in a blur. To Lacy, every step seemed to take an hour. Finally, she reached her daughter.

"Oh, baby, my baby," she whispered, her arms closing around the shaking child.

"Mommy," Joni sighed.

Tears of joy trickled down Lacy's face as she clutched her daughter to her chest. Once she had regained control of her own emotions, she stood and looked up. Marion had tied a rope around her waist and, with the help of the other woman, had made it halfway down the ravine.

With Marion's help, Lacy got Joni to safety, then concentrated on helping Boothe, who had somehow managed to get to his feet. His teeth gritted, he bore some of his own weight and relied on the rope, eventually climbing to the ledge.

"See to Joni," Boothe said, catching his breath as he leaned heavily against a tree.

Despite the harrowing fall, Joni wasn't seriously hurt. Only a few scratches marred her cheeks and legs. Lacy went giddy with relief as she squeezed Joni to her, their tears mingling.

Once her emotions were under control, Lacy looked around. The women had disappeared, thankfully giving them privacy.

Boothe! Where was Boothe? She twisted her head. He had dragged himself free of the tree and was standing valiantly on two legs, staring into space.

Lacy cringed inside, having never seen such bleak despair on another human's face. She wanted to comfort him, to tell him it was all right that he couldn't rescue Joni, that she loved him anyway. But fear that she'd make it worse by saying anything kept her quiet.

"Mommy," Joni said, "put me down."

"All right." Lacy sniffed back the tears.

"Mommy, please . . . don't cry."

"I can't help it, honey."

"Where's Boo?"

"He's standing over there."

The child turned in Boothe's direction, where she stared at him for a long moment. As if she sensed something was wrong, she trotted to his side and looked up at him. "Is your leg hurt?"

He peered at Joni through pain-ridden eyes. "A little."

"Want me to rub it, Boo?" Joni's tone was serious.

Boothe smiled. "I'd like that."

"It'll make it better, I promise."

Lacy watched while tears blinded her and her heart swelled with love for the small child and the tough man. Yet she was afraid to move or even breathe, for fear she'd start crying and not be able to stop.

Chapter Nine

Boothe stood before the window and stared out at the snow-littered ground. From the upper floor in the doctor's office complex, he could see the park below. Tourists were there in droves, some ice-skating on a nearby rink, some listening to a civic group sing carols and others simply milling about, enjoying the smell and feel of Christmas.

Too bad some of that spirit couldn't rub off on him, he thought, stretching his lips into a tighter grimace. He jammed one hand into his jeans pocket and turned just as the door opened.

"Sorry to keep you waiting," Dr. Hank Stewart said as he ambled to his desk and laid a folder down in front of him.

"No problem," Boothe said, feigning a nonchalant attitude that he wished he could feel but didn't.

It wasn't Hank Stewart, personally, that made his stomach feel like it was in a meat grinder. As far as doctors went, he was an okay guy—middle-aged, nice-looking, competent, the whole works. But Boothe didn't trust doctors, no matter how professional. Since his accident, he'd been prodded and poked by the best. To date, his leg wasn't a bit better.

"Sit down, Mr. Larson," Dr. Stewart said, following his own advice and sitting in his oversize chair.

"I'll stand, if you don't mind."

"Suit yourself."

"What's the verdict, Doc?" Boothe asked without mincing words. He wanted the truth; he was tired of doctors tiptoeing around the tulips.

"First let me ask why you didn't return to the specialist that treated you in Houston? He's one of the best."

Boothe shrugged. "I felt he'd done all he could do."

"And you expect I can do more?" Dr. Stewart asked with a smile that took the sting out of his words.

Boothe shrugged again. "Don't know. Can you?"

"No."

Boothe had prepared himself for that very answer. Yet when it came, he felt he'd taken a sucker punch to the gut. It took all his willpower not to lash out at the doctor.

Dr. Stewart sought out Boothe's gaze. "You weren't expecting that, were you?"

"Yes and no."

"Unfortunately there are no miracle cures for your type of injury. When there's muscle as well as bone damage, the only thing that will help is therapy."

"I've been that route, and it's not what it's cracked up to be."

"I'm afraid you're going to have to learn to live with it, then."

"Oh, I can live with it, Doctor," Boothe said tersely. "That's not the problem. What I want is to return to my job—fighting fires. That's the problem."

Dr. Stewart's gaze didn't waver. "I'm sorry, but that won't be possible."

"Well, I guess that's that." With a hollow-eyed stare, Boothe strode to the desk and held out his hand. "Thanks, Doctor, for your time."

"I'm sorry."

"Yeah, me, too."

* * *

The days following Joni's fall were the most hectic Lacy could ever remember. The small resort town, according to the old-timers, had attracted more tourists this year than ever before.

She wasn't complaining, of course. People meant money in the coffer, and since the majority of her year's receipts was amassed during this holiday period, she had to take advantage of the boom. The downside was that it left little time for Boothe. He'd been by the shop on several occasions and had even taken Joni to his place one afternoon to play with Spike.

His leg was better, though his limp seemed to be worse. Lacy had asked him about it the day after the incident at the party. He'd said the leg was fine. She'd sensed he hadn't wanted to talk about it, so she hadn't pressed.

When she saw him tonight, she'd ask him again, for her own peace of mind, if nothing else.

She'd decided to take the afternoon off from work. She'd had no choice, actually. Both Sue and Pam had shooed her out the door of the shop, told her if she showed her face again that day, she'd be in a heap of trouble.

Lacy's hands had shot up in mock surrender. "Okay, okay. You've made your point. I'm outta here."

So far she'd stayed away, having spent the early part of the afternoon with Joni. They'd gone to the park, then shopping. Joni had wanted to buy gifts for her teacher, Sue's daughter, Melody, and Boothe. Lacy had also wanted to shop for Boothe, hoping he'd receive their gifts graciously. With Boothe, one never knew.

"Mommy, do you think Boo'll love my present?"

Lacy smiled, then flipped an errant strand of hair out of her daughter's face. "How did you know I was just thinking about that?"

"I didn't."

Lacy didn't bother to explain herself to her daughter when she was waiting in giddy anticipation for the evening. She'd invited Boothe to dinner, and once Joni was in bed, she had plans for her and Boothe. She ached to make love again, to feel his muscled body blanket hers, feel his hot lips—

"Mommy, wanna see?"

"See what, honey?" Lacy asked in a faraway voice.

"Boo's presents."

"But we just bought them."

"Let's look again."

Lacy smiled to herself. "Oh, all right, but then I have to get busy in the kitchen."

Joni led her into the bedroom where Boothe's gifts were spread on the bed, waiting to be wrapped. Joni had chosen a small picture of an eagle. Because it was cheap and in a cheap wooden frame, Lacy hadn't wanted Joni to buy it. But the child had her own money, and she was so sure Boothe would like the picture that Lacy hadn't the heart to deny her.

Lacy's choice was more traditional, but not any more glamorous. She had spotted the knit sweater first off, thinking it was the exact color of his eyes and had bought it.

"When can we wrap them?" Joni asked, fingering the sweater.

"How 'bout right now?"

"Oh, boy!"

Lacy chuckled.

"You know what, Mommy, I can't wait for Boo to come."

Lacy squeezed her daughter's hand. "Me, either," she said huskily. "Me, either."

Boothe took the book from Joni's hand and began to read. " 'Twas the night before Christmas...' "

Earlier, they had eaten the hearty pre-Christmas dinner Lacy had lovingly prepared, which consisted of smoked turkey, candied sweet potatoes, dressing, two kinds of salad and pecan pie.

Once the kitchen sparkled, Joni had clamored to see the Christmas lights. They had piled into the Cherokee and driven through the town proper and the outlying neighborhoods. The tour had taken a little over an hour.

The instant they had returned to her apartment, Lacy had gone straight to the kitchen and popped a huge bowl of popcorn and perked wassail. They had just finished devouring both when Joni crawled into his lap with a book in hand.

Now, Lacy paused in the second clean-up process and listened to Boothe's deep voice as he read to Lacy.

"Do you like *Night Before Christmas?*" Joni asked when the poem came to an end.

"You betcha," Boothe said with feeling.

"Good, then you can read it to me again."

Boothe tapped her on the nose. "I have to tell you, Joni girl, you're a piece of work."

Lacy watched Boothe's smile, whose wattage had the power to turn her insides to putty. Suddenly she felt herself relax, where before she hadn't. She'd been uneasy. Something was different about Boothe but she couldn't pinpoint what it was. The feeling came from her gut and not her heart and she knew better than to ignore it.

But seeing him with Joni reinforced her confidence. Her imagination had played a trick on her. Nothing was wrong. In fact, everything was just right.

Boothe cared for her and Joni. Some people had difficulty putting their feelings into words, she rationalized. Boothe was one of them. She'd have to be patient and know that soon he would commit himself, that they would be together as a family.

"But it's not the night before Christmas yet, you know," Joni was saying in that grown-up voice she used with Boothe, as if to impress him.

Lacy chuckled silently while she listened for Boothe's reply.

"How do you know?" he asked, equally as serious.

"'Cause I just do."

Lacy shook her head. Boothe was right. Her Joni was some piece of work.

"Now, that's a dumb answer," Boothe teased.

Joni giggled.

"I bet you don't know when Santa comes."

"Do, too," Joni responded in a sharp, prissy tone.

Lacy walked back into the living room, her eyes on her daughter. "Watch it," she warned mildly. "That's no way to talk to Boothe."

Joni lowered her head.

"It's past your bedtime, anyway. Give Boo a goodnight kiss."

"Oh, Mommy..."

"Do what your mother says," Boothe put in, then hugged the child to his side and placed a finger in the middle of his cheek. "Lay it on me."

Joni grinned, puckered her lips and smacked him on target.

When Joni climbed down from the couch and followed Lacy from the room, Lacy realized her lashes were soaked with unshed tears.

"Is she asleep?"

"Out like a light, thank goodness," Lacy said as she sank onto the couch close to Boothe.

Boothe didn't say anything but Lacy didn't mind. Quiet felt good. They listened to the fire pop and sizzle in the fireplace. The twinkling Christmas-tree lights added more warmth to the room.

If Lacy hadn't been so aware of Boothe's vibrant presence beside her, she might have closed her eyes and drifted to sleep. But she didn't want to squander a moment of their precious time together. She wanted to feel his arms around her, his lips on hers. . . .

"Boothe."

"What?"

She stretched lazily, knowing that her full, aching breasts jutted wantonly against her knit blouse. "I've missed you," she said softly.

His gaze rested on her lips, then her breasts. A muscle jerked in his cheek, but he didn't reach for her. Instead he stood and walked to the fireplace.

Her nerve endings tingled an alarm. "What's . . . the matter?"

He turned and steadied his gaze on her, as if he were trying to commit her features to memory.

Alarm escalated to panic. "Why are you—" she paused, the tears she refused to shed ached in her throat "—looking at me like that?"

"After tonight, I won't be seeing you...and Joni anymore."

Shock stripped Lacy's face of color. "What— You can't mean that," she choked out.

"Oh, I mean it, all right," he said, twisting his lips into a bitter line.

"But—but I thought..."

His gaze avoided hers. "Well, you thought wrong."

Lacy jumped to her feet, though her flimsy legs barely held her upright, and forced him to face her. "Something happened, and I want to know what."

"Don't—" His throat hitched in a dry swallow. "Just let it go. Let *me* go."

For a moment, she was struck dumb by knee-jerk anger. "No, to both!" she finally said in a shrill voice. "I love you. You have to know that. So why—why are you doing this?" Her words ended on a whimpered sob.

"Because, dammit, you deserve someone who's not a cripple, who's whole and can earn you a decent living."

"Are you crazy? It's not your legs I love, but *you*, what's inside you, for God's sake. I don't care if you're crippled."

His eyes remained flat and cold. "Well, I do."

"You know what I think?"

He didn't answer.

"I'm going to tell you, anyway," she said fiercely. She was fighting for her sanity, for her future. "I think you like being the lone ranger, wallowing in your own self-pity."

"You don't know what I think," he countered in a voice that matched the intensity in his eyes.

"Is—is that all you have to say?"

"It's over, Lacy. That's all there is to say."

Lacy fought off the urge to scream, to launch herself at him, to plead, but she knew her words would fall on deaf ears. The harsh lines in his face were cast in granite. Her heart shuddered in her body; her stomach contracted to the size of a marble.

She was wasting her time; the bitterness, the scars had cut too deep. Drawing herself to full height, she said, "All right, if that's the way you want it, then go. But I want you to know that I think you're a world-class coward, Boothe Larson, and that you're right, I am ... better off without you."

He looked at her with dead eyes, then turned and walked softly to the door.

Only after she was alone did she grab her stomach. Everything that held her world in place had come apart, and there wasn't one thing she could do about it.

But she couldn't fall apart. She couldn't afford that luxury. She had Joni to think about. *Joni!* Oh, God. The box with Boothe's present in it that Joni had so lovingly wrapped sprang to mind. Her daughter would be heartbroken.

Lacy sat down on the couch, dropped her head in her hands and wept.

Chapter Ten

Desperation had driven Boothe to pick up the phone and call his boss at the Forestry Office. Max Helm had been delighted to hear from him, as Boothe figured he would be. But he hadn't wanted to talk over the phone; he'd insisted on talking face-to-face.

Boothe had told him to come to his place.

Now as the two men ambled back toward Max's truck, they still hadn't discussed the nitty-gritty reason for the visit.

Max rubbed the bald spot on the top of his head and took in his surroundings. "I can say one thing—you're in the boondocks."

"Ah, 'boondocks' is relative," Boothe replied with a benign smile that never reached his eyes.

"Well, I'll have to agree it's peaceful here and suits you to a T."

"There's no other place I'd rather be."

Max pawed a patch of ice with his boot, then threw Boothe an odd look. "What the hell's going on with you? We've circled the damn mulberry bush long enough. For someone who pretends to love the solitary life, you're a tad uptight."

Boothe grunted. "You know me too well, Max."

They had reached the front porch of the cabin and instead of going to Max's truck, they climbed the steps and sat in the glider. The afternoon was lovely—cold, but clear. For a moment both men breathed the pine-scented air and moved the glider back and forth.

"Don't you think you've beat up on yourself long enough?"

"It's not that, even though I still blame myself for Calvin's death and always will."

"Well, if you like being a martyr..."

Boothe shot him a hard look. "You always did cut to the chase, didn't you?"

"Don't see any reason not to. So I'll ask again, what's going on?"

"I won't be able to fight any more fires," Boothe said in a dull tone.

"Doctor tell you that?"

"Yep."

"So come back as a field supervisor. Old Charley is due to retire out of the Ozark office in about three months." Max sighed. "I know that's *not* what you want to do, but—"

"No, it's not," Boothe said flatly, "but will you let me think about it?"

"Take all the time you need."

Max stood. "As much as I'd like to stay, I gotta get back. Oh, by the way, you never did say what's got you stretched tighter than Dick's hatband."

"I'm not going to, either."

Max chuckled. "You were always a maverick, but the best at what you did. I guess that's why I take your bull."

"Go on, get outta here," Boothe ordered roughly, but smiled in spite of himself.

Boothe remained in the drive and watched until Max's truck disappeared. Then, with slumped shoulders and a set to his jaw, he trudged back to the porch and plopped back down on the glider. But he couldn't stay seated. His mind and body were possessed by demons who insisted on tormenting him.

It had been that way since he'd walked out on Lacy, since he'd flung her love back in her face. Still, he clung to the belief that he'd done her a favor. It had hurt; God, how it had hurt. When she'd told him he was a coward, pain and rage had battled within him. He hadn't been able to defend himself because there had been no words to describe the desolation he'd felt that day Joni needed him and he'd been helpless.

So he'd stood like a zombie, Lacy's pinched, white face devastating him, creating that dead feeling inside him. That same feeling now threatened to consume him.

He should have known better than to get involved. He'd known what would happen. People who dabbled in unnecessary emotions deserved to get hurt. His only alternative now was to block thoughts of Lacy and Joni from his mind and continue with his life as if nothing had changed.

Fat chance. No amount of reasoning could ease his torment. Thoughts of Lacy and how it felt to be inside her drove him crazy. He had tasted paradise and wanted more.

He lurched out of the glider, only to wince and feel sweat pop out on his upper lip, reminding him of his incapacitation. Yet he could work. Max had offered him a job, though not the one he wanted. Fieldwork was lost to him forever, but at least he could make Lacy a decent living and—

He chopped off his thoughts suddenly, brutally. Even if he wanted to approach Lacy to tell her what a hardheaded sonofabitch he was, she would refuse to see him.

Or would she?

He had everything he wanted—everything except someone to love, someone to love *him*.

Sweat trickled into his mouth. He swiped at it with the back of his hand, his mind on fire. What if he went to her and begged her to forgive him? If there was even the remote chance that she'd see him, he'd take it. He realized that now with a certainty born out of more loneliness and pain than he could bear.

With that admission came sudden peace and a determination to try again. This time he damn well wouldn't screw up.

"Mommy, why can't I go see Boo?"

Joni's pouting lips and whiny tone grated on Lacy's nerves. But instead of scolding her like she wanted to, Lacy bit her tongue and counted to ten. Joni's irritability was partly her fault. She'd been short-tempered and impatient, and the child sensed something was wrong. "Because I've been too busy at the store," she said at last, which was the truth, only it wasn't the real reason.

"Why can't Boo come see me?"

Lacy shouldn't have been surprised by that questions, but she was. She groped for an answer. "Well, I suspect he's busy, too."

"Why's he busy?"

Lacy gnawed at the inside of her mouth. "Making wood carvings, perhaps," she said, grabbing the first thing that came to mind. Soon, though, she was going to have to tell Joni the truth, that she wouldn't see "her" Boo anymore. Lacy knew she had to do that dreaded task before Christmas Day—because he wouldn't be showing up.

Lacy winced at the pain that stabbed her heart. She missed Boothe so much that the pain never subsided.

Had it only been three days since he'd rejected her? It seemed an eternity.

Joni hadn't helped. She continually talked about Boo and Santa in the same breath. Today proved no different.

"Why can't Boo be my daddy?" Joni pressed.

Lacy feared her heart might burst. "Can we talk about this later?" she pleaded. "Anyway, we're due at your party in twenty minutes."

The following day, Christmas Eve, dawned with a fresh snowfall, which meant Christmas Day would be perfect. White Christmases weren't something Lacy took for granted.

But the beauty outside had little effect on Lacy's numbed heart. Still...she had to pretend, for Joni's sake. Since it was Sunday and the store was closed, she had promised Joni they would make cookies, and Joni wasn't about to let her forget. In addition, Lacy had to prepare Christmas dinner for the two of them.

Sue had asked them over, but Lacy had declined. She wasn't fit company for anyone. Besides, she needed to stay busy, to do something constructive that would keep her mind off Boothe.

By the time evening rolled around, Santa-, Rudolph- and ornament-shaped cookies filled three tin boxes. The turkey and all the trimmings were in the refrigerator, ready to be baked the next morning. Lacy was exhausted, but not enough to sleep.

She could hear Joni splashing in the bath, readying herself for bed. When she was finished, Lacy planned to tell her that Boothe wouldn't be coming to see them Christmas Day.

Blinded by sudden tears, Lacy switched the kitchen light off and stumbled toward the living room. Instead of sitting down, she walked to the window and lolled her head against the pane. She couldn't see anything; the tears wouldn't let her.

She had to stop grieving. Life had to go on. She had a lot to be thankful for. Her shop had made a small fortune. And just yesterday, she had paid a healthy sum down on the business.

But her business, even her daughter—God forgive her—were no longer enough. When Boothe had rejected her, something had twisted inside her and she could no longer function.

So why hadn't she fought harder? He loved her, she knew. So why had she let him off the hook so easily? Those questions came out of the blue. She staggered against their blow. Feeling her head spin, she jerked upright.

Maybe when it came down to it, *she* was the coward. She had given up too easily. She should have tried harder to knock some sense into his hard head. Hadn't she learned long ago that if something wasn't worth fighting for, it wasn't worth having?

Should she try again to convince him that she loved him, no matter what? Yes! her heart cried. She owed it to herself and to Joni.

"Mommy, I'm finished."

Lacy swung around. Her daughter stood naked just inside the room, her curls in damp disarray.

"I see you are, sweetheart."

"Why are you crying, Mommy? Are you afraid Santa won't come to see you?"

"Hopefully, he'll come see us both."

"Is it time yet?"

"No, it's too early for Santa. Before he comes, we have to go somewhere."

"Where?"

"I'll tell you on the way," Lacy said, her voice unsteady, still reeling from the thought of what she was about to do. "Let's dress you in something nice and warm."

Ten minutes later, Lacy clutched her daughter by the hand and headed toward the door. The unfamiliar noise stopped them midstride. They listened. Bells. The sound of jingle bells filled the air.

"Mommy, Mommy, it's Santa!" Joni cried, then rushed to the window.

Lacy stood still, fearing she had lost her mind.

"Mommy, hurry!"

Joni's excited voice forced Lacy's limbs into action. She crossed to Joni's side and uttered a startled, "Oh."

A horse-drawn wagon, decorated with twinkling lights and bells, occupied the space in front of the shop. A person dressed like Santa sat atop it.

While Lacy and Joni looked on, the man jumped down, then reached for a sack that overflowed with toys.

"I told you it was Santa!" Joni cried again.

"It's...Boo...dressed like Santa," Lacy managed to say before her daughter dashed to the door and pulled it open.

By the time Lacy reached the sidewalk, Joni was clinging to his leg. But his eyes, glistening in the moonlight with unshed tears, were on Lacy.

"Will . . . you forgive me?" Boothe said simply.

"Do you love me?"

"More than life itself."

"Then that's all that matters."

"No, it matters that I'm a sonofabitch—"

"Mommy, what's a sono—"

"Never mind, Joni," Lacy said without taking her eyes off Boothe.

"Will you marry me?"

Joni tugged on Boothe's hand, distracting him. He lowered himself to her level. "What, sweetheart?"

"Are you gonna be my daddy?"

"Do you want me to?"

"Uh-huh." Joni placed her tiny palm on his cheek. "You aren't gonna leave me and go to heaven like my other daddy, are you?"

"Oh, Joni," Lacy whispered.

Boothe swallowed hard. "Not any time soon, I hope." He reached for the child and, with her in his arms, straightened to his full height.

Lacy could feel the blood pounding frantically in her head as his gaze locked on her once again. "Well, are you going to marry me?"

"Yes! Yes! Yes!" Lacy cried, and flung herself into his arms.

"Ouch, Mommy. You and Daddy are squeezing me."

Lacy and Boothe squeezed that much harder.

The house was quiet.

Once Joni and Boothe had exchanged presents, Joni had fallen asleep in Boothe's lap. Together Lacy and

Boothe put the child into her bed, then, hand in hand, they had gone into Lacy's room to her bed.

Their coupling had been swift, hot and complete.

Now they faced each other, content in their togetherness.

"Mmm, this is nice," Lacy said in a dreamy voice. "Tell me I don't ever have to leave you or this warm bed."

Boothe nuzzled her neck. "I'll never leave you again."

"What made you . . . change your mind?"

"And come after you, you mean?"

She nodded, her throat suddenly too full to speak.

"It's simple—I couldn't face another day without you . . . without Joni."

"I . . . was on the way out the door when you pulled up in that wagon and uncoordinated Santa outfit."

"Why, woman, them's blasphemous words. I worked hard on getting that outfit together."

"Yeah, right."

He nuzzled her neck again. "Okay, so it took all of two minutes."

She hugged him, and for a moment they were quiet.

He pulled back and looked at her, his eyes serious. "I have a job."

Lacy's breath caught. "You do?"

"Yep." His face clouded. "It's not my first choice—"

"There's no chance you can return to fighting fires?"

"None. The slip on the ice trying to get Joni axed that."

"I still blame my—"

"Shh, don't say it. It wasn't your fault—it wasn't anybody's fault."

"So what will you do?"

"Field supervisor, out of the main office about thirty miles away." He grinned. "It ain't the real thing, but close."

"Will you like it?"

"If I have you to come home to every day, I can love it."

"And I love *you,*" she whispered.

"Prove it."

It didn't take long for Lacy to fill the order, then find herself lying contentedly beside him again, just as before.

"Let's go play Santa," Boothe suggested. "Our daughter'll be up in no time."

Lacy's heart tripped. *Our daughter.* Already they were a family, and it felt good, oh, so good.

Boothe put on his jeans while Lacy slipped into a robe. Arm in arm, they went into the living room. The tree lights and the smoldering fire greeted them, bathing them in their warmth.

After a moment, Boothe disentangled himself and walked to the near-empty bag. "I have a present for you," he said, looking over his shoulder.

"You're the only present I want or need."

"Ditto," he said huskily. "So just consider this icing on the cake. Now, shut your eyes."

"You've got to be kidding."

"Nope. Go on, shut your eyes."

"Oh, all right."

She waited, but didn't feel him put anything in her hands.

"You can look now," he finally said.

She opened her eyes, gasped, then laughed. A box sat on the floor filled with the most exquisite wood carvings she'd ever seen.

He leaned and kissed her. "Merry Christmas, my heart."

*   *   *   *   *

A Note from Mary Lynn Baxter

Christmas for my family is a joyous occasion. While we love the hoopla that surrounds the holidays, we do try to keep our focus on the real meaning of Christmas.

This year will be extra special, since we recently moved into a new house. I'm eager to decorate it and fill it with the smells of Christmas.

However, on Christmas morning my husband, Len, and I turn off our tree lights, load the car with our presents and head to my parents' house. My brother, sister-in-law and their three children meet us there.

We then gather in the living room and pass out gifts. Everyone makes a big to-do over their presents, whether big or small. Following the gift-opening ritual, we gather at the table for our noon meal.

The main attraction there is my husband's smoked turkey breast, which has just come off the outside smoker, stuffed with jalapeno peppers. The extra added attractions are my mother's chicken-and-dressing, chicken-and-dumplings and various vegetables and sweets.

While we certainly enjoy the food the remainder of the day, the most precious moments are the time we share together as a family in loving thankfulness for our blessings.

My wish for each of you is a safe and happy holiday.

Mary Lynn Baxter

HEARTS OF HOPE

Sondra Stanford

A recipe from Sondra Stanford:

PEANUT MOUNDS

12 oz pkg butterscotch morsels
6 oz pkg semisweet chocolate morsels
12 oz salted Spanish peanuts

Melt combined morsels in top of double boiler over boiling water on stove, or melt in large bowl in microwave, following manufacturer's directions for melting chocolate.

When morsels are all melted and stirred together, pour in salted peanuts. Stir until all peanuts are coated. Drop by teaspoonfuls onto waxed paper. Let cool and harden. Then enjoy!

Chapter One

Mary Shelton pushed open the heavy door and stepped outside of Hope Elementary School. Her friend, first grade teacher Jan Crane, was behind her.

It was a brilliantly sunlit afternoon in early December, but its beauty was deceptive. The air had a chilling edge that hadn't been there earlier. Mary was glad for the jacket she wore over her straight black skirt and soft blouse. Jan, in only a silky dress, shivered as she dug inside her purse for her car keys.

"Can I give you a lift, Mary?" Jan asked. "It's pretty cold today."

"Thanks, but my place is only a couple of blocks away," Mary responded. "Anyway, it'll give me time to begin organizing my thoughts."

"Don't let the job throw you," Jan advised. "You'll do just fine as the new Christmas program director."

Mary grimaced. "I hope you're right. I'd just feel a little better about it if I had some experience in the department. From what I understand, Jackie Murphy is a hard act to follow."

During the faculty meeting that had just ended, Mary had been given the news by the principal that she was to take over running the school's annual Christmas show. The fifth-grade teacher who'd handled the task for the past twenty years was recovering in a Houston hospital from an emergency appendectomy.

"She does a wonderful job, all right," Jan admitted, "but so will you. And Lydia Willis will be a big help to you. She's assisted Jackie the last few years, so she knows all the ropes."

"I wish she could take over the program, and just let me be her assistant," Mary said. This was her first semester teaching at Hope Elementary and, as a newcomer, she didn't feel confident about being thrust into a leadership position yet.

"Lydia doesn't read music. Besides Jackie, you're the only musical talent on staff, so there was really no choice but to load the job onto your shoulders."

"I know." Mary's long blond hair, pinned back by a large black bow, swished against her shoulders as she nodded. "I just hope I can do Jackie justice. I hear practically the entire town turns out for the event."

Jan grinned. "There aren't a whole lot of entertainment options in Hope, Texas. We take our cultural stimulation wherever we can find it." At Mary's anxious expression, she laughed. "Honestly, Mary, there's no need to get into a swivet. Remember, you're merely the director, not the star of the program. The children are. *They're* the ones folks come to see, and a more tolerant audience you'll never hope to find anywhere than a bunch of doting mamas, papas, grandparents and assorted relatives and friends. Nobody'll be paying the least bit of attention to you!"

Mary laughed. "Thanks! My ego needed that!"

Jan laughed, too. "Well, I'm off to the supermarket. Pete had a job interview in Nacogdoches today, so he'll be late getting home. I want to have a good meal waiting on the table for him when he finally gets in tonight."

"I had no idea you were thinking of moving."

A shadow passed over Jan's face. Her husband had been out of work ever since the Ledbetter Refrigeration Plant closed seven months ago. "If he gets a decent-paying job somewhere else, we'll have to move. What choice do we have? A lot of other folks are hurting, the same as us," she said sadly. "If something doesn't change soon, the school's going to start losing a lot of its students as their parents find jobs elsewhere. Then where will *our* jobs be?" She shrugged, then added philosophically, "There's no sense standing here brooding about what can't be helped. See you tomorrow, Mary."

Despite the cold, Mary walked home slowly. She was in no hurry to shut herself inside the small house she'd rented on Oak Grove Street. She had moved to the small community of Hope just before the beginning of the fall semester in order to teach second grade. Growing up an only child on a West Texas ranch, she had never suffered from loneliness or boredom when she was alone, but for the past few months, ever since the fiasco in Abilene, she had discovered that she had far more solitude than was good for her.

The other teachers at school were friendly enough, but most of them were a good deal older than Mary's twenty-six years. Jan was the only one close to her age and was probably her best friend in town, but Jan had a busy life with her husband and their baby, so Mary didn't see much of her outside of school.

Mr. Starr, Mary's elderly, widowed neighbor across the street, was outside sweeping off his front porch when she approached her own house. He lifted one hand in greeting and Mary waved back.

The silence of the empty house felt like an assault to Mary when she entered it. Other people had busy, interesting lives to go home to after work—husbands, wives, children. She had no one at all to care about whether she came or went.

Mary kicked off her pumps and made herself a cup of hot tea. When it was ready, she carried it into the living room where she sat down at the piano. Listlessly she began picking out the notes to "Jingle Bells."

The piano was the reason Mary had rented this particular house. It had belonged to her landlady's deceased sister, along with the rest of the furnishings. The piano was a wonderful, unexpected bonus and it had helped her pass many a lonely hour. She could always lose herself in music or books.

For all her uncertainties about tackling the job of running the school Christmas program, Mary didn't mind the extra work. She much preferred staying busy to having too much free time to think... or to brood. No, what she did mind was the holiday itself.

Mary dreaded Christmas. How on earth would she ever get through it? Last Christmas there'd been her grandmother... and Wayne.

This year she had no one.

Her hand crashed down heavily on the piano keys, creating a discordant thud. Mary dropped the lid, stood up and, ignoring her untouched tea, thrust her feet back into her shoes, grabbed her purse and jacket and headed out the door.

The best weapon against the onset of depression was action. So what if she was alone this Christmas. So what if she had no one to exchange gifts with. She would treat herself to the finest Christmas she could afford.

Mary got into her gray three-year-old Honda and drove to Main Street. She passed the supermarket,

Hope's First State Bank, a service station and Green's Real Estate offices. Just past the drugstore was a lot that was normally empty. Now there was a small portable metal building on the site, surrounded by dozens of Christmas trees and a wire fence.

Mary parked her car and got out. She intended to buy herself the biggest, prettiest tree she could find.

Rob Green slouched in the open doorway of the portable building. His frayed jeans were streaked with axle grease and smudges of red soil. His blue T-shirt was as filthy as his jeans, but it was mostly concealed beneath a clean, though faded and old, flannel-lined denim jacket. His Western boots matched the rest of his appearance—dull and dusty, all mute testimony that he'd been working hard.

His dark brown eyes were hooded beneath the brim of a blue baseball cap as he watched customers inspecting the small forest of Christmas trees for sale. It amused him to watch an entire family huddle together to debate the merits of one tree over another before making a final choice.

Rob's friend and neighbor, Ed Watson, operated the Christmas tree lot. At that moment he was busy helping a customer load a large tree onto the bed of a pickup truck. Ed had managed only a brief nod in Rob's direction when he'd arrived.

The beautiful sunlit day had degenerated into a foggy, damp, cold evening. Misty halos surrounded the lights that were strung on poles around the lot.

When Ed was free, he joined Rob inside the small metal building that served as a temporary office. "There's fresh coffee I haven't had time to touch. Want a cup?"

"Sounds good," Rob replied.

The tiny room was crowded with two chairs, a card table that served as a desk and another small table with the coffeemaker.

"What are you up to tonight?" Ed asked idly as he poured some coffee.

"Hanging out until it's time to pick up Holly." Holly was Rob's eight-year-old daughter. "She's at a classmate's house. They're making a shadow box project for school. The other girl's mother invited her to dinner, so I told her I'd pick her up at eight." He glanced down at his less-than-impeccable clothes. "I didn't have time to shower and change before bringing Holly to town. I've been mending fences and working on the tractor this afternoon."

Ed nodded with complete understanding. The two men had grown up within a half mile of each other, both sons of farmers. Ed still farmed his family's land. He'd built a modern home for his wife and children across the road from the farmhouse where his widowed mother still lived. Ed also leased most of the farmland Rob had inherited from his parents. Rob still lived on the land in a new home he had built, but he'd given up farming in favor of operating a real estate company in town. He'd only kept a couple of fields for a few head of cattle and his horses.

"How's business?" Rob asked as he picked up his coffee.

"Not bad, considering it's so early in the month," Ed declared. "You want to pick out a tree?"

Rob grinned. "You know Holly. I'd never hear the end of it if we didn't go out into the woods and cut our own."

Ed nodded. Even though he sold Christmas trees every December, it was the same way with his family. He started to speak, but instead he suddenly whipped out a handkerchief and sneezed. He sneezed again. And again.

"Sounds like a bad cold," Rob murmured sympathetically.

"Yep. I can't seem to shake it, and this damp, cold air is not doing it a bit of good."

"Why don't you close early and get on home to bed?" Rob suggested. He peered out the doorway. "There are no more customers, anyway."

Ed sneezed once more, then murmured, "I think I will. I've been feeling worse 'n' worse all evening." He slapped his forehead. "Oh, I forgot! I promised Randy's teacher I'd deliver her tree to her house when I finish here tonight."

Rob was mildly surprised. "Since when did you start delivering trees to people's houses?"

"I don't really." Ed doubled over and sneezed a couple of more times. "Not as a rule, anyhow. Sometimes for someone like old Mrs. Phillips. But the teacher wanted that tree over there." He pointed through the doorway to a tall full tree with a red Sold tag dangling from a branch. "And there was no way that tree was gonna fit inside her little Honda, so I said I'd deliver it after closing." He grinned sheepishly. "I figure I owe her for coping with my rascally son at school every day."

Rob grinned. Randy was a livewire seven-year-old, all right. Poor Ed sneezed again and Rob glanced at his watch. "Where does this teacher live? I've got time to deliver the tree to her before picking up Holly. You just close up here and go on home."

"Bless you," Ed mumbled through his handkerchief.

Fifteen minutes later Rob arrived at the small, unpretentious house on Oak Grove Street. A Honda was parked in the drive.

Rob hadn't formed any particular mental image of the teacher, but he certainly hadn't expected the angelic vision that confronted him when she opened the front door.

She was young and extremely attractive, with long golden hair and a sensational figure beneath a straight dark skirt and a silky blouse. Rob wished he could make out the color of her eyes, but he wasn't near enough to her for that.

"Miss Shelton?"

She tilted her head up, but there was a wariness in her voice when she replied, "Yes. May I help you?"

Rob touched the brim of his cap and slightly inclined his head in that age-old Texas-gentleman custom of greeting a lady. He was completely unaware of the fact that he even did it. "I've brought your Christmas tree," he said.

"But...Mr. Watson...?"

"He sent me. Do you want me to carry it into the house for you, or leave it out here on your front porch?"

"Would you mind taking it to the back porch?"

"Of course not."

"I'll turn on the light for you," she told him.

As he ambled back to the truck, Rob carried the impression of a slightly upturned nose, generous lips and wide-spaced eyes. The teacher couldn't have been long in Hope, he mused, or he would surely have seen her before.

The outside light was on when Rob dragged the large tree around the side of the house toward the back porch. Miss Shelton was standing on the porch with her arms crossed beneath her breasts as though she were cold.

"I don't know where you plan to put it when you get it inside," Rob commented, as he mounted the steps to the porch. "This is a pretty large tree. You'll probably need to trim off some of the lower branches as well as part of the trunk before you can even get it into a stand, much less into the house."

"You're right," she replied, while Rob propped the tree in a corner of the porch. "I knew the tree was too big, but it was so beautiful I just couldn't stop myself from buying it." She gave a soft, self-deprecating laugh. "I'm afraid I've bitten off more than I can chew."

Rob liked the sweet, almost musical tone of the teacher's voice. He bet her students did, too. He dusted his hands against the legs of his jeans and stepped closer to her. Beneath the bright porch light, he was able to see her clearly. His earlier conclusions had been correct. Miss Shelton was more than merely attractive; she was downright beautiful!

Rob's blood heated up, catching him off guard. He found himself gazing at her lips and wondering what they tasted like, whether they were really as soft as they looked and what it would feel like to thread his hands through her silky spun-gold hair. He was amazed at his reaction to her. It had been a long time since he'd been this powerfully attracted to any woman.

And it was showing. Rob was unaware of it, but the fire in his blood ignited a telltale flame in the depths of his dark eyes as his gaze slowly rose to meet Mary's.

Rob collected his thoughts enough to form a coherent question. "Do you have someone to trim the branches for you?"

Mary was disconcerted by the raw, virile magnetism of the man. He was so large! And she scarcely topped five foot three. She supposed it was the sheer size of him causing the breathlessness she felt in his presence! But there was no rhyme or reason to her sudden, and entirely unexpected, attraction toward him.

She was shaken by the feelings he stirred within her. He towered above her, and his massive shoulders matched his impressive height. Mary wondered fleetingly whether he worked out with weights, but she rejected the notion immediately. This man plainly labored physically in his everyday work. His frayed, stained jeans, dirty boots and scraped hands were evidence of hard physical labor.

Her eyes lingered on those strong, work-hardened hands, and she found herself wondering what it would feel like to be stroked by them in the throes of lovemaking.

Mary was horrified at herself. Had she gone insane? She couldn't believe she was having such inappropriate thoughts about a man she'd never seen before.

"Are you all right?" Concern was evident in the man's voice.

He unnerved Mary by stepping closer to her. She hoped he couldn't sense what had just been running through her mind. Mary's face reddened and something caught in her throat as his compelling gaze met and held hers for a long moment. With tremulous effort, she mustered a smile. "I'm fine. Sorry...you were saying?"

"Do you have someone to trim the tree branches for you? I don't have time tonight, but if you need someone to trim them, I can bring my saw and come back tomorrow evening."

Mary was tempted to accept his offer. She didn't own a saw, and she definitely needed help with this mammoth-sized tree she'd bought, but she couldn't take advantage of the man's good nature. By the look of him, he'd probably been very tired tonight already from working hard all day, even before he'd brought over her tree.

"Thanks, but that's not necessary." Mary deliberately avoided answering his question directly.

Rob nodded briskly. "All right, then. Good night."

"Good night," Mary replied. "And thanks." As she watched him descend the porch steps, she remembered just in time the bill she clutched in her right hand. She had grabbed it from her wallet on her way through the house while the man was getting the tree from the truck. "Wait!" she called out.

Rob halted as his booted foot touched the bottom step and he half turned around. "Yes?"

Mary went to the top of the steps and extended her hand.

Rob was totally astonished when she said, "Here's your tip. I'm so sorry that I almost forgot it."

This Miss Shelton obviously took him for a common laborer employed by Ed Watson. He didn't know whether to laugh, play along or be insulted.

Trying to suppress a grin he felt tugging at the corners of his mouth, Rob held his hand upright in a negative gesture. "That's entirely unnecessary."

"Oh, no, please!" Mary pleaded in a voice filled with distress. "It was extra work bringing the tree to my house. I owe you something for your trouble. Please . . . I'll feel awful if you don't accept it."

Rob bit his lower lip to keep his amusement from bubbling over. "In that case," he said at last, "I'll accept it, ma'am. The last thing I'd want to do is to cause you to feel bad."

He took the folded bill from her fingers and, as his hand lightly brushed hers, he found that one of his assumptions had proven correct. Miss Shelton did indeed have very soft, very smooth skin.

Once more, Rob touched the brim of his cap. "Thanks very much, ma'am. Good night." He turned and strode quickly around the house and back to his truck.

Inside the cab of his truck, the dashboard light disclosed that she'd shoved a fiver into his hand. Rob sighed, stashed the bill in the breast pocket of his jacket and wondered how the devil he was going to be able to return the money to the school teacher without embarrassing her or offending her pride.

But as he drove away his thoughts weren't on the unnecessary tip, but on the unexpected woman from whom it had come. Rob had found Miss Shelton enormously attractive and that unsettled him. He didn't want to start having those kinds of feelings again.

They'd burned him once. They could burn him again.

Chapter Two

Mary graded the last of the arithmetic test papers and stacked it on top of the others. Sighing, she thrust the lot into her desk drawer. Then she pushed back her chair and went to the coat closet for her raincoat and umbrella. It had been raining all day. The playground outside her classroom window looked like a lake.

Mary's footsteps echoed loudly on the marble floor as she walked down the hall toward the main lobby. She glanced down at her red dress shoes and wished she had a pair of galoshes.

Evidently she was the last to leave the building today. Usually there was a custodian around, but she neither saw nor heard him.

When she rounded the corner to the lobby, she was surprised to see a little girl standing near the doors. She wore jeans and a heavy blue and pink sports jacket, and her nose was pressed against the wide glass window panel as she gazed at the driving rain.

At Mary's approach, the girl turned swiftly, startled. Mary recognized her as one of Mrs. Daniel's third-graders who had participated in the Christmas program rehearsal earlier this afternoon. She had a speaking part in the play.

She was a very lovely child with long, straight, almost-black hair and fluffy bangs over her forehead. Just now there was a woebegone expression on her face, and her dark eyes were filled with unmistakable anxiety.

Mary paused and smiled. "You're Holly Green, aren't you?"

The girl nodded.

"Why are you still here?" Mary asked gently. "It's after four o'clock."

"My daddy was s'posed to come for me." The child's voice quavered. "But he didn't."

The secretary's office, where there was a telephone, was locked for the night, so there was no way to call Holly's father. Obviously Mary couldn't go off and leave the child here alone.

"I'll take you home," she offered.

"Thanks, Miss Shelton," Holly murmured. She was plainly relieved. "But what about my daddy?"

"We'll leave him a note." Mary returned to her classroom long enough to jot down a note and grab some tape.

Mary ripped off strips of tape and handed them to Holly, who taped the note on the outside of one of the doors. When it was secure, they dashed across the parking lot to Mary's car.

Holly's home was several miles out of town. On the way there, Mary set the girl at ease by talking with her. "Is your father a farmer?" she asked.

"Sort of," Holly answered. "He has some cattle, but Mr. Eddie farms the land that my daddy got from my granddaddy."

"I see." Obviously Mr. Green had inherited his land and now leased most of it out to someone else. "Does your daddy have a job in town?"

Holly nodded promptly. "Uh-huh. He sells land and houses."

"Ah. Green's Real Estate Company?" Holly nodded, and Mary asked, "What about your mother? Does
she work in town, too?"

Holly didn't answer at once. Mary stole a quick
glance at her. The girl was staring down at her hands.
"I don't have a mommy," she said softly. "She died
when I was little."

"I'm sorry." Mary's voice was gentle. "You must
miss her very much."

Holly shrugged and said sadly, "I can't remember her
anymore."

Mary's right hand left the wheel to touch Holly's
shoulder. She knew firsthand what it was like not to remember your mother. Inside, you felt a big gaping hol-
lowness.

"How much farther to your house?" she asked, deliberately changing the subject.

"Not much. See that metal barn? It's just past that."

When they entered the driveway, Holly observed,
"Daddy's truck's not here."

"Can you get into the house?"

Holly nodded. "I have a key."

"I'll wait with you until he gets here."

That assurance won Mary a dazzling smile.

The house was a sprawling, modern brick structure
edged by shrubbery. The spacious yard boasted towering oak and pecan trees. Along the driveway were aromatic pines. Beyond the house were fields and
dispirited-looking cattle, heads drooping in the downpour.

Inside, the living room was attractive and comfortable. There were overstuffed sofas and chairs grouped
before a massive stone fireplace. The adjacent wall was

concealed by cabinets, shelves, a television and VCR, a cassette player, books and magazines.

Mary sat down on the sofa while Holly tried to call her father's office. She came back a moment later to say the phone wasn't working.

"That happens sometimes when it rains a lot."

Mary nodded. She'd grown up in a rural area. "Do you stay at home alone while your dad's at work?" Mary asked.

Holly shook her head. "I either walk to Mrs. Dudley's house from school and stay there until Daddy comes for me, or I ride the school bus and stay with Miss Maggie." She pointed toward a window. "That's her house down the road."

Mary concealed her growing irritation with Holly's absent father but beneath her outwardly calm demeanor, Mary was seething. How dare Mr. Green neglect his daughter like this and leave her to find her own way home on a freezing rainy day? The child couldn't be more than eight or nine at the most.

"I suppose you're looking forward to a big Christmas?" Mary asked conversationally.

The tires squealed as Rob's truck rounded the corner and sped toward Hope Elementary. Rob was terribly late. Holly must be near hysterics by now.

He tensed at the thought. He'd been about to leave the office to go for her when he'd received an important long-distance call. The Houston man had been long-winded, to say the least, and in the end he'd said essentially what he and his colleagues had been saying all along—that there were still many factors to consider before making a final decision. All he could do was assure Rob that his proposal remained under consideration.

The school parking lot was empty. Rob stopped in front of the main doors and dashed through the rain up the concrete steps. The building was dark, and when he tried the doors he found them firmly locked.

Where was Holly?

Rob's heart hammered as he ran back to the truck. He'd been in such a rush, he'd left the office without a jacket. Now his shirt was wet, making him shiver as he slid behind the steering wheel.

He forced himself to take a deep breath. There was no reason to panic. Holly was a sensible child. When he hadn't shown up on time, she must have run through the rain the three blocks to the Dudley house. Mrs. Dudley often looked after Holly for Rob whenever he needed a sitter in town. Realizing that Holly must have gone there brought him instant relief.

But a few minutes later, plump, middle-aged Mrs. Dudley was frankly surprised to find Rob on her doorstep. When he explained his mission, she shook her head. "Holly hasn't been here today, Rob."

Rob's heart plunged. Renewed alarm clamored through his veins.

"She probably just went home with one of her friends after you didn't show up," Mrs. Dudley said encouragingly.

"Sure," Rob replied at last. "That's it, of course." But he knew it was totally unlike Holly to go off like that without permission, whether he was running late or not.

"Would you like to use my phone to call around for her, Rob?" Mrs. Dudley offered.

"Yes, please. Thanks." He followed her into her house.

Ten minutes later Rob had tried everyone he could think to call—all of Holly's friends and Ed Watson's mom, Maggie. There'd been no answer at her house or his own. On most of the days Miss Maggie cared for Holly, they took the bus together after school while Rob was still at work, but today Rob had told Holly he'd pick her up. Now inside him was a hard knot of fear.

"Maybe we'd better call Charlie," Mrs. Dudley suggested softly.

Rob nodded grimly. Charlie was her son; he was also the sheriff.

"I need to get home and check just in case Holly managed to get there somehow. The phones out our way probably aren't working because of the rain. Call Charlie and ask him to get his men out looking for her, will you, Mrs. Dudley?" At her nod, Rob headed for the door. "Tell him she's wearing jeans, a blue and pink sports coat and sneakers."

Rob's teeth chattered on the drive home, and although heat blasted through the dashboard vents of the truck, it couldn't take away the bone-chilling cold. But then, the cold he was experiencing had nothing to do with physical conditions like being wet on a near freezing day. It was Holly—his baby, his love. His very life. If he lost her, too...

Please God! he begged silently. *Please don't take her away from me!*

Rob immediately saw the gray Honda when he turned into his driveway. The car seemed vaguely familiar, but in his frantic state of mind, he didn't attempt to place it. He switched off the ignition while braking, leapt from the truck and raced toward the house. The presence of the unfamiliar car filled him with fresh anxiety. Had Holly been injured ... or worse?

He burst through the front door with all the grace of a charging bull.

Holly came running toward him! Rob swept her up into his arms, whirled her around and squeezed her so tightly that she squealed in protest.

"Where were you darling?" he demanded gruffly. "I've been worried sick since I didn't find you waiting for me at school!"

Holly kissed her father's cheek. "I did wait for you, Daddy, for a long, long time. Everyone else had left, and when you didn't come, Miss Shelton brought me home."

"I love you, squirt," Rob murmured. He nuzzled Holly's neck.

"I love you," she replied. She leaned forward and rubbed her nose against his. Then she giggled and demanded, "Put me down, Daddy."

For the first time, Rob looked at the woman sitting on his sofa. It was the teacher with the gigantic Christmas tree.

Rob was still overwrought, and he lashed out at her. "How dare you take it upon yourself to remove a child from the school premises without so much as even leaving a note for the parent?" His voice grated harshly. "Do you have any idea what you've put me through? I've been out of my mind with terror that my daughter might have been kidnapped, or involved in some horrible accident!"

Mary had been touched, witnessing the reunion between father and daughter. But now she surged to her feet, glaring at the towering man. The same man, she realized with a jolt, who had delivered her Christmas tree last night. The same man she'd tipped because she'd figured he probably needed it! What a laugh! Today, instead of dirty, work-worn jeans and boots, he wore a blue pin-striped dress shirt, tie and dark tailored slacks. Moreover, he lived in a fine, spacious modern house and owned his own business. He must've snickered all the way home last night over that tip!

He wasn't snickering at the moment, however. He was wet and shivering, and he looked miserable, but Mary's icy-blue eyes held no sympathy for him as their gazes clashed.

"What about you?" she demanded. "What kind of father are you to be so negligent? Anything *could* have happened to her, even in a small town like Hope. You should be thanking your lucky stars that *I* came along and took care of her—and not someone else! Anyway, I did write you a note. Holly taped it to one of the doors. There's no way anyone could have missed it!"

"There was no note," Rob stated flatly. "I went right up to the door and there was no note there!"

"Well, I don't know what happened to it," Mary countered impatiently. "We left one."

"I'll just bet," Rob snapped sarcastically.

"Daddy," Holly's shrill voice interrupted them. "We did! I taped it to the door myself."

"Then what happened to it?" Rob demanded, still glaring at Mary.

"How should I know?" she shot back. "Maybe the wind and the rain blew it off! Maybe some joker took it!"

"Maybe I didn't tape it good enough, Daddy," Holly said tearfully.

"Are you happy now?" Mary challenged. "You've made your daughter cry!"

Rob tossed her a murderous look, before reassuring Holly that he wasn't angry with her.

"I wouldn't dream of going off like that with someone's child without leaving word," Mary commented stiffly. "But I also would never dream of going off and leaving a small child all alone in the school building, either. And it was already past four!"

"Please don't fight anymore," Holly begged. "Please, Daddy!"

Her plea effectively ended the argument. Both Rob and Mary glanced down at Holly and then back at each other.

"I'm sorry," Rob said in a reasonable voice. "I'm being a jerk. I truly am grateful to you for bringing my daughter home safely. I was just so..."

Something melted inside Mary. "I know," she said gently. "You must've been scared out of your mind when you didn't find her waiting for you. I'm sorry you didn't get my note. I didn't learn until we were almost here that you had an office in town, or I would've taken her there first. She did try to call you after we arrived, but your phone seems to be out of order."

Rob nodded, calmer now. "It happens every time we get a heavy rain. I tried calling here, too."

"Where were you, Daddy?"

"I got a long-distance call just as it came time to go for you, and I was alone in the office. There was nobody else to send to get you." To Mary he explained, "There's only my secretary and one salesman with me at my office. Beth's home with the flu and Jack had taken the day off on personal business. I tried to hurry the call, but it was an important one, so I was just stuck. The second I got off the phone I went to the school, but

Holly was already gone. I started calling around, and when I couldn't find her, I just...freaked."

Rob knelt and wrapped his arms around his daughter once more, this time in a cozy bear hug. "All that matters now is that she's safe and sound."

"I agree," Mary replied. "And that being the case, I'll be going."

Rob released Holly and rose to his full height. "Thank you again for taking care of Holly, and I'm sorry I behaved so abominably toward you."

"Never mind." Mary smiled, letting him off the hook.

Rob was enchanted by the dimple that creased her cheek. She was even lovelier than he'd thought last night. Today she wore cherry-red, reminding him of Christmas; reminding him that she had a Christmas tree that needed shaping and trimming.

"Wait!" Rob said sharply when Mary moved toward the door.

"Please...wait while I change out of these wet clothes, and I'll follow you back into town. It's still raining so hard, I'd rather you didn't go alone. I'd never forgive myself if anything happened to you on your way back."

"There's no need," Mary protested.

"Please," Rob said again. "Since my phone's out, I've got to return to town anyway to let the sheriff know Holly's safe. His deputies are out looking for her."

"In that case, I'll wait. It might not be a bad idea to travel in pairs in this weather."

"How about if I bring along my saw?" Rob grinned. "After I talk to the sheriff, I can stop by your place and get your Christmas tree ready to put up."

Mary's face reddened as she remembered the tip she'd thrust upon this obviously affluent man. "I can't ask you to do that. I'm sure I can manage."

"I know. You said so last night," Rob replied. "But I'd really like to do it as a small way of saying thank you, if you'll let me."

"But... the weather is so awful."

"So what? I'll work on it in your garage. It won't take long. That is, if you'll let Holly stay inside the house with you, while I go about my business."

Mary hesitated, and her eyes narrowed as she assessed him. "Do you like homemade chili, Mr. Green?"

"Love it, Miss Shelton," Rob replied. Hope rose within him at the surprising question.

"And you, Holly?" Mary smiled down at the girl.

Holly's head bobbed up and down.

"Then I'll make you a deal." Mary's gaze met Rob's once more. "You shape up my Christmas tree, and I'll make supper. Afterward, you and Holly can help me decorate the tree. Huge as that thing is, I need all the help I can get."

Rob grinned and appealed to his daughter. "What's the verdict, small fry?" he asked.

"Yummmm!" Holly stated before subsiding into giggles.

"Then it's settled," Mary declared. "Let Holly ride with me back to town," she suggested to Rob. "While you're at the sheriff's office, we girls can shop for groceries and some new ornaments. I don't have nearly enough for such a big tree, and I have a strong hunch Holly's an expert at choosing just-right Christmas decorations."

"She is," Rob confirmed. He reached into his pocket and extended some money toward Mary. He grinned as he said, "Here's my contribution to the ornament fund."

Mary's face heated even before she looked down at the bill. Sure enough, it was the five dollars she'd tipped him with last night.

Rob roared with laughter, but before she could cut him down to size, he was striding toward a hallway, presumably to his bedroom to change his clothes.

Chapter Three

They gazed with awe at the enormous Christmas tree in its place by the corner windows. One spiky branch stretched almost to the front door; another overhung one arm of the sofa. The tree also dominated fully half of the floor space of the small living room. Despite the clipping Rob had given it, the top of the tree still brushed the ceiling.

"Why did you want such a big tree, Miss Shelton?" Holly ventured to ask.

"Isn't it obvious?" Mary responded weakly. "I completely lost my mind! What other explanation could there be?"

Holly subsided into a fit of giggles. "Teachers don't lose their minds! They're smart!"

"Hmmph. I'm not so sure about that," Mary declared tartly. "Oh well, now that I've got it, I'll just have to live with it."

"We can take it back to Ed and swap it for a smaller one," Rob offered.

"After all the work you've already invested in it, trimming the trunk and branches and setting it in the stand?" Mary shook her head. "No way! Besides, this will teach me a valuable lesson every time I have to ease around it to get through the room."

"Yeah?" He grinned. "What lesson is that?"

"Not to become too greedy. Bigger isn't *always* better."

"Hear that, small fry?" Rob asked Holly.

"Awww, Daddy!"

"Holly has a pony, but she's been begging for a horse of her own. I say she ought to wait another year, when she'll be a little older." Rob winked at Mary, a wink that his daughter couldn't see. "I'm sure you agree with me, don't you, Miss Shelton?"

"I'm in the third grade and I'm almost nine! So, I am too, big enough to have my own horse! Aren't I, Miss Shelton?"

"Oh, no you don't!" Mary laughed and shook her head. "You're not dragging me into the middle of a family argument. What I think is that I'd better go check on how the chili's coming along."

"Wise woman," Rob murmured with a chuckle. "Even if you are a bit nutty over Christmas trees."

Mary glanced toward the gigantic tree. It totally dominated the room. Her gaze shifted back to Rob, and she sighed. "You're not planning to let me live this down, are you?"

"Not a chance," he admitted cheerfully. "The Christmas-tree-that-swallowed-the-room story combined with the tip story should earn me free cups of coffee at Ella's Café for months."

"You've got quite a mean streak in you, Mr. Green," Mary said in a withering voice.

"So I've been told from time to time," he retorted. "Still, it's a lot more fun than being labeled a boring nice guy."

"Like the sort who delivers a huge Christmas tree to a stranger as a favor, and then returns the next day to spend an hour in a cold garage getting it in shape to use?" Mary nodded. "If word like that got around

town, it could do severe damage to a man's reputation.
Maybe even for life.''

Rob stepped toward her in a threatening manner and
his large hand swallowed Mary's slender wrist. "You
wouldn't dare," he said in a low, deep growl.

"You tell your tales, and I'll tell mine," Mary
taunted.

"Daddy!" Holly cried. "Why are you fighting with
Miss Shelton?"

Rob released Mary at once and stooped to his
daughter's level. It was important to reassure her.
Though he and Holly often teased and joked with each
other in light-hearted banter, when his daughter was
genuinely concerned about something, Rob always tried
to be straight with her. There had to be honesty and
trust between them, or they'd never make it for the long
haul, and they *had* to make it. All Holly had was him.

"We were just play-fighting, honey. The way you and
I do sometimes."

Holly gazed at him solemnly, searching his face for
the truth. Rob gazed solemnly back. He couldn't fault
his daughter for believing he was truly quarreling with
the teacher. After all, they'd exchanged honest-to-
goodness sharp words this afternoon at the farm.

"Cross your heart and hope to die?" Holly asked in
the age-old childhood vow.

Rob nodded and drew an imaginary cross over his
chest. "If you don't believe me, ask Miss Shelton."

Holly's eyes were questioning when she looked at
Mary. Mary nodded. "He's telling you the truth, Holly.
We were just joking around."

Satisfied, Holly decided to get in on the fun herself.
She wagged a finger at both of them and said sternly,
"Okay, but no real fighting allowed."

"Yes, ma'am," Mary replied smartly.

Holly giggled. Rob chuckled, ruffled Holly's hair, then rose to his full height. He smiled at the light dancing in Mary's eyes.

"I really must check on that chili," Mary said. "Holly, how about unwrapping my old ornaments in that box on the sofa?"

"Sure."

"I'll be the official chili-taster," Rob declared, following Mary into the kitchen.

"Who said we need one?" Mary asked.

"Every kitchen needs one."

"In that case, you're elected." Mary removed the lid on the large cook pot, stirred the contents, then offered Rob a large spoonful.

He tasted, squinted his eyes and gazed off into space, trying to look thoughtful—and failing at it. Mary hid a grin and demanded, "Well?"

"I need a second taste, just to be sure."

She gave him a second spoonful. "Well?" she asked again.

"How about a third taste? As a chili specialist, I like to be thorough."

"Hmmph. If you're any more thorough, Holly and I won't get a bite to eat!"

Rob grinned. "I was hoping you wouldn't catch on." He stole the empty spoon from Mary's hand, dipped it into the pot once more and added, "But as Holly says, school teachers are smart." He put the spoon in his mouth and a moment later murmured, "Ummmm. You, Miss Shelton, are one terrific chili maker."

"Thanks." Mary wrested the spoon from him before he could dip it into the spicy concoction again. "But if you call me Miss Shelton one more time, you won't get anything to eat at all! I hear Miss Shelton this and Miss Shelton that all day long from my students. It wears thin after a while."

"Thank goodness!" Rob exclaimed. "I'm heartily sick of trying to remember it's me you're talking to when you say Mr. Green. That was my dad's name, and nobody in town calls me that. So, what should I call you...'Teacher'? Or 'Hey You' perhaps?"

"Mary will do. And you?"

"Robert's the name, but everyone calls me Rob. Do I know you well enough to be honest with you yet, Mary?"

"Certainly."

"There's a smudge of chili on your chin. Beats me how it got there, when I'm the one who was doing all the sampling."

"Oh." Mary grabbed a kitchen towel and dabbed.

"Wrong spot." Rob took the cloth from her and, cupping her face in his hand, dabbed at the left side of her chin.

His face was now so close to hers, she caught her breath and held it. Unable to meet his eyes, Mary's eyes rested on his neck. His touch was gentle, and it seemed to be taking him an inordinate amount of time to clean one small spot.

At last he released her and stepped back. Mary dared to look at him again.

"Thanks," she said briskly. Then she moved to the counter, relieved that she could legitimately turn her back to him. "I haven't mixed the corn bread batter yet. I'd better hurry and get it into the oven."

"Corn bread, too?" Rob asked, pleased. "You're a gal after my own heart. Jalapeño or plain?"

"Jalapeño, if you like hot."

"I love hot, and so does Holly."

Rob admired Mary's efficient movements as she measured flour and cornmeal and poured them into a mixing bowl. It was plain she knew her way around a kitchen. "Is this your first year teaching here?" he asked. "I've never seen you around town."

"Yes. Get me a couple of eggs and the milk from the fridge, okay?"

"Sure." Rob gathered the items and carried them to the counter. "How do you like living in a small town like Hope?"

Mary shrugged and added baking powder to the bowl. "Fine," she answered. She sensed that Rob was waiting for her to add something to her one-word reply, so she added, "I grew up on a ranch near a small town. The biggest place around was Abilene and that was forty miles away."

"Ah, a country girl. Then you're used to small-town life."

"Yes. But people in small towns can be hard to get to know, when you're the outsider moving into their territory." She didn't mention the loneliness she'd suffered these past few months. Her colleagues at school were kind to her, as were the few people she'd met around town, but Mary wasn't a part of their lives. It suddenly occurred to her that Rob and Holly Green were the first guests she'd entertained since moving here.

"People can be clannish until they get to know you," Rob agreed. "Lynn used to complain about that. Lynn," he explained, "was my wife. She died four years ago."

"Holly told me. I'm sorry. It must be hard raising your daughter alone."

"It's not always easy," Rob admitted. "Anyway, you were saying, about small towns?"

"Actually," Mary said, "I do miss the community where I grew up and went to school, and I certainly miss my grandparents and their ranch, but I have to admit, I thoroughly enjoyed the years I was away at college and the three years I taught in Abilene."

"Then why did you come here?"

Because I needed a place where I could lick my wounds in private. Because Hope was the first job offer I received when I was desperate to get away from Abilene... from Wayne. Mary couldn't voice such thoughts to a stranger, so she shrugged instead and said lamely, "It just seemed time for a change."

Rob had a hunch there was more to it than that. It probably involved a man, but he didn't press for the real reason. Actually, he didn't want to know, any more than he felt like explaining to Mary that Lynn had divorced him and remarried long before her death.

Mary appealed to him somehow in a quiet, subtle way. There was a wholesome loveliness about her that was completely different from Lynn's hard sophisticated beauty, and she was far more attractive than any of the women he'd dated now and then in Houston or Dallas these past few years. All the same, there was no point in getting to know her too well or getting to like her too much. After his experience with Lynn, Rob had vowed never to get that close to a woman again. It hurt too much when it ended.

He was startled at where his thoughts were leading. "I'd better go string the lights on the tree," he said abruptly. Without waiting for her reply, he left the room.

Mary was taken aback. One minute they'd been talking in the friendliest fashion, and the next, Rob had suddenly left the room. Had the subject of his deceased wife bothered him that much?

Whatever the reason, Mary wasn't sorry to have a few minutes to herself. She needed to get her bearings. Last night she'd thought Rob was a hired helper to the operator of the Christmas tree lot; this afternoon she'd thought he was an irresponsible father and a jerk with no sense of gratitude; now she thought he was one of the most exciting and attractive men she'd met in a long time, bar none, and that alarmed her. She'd come to Hope to get over the pain of the treachery one man had inflicted upon her. The last thing she needed was to get interested in another. She'd be a fool if she did.

Thank goodness for Holly, Mary thought later as the three of them were eating. A reserve had crept between her and Rob and they seemed to be finding conversation difficult. Holly, bless her, artlessly chattered on about school. She kept the table talk bouncing instead of running out of air like a deflated balloon.

"Mrs. Murphy's sick in the hospital, Daddy. She had to have an op-pour-a-shun." She pronounced the word carefully. "Miss Shelton took her place in charge of this year's Christmas program."

"Sounds like a big responsibility," Rob commented.

"It is," Mary replied. "Every child in school is included in the program one way or another, even if only to carry something on and off stage."

"I know." Rob grinned. "No one can be left out. It was that way when I was a kid, too. The elementary

school Christmas program is one of Hope's biggest so-
cial events of the year.''

Mary laughed. "So I've been told. What worries me
is getting the sets built. Mrs. Murphy's husband always
built them before, but as you probably know, he died
earlier this year. I don't know who to ask for help, and
no one seems to know what happened to the old sets."

"What do you need?"

"Two simple backgrounds that can be easily moved.
One an indoor scene with a typical living room—a window, a door, a fireplace—and for the other, an outdoor scene—a main street with storefronts. I have no
artistic ability whatsoever, much less building skills.''

"It doesn't sound too complicated," Rob mused.
"Let me see if I can come up with something. If you like
my designs, I'll put it together. Green's Realty will do-
nate the cost of the materials.''

Mary's expression brightened. "Thank you, Rob. I
can't tell you how grateful I am!''

"Don't thank me too soon," he cautioned. "You
haven't seen my designs yet."

"Oh, I'm certain they'll be wonderful!" Mary's blue
eyes sparkled, and Rob found himself hoping he could
please her with the Christmas sets—and maybe even on
a more personal level, as well.

After supper the three of them decorated Mary's
Christmas tree. At Mary's insistence, Rob lifted Holly
so she could have the honor of topping the tree with a
gold star. Because the tree was so tall, the star listed
slightly, but it didn't matter. When they were finished,

they all agreed that it was one of the most beautiful trees they had ever seen.

Afterward, Mary made hot chocolate and popcorn. While they were enjoying their snack, Rob said, "I suppose you must play, or else you wouldn't have a piano."

"Nor would I have inherited directing the Christmas program." Mary laughed. "The piano came with the furnished house. That's why I rented this place instead of a garage apartment over on Pine Street."

"I can play, too," Holly stated. "I've been taking lessons for two years."

"Play something Christmassy for us," Mary invited.

Holly went to the piano and played "Jingle Bells." Rob and Mary sang along to the music. Then she played a simple version of "Silent Night" and they sang that, too. Mary sang well, but she was especially impressed by Rob's deep baritone.

It was Mary's turn at the keys next. For the next half hour, the three of them sang most of the standard Christmas songs.

"That was fun," Rob declared when their songfest ended. He smiled at Mary. "In fact, this entire evening's been fun."

Mary smiled back. "For me, too."

Their gazes met. There was a sense of intimacy they shared that couldn't be denied. Something had happened between them, without a touch, without a word, but very real all the same.

Finally Rob ended the extraordinary moment. "This is a school night. I'd better be getting Holly home to bed."

A few minutes later Mary was alone with her enormous Christmas tree and its twinkling lights. The silence left by Rob and Holly's departure made her solitude so stark and bleak that she almost wished they hadn't come at all. Renewed loneliness crept over her, dampening her spirits the way the sleet was dampening the world outside her windows.

Chapter Four

Thursday afternoon Mary perched on a stepladder, tacking tinsel swags above her classroom windows. Twenty minutes ago the school day had ended and the children had rushed out in their usual boisterous high spirits.

Mary had stayed behind, finishing her work plan for tomorrow, and then she'd decided to hang the swags. Tomorrow the students would decorate the classroom. All week long they'd made construction paper chains and cut out and colored paper bells, stars, drums, stockings, angels and any other Christmas symbols they could think of for hanging on their artificial tree.

Rob entered the classroom and pulled the door closed behind him, but apparently Mary didn't hear him. He set the object he carried on her desk, and then he headed toward the back of the room where she was working.

Long streamers of golden tinsel draped over Mary's left arm as she reached to tack a section of the swag to the wall. She looked outrageously sexy, Rob thought, and she was completely unconscious of it. With her arms raised above her head, the pink sweater she wore hiked up in the back, revealing a small, but very luscious, patch of peaches-and-milk-colored skin just above the waistband of her straight black skirt. The skirt itself had inched enticingly above her knees. It was strained to the limits across her curvaceous hips as she pressed one knee against a rung of the ladder. Her other leg, alluringly shaped, stretched downward. Rob's gaze fell, following the line of the stockinged foot which was firmly planted on a lower rung.

"Hello," Rob said when he was halfway across the room.

Mary was so startled by his voice that she lost her balance as she twisted around, trying to see who was behind her. She fell, frantically grasping at air.

In a split second, Rob pushed his way through the barricade of neatly lined student desks, knocking over three of them in the process in order to reach Mary.

Somehow he managed to catch her. His arms closed about her, and his grip was firm as he pressed her tightly to his chest. Mary's eyes were wide with fright.

They were both breathing heavily, and their faces were close, so very close. For a long moment they gazed, mesmerized, into each other's eyes. Rob ached to kiss her... to taste those beautiful soft pink lips that were so close to his. But fortunately his common sense came back to him. This was a schoolteacher he had promised to assist. Even though she taught second grade now, there was always the potential that she might teach a higher grade in the future and become Holly's teacher. There was no need to create a possibly embarrassing situation between them and perhaps make things awkward for his daughter, as well. Rob was acutely aware that he had Mary in a very compromising position just now. And anyhow, he'd never had the least indication that she would welcome any kisses from him.

"Are you okay?" His voice was thicker, more uncertain than he would've liked it to be.

"Yes," she whispered unsteadily. "I think so."

Slowly and carefully Rob lowered her until her feet touched the floor.

The instant he released her, Mary moved a few steps away from him and slipped her feet into her black leather pumps. Her heart was beating erratically and she was grateful to have something to do with her attention for even a brief moment, besides looking at the tall man who had just held her so intimately. She also felt better able to face him once she had her shoes on.

She told herself she should be relieved that Holly's father hadn't kissed her in those few magical moments when she'd been practically certain that he was going to do so. She *was* relieved, she insisted to herself. Honestly.

But the whole truth was less simple. Disappointment vied with her relief. She felt almost overwhelmed by his appealing masculinity. Today he wore neat brown slacks with a tan corduroy blazer that fit perfectly across his strong shoulders, and the scent of his after-shave cologne tugged powerfully at her senses. She had tingled everywhere their bodies had touched when he'd held her against him so tightly. Heat still coursed through her veins. His lips had been so near, so inviting. Her heart had fluttered with excitement and anticipation as they'd subtly leaned into each other.

Mary's face still felt hot, and her body was oversensitive to Rob's proximity. Thank goodness he had broken the spell and set her down firmly on her own two feet! How humiliating it would have been if they had kissed and later he'd regretted it, and they still had to see each other from time to time. In a small town and a small school like this, running into each other now and then would be inevitable, and she'd already suffered more than enough embarrassment last term in Abilene.

She'd had no choice but to finish out the school year there, forced to see Wayne every day. It had taken superhuman effort to pretend his presence hadn't affected her. The last thing she wanted was to repeat her past mistakes. Being in love was a dismal, painful business. She didn't intend to allow it to happen to her again.

Mary suddenly busied herself righting a chair and desk.

Rob quickly moved to straighten up the others he'd knocked over in his haste to reach her.

Mary turned to go to her desk in the front of the room. In a studied, yet casual, voice she began, "What is it you wanted to—?"

She broke off as she spotted an exquisite poinsettia plant on her desk. It was at least two feet tall and equally as wide, full of lush red and green leaves. A wide red-velvet bow with a pinecone was attached to the front of the basket in which the plant came.

"How beautiful!" she exclaimed. When she reached the desk, she touched one red leaf ever so gently, then turned toward Rob. "Did you bring this?" she asked.

He nodded.

"Well, thank you very much," she said uncertainly. "But why?"

"For rescuing my daughter yesterday," he answered with a smile.

"Don't be silly. There was no need for you to do this." But then an impish grin robbed her of any schoolteacher sternness. "All the same, I'm glad you did. I'll enjoy it tremendously."

"Good. That's the idea," Rob replied heartily. "Are you about finished up here for the day?"

"Yes, thank goodness!" Mary sighed as she opened a desk drawer and pulled out her purse. "It's been a long, trying day."

"A tough one, hmm?" Rob murmured sympathetically. When Mary took her suit jacket from the coatrack in the corner, he gently removed it from her hands and held it open for her.

Mary thrust her arms into the jacket sleeves and felt flustered all over again as he straightened the back of the collar and his large fingers lightly brushed against her neck.

When she turned toward the door a moment later, Rob asked, "Aren't you going to take your poinsettia home?"

Mary shook her head. "There'd only be me to see it, and I have that huge tree taking up most of my living room already to remind me of Christmas. Here my students will be able to enjoy your gift as much as I will. It really does brighten up the classroom, don't you think?"

Rob silently conceded that she had made a valid point. As they left the room and walked along the hallway, he couldn't help admiring Mary's thoughtful, sharing nature. He bet her students were crazy about her.

When they got outside, Holly was nowhere around. Mary had vaguely assumed Rob's daughter was waiting for him.

"Where's Holly?" she asked. "Didn't you come to pick her up?"

"Nope. I only stopped by to bring you the plant. On Thursdays, Holly has piano lessons. Her teacher only lives a block from school, so she walks over. When she's finished there, she'll go another couple of blocks to

Mrs. Dudley's house. I have a meeting every Thursday evening, so Holly always stays there until I'm done.''

Mary nodded and turned away from the parking lot toward the sidewalk. "Here's where we part," she told him. "I'm walking today. Thank you again for the gorgeous poinsettia."

Impulsively Rob said, "I'm at loose ends right now. I've still got some time before my meeting. How about coming with me to Ella's Café for coffee and a piece of pie?"

Mary hesitated, knowing she was finding this man entirely too attractive for comfort, knowing that out of sheer loneliness she might too easily become susceptible to such beguiling, friendly ways.

But she also knew that she was in no mood to rush home and be alone. Just for a little while, at least, she wanted to enjoy Rob's company, to bask in the light of his warm smile, and hang the consequences.

"All right," she heard herself agreeing. "I'd love to."

The café, plain as they come, was nevertheless spruced up for the holiday season. Fake snow decorated the windows; red paper bells and shiny ornaments dangled above the counter; a slightly worn silver imitation tree stood in one corner. Red glass balls dangled from its branches.

Rob and Mary immediately drew the undivided attention of the other café patrons. Rob nodded, howdy'd and Merry Christmased everyone, while he guided Mary to a table against the wall. She was intensely self-conscious of the openly speculative gazes she received.

"They're pairing us off!" she hissed to Rob as they sat down.

He chuckled. "Don't let it bother you. You know how small towns are. They'll forget about us once something else grabs their attention. Now tell me about the tough day you had."

For the next half hour they got on with remarkable ease, in spite of the curious gazes that occasionally came their way. Mary was glad she had come.

One of a small group of men near the front rose from his table and came to theirs. Rob politely introduced him to Mary as Dan Baxter, and then the two men chatted casually for a couple of minutes.

When the other man started to leave, he nodded to Mary and murmured a polite, "Pleased to meet you." To Rob, he added, "See you later at the council meeting."

"Sure thing," Rob replied.

"Council meeting?" Mary repeated when they were alone again.

Rob nodded. "We're both members of the town council."

"Oh. I didn't know. How nice."

Rob sighed. "It's not particularly nice these days, but it's a duty I feel obligated to perform. A major employer here in Hope closed its doors earlier this year. A lot of people lost their jobs."

"Yes. I've heard about that. It's a real shame."

"Yes, it is," Rob agreed sadly. "A lot of folks around here are hurting and desperately need jobs. The council's been working hard trying to lure new businesses to town. We've been putting in our bids toward several companies that are in the stage of choosing locations to build new manufacturing plants. I've been negotiating with a company in Houston that is planning to build a new vinyl products manufacturing plant next year. Dan is wooing a company based in Colorado, and other members are trying the same thing with various other companies." He sighed again. "Believe me, it's not easy for a place as small as Hope to attract large businesses. Most want to locate where there's plenty of entertainment, cultural and higher education facilities."

Mary nodded. "It's sad the way so many small towns are dying. I hope you succeed, for everyone's sake. One of the teachers at school was telling me she and her husband might have to move away. He's trying to find a job elsewhere. Multiply them by a good number of other families and it'll soon affect businesspeople like you and schoolteachers like me. If the school loses many students, as the newest teacher, I'd be the first to be let go."

"It's already affected my business," Rob admitted solemnly. "These days I've got more sellers than buyers. This year's been hard on everybody." He suddenly dispelled his gloomy mood and smiled at her. "Are you saying you've already grown so fond of Hope that you'd hate to have to leave it?"

Mary smiled back. "That about sums it up."

"Might there be any particular individual in town you'd hate to leave more than any other?" he challenged in a suggestive, teasing voice. "Someone you met only recently, perhaps?"

Rob could scarcely believe himself. He was actually flirting! No woman since Lynn had been able to pierce his iron heart. Neither would this one, he hastily reassured himself. Yet when Mary laughed at him, he found that he was thoroughly enjoying the sound of it, thoroughly enjoying her company.

The man was outrageous—blatantly flirting with her right here in Ella's Café, in front of some mighty curious townsfolk. As wary as she was of attractive single men in general, Mary was amazed to find herself hugely enjoying his flirtations. She tilted her head and, with great exaggeration, fluttered her eyelashes. "Maaaybe," she taunted in a long drawl.

Rob chuckled. Mary could give as good as she got. "And who might that individual be?" he asked. "If I'm not being too nosy."

"Oh, you're definitely being too nosy," she stated in a voice that cracked with amusement. "But if you must know, that person is Holly Green, of course. I so enjoyed her visit with me last night, and I look forward to many more."

"Anyone else you'd miss?" Rob prompted.

Mary gazed off as though in deep thought. "No," she answered at last. "I can't think of anyone. Besides, you asked me only if there were one particular individual I'd miss, not two."

"Okay, okay, I concede! You got me."

"You deserved it," Mary returned pertly. "When you go fishing in a cattle watering tank, don't be expecting to catch a whale."

Rob threw back his head and laughed heartily. He was starting to get darned fond of the town's newest second-grade teacher, and he had a suspicion that he would miss her very much if she moved away.

He disapproved entirely of his feelings, but there they were, all the same.

Chapter Five

Friday morning was bright and sunny, so Mary chose to walk to school. When she left the house, she saw Mr. Starr in his yard, busily unwinding a string of outdoor Christmas lights.

Mary crossed the street to speak to him. "Good morning. Getting into the spirit of the season, I see."

"My wife always loved the outdoor decorations even better than the ones inside the house, because she liked everyone to be able to enjoy them." Mr. Starr's voice thickened. "She died last fall, you know."

Mary nodded. He had told her the first time they'd met.

He continued, "I'm doing this because I know Wilma would want me to."

Mary was touched. "That's a very loving thing to do in her memory," she said gently.

They said goodbye and Mary walked on to school.

The children were excited all morning, knowing that after lunch they would decorate their classroom for the holidays. Somehow even Mary managed to catch a little of the children's enthusiasm.

The decorating went well, and afterward it was time to practice for the Christmas program.

Mary was sorting her music in the auditorium as the children arrived and Holly Green approached her. "Hi, Miss Shelton."

"Hi, yourself," Mary replied, smiling.

Holly thrust a white envelope toward her. "I brought you a note from my dad." Artlessly she spilled the message before Mary could open the envelope. "We want you to come to supper tonight and help us decorate our Christmas tree."

Sure enough, Rob had written, "We owe you a dinner, so don't say no. Come early, around six. Jeans will do." A postscript added, "The set design sketches are done, but I can't start construction without your approval."

Mary told herself she shouldn't go. She was seeing Rob Green entirely too often, and her growing attraction toward him was happening so fast it unnerved her. She didn't want to set herself up for another fall, another rejection.

But his invitation pulled at her like a magnet. Holly's cajoling did her in altogether. "Please come, Miss Shelton. It'll be fun if you're with us. Daddy said you can help us decorate our tree. Please."

Mary's meager resistance dissolved. "All right. I'll be there."

When Mary arrived at the Green home that evening, Rob greeted her at the door wearing an apron over his sweatshirt and jeans, which read, Kiss the Cook. Without speaking, he pointed to the words.

Mary tried not to laugh, but failed. "Must I?" she asked.

"Absolutely, if you expect to be fed."

Delicious anticipation shivered through her, and Mary threw caution to the winds. With pretend resignation, she sighed. "Well, I *am* hungry." She placed a chaste kiss on his cheek.

"That won't do," Rob said sternly. "It won't do at all." This time he pointed to his lips. Reinforcing his demand, he displayed a sprig of mistletoe in his hand and raised it above his head.

Mary suddenly found herself leaning toward him, and this time her lips met his.

The kiss lasted only seconds, so it couldn't have been all that profound, Mary told herself when it was over. But for long moments afterward, they stood gazing deeply into each other's eyes. Rob looked as surprised as she felt. The kiss they'd just shared had packed a wallop, no doubt about it. They were both rocked off balance by the warmth, the wealth of emotion, that had been contained in that brief contact. A stunned silence followed.

Rob found his voice at last. "Come in," he said huskily.

"Thanks." Mary despised the weakness in her voice.

A bare pine tree stood before the living room windows, awaiting adornment. Mary inhaled the tangy scent with appreciation as Rob took her jacket.

"Hope you brought your appetite," Rob told her. "We're having fried chicken. Come out to the kitchen. You can supervise."

Holly and her friend, Amy Grant, were there chopping salad ingredients. "Hi, Miss Shelton," they greeted in unison.

"Hi, girls. What can I do to help?"

"Daddy said not to ask you to do anything. You're company."

"I'd rather help than stand around doing nothing." Mary swung around to Rob who was at the stove turning the chicken. "Honest. Give me a job."

"Okay, you can set the table. By the way, can you make cream gravy?"

"Can I make cream gravy?" she retorted lightly. "That's like asking if there's really a Santa Claus!" She winked at the girls. "I'm world-famous for my cream gravy."

"Your humility is so becoming," Rob tossed back. "All right, you're hired as our cream gravy maker this evening."

"Daddy can't make gravy, no matter how hard he tries," Holly confided. "He makes lumps and burned gunk."

"That bad, hmm?" Mary laughed.

Dinner was not only delicious, but also a light-hearted affair. Rob joked with Mary and the girls and they teased him back, sometimes all three of them ganging up on him. Rob had a very relaxed, easy rapport with his daughter and her friend, as well. Mary liked that.

After dinner Mary insisted she and the girls clean the kitchen alone, considering Rob's hard work preparing the meal. With alacrity, he vanished into the living room. The girls weren't quite so enthusiastic, but they good-naturedly went along with Mary's plan. While they worked, they became more familiar, and Mary told them they could call her by her first name, as long as they didn't do it at school or in the presence of other students.

After the kitchen was cleaned, while Holly and Amy pulled boxes of Christmas ornaments from a hall closet, Mary approved Rob's set designs. He promised to begin construction the next day.

Decorating the tree was a hilarious affair. Rob clumped silver icicles on a few branches and hung several ornaments close together. When the girls protested, he pretended he thought the tree looked better that way. Of course they kept having to fix his "mistakes." He finally retired from the job of decorating in favor of building a fire in the fireplace, and he occasionally pestered them by swiping the candy canes they hung on the tree.

When they were done, despite Rob's efforts at sabotage, the Christmas tree was beautiful. The lights blinked on and off, casting magical, ever-changing colors on the shiny round glass ornaments. Holly declared herself satisfied that Santa wouldn't find her tree wanting.

The doorbell rang and the two girls raced to open the door. "Hi, Mom," Amy greeted the woman at the threshold.

"Are you girls ready to go?" she asked.

"Almost," Holly replied.

"Don't keep her standing out in the cold," Rob called to his daughter. When the woman came inside, he said, "Hi, Joanne. Have a seat."

"Can't. Brad's waiting in the car. Hurry, girls," she added. "We rented a Disney movie to watch when we get home."

The girls squealed with delight and dashed off to collect Holly's things.

Rob introduced Mary to Amy's mother, and Joanne Grant gave her a friendly smile. "I've seen you around school. I'm the secretary of the PTA."

"Ah, yes. I knew you looked very familiar," Mary replied.

Rob extracted money from his wallet and handed it to Joanne. "That ought to be enough for Holly's lunch and gift buying. If she runs short on something you consider reasonable..."

Joanne laughed and nodded. "I'll advance her an emergency loan if necessary." At Mary's questioning expression, she explained, "I'm taking Amy and Holly Christmas shopping in Houston tomorrow."

"Brave woman," Rob said with a grin.

The girls returned with Holly's duffel bag, and there was a general bustle over their departure.

Suddenly Mary and Rob were alone. The only sound was the crackling fire. Mary tensed, realizing she'd been had.

"Well..." Rob began.

Mary interrupted him. "You set me up," she declared flatly.

"Who? Me?" Rob feigned innocence. His expression was so mischievous, Mary almost laughed. He looked like a little boy caught with his hand in the cookie jar.

"You deliberately deceived me," she accused. "You know very well you gave me the impression that I was to spend the *entire* evening in Holly's company, as well as yours."

Rob denied it. "I just sort of forgot to tell you the whole truth." He slowly advanced on her. "Was it really such a terrible crime? Is it so awful... being alone with me?"

Confusion and uncertainty sped through Mary's veins. Her pulses throbbed because of what was about to happen. It had, she thought fatalistically, been inevitable from the first. The only unknown factors had been *when* and *where*... never *if*.

Rob pulled her into his arms, bent his head toward her with quiet deliberation and proceeded to kiss her thoroughly. This kiss bore as much resemblance to the one they'd shared when she first arrived as Christmas Eve did to the Fourth of July.

Heat coursed through Mary, quickening feelings she had ruthlessly submerged ever since meeting Rob. For the space of a heartbeat, she resisted. But then her lips parted, and her hands fluttered up to timidly caress his face. When she touched him, yielding to his embrace, they both trembled with emotion.

"Thank you for coming into my life, Mary Shelton," Rob murmured against the softness of her lips.

She caught her breath at the sweet, unexpected words, and she pulled back to gaze at him in wonder. "Nobody has ever thanked me before...just for being," she whispered hoarsely.

"Blind, unappreciative people you've known, then, I'd say," Rob murmured. He threaded his fingers through her hair and brushed it away from her face. "I've been so lonely...for such a long time. I'm very, very glad you're here."

Mary went up on tiptoe to kiss him.

Her spontaneous action enflamed Rob, and his arms tightened about her, crushing her soft body to his. His hands roamed up and down her back, pressing her closer and closer. In that moment he was surprised to discover he never wanted to let her go.

"I'm glad I'm here, too," Mary finally whispered. "But I didn't expect to feel like this about you...about anyone."

"Neither did I," he answered huskily. "But it feels wonderful to me." Rob kissed Mary's cheek, her temple, and buried his face in her gorgeous silky hair. He sought and found her lips again, and capturing them, he pulled her down to the sofa.

A moment later Mary's head was cradled by a mound of pillows and Rob lay beside her. They were both fully clothed, yet he became familiar with her graceful, feminine body as his hands explored the length of her.

Slowly his hands slid beneath her sweater and were warmed by her toasty skin. Moving upward, his fingers encountered a tantalizing barrier of lace covering the soft swelling of her breasts.

When Rob's fingers slipped inside her bra and began to circle her nipples, Mary shivered with wanton pleasure. Her entire being was suddenly afire. A terrible ache set into her lower limbs. She moved against him with sudden urgency.

His desire for her became a sweet excruciating pain. He wanted to see her, to kiss her everywhere, to make love with her.

Rob began working at the clasp on the waistband of her slacks, but his movement was restricted by the back cushions of the sofa. "We're too crowded here, sweetheart," he whispered. "Let me carry you into the bedroom."

Mary wanted to acquiesce. There was no doubt about her feelings for Rob. He'd aroused her to a fever pitch of excitement. She'd never experienced such powerful sensations before.

Rob rose from the sofa and held out his hand to her. Ignoring it, Mary sat up and tugged at the bottom of her sweater.

Her throat felt hot and dry and it was hard to speak. Her desire for Rob was so undeniable, she almost didn't have the strength to resist. But she had to!

"I'm sorry," she murmured unhappily. "I'm truly sorry, Rob, but I just can't do this."

Concern darkened Rob's eyes. "Did I misread the signs somehow? I thought you wanted me, too. Was I forcing myself on you?" He ran his hand agitatedly through his hair. "God, what a jerk you must think I am!"

"No!" she exclaimed sharply as she got to her feet. "I didn't think that at all! You didn't do anything wrong. And yes, I...I wanted you, too." She lowered her head and confessed raggedly, "I still do."

Rob took a step toward her, as though he were about to take her into his arms again. Mary hastily backed away.

Rob's eyes widened. "You say you want me, but then you tell me no. This is plain crazy. Unless," he added with sudden suspicion, "you've got a husband around somewhere?"

Mary shook her head. "There's no one," she answered truthfully.

"Then what's to hold us back?" Rob's voice took on a tinge of anger.

"I simply can't. I don't...I don't want to fall in love with you," she said brokenly.

Rob was stunned by her reply. He lifted both his hands in a wordless gesture that meant he wouldn't touch her again.

"I'm so sorry," Mary murmured. She was dangerously close to tears.

"Don't be," he said harshly. "It's my fault. I shouldn't have even kissed you, much less—" He broke off and looked away as her face reddened. Then he admitted baldly, "I don't want to fall in love with you, either. Or anybody else, for that matter. We would both be a lot happier if I had only remembered that, before inviting you here tonight. So, if anybody needs to apologize, it's me."

Their melancholy gazes met. There remained nothing more to say, except goodbye.

Mary collected her jacket and purse. Rob didn't attempt to help her put on her jacket as he had yesterday afternoon at school, and she felt a sharp pang of regret. When she was ready to leave, Rob's jaw was rigid as he opened the door for her.

"Forgive me," she whispered.

"Good night," he replied bleakly.

Chapter Six

On Saturday Mary stayed as busy as she could with her household chores and errands to keep her mind off Rob and the disastrous end to their evening last night.

Now and then she glanced out her window and watched in fascination as Mr. Starr kept adding lights and decorations to his lawn. Every tree and shrub, all the edges of his house and roof, were now outlined with strings of lights. Even the rural mailbox out by the road was outlined, as was the post beneath it. Mary had never seen anything quite like it on such a simple, ordinary home. He must have been working night and day to put it all up.

Sunday morning, feeling the need for inspirational uplifting, Mary attended church. Arriving ten minutes early, she sat down at the end of a pew about midway toward the front. A few minutes later she was surprised when the pastor approached her.

"Mary," Reverend Harwick greeted, offering her his hand.

"Good morning, Reverend."

"Someone told me you play the piano. Is that correct?" At Mary's nod, he asked, "Can you also play an organ?"

"Yes."

"Would you be so kind as to play for our services today? Jackie Murphy, whose place you've taken as director of the school Christmas pageant, is our regular organist. Without her, we're rather badly off.''

''Certainly.'' Mary immediately followed the pastor to the front of the church.

A while later, after several hymns, it was time for the sermon. Mary left the organ bench to move over to the front pew, and her gaze swept over the congregation. As though drawn by a magnet, her eyes discovered Rob on the opposite side of the aisle sitting with his daughter.

Their gazes collided and there was an eternity in the brief glance they shared. It seemed to Mary that Rob appeared as dispirited as she felt.

It was impossible for her to fully concentrate on the sermon after that. She was too aware of Rob's presence. She could feel the heat of his unwavering gaze upon her.

Mary's throat tightened. Oh, God, she didn't want to fall in love with the man, but apparently she already had stronger feelings for him than she'd believed. Knowing that there wouldn't be any more cozy dinners together or shared laughter or—she might as well admit it—wild passionate kisses, hurt badly. Yet, this way was best. A little pain now was better than a big heartbreak later. Mary had been rejected too many times in her life to open herself up for more.

She was relieved when the services were over. One final piece. Then she placed the sheet music on top of the organ, closed the lid and rose.

''Hi, Miss Shelton.'' Mary recognized the sound of Holly Green's voice.

''Good morning, Holly,'' Mary answered. She knew, even before she turned, that Holly's father would be standing behind her.

Sure enough, there was Rob, looking extraordinarily handsome in a dark gray suit, a snowy white shirt and a red-and-silver-striped tie.

"Hello, Mary," he said in a low voice.

"Hello, Rob."

Holly darted off to talk to a friend, and abruptly they were left alone together.

"You're looking very lovely today," Rob finally said after an awkward silence. "And your playing was wonderful."

"Thanks. You look great yourself," she said softly. It was only fair to repay him the compliment. After all, it was true, he did look wonderful to her eyes.

The conversation degenerated after that. They were gazing at one another unhappily, each trying to think of a way to gracefully walk away, when the pastor joined them.

"Thank you for playing for us today, my dear. Until Mrs. Murphy is well enough to return, could we prevail upon you to continue, not only on Sundays, but for the children's Christmas choir practice and Christmas Eve performance? We'll pay you, of course."

"I'll be happy to help," Mary replied, "but without pay. Let it be my Christmas gift to the church."

"We appreciate it very much." Reverend Harwick was then distracted by an elderly parishioner who wished to speak with him. Once again Mary and Rob were left alone together.

There she went, giving of herself again, proving what a generous spirit she had. Rob's warm feelings toward Mary returned, in spite of his resolve not to permit it to happen.

The other night Mary had stopped him before things could get completely out of control, painfully insisting that she didn't want to fall in love with him. *As if it were a distinct possibility!* Rob's retort that he didn't want to fall in love, either, had been a swift and proud defense of his shattered ego, but actually, those were his true feelings, as well. After Lynn, he'd promised himself never again.

Now, as he looked at Mary, so pretty in a blue silk dress, Rob wondered what invisible wounds had scarred her.

She turned to walk up the aisle and Rob followed her out of the church. It was an exquisite day. The air was still cool but with a promising hint of warmth for the afternoon. The sunlight was brilliant.

On the grassy lawn just ahead of them, Holly was chatting with several friends.

Rob paused beside Mary, feeling awkward again. How he hated this awful tension that was between them.

"It's a gorgeous day, isn't it?" Mary ventured.

"Yes. Too beautiful to waste." Impulsively Rob asked, "What are your plans for the afternoon?"

Mary shrugged. "Oh, I've got a number of chores that—"

"Forget them," he interrupted her. "We don't get December days like this very often. You said you grew up on a ranch, so you must like horses, right? Let's go riding this afternoon."

Mary hesitated for a fraction of a moment. She shouldn't accept the invitation. She knew it would only make it that much harder to do without Rob's companionship later. But riding! It had been so long!

Rob saw desire and doubt battling it out in her eyes. "No ulterior motives," he hastened to assure her. "Holly will be our chaperon."

Mary's eyes took on a twinkle that delighted Rob, even before she smiled. "I'd love it," she told him with an eagerness that caused his heart to leap.

Two hours later they sat on a blanket beside a tiny winding creek. Their mounts were tethered to a tree a few yards away. Holly and her friend Amy were riding across a field to Mrs. Watson's house in the expectation that they'd be welcomed, perhaps even with Christmas cookies and milk. Instead of taking Holly's pony today, Rob had put both girls on the back of a gentle nag appropriately named Honey. He'd ridden his own stallion and he'd mounted Mary on a spirited mare called Winnie, after she'd assured him she was equal to it.

She had handled the horse with the easy confidence of an expert. Now Rob's gaze slid appreciatively over her attire—great-fitting faded jeans, a blue Western shirt topped by a suede vest and well-broken-in boots. The outfit was unpretentious and natural. It was clear that she was perfectly at ease, both with her clothes and with riding a horse.

"You ride with such confidence," Rob said with admiration. "You must've been born in the saddle."

Mary smiled. "Almost. My grandfather taught me to ride when I was very small. When I was Holly's age, I was participating in rodeo barrel races. I won a few trophies in calf-roping events as a teenager." She sighed. "I do miss the excitement of rodeos sometimes. And I especially miss my horse, Champion."

"What happened to him?" Rob asked.

Mary smiled again, and the soft glow of affection in her eyes was bedazzling. "Just old age, same as with your Honey. When I went off to college, I gave him to our nearest neighbor's young daughter. They still have him, but nobody rides him anymore."

"Sounds like you had a great childhood. Did you live near your grandparents?"

Mary shook her head. "No. I lived with them."

"What about your parents?" Rob asked gently.

Mary gazed off and focused her eyes on the distant forms of Holly and Amy astride the slow-moving Honey. They were almost to their destination. At no time had the children been out of Rob and Mary's sight.

"I never knew my father," Mary answered. "My parents weren't married. When I was seven, my mother went away with a man she hoped to marry. He didn't want the burden of me being with her, you see."

Rob heard the deep pain in her voice. He reached out and laid his hand over hers.

"I'm sorry," he murmured. "Your mother...is she still alive?"

Mary shrugged. "I have no idea. While I was growing up we used to receive occasional postcards from her, but they were always from different places and there was never a return address. The cards stopped coming by the time I was a teenager."

Rob's hand closed around hers and squeezed. "God, what a rotten thing to do to a kid."

She shrugged again and there was a defensive thrust to her chin. Her reply was curt. "It happens."

"Believe me, it's your parents' loss!" Rob burst out forcefully. "They've missed out on knowing a very special person who's as beautiful on the inside as she is on the outside."

"Thanks." Mary's voice was raspy. "But if there's any good in me, it's entirely to my grandparents' credit.

They were always good to me. They were the only people who ever loved me.''

"I don't believe that for one minute." Rob withdrew his hand from Mary's, feeling that was the safest way to restrain his urge to kiss away her pain. "You can't tell me," he challenged, "that no man has ever loved you, because I just can't believe it!"

Rob had meant the statement in a half-teasing vein, hoping to pull Mary out of the anguished memory of her parents' rejection. The last thing he expected was a sudden burst of anger.

"It's true!" she declared. "Do you want to know the whole sorry story of my love life now?" Not pausing for a reply, she said in a hard, straightforward voice, "I never dated during high school. I lived too far out in the country for any boy to want to go to the trouble of driving back and forth for me. At college I was so shy and inexperienced it turned guys off. They went for the outgoing party girls, and I just didn't know how to be like them. I think I had a total of three dates during all my years at college."

"What about later?"

Mary shrugged. "After graduation I got a job teaching in Abilene. The location was perfect because I was close enough to visit my grandmother on weekends. She was in failing health by then, and I worried about her living all alone so far out in the country. My grandfather had died during my senior year in high school."

Mary sucked in a deep breath before plunging on. "Anyway, at the grammar school where I taught, a new teacher named Wayne came to work during my third year there. For some reason he seemed to like me, and we started dating. I even took him home to my grandmother's a couple of weekends, but most of the time we just saw each other on weeknights, and I went home on weekends alone.''

Her voice wobbled a bit as she quickly finished the story. ''We became engaged and were planning a summer wedding. In all honesty I can't say I was passionately in love with him, you know...the stars and fireworks sort of love you read about...but I did love him. And I trusted him.''

Rob's hand covered hers again. ''Let me guess the rest. The jerk cheated on you,'' he muttered grimly.

''Oh, better than that!'' she exclaimed. ''One weekend while I was visiting my grandmother, he married the other woman. She was pregnant, you see. While we— while he and I had never even—we'd agreed to wait until our wedding night—'' She broke off on a ragged sob.

Rob was stunned. Mary was telling him she was still a virgin! A rejected virgin!

Without even pausing to think, he wrapped his arms around her and she dropped her head to his shoulder. His hand made circles on her back, gentle and soothing, the way one would calm an unhappy infant. ''It's all right, now,'' he whispered. ''The two-timing creep didn't deserve you, Mary, I swear he didn't.''

That made her chuckle. ''Oh, I agree with you completely. I'm far too good for the likes of him. But that doesn't stop me from being hurt...or lonely, you know?''

''Yes,'' he agreed somberly. ''I do know...about pain and about loneliness.''

Mary believed he was speaking of his grief and loss over his wife's death. She sniffed but said nothing.

Rob released her hand and offered her his handkerchief. ''Blow your nose,'' he instructed.

Mary did as she was told and then sniffed with feigned indignation. "You're getting bossy," she complained.

Rob grinned. "Force of habit when you have a kid Holly's age. Feel better now?" When she nodded, he asked, "Are you going to visit your grandmother for the holidays?" He thought about how dull Hope would be if she went away for two long weeks.

But Mary shook her head. "She died a month after Wayne dumped me," she said softly.

"Ouch," Rob murmured sympathetically. "I suppose you moved here to get away from everything?"

"Yes. It was an impossible situation, seeing him at school every day after he'd married someone else. I could've transferred to a different school in town, but by then I'd sold the ranch and there was nothing to keep me in the area any longer. I sent out letters of inquiry to different school districts. It didn't really matter to me where I went as long as it was away from Abilene. Hope Elementary was the first offer that came along, and I took it."

"Have you regretted it?" Rob asked.

Mary dabbed away the last of her tears and shook her head vigorously. "No. I'm glad I came here. Very glad. Rob, I'm sorry about the other night, but I just... panicked."

"No explanation is necessary," he assured her gently. Looking over her shoulder, he added in a very different tone, "Here come the girls."

Chapter Seven

When Rob took Mary home that evening, they were all enthralled by Mr. Starr's lights. His work extended even farther than Mary had already seen. Tonight the tall pine tree out by the street made a perfect Christmas tree. Dangling from its branches were large, brightly colored wooden toys and, of course, plenty of twinkling lights. Topping the tree was a golden star, outlined by tiny white lights. It shone brightly against the dark sky.

Holly said knowingly, "All of the decorations aren't even up yet. The crèche and Santa and his sleigh and reindeer are still missing."

"Give him time." Rob laughed. To Mary he explained, "Every year Mr. Starr's decorations grow more lavish. Everyone drives by to see his display at least once before Christmas Day."

"I had no idea he went to such lengths," Mary said, impressed.

Rob walked Mary to her front door. With the two little girls in the car watching them, he refrained from following his inclination to kiss her. Besides, he'd promised Mary he wouldn't make any advances toward her today.

Mary was equally aware of their audience. She wished Rob could kiss her good-night yet wondered if he'd even want to if he did have the opportunity, after the hysterical way she'd reacted the other night. Today he'd treated her with only friendship and kindness. There'd been no hint of the passion he'd exhibited that other memorable evening.

Monday morning, when Mary's class went outside for physical education, she went to the teachers' lounge for coffee. She was surprised to find Rob there waiting for her.

"Is something wrong?" she asked.

"No. I came to ask you a favor," he said. "I have to go to Houston for an important meeting this afternoon with representatives of the company I told you about."

"The one you're trying to win over for Hope?"

Rob nodded. "It just came up, and it looks like I'll need to stay overnight. I had promised Holly that I'd take her shopping today for a new outfit for the Christmas program on Friday, but now I can't. Could I impose on you to take her to either Betsy's or Hope's Dress Shop and then drive her out to Mrs. Watson's afterward, where she can spend the night?"

"Of course," Mary agreed at once. "But why not just let Holly stay the night with me here in town? I've got a spare bedroom. After we finish shopping I can drive her out to your house to pick up her night things and school clothes for tomorrow."

Rob smiled. "Are you sure you want to be bothered to that extent? There's no problem about leaving her with Mrs. Watson."

"Only if you think Holly would prefer it."

Rob chuckled. "Holly loves her, but she claims Mrs. Watson makes her go to bed too early."

"Then it's settled," Mary declared. "I'll enjoy the company. Holly's a terrific kid."

Rob's smile stretched. "I'm compelled to agree with you on that."

They both fell silent, gazing at each other. Mary fancied she could see the same frustrated longing in his eyes that she felt herself, and her heart began to skip beats erratically. Why couldn't she seem to keep in the forefront of her mind the fact that she was bound to be hurt again if she let herself care for him too deeply?

"Well," he said, finally. "I'd better go find Holly and tell her and then get a move on, or I'll be late."

Mary nodded and said, "Drive carefully."

After school Mary and Holly had a wonderful time shopping. They found the perfect dress for the Christmas program—red velvet with a snowy-white lace collar. Rob had also told Mary to pick out shoes and underwear as well, so now Holly had new black patent shoes, a ruffly slip and white lacy tights. The entire ensemble would be crowned by a huge, red hair bow. Holly would look like an angel on Friday evening, and Rob would probably burst with pride, as well he should.

When darkness fell and they drove out to the Greens' house, they were both tired, but pleased with their purchases. They went straight to Holly's room to put away the new things and pack what she needed for overnight.

The room was a typical young girl's room, pink and white and flowery. On the bed was a zoo of stuffed animals; on the dresser was a photograph of a beautiful woman. "That's my mommy," Holly said when she saw Mary looking at it. "Wasn't she pretty?"

Mary nodded. "She certainly was. And so are you. You favor her very much." As she gazed at the photograph, she felt sad for the woman who had died so young, who'd been cheated out of the joy of watching her daughter grow up.

While Holly was searching for a pair of socks in a bureau drawer, the telephone rang. She dashed from the room and ran down the hall. Soon afterward Mary heard an enthusiastic "Hi, Daddy!" followed by a brief silence and then an excited description of Holly's new clothes. Mary smiled to herself and began to fold the pajamas that had been tossed on the bed.

Holly came back and said, "Daddy wants to talk to you. The phone's in his room."

Mary went down the hall and felt like an intruder as she entered Rob's bedroom. Her first quick impression of it was one of masculine solidity etched with accents in medium brown and sky blue.

The telephone was on the night table beside the king-size bed. Mary crossed the room and sat down on the side of the bed. "Hello, Rob," she said into the receiver. "How'd your meeting go?"

"I'm cautiously optimistic," he replied. "They're not ready yet to commit themselves to us, but they're interested enough that they want to meet with other members of the city council. Tomorrow the mayor and two other council members will arrive and we'll have another meeting. It's looking as though I may have to stay over tomorrow night, too. I hate to admit it, Mary, but at this rate I may not get back in time to build the sets before Friday night. I got a good start Saturday, but I didn't expect this, or I would've worked at it all day Sunday instead of going riding. I'm really sorry about letting you down."

"I realize you can't help it," she assured him. "Attracting new business and jobs to town is slightly more important than the sets for a grammar school pageant.

We'll make do with just our Christmas tree, that's all, and maybe I'll be able to hang some tinsel and bells and things. We'll get by, so don't worry about it. The audience only comes to see the children, anyway. They won't care about the background."

"You're very understanding and forgiving," Rob murmured.

"Of course I understand. And there's nothing to forgive."

"Thanks. Holly tells me you found her the perfect dress for Friday night."

"I think you'll be pleased," Mary told him. "She looks beautiful in it."

"I really appreciate you taking on that job for me. Thanks."

"It was my pleasure." Mary laughed softly. "I enjoyed spending your money for you."

Rob chuckled. "I'm sure Holly enjoyed you spending my money, too—a lot more than if I'd been there to do it myself."

"Certainly!" Mary declared. "Armed with a credit card, and without you along to restrain us, the sky was the limit!"

"Uh-oh, it sounds like I've been bankrupted!"

Mary laughed again. "Close to it."

Rob laughed, too. "Have you had dinner yet?"

"No. We'll pick up something when we get back to town. Holly's leaning toward pizza."

"I wish I were there with you," Rob said softly. "I'm committed to taking two of the Prichart Vinyl Company reps out to dinner tonight. It'll probably be eleven or later before I can finally kick off my shoes and relax."

"You sound tired," Mary said.

"I am," he agreed.

"Perhaps you'll enjoy your evening more than you think."

"I doubt it," Rob responded. Then he lowered his voice and asked in a suggestive tone, "I'll bet you're sitting on my bed right now, aren't you?"

Mary felt her cheeks warm. Unconsciously her free hand had been touching, almost caressing his pillow. Now she jerked the hand away as though she'd been caught stealing.

"Er...yes, I am," she finally admitted.

"I can picture you there," he murmured. "All stretched out, with your hair spread over the pillow, wearing nothing but..."

"Rob!" she gasped. Primly she corrected his mental image. "I'm fully dressed and sitting on the edge of the bed, with my feet on the floor. I would never presume to—"

"Ummm. Too bad. You know, you could presume to sleep in my bed tonight. I wouldn't mind. Matter of fact, I rather like the thought of it."

"Hush!" she pleaded. "Yesterday you promised you wouldn't say things like that anymore."

"No, I didn't," he denied swiftly. "I said I wouldn't make any advances toward you while we went riding, and I didn't. But I don't recall making any promises about the future. I like imagining you in my bed, so why shouldn't I?"

"Please," she began breathlessly. "I told you before. I don't—"

"I know," Rob interrupted. "You got burned once, and you're afraid to play with fire again. I understand that. I'm not in the market for a long-term commitment, either, but, Mary, I'm finding that I'm liking you more and more. I think you like me, too. We're two lonely adults with perfectly normal desires and needs, we're both free agents and we're attracted to each other, so why shouldn't we enjoy each other's company?''

"I don't want to get hurt again," she whispered.

"Neither do I, believe me," Rob said with heartfelt accord. His voice filled with a strange anguish. "I don't think I could bear it," he added. "Especially not from you."

"What...what do you mean?" she asked uncertainly.

"Never mind. Good night, Mary. Sweet dreams."

After they hung up, Mary gazed slowly around Rob's bedroom. There was no photograph of his deceased wife, Lynn, and she wondered why. Was it because it was still too painful for him? When Rob had said he couldn't bear to be hurt again himself, Mary had recognized genuine pain in his voice.

Swiftly she got up and returned to Holly's room.

In town Mary picked up a pizza before going home. When they pulled into her driveway, Holly was thrilled. "Look! I told you! There's Santa and his reindeer!" As soon as the car stopped, she hopped out and ran across the street to Mr. Starr's yard. Mary followed more decorously.

On one side of the yard was a candy cane house with Mrs. Santa Claus waving through the window; Santa himself sat in his sleigh. On the opposite side of the lawn was a large straw-roofed crèche, with life-size wooden sculptures of the holy family. Nearby were figures of the three wise men, shepherds and a few sheep. All of the figures were spectacularly beautiful, lovingly crafted.

Holly headed for the candy cane house. Mary joined Mr. Starr, who sat in a rocking chair on his front porch.

"Evening, Mary," he said, nodding.

"Evening, Mr. Starr. Your Christmas display is nothing short of magnificent."

He nodded, silently accepting the tribute.

"Did you carve the wooden sculptures of Mary and Joseph and the rest of them?" Mary asked in wonder.

"Oh, no," Mr. Starr replied. "I'm not so talented. My wife, Wilma, carved, painted and lacquered them all."

Mary shook her head, marveling.

Holly dashed across the lawn from the candy cane house to the crèche, and Mary made a startled move to follow her. "I'd better make sure she doesn't break—"

"Let her be," Mr. Starr ordered gently. "She's fine. The displays are all for the children to touch and enjoy, particularly the manger scene. Wilma was always very insistent about that. Now, tell me about your Christmas plans."

Mary spread her hands. "I don't have any. What about you?"

"Nope."

"Are you going to be alone?" she asked.

He nodded curtly.

"Then let's make a dinner date for Christmas afternoon," Mary suggested.

Mr. Starr nodded and came close to smiling. "I accept," he answered.

"Mary, come see the manger," Holly called.

"Excuse me, Mr. Starr," Mary said.

He waved a hand. "Browse as long as you want, my dear."

Inside the stable, the beautiful figure of Mary, the mother of Jesus, gracefully sat on a bale of hay. Nestled in the straw-filled manger beside her lay her infant son. She gazed at her holy child with joy and adoration. Her husband, Joseph, hovered protectively behind them.

Holly reverently stroked one of the child's out-thrust arms, and her smile was radiant when she looked up at Mary. "Aren't they beautiful?" she whispered in awe.

"They are indeed," Mary replied softly.

"I told Baby Jesus what I want for Christmas," Holly said, "because what I want is too big a job for Santa all by himself."

"And what is that?"

Holly replied simply, "*He* knows." Abruptly she left Mary alone in the crèche. Her voice grew distant as she called out to Mr. Starr.

Mary remained a few moments longer, touched by the beautifully crafted symbols of the essence of Christmas. Surprising herself, she followed Holly's example, whispering the secret hopes and wishes of her heart.

After all, it was Christmas, a time of miracles.

Chapter Eight

Kneeling on a chair, Holly concentrated fiercely on wielding the wooden spoon through the thick mixture in the saucepan on the table before her. She'd just added peanuts to melted chocolate chips, and she found that stirring them together was a bit of a task. They were making peanut mounds, Mary's favorite candy. It was delicious, as well as easy to make.

It was Tuesday night, and Rob was still in Houston. He'd called Mary at school during lunch break to say he wouldn't make it home today, either. They'd agreed that Holly would stay another night with Mary.

This evening, after a simple meal, Mary had decided to teach Holly how to make the peanut mounds. Both of them had a bit of chocolate smudged on their faces, but it didn't matter. They were having fun.

"Ready?" Holly asked when Mary spread out a long strip of waxed paper on the table.

"Let me put down a second layer," Mary said. She overlapped the edges of the paper, then nodded. "Okay, go to it."

Holly filled a teaspoon with the chocolate mixture, then deposited the contents onto the waxed paper. It made a small irregularly shaped mound.

"Perfect!" Mary declared. "When it cools, the candy will be firm."

"Will we be able to eat some before bedtime?" Holly asked.

Mary frowned. "I'm not sure. It'll be cutting it pretty close, but we'll try."

Holly carefully deposited another spoonful of chocolate-coated peanuts onto the waxed paper. Without warning, she asked, "Do you like my daddy?"

Mary was startled. "Of course I do."

"But do you like him a whole, whole bunch?" Holly asked with an odd seriousness to her voice.

Yes, I like your daddy a whole, whole bunch, Mary's heart silently whispered. *In fact, the thing I feared most has happened. I've fallen in love with him.* But naturally she couldn't say such things to Rob's daughter.

Holly watched her closely, waiting for a reply. Mary forced herself to smile. "I'm not certain exactly how much a whole, whole bunch is, but yes, Holly, I like your father very much." A sudden question came to mind and Mary asked pointedly, "Is that all right with you?"

Holly grinned impishly. "It's okay with me, even if you like him a whole, whole, *whole* bunch!"

If Holly didn't mind Mary liking her daddy "a whole, whole, *whole* bunch," did that mean the child was actually trying to play Cupid? Mary wondered.

Wednesday afternoon Mary and the children took time out from rehearsing the Christmas program to decorate the stage Christmas tree. Mary also draped the tinsel and paper bells above the front of the stage. Somebody had found a small table and placed on it a lantern-shaped lamp next to a folding chair. That was the best they could do for an indoor scene. All they had for an outdoor scene were several boxes of small bits of tissue paper, which would become "snowflakes" when dropped from the rafters by the fathers of a couple of the children.

Again Rob telephoned with an apology, saying he would not be home before tomorrow. He and the other city council members were to have one last meeting tomorrow morning with the Prichart company representatives before heading back.

"Looks like I'm going to be really indebted to you," Rob said. "I can't thank you enough for taking care of Holly. I know from talking with her that she's happier staying with you than she would have been with Mrs. Watson."

"It's been fun having her," Mary replied honestly.

The following afternoon, when school was out, Mary left the building, expecting Holly to be waiting for her so that the two of them could walk together to Mary's house. Ordinarily Thursday was the day for Holly's piano lesson, but it had been canceled this week because the teacher was out of town.

The instant she stepped outside, Mary saw Rob across the parking lot, standing next to his car. Holly raced toward him. Rob stooped, caught her up in his arms, and they hugged and kissed with open affection. It was a heartwarming scene.

Mary's own heart raced at the sight of Rob. Her body went suddenly hot despite the fact that it was a chilly afternoon, especially when, after setting Holly on her feet, Rob rose to full height and turned that warm, magnetic smile on her.

Mary wished she could go dashing willy-nilly into his arms the way Holly had. Instead she walked toward him with all the sedate poise and decorum she could summon.

His smile broadened, and his sweeping gaze was bold. When she stood beside him, Rob took Mary's hand into his and said, "You're a beautiful sight for sore eyes."

His words made her heart sing.

But then he spoiled the effect by saying, "Hop in. I'll drive you home and collect Holly's things, and I'll pay you for taking care of her for me."

The song in Mary's heart stilled. "You owe me nothing," she said coldly.

"Of course I do!" Rob insisted sharply. "She stayed three nights with you, instead of one. I can't take advantage of your generous nature. Besides, if it was Miss Maggie or Mrs. Dudley, I'd have paid them."

To Mary his voice seemed distant and businesslike. She stiffened her spine and answered him in kind. "I'm neither of those ladies," she said implacably, "and I won't accept one penny."

Rob realized he'd offended her, when that was the last thing he'd intended. "If it's a matter of principle with you," he said gently, "then I won't offer again."

"Good!" Still hurt and angry, Mary jerked her hand from his, as though his touch were poison.

With a worried frown, Holly asked, "Are you mad at each other?"

"How could I possibly be mad at Mary, when she's been showing you such a good time?" Rob countered lightly. He opened the car's back door. "Climb in."

Holly stood her ground. "You sounded like you were mad," she said bluntly. Her uncertain gaze was on Mary.

Mary smoothed Holly's hair. "Your dad's right. We're not really angry. We were just having a sharp disagreement."

Holly seemed doubtful, but finally she said, "Okay," and slid into the back seat of the car.

Rob closed her door and opened the front door for Mary. There didn't seem much choice but to get in. At least, Mary reminded herself, the drive would be mercifully brief . . . only two short blocks. She wouldn't be confined in such close quarters with Rob for very long.

On the short drive Mary thought Rob looked very tired, but she said nothing. She couldn't possibly have squeezed in a word, anyway. After three days without her father, even though she'd spoken with him on the telephone each night, Holly was bubbling over in her rush to tell Rob all her news, from making candy to Timmy Bates throwing up in class today to seeing a photograph of Mary, at age fourteen, with her horse, Champion, after they'd won a trophy for calf-roping at a rodeo contest.

"I'd love to see that sometime," Rob replied, favoring Mary with such a heart-stopping smile that she caught her breath. But before she could respond, Holly was off and running on a different subject.

When they entered the house, Mary felt obliged to offer Rob coffee, while Holly packed her things. He accepted, and when he sat at the kitchen table, Mary set out a plate of peanut mounds.

"Ummm," he murmured after the first bite. "This stuff is great. How about another piece?"

"Help yourself," Mary said, while she poured the coffee.

When she brought Rob his cup, he was happily licking chocolate from his fingers. When he saw her grin, he grinned back, declaring, "Good to the last lick. Mind if I try one more piece?"

Mary chuckled. "A teeny-weeny one. Then you've got to quit. I don't want you to overdose on chocolate."

"Thanks for being so concerned about my health and well-being. I'd say that's a good sign, don't you think?"

"A good sign of what?" Mary challenged.

"A good sign that maybe you care about me . . . just a teeny-weeny bit?"

Mary was spared having to reply. Holly was calling out to them from the living room.

Mary called back, "We're in the kitchen, Holly." To Rob she said in a low undertone, "Rave about the candy to Holly. She made it."

"Did she, really?" He grinned. "With a bit of help, I imagine."

Mary smiled back. "Only a little. Now don't forget!"

When Holly came in, Rob dutifully praised her candy-making skills, and she beamed with pride.

Mary poured a glass of milk to go with a couple of pieces of the candy for Holly and then refilled Rob's coffee cup.

"Tell me the outcome of all those meetings," she invited.

Rob grimaced. "We still don't know whether they'll come here or not, but we've offered all the incentives we possibly can. There are still other towns in the running, so who knows?" He shrugged wearily. "The only positive thing I can say is that Hope still has our hat in the ring, and the company officials promised to let us know one way or the other before the end of the year. At least we won't be left dangling much longer."

"You're discouraged because you're tired," Mary said gently. "You just said Hope's still in the running—that's positive. Try not to let yourself get too down."

Rob smiled. "You're right, of course. Thanks." It had been a long, long time since anyone had tried to encourage him and lift his spirits. He hated ruining the moment, but he had no choice. "I do have some bad news to tell you," he said slowly.

"To tell me?" Mary asked, surprised. "What is it?"

"When I got home today, I went out to the garage to look over the sets and try to gauge whether I could finish them before tomorrow night."

"And you can't?"

"Everything's missing—the plywood, paint, even the design sketches!" He shook his head. "What really puzzles me is that none of my tools or fishing gear was taken. The only things missing were the project materials. Did you find someone else to build the sets and send them out to my place for the materials?"

"Why, no," Mary replied. "I thought you'd be back in time to do it yourself. By the time I knew you wouldn't, it seemed too late to find someone else. Anyway, I don't know anyone well enough to ask."

"It never occurred to me to lock my garage," Rob mused. "Nobody ever steals anything around here." He sighed. "There's no way I can start all over now and get the sets done in time for tomorrow night. I'm really sorry I let you down, Mary."

Rob seemed genuinely distressed. "It doesn't matter," Mary insisted. "I believe everyone would agree that trying to draw new jobs to town is a lot more important than whether we have background sets for the grammar school Christmas program. Besides, I've been assured on good authority that the parents only pay attention to their children, anyway," she ended with an amused smile.

Rob laughed shortly. "I suppose there's a measure of truth in that." He thrust back his chair and turned to his daughter. "We'd better be getting home, Holly. Mary, thanks again for taking care of my girl for me."

"Don't forget my birthday party Saturday," Holly reminded Mary.

"I'll be there," Mary promised.

"Go ahead to the car," Rob told his daughter. "I'll be there in a minute."

"Okay. Bye, Mary." Holly scampered through the door.

With Holly gone, Mary was acutely aware of being alone with Rob. He'd been standing just inches away from her, and now he moved even closer.

He tilted her head and gently kissed her. "I missed you," he whispered.

"Rob, please . . ."

His lips possessed hers again, and Mary began to feel light-headed. She was so weak that his slightest touch, his briefest kiss, profoundly affected her. She was that far gone.

From outside came Holly's voice shouting, "Daaad, come on!"

Rob and Mary both smiled.

"Seriously," Rob said, "one of these days—or nights—you and I are going to be alone together, uninterrupted."

Mary's heart raced and she laughed. Boldly she asked, "Is that a threat?"

"Oh, no," he returned quickly. "It's a promise."

Friday evening Mary was just about to leave her house for the school Christmas program, when a knock fell on the door. When she opened it, a deliveryman handed her a box containing a beautiful white rose corsage. It was tied with a red ribbon and completed with baby's breath and silver jingle bells. Scrawled on the accompanying card was one word: Rob.

Telling herself it was nice of him, and nothing more, didn't quite convince Mary. She was deeply touched. The man was firmly lodged in her heart and in her mind, no matter how hard she might wish he wasn't.

She went to the mirror and smiled. Like Holly, Mary had also chosen a red dress of her own for tonight's occasion, and the fragrant roses added the perfect touch when she pinned the corsage to her dress.

Mary picked up her purse and went out the door. As usual, Mr. Starr was outside, fussing with his holiday display. She waved to him as she went toward her car.

"You look mighty fine, Mary," Mr. Starr called to her. "Good luck with your program tonight."

"Thanks," she called back. It was the mark of a small town, Mary thought as she got inside the car, that an elderly man with no children would be aware that she had taken on directing the grammar school Christmas program.

Mary was the first to arrive at the school auditorium. She was shocked to see that her tinsel swags were gone. So were the paper bells. Enhancing the stage was a comfortable armchair to replace the folding chair they'd planned to use. The table, lamp and Christmas tree were still there, looking beautifully homey before a beautiful background set of a living room. There was a realistically painted fireplace, complete with leaping flames in the grate. On a real mantel above the fireplace were tall, red candles and a centerpiece of pine boughs. Near the right end of the set was a window with real curtains; on the left was an impressively drawn doorway, painted and edged with real moldings.

Bemused, Mary went backstage. Sure enough, there she found an equally wonderful Main Street set boasting a pet shop, a candy shop and a toy store.

When the students arrived, they were as enthralled over their new stage sets as Mary was.

A few minutes later Rob arrived with Holly, who looked adorable in her new outfit. "Look, Daddy!" she exclaimed. "I knew it! I just knew Santa would see to it that our stage looked nice for Christmas!"

Rob gave Mary a startled look. "Who did this?"

She spread out her hands. "I wish I knew. Aren't they beautiful?"

He nodded. "Whoever did it followed my design, but improved it a hundred percent. The only person I can think of who can take next to nothing and turn it into a thing of beauty is your neighbor, Mr. Starr."

"You think...?"

Rob shrugged. "It's possible. He's a retired master craftsman and cabinet maker. He built all the cupboards and bookshelves in my house. And look at all those original Christmas decorations in his yard. He made them, you know."

Mary shook her head and marveled. "I didn't know, although he did tell me his wife carved the wooden figures in the manger scene. How could he have known we needed help?"

"Beats me." Rob smiled. "Let's just be grateful and enjoy it. And may I say how beautiful you are tonight?"

Mary's face warmed with pleasure. "Thank you for these lovely roses." Her fingertips lightly brushed the delicate petals.

"I'd rather be thanked with a kiss."

"Here?" Mary asked, shocked.

"Well, maybe not here. But soon, somewhere else."

A tiny smile curled her lips. "I'll think about it." Just then, she was distracted by a question from one of her students.

To Mary's relief the Christmas program went well, with only a few hitches. A first-grade girl forgot her speaking lines and burst into tears; a fourth-grade boy bumped into the Christmas tree, rocking it so hard it would have fallen if a fast-thinking father hadn't leapt to the stage to steady it. A few children sang off-key, but all in all, the program was a great success.

Afterward, refreshments were served, and Santa Claus made his appearance, giving all the students and their siblings candy.

Mary thought that Santa looked suspiciously like her neighbor, Mr. Starr, with a pillow stuffed inside his jacket.

The following afternoon Mary took extra pains with her appearance as she dressed for Holly's birthday party. But it wasn't on Rob's account, she assured herself. It didn't matter a whit what he thought about her.

Sure, sure, and the earth's not round, the scrupulously honest side of herself sneered. *And don't give me any of that nonsense about not being in love with him, either!*

Mr. Starr was in his yard, as usual, when Mary went outside. She crossed the street to speak to him before she left. "You made a great Santa Claus last night," she told him.

Mr. Starr was poker-faced. "Santa?" he inquired.

Mary grinned. "I recognized you beneath the beard and the pillow."

"Maybe you just think you recognized me," he told her.

"Won't admit to it, huh?" Mary laughed. "All right. What I came to say is thank you for the beautiful stage sets you made for us."

"Sets? What are you talking about?"

If she didn't know better, Mary might have been duped by that innocent expression, but she did know better. Another look at Mr. Starr's lawn convinced her. The same hand that created the Christmas sets had also created this Christmas wonderland.

Now it all made sense. When Holly had stayed with Mary, she'd made a point of visiting Mr. Starr and his delightful Christmas display every evening. At some point she must have mentioned the unfinished sets in her father's garage.

But who was Mary to call Mr. Starr's bluff? If he wanted his good deeds to remain anonymous, so be it. Still, she thought she detected a mischievous twinkle in his eyes before she said goodbye.

Holly's birthday party was a riotous success. Ten little girls were present, and a clown entertained them.

Mary assisted Rob. While he grilled hot dogs, she poured drinks and filled bowls with chips and dips.

After the meal the girls voted to watch Holly open her gifts before they ate birthday cake.

The gifts ranged from a purse to a new puzzle. Mary gave Holly books and was gratified by the little girl's smile when she unwrapped them.

"You couldn't have made a better choice," Rob whispered in Mary's ear. "She loves to read."

Mary nodded. "When we came out to pick up her clothes the first night she stayed with me, I could tell that, by the number of books on her shelves. Naturally the schoolteacher in me has to encourage a habit like that."

"Naturally." Rob grinned. "Well, it looks like my turn now." He pulled a small package from his shirt pocket and went to Holly. "Happy birthday, sweetheart."

Holly gasped when she opened the box. "Oh, Daddy..." Her voice trailed off as she gazed in fascination at the contents.

"Like it?" Rob asked.

"I love it!" Holly held the box out so that everyone else could view the heart-shaped golden locket inside.

Rob took the trinket from the box and said, "Stand up, honey, so I can put it on for you." As he clasped the chain around her neck, Rob added, "This belonged to your mother, Holly, when she was a girl."

"Really?" Holly's dark eyes rounded and her hand gently touched the locket.

Rob nodded. "I was planning to wait until next year to give it to you, but I decided a grown-up young lady of nine should enjoy it now. Open it up and look inside."

Holly opened it and said in wonder, "There's a picture of Mommy. And me." She carefully closed the locket, then flung her arms around her father.

It was a touching scene. Although the other children were also present, Mary felt like an intruder upon the private moment of a father and daughter remembering their beloved wife and mother.

She was starkly reminded that Rob had loved his wife so well that he could never love again. All he wanted with Mary was a relationship without commitment.

Once again she was on the outside looking in, the rejected one. The pain of it was intense.

Chapter Nine

It was almost nine o'clock that evening when Mary heard a knock at the door. She was surprised to find Rob there, smiling that lazy, devastating smile of his that twisted her heart.

"Mind if I come in?" he asked. "It's cold out here."

"Where's Holly?" Mary asked as she admitted him. She felt suddenly breathless.

"Spending the night with Amy," he replied. Without warning he pulled Mary into his arms.

She inhaled deeply as he molded her body to his. Finally she managed to speak. "What're you doing here?"

"What does it look like?" Rob countered. His dark eyes were blazing with such desire that it set her blood sizzling. The next thing Mary knew, she was being thoroughly and excitingly kissed.

The kisses went on and on, alternately rough and tender. Mary knew she ought to put a stop to it. She would, she determined hazily, as soon as she could get her body to obey her will. It was just that right now she was so languorously cozy, wrapped in the warmth of his arms.

"I want to make love with you, Mary. Very much. And I know it doesn't come as any surprise."

Anguish squeezed Mary's heart. She tried to pull away, but Rob's embrace was strong. She did manage to turn her head so that their lips were no longer so kissably close, but now his cheek, with an enticing hint of after-shave, caressed hers. "It's no surprise," she admitted. Her voice held genuine regret. "But my answer still has to be no."

"Why?" he murmured persuasively. "We care about each other. I'm crazy about you, and you care for me, too. Don't pretend that you don't."

She moved her cheek against the hardness of his and then dropped her head to his shoulder. It felt so safe there.

"I won't try to pretend anything," she said sadly, "because you're right. I care for you very much, Rob. Maybe too much."

"Then why are you still holding me at arm's length? Okay, so we've only known each other a very short while...so what?" Now Rob set Mary away from him, hands on her shoulders, so that he could look deeply into her eyes. "I *care* about you," he said again, with emphasis. "I know you've been hurt in the past, that you're afraid to fall in love, but Mary...darling, you're not alone. So am I. But it hasn't stopped the growing feelings I have for you. All I can say is that I'm not like your ex-fiancé. I would never deliberately hurt you."

Mary's eyes filled with tears. "That's no guarantee," she whispered huskily.

Rob's hands dropped from her shoulders. He stepped away from her and his manner was suddenly distant. "If it's guarantees you're looking for, you'd better stay away from me and every other man, as well, for as long as you live." He lowered his head for a moment. His expression was bleak when he looked at her again. "I thought I had a guarantee when I married Lynn, but it didn't turn out that way. I certainly never expected to deal alone with all the challenges of raising a child.

It's . . . hard, really hard sometimes. I can't say I blame you for not wanting to get mixed up with a man who's raising a child, but I thought maybe, since you seemed to like Holly, that—''

"This has nothing to do with Holly!" Mary exclaimed.

"No?" Rob challenged. "Can you honestly say that if there were no Holly, you'd still turn me down?"

"Yes! I think Holly's adorable!"

"Just . . . not her dad? Well," Rob added heavily, "I must be crazy for daring to love again. After Lynn, I'd been too wary to get this close to another woman, but you just sneaked under my defenses somehow. I guess it's partly because you were so vulnerable, too. Goodbye, Mary." He ended with crisp words and a sharp nod. "I won't bother you with my unwanted attentions again."

He was gone before Mary could move. As though from a very great distance she heard his car backing out of the driveway, moving down the street. At last she heard no sound whatsoever, except the thudding of her own heart.

Rob had said he must be crazy for daring to love again.

Love!

Rob loved her! He loved her, and she had just let him walk out of her life! She had rejected him just as she'd been rejected in the past. How had it happened? How had she *let* it happen?

This wasn't Wayne, the man for whom she'd felt lukewarm affection and called it love. This was Rob, the man who had stormed right into her life and heart. What she'd once felt for Wayne had been such a pale

imitation of what she now felt for Rob that it would
have been laughable if it weren't so pathetic. She'd
known for days that she was deeply, irrevocably, in love
with Rob, but she hadn't believed it was possible that he
could love her back. He'd even said as much. That was
why she'd had to resist giving in to her natural instincts
to make love with him. If she had, she wouldn't have
been able to conceal her real feelings for him, and she'd
been too proud to accept his pity.

Darn the man, she thought almost angrily. Why
couldn't he have plainly told her he loved her before
now? But then she wasn't being fair. She hadn't told
him she loved him, either…only that she feared it might
happen.

So what if Rob still missed his wife and carried loving memories of her? The only thing standing in Mary's
way of a relationship with him was her own insecurity
based on her painful betrayal by another man. She re-
called Rob's voice saying he was *crazy for daring to love
again*. He'd also said he would never deliberately do
anything to hurt her.

How much more could any woman ask? She'd been
so afraid Rob would hurt her, that tonight she'd gone
and hurt him.

It was high time to seek his forgiveness.

Mary's gaze swept frantically around the room as she
tried to collect her thoughts. Jacket. Purse. Keys.

Rob's face was forbidding when he opened his door.
Mary's heart sank. This was not going to be easy. He
wasn't going to give an inch.

"What do you want?" he asked ungraciously.

"I need to talk to you. Please," Mary said softly.

His jaw tensed, and he shook his head. "I'm done talking."

"Please?"

Implacable and stony-faced, at first he blocked the door, but he finally relented and allowed her into the house. Inside, Rob turned his back to her and went to the fireplace, where he shoved the poker into the fire, stirring up the red-hot embers.

"I'm listening," he said over his shoulder.

Mary gathered her courage and went to stand behind him. She longed to run her hands freely over his back and shoulders, but she didn't have that much courage.

Her heart raced. Now that she was here, she didn't quite know how to start. But she had to speak soon. Rob didn't seem to be in a very patient mood.

At last she simply blurted it out. "I love you, Rob."

His shoulders jerked as though he'd been taken by surprise. But then Rob shook his head, still with his back to her. "I'm too old for fairy tales, Mary. A woman doesn't keep turning away from the man she loves."

Mary's throat was dry. "I . . . I believed you could never love me back, because of the love you shared with your wife, because of the memories you have of her. How could I ever win your love after you suffered such a tragic loss? I thought you only wanted to have a temporary fling, and I couldn't bear for you to abandon me one day the way Wayne did, the way my parents did. I was afraid to let myself love fully. But I know now that you're right, Rob. Life offers no guarantees. I was wrong to demand them. I know you can't promise to love me forever, but I'll take what you can give me, for as long as you're willing to give it to me."

Rob turned and his eyes were dark and somber. He came to her and cupped her face with his hands. "Do you mean it?" he asked gruffly. "Do you really love me?"

Mary nodded, too choked by the longing she saw in his eyes to speak.

Rob's kiss was gentle. His thumbs tenderly caressed her cheeks before his hands slid into her hair, then down to stroke her neck and shoulders. "Tell me again," he murmured against her lips.

"I . . . love . . . you," she said between kisses.

The kiss deepened and Rob's embrace grew stronger as he pressed her tightly to him. "Ahh, Mary . . ." he whispered.

He pulled her down to sit on his knees in an easy chair, and his arms cradled her tenderly as though he cherished her more than anything. "You have everything all muddled, darling," he chided softly. He nuzzled Mary's neck. "Except the part about my loving you. I do . . . madly."

"Then what are you saying?" Mary asked warily.

Rob's forefinger lightly traced Mary's hairline and ear. It was such a pretty ear. He was tempted to explore it with his tongue, but he saw the uncertainty in her eyes and decided he'd better deal with that first.

"Lynn and I were divorced. Our love ended long before she died."

Mary's lips rounded in surprise. Rob's restraint was sorely tested. He ached to kiss her again.

"Holly was only two when Lynn moved back to Dallas to be near her parents. She remarried a year later and died in a traffic accident almost a year after that."

"I . . . see," Mary murmured.

"Despite our differences, we worked hard to have a friendly divorce for Holly's sake. Lynn had custody, but she never gave me any trouble about visiting rights. I saw Holly almost every weekend, and several times a year she came her for a week or two at a time." He sighed. "She was so little when Lynn died. She can't remember much about her. I've done my best to teach her to love her mother's memory. Lynn deserved that much. She was a good mother. She was just unsuited to be my wife . . . and I was not the right husband for her, for that matter," he added honestly.

"What happened between you?" Mary asked. She gave in to temptation and allowed her fingers to stroke away the frown lines on Rob's brow.

His lips grazed the palm of her hand. "I'm a country man," he stated. "Always have been, always will be. Lynn was a city girl. She was stifled here, and she came to hate it. When the hate started creeping into our relationship, we called it quits. We met and fell in love at college, when we were young and idealistic. The differences between us just didn't seem to be so enormous then as they became later." Rob's arm, encircling Mary, tensed. "When we first separated, my whole world collapsed. I felt a terrible sense of failure as a husband and as a man. And I missed my daughter dreadfully."

"Your marriage may have ended, but you're a wonderful man and a wonderful father, Rob. Never doubt that!" Mary fiercely insisted.

"Thanks." Rob's voice broke. "I can't tell you how much it means to hear that from you. Holly was only four years old when Lynn died and I brought her home for good. Even though I'd always spent as much time with her as I could, raising her all alone is an entirely different thing. I do my best to be a good father, but it's not the same for her as having both parents. Lynn's parents offered to raise her, but I couldn't let them do that. I couldn't let Holly grow up feeling that I didn't want her."

Mary nodded with approval. No wonder she adored this man. Rob was the kind of parent to Holly that she herself had never had, and on Holly's behalf, she was very, very glad. No child should ever have to endure rejection by their parents.

"Do they still see her?" she asked. "Holly's grandparents?"

"Oh, sure." Rob nodded. "They're the only grandparents Holly has, and she's their only grandchild, so I make sure they have the opportunity to spend plenty of time together. As a matter of fact, the day after Christmas they'll arrive here to take her home with them for a week. I'll go to Dallas and pick her up the day after New Year's."

"It's kind of you to share her with them," Mary commented.

"They're good people," Rob answered. "They adore Holly, and she's crazy about them. It wasn't their fault Lynn and I didn't make the long haul together." He smoothed Mary's hair from her forehead and said solemnly, "Mary, you say you love me, and God knows I love you, but...well...Holly and I are a package deal. You've been wonderful, allowing her to stay with you while I was in Houston and even attending her birthday party. But I've found most women quickly lose interest in me when they find out I'm raising a daughter. Can you accept her completely?"

"Robert Green, are you *proposing* to me?" Mary's eyes widened in astonishment. She was still trying to get used to the idea that he loved her, and now this!

Rob's smile was tender. "Yes, Mary Shelton, that's exactly what I'm doing. I realize we haven't known each other very long, and if you need time to think things over, I'll understand. But I want you to know I love you with all my heart, and if you can accept Holly... and spend the rest of your life here, I would be most honored if you would marry me."

Mary leaned forward and kissed Rob. "Yes." She kissed him again. "Yes." She kissed him yet again and murmured, "Yes."

"Thank God!" Rob exhaled loudly. "I was so afraid you'd say no."

"And I was so afraid you couldn't really love me enough to want to marry me."

"We've both been afraid to hope for too much," Rob said. "Afraid of rejection. But never again. I promise you this—I'll always want you at my side, as long as I live."

"That's all I want," Mary replied softly. Her eyes suddenly sparkled. "What will Holly say? She told me once that it was okay with her if I liked you a whole, whole, *whole* bunch."

"Is that a fact?" Rob grinned. "Why, that cunning little imp! She told me the same thing about you."

They laughed, and then Rob became serious. "Will you marry me soon, Mary Shelton?"

"As soon as you like, Robert Green," she promised.

Rob stood up, lifting her in his arms, and he carried her toward the bedroom.

This time Mary was content to let him. This time she belonged.

Epilogue

It was Christmas afternoon, and for a bride-to-be with no relatives to call her own, Mary had a large, self-appointed adoptive family, consisting of many well-wishing citizens of Hope. In the beginning she and Rob had planned a tiny private wedding, but the townsfolk had raised such a ruckus, they'd been forced to alter their plans.

The community of Hope was just that—aglow with fresh, exhilarating new hope. The Monday following Rob and Mary's engagement, word came that Prichart Vinyl Products would build its new manufacturing plant in Hope. Construction was scheduled to begin early in the new year.

It was common knowledge that Rob had been chiefly responsible for attracting the new business and had even sold some of his own property to the factory at a substantial loss to himself as an added inducement. The town was grateful and ready to celebrate this Christmas gift in a special way. When the residents learned Rob was about to be married, many of his lifetime friends wanted to participate in the occasion, and they'd showered gifts and assistance upon the couple.

Mary had also won herself many new friends by taking on the school Christmas program and playing the organ at church when there was a need. Word spread that she was without family, and almost magically many of the tasks and expenses accompanying the wedding were taken care of.

Jan Crane, Mary's closest friend from school and her matron of honor, entered the anteroom and gave one last adjustment to Mary's veil. "The church is packed," she announced. "It's time, Mary." Jan handed the bouquet to her and gave her a careful hug. "I'll step out and tell Reverend Harwick you're ready."

Holly, gorgeous in the red velvet dress they'd bought for Christmas, which was now serving her well as flower girl, gave Mary an unexpectedly shy smile. "Remember when I said my Christmas wish was too big for Santa, so I told it to Baby Jesus instead?" Mary nodded, and Holly beamed. "I asked for Daddy and me to be a real family, with a mommy like all my friends have, and now we are."

Mary stooped down and hugged the little girl. "I love you, Holly," she said earnestly.

"I love you, too...Mom." Holly said the word experimentally, then cast Mary an anxious glance. "Is it okay to call you that?"

Mary blinked back tears. "It's more than okay, sweetheart. It's the greatest honor I've ever received. I'll always be here for you, Holly. Always."

There was a knock at the door, and Mr. Starr entered, looking spiffy in a black tuxedo and wearing a large smile on his face.

He had never admitted to constructing the sets for the school Christmas program, or to playing Santa Claus, either, but maybe that was best. It left ample room to believe in the miracles of Christmas.

He gave a courtly bow. "You're a beautiful bride, my dear," he told Mary. "I only wish my Wilma were here. She loved weddings. A Christmas wedding and my enjoying the honor of giving away the bride would've thrilled her."

Mary smiled, accepted his arm, and they went out to the vestibule. There came the strains of music. Jackie Murphy had recovered from her surgery at last, and today she was playing for Mary's wedding.

At Mary's nod, carrying a small basket filled with vivid green holly and its bright red berries, Holly entered the sanctuary and proudly walked down the aisle. Jan followed. To Mary it all seemed to happen at a torturously slow pace.

Finally it was her turn. Escorted by Mr. Starr, Mary joyfully walked toward the man who waited for her at the altar.

Her own Christmas wish had come true. Now, and for the rest of her life, there was someone for her to love; there was someone who loved her back.

Rob gazed upon his approaching bride with as much love and pride as it was possible for one man to contain. He'd never expected to love again, much less so strongly.

What a Christmas! There would never be another quite like it. On this day many hopes were being fulfilled—for himself, his bride, his daughter...even for the town of Hope itself.

His heart overflowed with happiness and heartfelt gratitude as Mary, smiling and more beautiful than an angel, joined him at the altar. He took her hand and together they turned toward Reverend Harwick.

The pastor smiled and began, "Dearly beloved..."

* * * * *

A Note from Sondra Stanford

Christmas is the most special time of year to me. I'm a sucker for Christmas carols, twinkling lights, the fresh scent of evergreen, secrets and mysterious, enticingly wrapped packages beneath the tree. Mail is an exciting event, too, as cards and letters pour in from friends and relatives.

Practically from infancy, my daughters "helped" cut out and ice Christmas cookies every year, in addition to all the other baking we did. The kitchen would be an unbelievable mess by the time we were through, but the fun and love we shared always made it worth the bother. On Christmas Eve, they always left a plate of the cookies and a cup of hot cocoa on the table for Santa Claus, and during his secret visit in the middle of the night, he always enjoyed a bite or two of a cookie and a few sips of the hot cocoa.

In our house, the custom was for the girls to help Dad choose the Christmas tree. Since it was also his job to string the lights on the tree and outside, as well, it was up to Mom and the girls to decorate the tree while Dad supervised.

Through the years, we've accumulated quite a collection of decorations with personal meaning to us. We've got pretty ceramic tree-shaped ornaments with our names on them, crocheted wreaths made by a neighbor, a delicate wreath and bell woven of Kansas wheat and sent to us by a relative, twenty-year-old pine cones collected by the girls on a visit to family in Louisiana, as well as fragile, old glass ornaments from my parents' collection.

The tree itself must be real. We tried the artificial route for a year or two, and our oldest daughter, in grammar school at the time, almost threatened to run away from home. To this day, she dearly loves everything about Christmas and is a die-hard traditionalist. None of that fake stuff for her, thank you very much.

Tampering with the Christmas dinner menu is absolutely forbidden. Additions are permitted, but old favorites must be served. In our family, all the relatives get together for a big meal, each contributing special dishes, from Gran's corn bread dressing to go with the turkey, to my sister's cherry cheesecake, to my aunt's ambrosia fruit salad, to my broccoli casserole and pecan pies. It wouldn't be Christmas without each of them.

Even though my children are grown now and the magic of expecting Santa's visit is past, Christmas is still very special to our family. There's lots of baking for gift-giving to neighbors and friends, cards and letters to send, shopping to do. And, of course, there are still secrets and mysterious packages under the tree and too much delicious food to eat at Christmas dinner.

May your Christmas stocking be filled with the rich blessings of family and love, joy and peace.

Sondra Stanford

THE NIGHT
SANTA CLAUS
RETURNED

Marie Ferrarella

To Mama,
Who Always Made
Christmas Special
Even When All We Had
Was Each Other;
And
To Lucia Macro
Who Made This Christmas Special

A recipe from Marie Ferrarella:

SAUERKRAUT PIEROGI

Dough:
1 egg
3 ¼ cups flour
½ cup water
⅛ tsp salt

Combine ingredients. Knead dough. With rolling pin, flatten dough until almost paper thin. Cut into 3″ squares.

Stuffing:
2 lb sauerkraut
1 onion, chopped
oil for frying

Boil sauerkraut. Drain. Squeeze out excess water.

Fry onion until golden brown. Add sauerkraut. Fry for 5 minutes. Salt to taste.

Assembly:
Water for boiling
melted butter

Put a teaspoon of stuffing onto each square of dough. Moisten two ends of each square and press together, forming a triangle.

Put pierogi in rapidly boiling water for 5 minutes. Drain. Serve with melted butter.

Don't worry about leftovers, if you're so lucky. These pierogi make a wonderful breakfast the next morning. Just fry with a little butter or margarine.

Chapter One

There was something about the suit.

Initially nothing had seemed unusual about it. When the assistant floor manager handed the box to him in the dressing area, the outfit inside had appeared to be the typical size-forty-two bright red Santa Claus costume.

It was when he put the suit on that it began to happen. As he slipped his arms into the sleeves and closed the jacket, vivid memories suddenly came flooding back in a tidal wave of magic. Magic that went hand in hand with a child's view of Christmas.

Timothy Holt looked into the dressing room mirror, adjusting the white wig and flowing white beard that hid his slightly unruly blond hair and superherolike square chin. As he did, he could have sworn he smelled sugar cookies baking. His mother had always baked sugar cookies during the Christmas season. He'd forgotten how good that aroma had made him feel. How special Christmas had always been to him. Special and full of magic.

Gerald Lakewood looked Tim over with a quick, nervous eye. The man had gratefully hired him less than an hour ago. "Do you have enough padding?" he asked.

Tim nodded, moving his hips slightly from side to side, trying to get comfortable with the extra bulk that hung in front of him. He patted his stomach. "I just hope it doesn't come loose."

Gerald pushed open the dressing room door. The noise of the pre-Christmas shoppers filling the aisles of Mattingly's Department Store suddenly assaulted them. ''All you've got to do is sit and listen. And smile for the photographer.''

And take notes, Tim added silently as he stepped past Gerald.

Tim moved down the nearest aisle, taking small, rolling steps toward the toy department. Children all along his path smiled and waved or called out to him. Tim waved back, a strange warmth taking hold of him. Encased in wig, beard, red suit, boots and padding, Tim estimated that he was at least fifteen pounds heavier. Yet somehow, despite the bulkiness, he felt freer than he normally did. Lighter. He waved at a little girl who couldn't have been more than three, and she stared at him with wide, delighted eyes. It had been a very long time since he had experienced this sort of buoyancy. It felt wonderful.

He reminded himself that he had a job to do. This wasn't for fun and games, or even just a whim. This was research.

''Here, you'll sit here,'' Gerald said, repeating himself needlessly as he gestured at a red velvet, thronelike chair that sat on a raised platform. To the left of the chair was an elf's hut complete with elf and ready camera. Photographs of Santa and toddlers cost six dollars.

Everything, Tim thought with a sudden twinge of sadness, had a price to it. But if it didn't, he would've been out of a job.

''I don't know what came over Jack, taking off like that,'' Gerald muttered under his breath to Tim. ''He's been our Santa for five years now.'' Gerald glanced at

Tim's waist as Tim made himself comfortable. "And he doesn't need padding."

No, but he did need the extra three hundred dollars Tim had given him to suddenly vacate the position. That and the promise of getting his customary salary had done the trick. Tim had no interest in the department store's paychecks. All he wanted was the vantage point of being Santa Claus in a popular department store.

"Appendicitis," Tim said, suddenly inspired. After all, Jack might need the job again next year. And Tim just needed it for the next three weeks, long enough to complete his marketing report.

"Yeah, well—" Gerald mopped his brow "—lucky you could fill in for him."

"That's what nephews are for," Tim murmured. That was the excuse he had given Gerald for appearing in the other man's place. It had gone over easily enough.

A dark-haired boy approached him, pulling his hand free from his harried looking mother.

"Are you Santa's nephew?" The boy appeared to seriously study Tim.

"Me?" Tim coughed, lowering his voice until it sounded gravelly. "No, I'm the real guy. I was just talking about my nephew."

The boy pursed his lips. "I didn't know Santa had a nephew."

"Sure." Tim beckoned the boy forward as Gerald melted away behind him. "But let's talk about you, okay?" The boy settled happily into Tim's lap. "What would you like me to bring you?"

Tim listened to small, childish voices for the better part of three hours. The experience was different than he had imagined. There was no reserved hesitation on his part the way he had anticipated. It was odd, and he had no explanation for it. He felt relaxed, as if this was where he was really supposed to be. But not as Tim Holt, president of Holt Enterprises, a marketing firm that in six short years had risen from obscurity to become a leading contender in its field. And especially not as a researcher hired by Imagination Toys to discover what it was that children, not their parents, *really* wanted to get for Christmas.

Tim felt he belonged here as . . . *Santa Claus?*

It had to be the mothballs or whatever it was the store used to preserve the suit from year to year that was giving him this strange, euphoric high.

The feeling intensified rather than diminished as the hours went by. He didn't understand it and eventually gave up trying to analyze it. Whatever was causing the sensation, he felt comfortable sitting in the roomy velvet chair, letting Mrs. Claus, a gray-haired woman in rimless spectacles, lead children to him. Very comfortable. Certainly more comfortable than he did when he was in his office. Children looked up at him trustingly, and he liked that, liked listening as they giggled and told him about presents they hoped would be under their trees Christmas morning.

Through the gift of a photographic memory, Tim noted and retained the wealth of information that came his way, aptly cataloguing the types of toys that were requested over and over. The minutes merged into hours and, caught up in his task and in the magic, Tim lost track of time.

That was why he didn't know when he first became conscious of the blond-haired boy. By the time he had,

Tim realized that the child had been standing there, leaning against the side of a counter for a while, eyeing him with a smug, knowing look. He couldn't have been more than six. And he was alone.

Six was a very young age to have lost one's grasp of make-believe. He had believed in Santa Claus long after he really shouldn't have, Tim remembered, unwilling to give up that last vestige of childhood.

The strawberry blonde in the ruffled polka-dot dress wiggled off his lap, satisfied that Santa would grant her every wish. Tim was turning to look at the boy at the counter again when he felt a tap on his shoulder. Mrs. Claus smiled at him kindly.

Tim blinked. "Yes?"

"You can take another break, Santa," she informed him. Several children at the front of the line groaned.

"I'll be right back," Tim promised them with a wink.

Tim pushed himself up from the chair. The padding had been flattened somewhat by all the children who had sat on his lap, leaning against it. He patted his stomach repeatedly, subtly reshaping it. Stepping off the platform, he crossed to the little boy at the toy counter. As he approached, Tim saw large, clear, water-blue eyes looking up at him defiantly.

Tim grinned, the beard moving slightly on his broad, chiseled cheeks. "Hi."

The luminous eyes looked Santa over once before an indifferent . . . no, almost hostile, "Hi," echoed back. The boy shoved his hands into his pockets and turned away. Tim would have bet that the small hands were doubled up into fists. He couldn't help wondering why.

He tried not to sound patronizing as he asked, "Do you know who I am?"

The boy turned away and began to examine a toy truck with wide tires. He tested one wheel with his thumb, moving it back and forth. "Yeah, some guy pretending to be Santa Claus."

Tim knew it was useless to claim to be the genuine article. The boy had already made up his mind about that. "Well, he's kind of busy this time of year, so he has people stand in as—"

The boy replaced the truck on the counter and looked at Tim with eyes that were older than they had a right to be. "No, he doesn't."

"He doesn't?" Tim echoed, stumped for a better answer.

The boy set his mouth hard. The words he uttered hurt. "No. He doesn't exist."

Because the conversation was too serious to carry on with so much distance between them, Tim bent down to the boy's level. "Really?"

The anger and hurt were on the surface, so tangible that Tim could have touched them. "Sure. Don't you know that?"

What had happened to make the child feel like this? "How old are you?"

The boy raised himself up on his toes. "Six."

He was a very small six. "And you don't believe in me—umm—in Santa Claus?"

"No." But this time, when faced with authority, there was just the slightest waver in the boy's voice.

Tim kept his voice gentle. "You're absolutely sure about that?"

The little boy shoved his hands back into his pockets, as if that gave him strength. "Yeah."

Tim had no idea what made him push the matter. Maybe it *was* the suit. Or maybe it was the fact that he didn't like seeing someone so young so stripped of hope. "What makes you so sure?"

The boy took a deep breath, creating a barrier between himself and the weight of the words. "Because last year I asked him for a dad and he didn't bring me one."

Tim stroked his beard thoughtfully, taking care not to move it. "A dad's a tall order."

The boy raised his chin. "Not for Santa Claus. If he was real." His voice dropped. "But he's not."

Tim placed his hand on the boy's shoulder and was happy to see that the child didn't shrug him off. "What happened to your dad?"

"I don't know." The boy's voice was small, helpless. As small and helpless as his pain had made him. "He's been gone for a long time. Longer than I can remember." The words gained speed. "I asked for a dad so he could bring me a train and play with me. And make my mama stop looking so sad." The sudden torrent of words stopped as the boy frowned. "But I didn't get one."

"Maybe this year." Somehow, Tim felt compelled to voice the optimistic words.

But the frown on the boy's face remained. "No. We've moved."

Tim searched for the logic behind the statement and found none. "And that makes a difference?"

The boy sighed impatiently. "We moved a long way. We don't know anyone here, not really. All the dads on the block already have kids. We're from Ohio." The state's name was said wistfully. "And I don't like it much here."

Tim was a native Californian and loved it. "California's great."

The young eyes were unconvinced. "It doesn't snow here."

"Well, yeah, but—"

"I know you're not real—I mean Santa isn't," the boy corrected himself, "but I sure did like snow for Christmas." His frown deepened. "This year we've even got a fake tree. Mama says it'll be cheaper that way after a while." His lower lip trembled as he tried to be older than he was. "Nothing's real anymore."

It had been a long time since Tim had felt so moved. He wanted to gather the boy to him, to tell him that things would turn out all right in the long run if he had faith. But he couldn't very well pull a daddy out of a hat. "What's your name?"

Rubbing a telltale tear from his cheek with the back of his hand, the boy answered, "Robbie. Robbie Lekawski."

"What are you doing here by yourself?" Tim glanced up, but though there was a throng of shoppers, no one seemed to be searching frantically for a small, blond-haired boy.

"I'm not by myself. My mama's here." Robbie looked around and saw only bodies. "Somewhere."

"Somewhere?"

Some of the bravado left the set of his shoulders. "She got lost." Robbie looked around again, his eyes growing uneasy.

Tim took the small hand in his large, gloved one. "Then we'd better find her before she gets frightened,'' he told Robbie gently. Mrs. Claus would know what to do with a lost child, Tim assured himself. He looked around for her, but the woman had apparently taken her break, as well.

"I'm not supposed to talk to strangers," Robbie told Tim, unwilling to move.

Tim smiled down at him. "But I'm not a stranger. I'm Santa's earthly representative."

"I already told you," Robbie insisted stubbornly. "I don't believe in Santa Claus."

"That's okay. I do." Tim began to lead Robbie back to Santa's platform. Maybe the elf's sphere of knowledge went beyond photography.

"Robbie!"

The loud, relief-filled cry had Tim turning around and searching the crowd for its source.

He had always known that he was strictly a one-woman man. He had never found that one particular woman, but he hadn't worried. He knew that she was out there somewhere. It was only a matter of time. Someday, some way, when he least expected it, he would see her.

And he would know.

But he never expected to see her while he was swaddled in a long, flowing white beard with bushy eyebrows dipping into his eyes.

"Robbie, where've you been?" Laura Lekawski dropped to her knees and threw her arms around her only son. Tears stung her eyes. She didn't know whether to cry and hold on to Robbie, or to shake him for scaring her so badly. She had envisioned all sorts of horrible things in the twenty minutes she had been searching for him.

Hugging won out. It always did.

"Here. Talking to him." Robbie's voice was muffled against his mother's chest. Squirming loose, Robbie pointed at Tim.

Laura looked over her shoulder and saw Santa Claus grinning at her.

Chapter Two

Tim had always thought that when he fell in love, it would happen slowly, like the gradual unfolding of an interesting novel. Instead, it seized him on the very first page, like a suspense thriller. He had thought that falling in love would be like learning to appreciate a soft melody. It would grow on him as the refrain played over and over in his head. This wasn't anything like a lyrical song. It caught him up like a march by John Philip Sousa, right from the first thundering note that drummed through his entire being.

There was no rhyme, no reason for it. One moment love wasn't there, the next it was, fully grown and alive, holding him prisoner in the palm of its hand. The feeling swept through every fiber of his Santa-suited body like wildfire as Tim took in and instantly memorized every detail of the attractive woman before him. The initial fear of losing Robbie that had left her flushed and slightly disoriented looking only served to heighten Tim's reaction to her.

He had it bad.

Laura rose to her feet, holding Robbie by the hand. She was clearly aware that he—Santa Claus—was staring at her, almost staring right through her. It seemed to be making her a little uneasy. But there were questions Tim wanted to ask this woman who had materialized from the crowd and turned his whole world upside down by her mere existence. All sorts of questions, beginning with her name and verification of the fact that she really wasn't married.

He didn't get the chance. Mrs. Claus was tapping him on the shoulder, her small lips pursed in a tolerant, half smile. "Santa, I'm sorry, but your break is over. The children are waiting."

"He wasn't afraid," Tim told Robbie's mother, desperately searching for something to say that sounded halfway intelligent.

Laura looked at her son. Her expression softened. "No, but I certainly was." She spared the odd Santa Claus one last glance. "Thank you for finding him." Turning, she began to walk away, packages in one hand, Robbie's hand in the other.

"He found me," Tim called after her as Mrs. Claus tugged on his arm, drawing him back to the restless, noisy line of children.

As he mounted the platform to his chair, Tim helplessly watched the woman of his dreams slip right through his fingers, knowing that he'd regret letting her go all the days of his life.

Those were Timothy Holt's thoughts on the subject. The man in the red suit, however, had another feeling about the matter, a feeling that told him he hadn't loved and lost in the space of three minutes. There was no basis for this feeling, but it didn't matter.

Tim had absolutely no idea how he knew he'd see her again. He just knew.

He thought about her during the rest of his shift, thought about her as sticky-fingered children, clutching red-and-white striped candy canes, poured out their dreams to him. Thought about her as one very small child became so excited upon seeing Santa for the first time that she left a little wet circle commemorating their encounter. Thought about her as he smiled for the elf and his camera. The part of Tim's mind that was so good at tabulating things kept meticulous track of what each child asked for. That was his job, and Tim always kept his priorities straight.

But another part of his mind, the part that had once dreamed fantasies, that had clung to make-believe longer than the other kids in his class, the part that had been denied for so long in this adult life he was leading, kept drifting off, thinking of the woman with the soft, blond hair and liquid blue eyes like her son's. The woman in the navy blue suit that was subdued and practical and yet still managed to show off her soft, supple curves.

Tim was still thinking about her when he walked out to the parking lot. He was so preoccupied that he had forgotten to return to the dressing room and change out of his costume.

"Hi, Santa Claus!" twin boys yelled from across the nearly deserted parking lot as their parents hustled them into a minivan.

Tim waved back, told himself he was an idiot and turned around to return to the store and change into his street clothes before it closed.

That was when he saw her.

Laura had completed her shopping in more time than she had anticipated. The packages were all neatly deposited in the trunk of her car. A car that stubbornly refused to do anything when she turned her key in the ignition. Repeated tries had yielded absolutely no response other than a dull whine. She got out and circled the car, eyeing it like an opponent to be outsmarted.

Robbie trailed after her, complaining that he was hungry. Laura was very close to kicking the car's front tires, even though it would accomplish no earthly good except, perhaps, to make her feel better. And scrape the polish off the toe of her navy high heels.

But Robbie was with her, so she couldn't vent her frustration. It wasn't reassuring for a child to see his mother act like an irrational fool, she thought, glancing at him.

With a sigh, she took Robbie's hand. "Come on, we're going to have to call a tow truck."

Robbie was already anticipating the ride home. "Wow!"

"Yes, wow," Laura echoed without his enthusiasm. She dragged her free hand through her hair, feeling just this side of overwhelmed.

"Something wrong?"

She gasped, startled as she swung around to look up into crinkling green eyes and bushy white eyebrows. Another Santa Claus, she thought. Or was it the same one? She peered closer.

It *was* the same one. Uneasily, she glanced around, but most of the parking lot was empty. With the mall closing, everyone was going home. Where were the holiday throngs when you needed them?

One hand hovered protectively in front of Robbie as she pushed the boy behind her. "Yes," she answered Tim's question. Then, because she couldn't help herself, she asked, "Who *are* you?"

He saw the mistrust in her eyes. Like son, like mother, he thought. "A good samaritan," Tim answered cheerfully, glancing at her. "Santa Claus. Some call me Kris Kringle."

Why wasn't he dressed in normal clothes? Laura wondered. Did he get some kind of perverse pleasure out of parading around in a Santa Claus suit? "Some probably call you crazy." The words slipped out under her breath before she realized it.

Tim caught himself grinning. "No, but I was told just today that I didn't exist."

He looked pointedly at Robbie, who clearly didn't know what to make of the situation. The boy glanced from his mother to Tim, curious to see if this Santa could work magic and get the car going. He had said he didn't believe in Santa Claus, but he was willing to be persuaded otherwise. Especially if reindeer came to the rescue.

Laura wished there was someone else close by. It would have made her feel more in control. She ran her tongue along her lips and decided to brazen the situation out. "Look, Mr.—" she faltered, not knowing what to call him. Santa Claus sounded ridiculous.

"Holt. Timothy Holt." He saw the knowing smirk on Robbie's face. *Just you wait, Robbie. I'm going to make you believe. In time.*

"Mr. Holt, I, umm—" Laura felt her throat grow dry as she began to edge her way back to the driver's side. *Then what? The car doesn't work, remember?*

Oh, why hadn't she gotten that car phone the way her mother kept badgering her to? Because car phones were expensive and money was an object these days, she reminded herself.

Tim had a feeling that if he told her he was harmless, that would only make her edgier. Instead he turned his attention to her car. "What's wrong with the car?"

"It won't start," Robbie offered.

Laura wondered if it was a mistake to admit that to this man. She held her breath, nervous, as the green eyes turned to her.

"Have you tried your lights?"

"No." She realized that the word had come out in a whisper. "No," she repeated more forcefully.

Tim gestured to the car. "Try them."

Opening the door, Laura leaned into the car and turned the key. Tim watched the straight skirt ride up a long, slender leg. The car's lights turned on, but dimly.

Reluctantly, Tim drew his eyes away from her legs to her face. Not a bad trade, he decided. The woman took his breath away. It was a moment before he found his voice again. "It's your battery."

Laura sagged against the car. "Swell."

He had never played a knight in shining armor before. He wanted nothing more than to play one now, even if his armor was a red suit with fur trim and a huge, square buckle. "I've got jumper cables."

Laura didn't like to ask for favors from strangers, especially *strange* strangers wearing Santa Claus costumes, but it was getting late and she knew her mother would be getting worried. She always worried—it was one of her hobbies.

Squeezing Robbie's hand more tightly, Laura gave in. "Would you mind?"

"Mama, my fingers are getting tingly."

Laura released her hold on Robbie's hand. She saw a smile materialize beneath all that white hair on Santa's face.

"My pleasure." Tim held up his hands, willing her not to move. "Wait right here."

Laura leaned against the hood of the dormant car. "As if we had a choice," she muttered to Robbie, hoping she was making the right decision.

"Thank you, Santa Claus, wherever you are," Tim murmured under his breath as he hurried to his Jaguar.

Laura's car came to life on the second try.

By the time Tim removed the jumper cables from her battery terminals, Laura was hustling Robbie into the front seat.

"Well, thank you very much," she said quickly, her voice higher than she would have liked it to be. Her voice always went up an octave or two whenever she was nervous.

Laura got in on the driver's side and started to close the door. Tim impulsively placed his hand in the way, stopping her. It wasn't like him. But then, he had never been in love before, either.

"The least I can do is follow you home. To make sure you make it," he added when he saw the guarded look come into her eyes.

Laura hesitated. After all, he had helped her. But still, what did she know about him? Absolutely nothing. "I don't want to cause any trouble."

"No, this won't be any trouble."

She watched the tip of his beard flutter in the wind. Maybe she was just overreacting. But why didn't he at least take his beard off? Was he disfigured? Did he have a weak chin he was ashamed of? Or was he hiding something far more serious?

"You're sure?" she asked slowly.

He wondered what had put the wariness into her eyes. He knew he wanted to erase all traces of it. "Scout's honor." He held up three fingers, and then let them drop as he leaned forward. "Not very trusting, are you?"

Laura lifted an eyebrow. *Was* he after something after all? "I've no reason to be."

It didn't take a psychiatrist to know that she meant the words from the bottom of her soul. Why? What could have happened to a beautiful woman like Robbie's mother to make her so suspicious?

Laura wished he'd let go of the car door.

"Maybe we can change that," Tim said softly. It occurred to him that he still didn't know who she was. "What's your name?"

Laura hesitated for a moment, then decided that perhaps she owed him that much. Maybe he was just what he said he was, a good samaritan. She didn't particularly like the fact that he was going to follow her home, but her mother lived with her, and she could always summon the police if need be. Besides, Laura thought, shifting slightly in her seat, she could take care of herself. Now. That hadn't always been the case, but then, everyone had to be idealistic at one point in their lives, she supposed. Before reality set in.

"Laura Lekawski." Unconsciously, she reached over and placed her hand over her son's.

"Laura." Tim repeated the name slowly, rolling it around on his tongue. It filled his head like a melody. The woman he was in love with was named Laura. "That's a very pretty name."

Laura looked straight ahead as she shifted the car into drive. "My mother will be glad that you approve."

He tried again. "It suits you. The name, I mean."

Laura glanced at him impatiently. "Look, I don't like compliments." That was the way it had started the last time. With compliments. Empty compliments.

Tim smiled. "Everyone likes compliments."

"I don't." She had believed in them once, believed in love once. And though she didn't regret what happened, because it had brought Robbie into her life, she regretted being a fool. She would always regret that. "Perhaps I'd just better go home alone."

Tim shook his head. "I have to do one good deed a day or turn in the suit."

"You've already done a good deed," she pointed out. "You started my car."

He nodded. "Half a good deed. It gets negated if you don't reach your destination." He slung the jumper cables over his shoulder. "I'll just put these in the trunk and then—"

But Laura was already driving away. Tim threw the cables onto the front seat of his car, wincing slightly as he thought of the mark they would probably leave on his leather upholstery. But this was more important than immaculate upholstery. This was his future.

He started the car and drove after her.

Laura glanced into her rearview mirror and saw the white car following her. The tip of Santa Claus's beard was blowing out the open window, fluttering in the breeze. She shook her head.

"He's not real, right, Mama?" Robbie asked uncertainly, looking over his shoulder.

"What?" She glanced at Robbie and gave him a forced smile. She didn't want him to worry, even though she still had her doubts about the man behind them. "Sure he is."

Robbie's brow puckered as he looked at her, confused. "Santa Claus?"

They had already agreed that Saint Nick was nothing more than a fable when Robbie had insisted on the truth last Christmas. He remembered that his mother hadn't been happy about the admission. Was she changing her mind now? Was Santa Claus real after all?

"No, not Santa Claus. The man following us." She nodded behind her. "Santa Claus doesn't drive a white '92 Jaguar."

Chapter Three

Janka Lekawski rubbed her hands up and down the sleeves of her green sweater. Southern California winter nights were a lot warmer than those she remembered enduring as a young girl in Poland, but there was no denying that there was a chill in the air. And in her heart.

She knew it was foolish to worry. Laura was a grown woman of twenty-six, fully capable of taking care of herself and Robbie. There were any number of logical reasons why she was almost an hour late. But she *was* late, and Janka couldn't elude a lifetime habit of worrying.

Besides, the night somehow made it worse, making all her fears more vivid. Janka sighed and stepped out into the street, willing the car to appear.

Squinting toward the end of the residential cul-de-sac, Janka thought she could make out a car turning down the block. A huge sigh of relief escaped her as the silver Toyota drew closer. Janka's expression turned thoughtful when she saw that her daughter's car was being followed. Her knowledge of different makes was limited to the cars that occupied the garage directly behind her, but Janka knew that the second car was an expensive one.

The garage door yawned open behind her as the Toyota pulled up the driveway. Janka was at Laura's door before the car came to a full stop. "Where have you been? You are more t'an an hour late."

Laura got out and slammed the door a little too forcefully behind her. Robbie tumbled out from the other side and joined them. He held up a new action figure for his grandmother's examination.

"Very nice, dear," Janka said. "And scary." She knew what was required of her. Robbie grinned and proceeded to have his renegade soldier fight imaginary battles with invisible opponents.

Laura saw that her mother was still waiting for an answer. "The mall was crowded, Mother. And then the car wouldn't start." She heard Tim's car pull up behind hers in the driveway, but refused to turn around. Maybe he'd go away if she ignored him.

Janka looked down at the silver car's hood. "But you got here."

The soft thud of a car door closing told Laura that Tim had gotten out. He was joining them. She nodded her head in his general direction without looking. "He jump started it."

Janka left her daughter's side and drew closer to the tall stranger. Tim smiled and nodded a greeting. Janka looked over her shoulder at Laura, and then back at Tim. "San-ta Klauss?"

Laura gave up and turned around. She saw that her mother was, indeed, face to chest with the red-suited samaritan. "Claus, Mother. Santa Claus."

Twenty-two years in the country and her mother still mispronounced and inverted words. Usually, Laura found it charming. Tonight, for some reason, it irritated her. There was an uneasy itch traveling through her, and she had no idea why.

Janka peered up at Tim, intrigued by his eyes. "But San-ta Klauss is centuries old." Janka gently tugged on the beard until it slipped down. The face she discovered beneath made her smile broadly. "Not a handsome young man."

Laura looked, speechless, as Tim pulled off his wig. Her mouth fell open. He *was* handsome. Too much so. Until this very moment, she had thought of him as some older, retired man, possibly plain—definitely old. The white, even teeth, and the broad smile unnerved her, as did the chiseled features that were incongruously coupled with a gentleness that tempered them and kept him from looking hard. Only gorgeous. How could so much have been hidden by tufts of fake hair?

Laura didn't like the reaction skimming through her. She felt a tightening, almost a yearning, in places that she didn't want awakened to this sort of sensation. Laura had felt better when he was hidden behind his beard. At least then her uneasiness had a reasonable basis behind it. She couldn't put a name to the shaky sensation jumping through her now.

Or didn't want to.

Tim grinned at the small, dark-haired woman with the lively hazel eyes set in a round face. "I like your mother, Laura."

For just a moment, Laura put her wariness aside. She smiled fondly as she looked in her mother's direction.

It was the first smile he had seen on her face. A genuine smile. Somehow, he had known she'd smile that way. Guilelessly. The smile went right through him, into him, branding his heart as it filtered through every vein in his body. It was a smile that would last him for all time, a smile that made him look forward to forever. With her. Tim fell in love all over again. If the pulses in his body were hammering any harder, he was certain that the women in the driveway would hear them.

"Most everyone does," Laura answered. And it was true. When they'd moved from Ohio in the summer, they hadn't even been in the house for a week before Janka had made friends with everyone on both sides of the block. Everyone had come over to pitch in and help when the movers arrived the following Saturday.

She looked back at Tim. Enough was enough. Laura took a step closer to the house, ready to separate herself from this strange good samaritan, even if he was heart-stoppingly handsome.... She placed one hand on Robbie's shoulder. "Well, I'd better—"

Janka knew that tone. Laura was withdrawing. The older woman looked from the tall man to her daughter and then smiled. There was a certain light in the young man's eyes she found very interesting. "You will not introduce me to the man who jump-started you?"

Laura swung around in time to see Tim unsuccessfully trying to hide his grin. "The car, Mother, he jump-started the car."

Although, Tim silently acknowledged Laura's correction, he certainly wouldn't have minded trying his hand at jump-starting Laura in the bargain.

Janka shrugged away the correction. English was always so confusing anyway, what with words that were said the same way and meant different things. "Whatever." She looked at her daughter expectantly, waiting.

Laura knew they were going to stand there until she introduced her mother to Tim. The woman could be incredibly stubborn at times.

"As you must have already gathered—" Laura gestured to Janka "—this is my mother, Janka Lekawski. Mother, this is Timothy Holt."

"Hello, Timot'y." Janka took the hand Tim offered and shook it. He had a good, firm handshake. She liked him instantly. Liked the kindness she saw in his eyes. And the love.

She glanced down at Robbie, who had come to stand at her side, and then back at Tim. She made a decision. "So, what do you know about Christmas lights t'at stay dark even when you plug t'em in?" She pointed to the darkened frame of the house.

On closer scrutiny, Tim saw that the house was outlined in unlit Christmas lights.

Oh, God, Mother, don't do this to me. Laura tried to shake the sinking feeling that was gnawing at the pit of her stomach. "Mother, I'm sure that Mr. Holt—" she began just as Tim opened his mouth.

Janka waved her daughter to silence. "Shh, he was about to answer. Do not interrupt Timot'y." She turned her face toward him, smiling encouragingly.

Tim saw where Laura got her smile from. Janka's was radiant. "I can take a look at it for you." Janka looked pleased.

Laura, on the other hand, only looked suspicious. She ignored the expression on her mother's face. "Don't you have a home to go to?" she asked Tim pointedly.

Tim was already examining the string of lights closest to him. Everything appeared all right at first glance, but that didn't mean anything.

"Yes, but it's dark and empty." He looked at Laura over his shoulder. She was only a few inches away. He could smell her fragrance. Light and airy and incredibly sweet. And spellbinding. It suited her. "And I'm used to a lot more noise around Christmastime," he added more slowly. He felt, suddenly, as if the blood in his veins had been set on fire.

The look in his eyes held her captive even as it weakened her knees. It was a moment before she found her voice. Laura pulled her suspicions to her like a shield, wanting to deflect his gaze and the feelings it was generating. She felt a very definite hum of sexual tension in the air. And more than a little attraction. She couldn't let that take root. "Divorced?"

He grinned and shook his head as he jiggled the string a little. "Displaced."

He was making about as much sense as her mother was. "What?"

Tim let the string drop and followed it with his eyes to the next connection. "I just moved to Huntington Beach from L.A. The rest of my family—parents, brothers, sisters, nieces, nephews—all live in the Santa Barbara area. I'm usually there around Christmastime, but this year I've got a project to work on." It was his work that had taken him away from the bosom of his family. There was precious little use for his type of business in Santa Barbara. The midst of a large city was where he was needed.

Laura's eyes narrowed as she looked at his costume. "Playing Santa Claus is a project?"

He stepped back and looked to see where the light string ultimately fed into. "It's a little more involved than that."

How involved could it be? He was playing Santa Claus for a department store. Probably out of work and needed the money to support his car. Everyone had lies they used to save their pride, she supposed. There had been no lie to save hers, but at least there had been Robbie.

Janka moved around eagerly to Tim's other side. "When I put in t'e plug—" she pointed to the inside of the brightly lit garage "—poof." She brushed her thumb along her fingers, but no snapping sound followed. "Not'ing."

"So I see." Playing a hunch, Tim walked into the neatly swept garage and picked up the extension cord. "Who put the lights up?"

"We did," Robbie chimed in, pointing to himself and then his mother.

Tim curbed the impulse to ruffle the boy's hair. "Nice job." He bent down and saw that the extension cord had an On/Off switch. And it was turned off. "I think I found your problem." He flipped a switch. "How's that?"

"Beautiful!" Janka clapped her hands together as she admired the lights. Ignoring the warning look on her daughter's face, she went into the garage, took Tim by the arm and dragged him outside again. "Come see what you have done, Timot'y." She waved a hand around at the exterior of the house. It was ablaze with red and green lights.

"I just flipped a switch."

"Never play down what you do." Janka wagged a finger at him, her expression stern. But her eyes were dancing. "Would you like some eggnog? For fixing t'e lights and jump-starting my daughter?"

He grinned, aware that Laura was glaring at them. "I'd love some." It was clear that Janka was on his side, even if Laura wasn't.

Yet.

Maybe it was the suit, he mused, opening the top two buttons as he allowed himself to be ushered into the brightly lit house. It made him feel that however impossible it seemed at the moment, Laura Lekawski could be won over to his way of thinking.

And soon.

As they walked in the front door, Tim saw an eight-foot tree, symmetrically perfect and barren, standing in the living room. "That's a nice tree," he commented to Robbie as they passed it.

Robbie hardly spared it a glance. "It's fake," he grumbled as his grandmother walked intő the kitchen.

"It's pretty and practical," Laura insisted. And cheaper in the long run. Still, she had to admit that she did miss the wonderful scent of pine that had always filled the house when she was growing up. A twinge of guilt pricked at her for depriving Robbie of the same kind of memories she had.

Robbie looked as if he wanted to kick the tree over. "It's still fake."

Tim stopped and looked up at the tree, studying it. "Sometimes things that aren't real can be just as good as the real thing. Maybe even better."

"Like what?" There was no missing the challenge in Robbie's eyes.

Timothy Holt would have been hardpressed to answer the question. The man in the Santa suit, however, was not. It just seemed to come to him. "You know that amusement-park ride that has you thinking you're in a real spaceship?"

Robbie knew immediately the one Tim was referring to. He'd been on it just last week. It was all part of his mother's plan to make him feel happy about moving to Southern California. It had worked. For a while. And then he remembered that this Christmas there would no snow to look forward to, no snow to watch as it fell from the sky, no snowflakes to catch on his tongue. "Yeah?"

Laura crossed her arms before her, listening and wondering what Tim was up to despite herself.

"You get to enjoy the thrill without putting up with any of the problems," Tim was saying.

Robbie looked confused as he frowned. "Problems?"

Out of the corner of his eye, Tim saw that Janka had emerged from what he assumed was the kitchen, a large mug gripped in her hand. The woman had stopped and was apparently waiting to hear his explanation.

"Having motion sickness. Having to deal with cramped quarters. People floating around in your space." Tim lowered his voice to add gravity to his statement. "Having to worry if your ship'll land all right." To his satisfaction, he saw a hint of a smile on Laura's face. He was making points whether she wanted him to or not.

Robbie looked up at the tree, as if he was reconsidering his feelings about it.

The expression on Janka's face was one of admiration as she approached Tim. She looked at him and then nodded toward her grandson. "You are very good at t'is."

Yes, he was, wasn't he, Tim thought, pleased with himself. He wasn't altogether certain where his answer had come from, but all that mattered was that it had come. He saw Laura looking at him thoughtfully as he accepted the cup of eggnog that her mother was pressing into his hand. Tim glanced down at his suit, then at Janka.

"It's my job. Santa Claus knows everything there is about make-believe and magic."

Chapter Four

Tim felt his eyes water as his first swallow of eggnog flamed its way down to his stomach. He cleared his throat and wondered if he had a voice left. Janka was watching him attentively. He held up the mug toward Laura. "This isn't store-bought, is it?"

Laura couldn't help the smile that rose to her lips. "No." Served him right for being so pushy. And so damn good-looking to boot.

Janka gestured upward with her hand, indicating that he should continue drinking, and smiled when he obeyed. "It is my own recipe, Timot'y."

And a hell of a recipe it is, Mrs. Lekawski. "This could have brought about détente a lot sooner," he murmured, warily studying the inside of his cup. He was somewhat surprised that the eggnog hadn't burned a hole clean through it by now.

"Come," Janka urged, linking her arm through his. She led him to the kitchen. "I give you more."

This was too much, Laura thought, refusing to be part of it. She hung back.

"You come too, Laura," Janka said without turning around.

She could have protested. Laura knew that. She could have staunchly refused to join them. After all, she wasn't a child anymore, to be ordered around. No, she didn't have to go into the kitchen at all.

But she started to follow anyway. She refused to admit, even to herself, that she wanted to.

Robbie and his action figure were still fighting for freedom, justice and the American way. Laura kissed the top of his head. "Go get ready for bed, Robbie."

He looked toward the kitchen. "I want to stay and watch."

I'm sure you do. "It's past your bedtime."

Robbie pouted. "Aw, Mama, it's Friday."

Laura pointed toward the stairs. "Go. I'll be up in a little while to tuck you and your soldier in."

"Yes'm." Robbie looked crestfallen for approximately half a minute before he devised another adventure for his soldier and bounded up the stairs. With any luck, his mother wouldn't be up to check on him for some time.

Laura sighed, resigned as she turned toward the kitchen. There was no stopping her mother once she got rolling. The best Laura could hope for was just to live through it.

She walked into the kitchen, telling herself it was because she was afraid that if she wasn't there, her mother would be arranging for dowry payments by midnight. She also told herself that she didn't like leaving her mother alone with a stranger.

She told herself a lot of things.

Except the truth.

As she entered the warm kitchen, Laura saw her mother at the stove. Something was always either coming out of the oven or going in. Around the holidays, her mother seemed dedicated to baking around the clock. And to making her gain weight, Laura thought, running her hands down her hips nervously.

Reluctantly, Laura looked toward Tim, who was sitting at the table. For an intruder, she grudgingly admitted that he did have his merits. Especially when he smiled. There was a mischievous little-boy quality about the smile that made it almost impossible not to trust him.

But she didn't. Things were not always what they seemed. She had learned that the hard way.

The air was pungent with the smell of cookies, just the way he remembered from his own childhood. But even though he was preoccupied with memories, he was aware of her fragrance as soon as Laura walked in behind him. Cookies and roses. An interesting combination.

He turned his head toward her. "Your mother's charming."

Because there seemed to be suddenly nowhere else to go, Laura sat down opposite him.

Tim lowered his voice slightly as he leaned toward her. "But, umm, is it just me, or does she seem to have a little trouble with her th's?"

Laura didn't mean to laugh, but she did. "Mother came to America when she was in her twenties. There are no th combinations in Polish. She can't pronounce that sound to save her life, which is why Robbie is Robbie and not Theodore." Laura grinned to herself as she remembered her mother struggling with the first choice of name Laura had picked for her new baby. "Her tongue wouldn't wrap itself around the letters." Aware of the way he was looking at her and the fact that it was making her uncommonly warm, Laura looked away.

Tim glanced at the cup he held in both hands. The liquid was still heating up all his extremities. "Her tongue seemed to be doing just fine."

Laura nodded absently. Her mother could go on talking for hours once she got started. "She can talk your ear off."

He wasn't certain if Laura was apologizing for her mother or not. In any case, there was no reason to. "I don't mind. She reminds me of my Aunt Elizabeth."

Laura didn't want to know any more about him than she already did. The less she knew, the less there was to like. And she didn't want to like him. "Does Aunt Elizabeth live near the rest of your family?" So much for maintaining disinterest.

"Yes." It was all he had time to say. Janka was at his elbow, a tray of fresh sugar cookies between her oven mittened hands. She set it down gingerly on the table between them.

"Did you know t'at Laura runs her own business?" Janka cast a sly glance in Tim's direction as she gently shook the tray, loosening the cookies.

Next her mother would be showing him the results of her last dental checkup, Laura thought. "Mother," she said very firmly, "he doesn't want to know that I run my own business."

Unable to resist, Tim picked up a cookie from the tray and blew on it before breaking off a piece. "Yes, I do." The cookie was still hot to the touch. He blew again. "What kind of business?"

Oh, well, it made no difference if he knew. Laura shrugged carelessly. "It's a secretarial business. Have fingers, will type." Raising her hands, she wiggled her fingers, then dropped them in her lap, suddenly self-conscious. What had possessed her to do that? "We provide temporary service."

He misunderstood the source of her embarrassment. "Don't denigrate a small business." His had been almost nonexistent when he had started it.

Laura's head shot up, a touch of fire flickering in her eyes as pride reared its head. "I wasn't denigrating it." She was very proud of what she did, of the business she had put together single-handedly. She already had three other women working for her.

"Sorry." He looked at Janka, who was still hovering between them. "Is she always this touchy?"

"No." Janka removed the last of the cookies and placed them onto a festive plastic plate she had saved from last year. "I t'ink you are making her nervous." Approving, she patted Tim's hand and nodded. "T'is is good."

Laura waved her hand in front of her mother's face. She absolutely hated being discussed as if she wasn't even there. "I'm not dead. I'm right here."

Janka turned to her daughter, a wide, tolerant smile on her lips. "Of course, you are, dear." She brushed away the wispy bangs from Laura's eyes. "Have another cookie."

"I don't want another cookie." She did, but having one now somehow made it seem as if she was giving in to everything her mother was attempting to do. She wanted no part of any of it, most of all, not this wayward Santa Claus who was sitting in her kitchen, munching.

"Do you do free-lance work?"

Laura was so entrenched in her own thoughts, the sound of Tim's voice startled her. "What?"

"The typing—" he bit into another cookie and waved it to emphasize his question "—are you contracted to a specific company or do you do free-lance work?"

Laura watched, fascinated, as he polished off a fifth cookie. They were huge. Where was he putting all this? Was that padding under his jacket, or was that all him? "A little of both. I was just finishing up a job for Mattingly's Department Store."

Small world. And it was getting nicer all the time. "I need someone to do a little light computer work for me." Out of the corner of his eye, Tim saw Janka flash an approving smile that had encouragement stamped all over it.

Laura leaned back in her chair, her arms crossed before her, and eyed him. "What would Santa Claus have that needs typing?"

"It is t'e nineties, Laura," Janka said with a sniff. That seemed to be a standard answer these days.

Why did her daughter insist on making things so complicated? Janka wondered. It was evident from where she stood that the young man was crazy about Laura. And whether she knew it or not, Laura was attracted to him. If she wasn't, he would have never gotten in the front door. They both knew that. So why was she fighting this so hard? Why didn't she give it a chance?

Because she was afraid, that was why. That no-good louse who had fathered Robbie had scarred Laura and made her afraid. She needed to be pushed. And that's what mothers were for.

"Even San-ta Klauss is getting computered," Janka told Laura knowingly, winking at Tim.

"Computerized," Laura corrected without thinking.

Janka nodded toward Laura. "She takes after her fat'er."

Tim dug deep for his most sympathetic look. "He always corrected you, too?"

"No, but he always t'ought he was right." Janka smiled smugly. "I let him."

And Tim had every reason to believe her. If Janka Lekawski hadn't wanted Mr. Lekawski to think he was right, she would have easily set him straight.

Mr. Lekawski.

Laura had introduced herself as Laura Lekawski. Tim paused and wondered if Laura was the type to take her maiden name again after a divorce. He realized that she was looking at him, waiting for him to go on.

Tim did some quick mental calculations. Shirley could use some time off right about now, he judged. She was complaining about not having enough time for her family. He could give some of her work to Laura. He grinned. After all, he was president of the company. He could hand out work any way he wanted to. "How does twelve o'clock on Saturday afternoon sound?"

Laura was still convinced that this was a ploy. But she really could use the money. There were all those bills cropping up everywhere, and she had three mouths to feed. "You keep very unusual hours, Mr. Holt."

He wondered if the eggnog was interfering with his senses, or was that still frost he heard in her voice? He hoped not. "Yes, I do."

"All the women who work for me are busy for the next week."

"I'd like you."

There was something in the way he said the words that brought a hot shiver to the base of her spine. "I'll have to check my schedule," Laura said, not wanting to seem eager. She wasn't eager at all.

She had no idea why she had to reassure herself about that.

Laura realized that her mother was still standing there, the tray in her hands. "What?"

Janka's expression was nothing short of angelic. "You do not work on Saturdays, Laura."

She noticed that Tim had the good grace not to smile. "This is my busy season," Laura said between her teeth. "And I can make my own arrangements."

"Apparently not," Janka answered stubbornly. "You left your calendar book open on t'e sofa t'is morning. You are free on Saturday."

It was time to intervene before an argument got under way. "I'd really appreciate it, Laura. I have this report that's due soon, and my secretary is sick. I'm desperate."

She didn't believe a word of it. "Whatever you say."

"I pay well," he added.

"Good, I don't come cheaply."

This time, he did grin. "I never doubted it."

Laura didn't know if he was laughing at her or not. She pressed her lips together and held on to her temper. She needed the money. Her business wasn't strong enough for her to turn her back on legitimate work, and she could check him out by tomorrow. Maybe she'd get a train set for Robbie out of this. That would make it all worth it. He'd been asking her for a train, but she hadn't been able to budget things well enough to afford one this year. "Santa Claus" would provide it.

She raised her eyes to Tim's. "I'll get back to you."

Tim took out his wallet from the inside of the jacket. Flipping through it, he found his business cards. He took one out and wrote his home address on the back.

"Here's my address and phone number. I work at home on weekends." Tim leaned over to hand the card to Laura, but Janka intercepted it. He looked up at the woman questioningly as she deposited it into her apron pocket.

Janka patted the pocket. "She loses t'ings, sometimes."

He needed nothing more to assure him that Laura would be there. He nodded to Janka. "Thank you."

Janka looked at the empty plate and cup in front of him. She beamed as he rose from the table. "You eat well."

By the sound of it, she had given him her seal of approval. "That's because everything tastes so good. Well, I'd better be going."

"Yes." Laura stayed seated, though her mother took Tim's arm. "You'd better."

She contained her anger until her mother returned. Laura rose from the table as embarrassment and something far greater, which she couldn't put a name to yet, bubbled to the surface.

"Mother!" Janka's dark eyebrows rose in a silent, innocent question as she walked into the kitchen. Laura thought she was going to scream. "Stop matchmaking."

Janka cleared away the dishes from the table and placed them in the sink. "I am not doing anyt'ing wit' matches. I am doing somet'ing wit' people." She looked over her shoulder at Laura. "He is a nice man, yes?"

"No." Laura unclenched her hands at her sides. Why couldn't her mother leave things alone? "I don't know anything about him."

"So you will learn. Saturday." The simplicity of the situation was evident in Janka's voice.

How could someone who worried so much be so trusting? But then, her mother had always been a paradox. "Why aren't you worried? He might be Jack the Ripper."

Janka knew better. "He does not rip anyt'ing, t'is Timot'y. He fixes t'ings, like cars and lights and perhaps—" she cocked her head, looking at her only child "—a heart."

Laura's expression grew icy. That was the last thing she wanted. "Leave my heart alone, Mother."

Though her own heart ached at the rebuff, Janka stood her ground because she knew the hurt that had prompted the words. "It beat under my heart first." She tapped a thumb at her breast. "It was part of me before it was part of you. When it is happy, *t'en* I will leave it alone."

Laura sighed. She hadn't meant to hurt her. She tucked her arms around the short, ample figure and brushed a kiss on top of sleek, dark hair that was just beginning to turn gray. "You are a pest, you know that, don't you?"

For a small woman, Janka's shoulders were broad. They rose then fell as she considered Laura's words. "Maybe. But I am also lovable."

Laura laughed. "That you are, Mama. That you are."

"Come, we tug Robbie into bed."

"That's tuck, Mother," Laura corrected, linking her arm through Janka's.

"Tug, tuck, as long as we get him to stay in bed, what does it matter?"

Laura gave up, as she usually did. It was easier that way, at least in matters of English. "I haven't the foggiest, Mama."

"Why should you have a fog?"

"Never mind, Mother. Never mind."

Chapter Five

Tim had spent half the night writing data for his survey so that Laura would have something to input into the computer when she arrived. His secretary was too efficient, and everything that he had dropped off earlier that week was already written up. Except for a few hours of restless sleep, Tim had spent the remainder of the night clearing away the telltale signs of a not-so-neat bachelor who lived alone and hated housework.

He was nervous. As he hurriedly threw a few items into his closet, his attention was drawn to the Santa Claus suit hanging off to one side. He was tempted to touch a piece of it as a talisman for luck. For confidence.

Shaking his head at his uncustomary jitters, he closed the door again.

It seemed like an eternity before Laura was finally standing on his threshold. She walked in slowly, wearing a simple, light blue skirt and blouse that could easily be found on any department store's sale racks.

She looked like a queen.

As for Laura, nothing had prepared her for what Tim actually looked like. He had the lean, firm body athletes trained vigorously to maintain. In jeans and a casual white-and-blue, pin-striped, fitted shirt with the sleeves rolled up, he looked like every woman's dream.

Laura felt precious ground slipping away from her by the moment.

He took her sweater and closed the door behind her, afraid that if he didn't, she'd leave. "How's your mother?" The question sounded stilted, but without Janka around to fill in the gaps, Tim suddenly felt awkward, tongue-tied.

Laura looked around. It was a pleasant room, bathed in gold by the incoming sun that had access to it on two sides. It was an apartment that belonged to a successful businessman. She had verified the business part last night. He was listed in the phone book under Marketing, just as his card said. Even so, twice this morning, she had picked up the phone to cancel the session. On both occasions, she had changed her mind. She wanted this job, wanted to see him, and yet she felt anxious, almost afraid, but afraid of what?

Something had made her come here when she knew that it was crazy. There was something about this man, no matter how much she denied it, that drew her to him.

The same something that told her he was dangerous to her peace of mind. To her very way of life.

And yet, she came.

"Still talking about you," she answered with a nonchalant air she didn't feel. "You've impressed her."

"How about her daughter?"

He was still behind her, but when he spoke, he seemed to fill the entire room. There was nowhere to run, nowhere to hide. "Her daughter needs to earn some money for Christmas." Laura held her purse a little too tightly to her as she turned around to face him.

"You look nervous." He suddenly realized that she might be experiencing the very same feelings that he was.

"I'm not." The words were almost fiercely uttered. She said them as much to convince him as herself. She saw a smile enter his eyes, a smile that somehow managed to put her at ease even while the excitement, the anticipation of something to come still hummed through her.

"That's good," he said softly, somehow cutting the space between them down to nothing without moving a fraction. "Because there's nothing to be afraid of."

Oh, yes, there was. But it wasn't the regular kind of fear. She knew that. She wasn't afraid of him being a serial killer. She was afraid of something far more complex. She was afraid of liking him.

Licking her lips, she pressed on. "So, when do we get to work?"

He couldn't resist any longer. He had waited a lifetime already. "Right after this."

She was about to ask what, but the question died, unborn, on her lips as her purse slipped from her hands. It was as if she was suddenly glued to the carpet. His eyes held her in place.

His fingers dived into her hair. Soft. Silky. Just as he had imagined. He felt something quiver within him as he drew her mouth closer to his. Was this what it was supposed to feel like? He had no idea. He had never been in love before. He rather liked it. A lot.

Laura's heart pounded, drowning out all other sounds as she looked up at Tim. She was caught in his gaze, in the heated look in his eyes. She knew four different judo blows, all of which would have rendered him totally immobile. She executed none of them. Instead, she stood there and raised her mouth to his, not having a single idea why she was doing something so very foolish.

Except that she wanted this and needed this. If only for one tiny second in time, she needed to feel like a woman again, and, oh, he did that to her. He made her feel like a glorious woman.

The rush his kiss created within her stunned Laura. She forgot that it was a kiss at all. And it wasn't. It was an adventure, an experience, one that melted her limbs, upset her equilibrium and made her throw her arms around his neck for support. She felt like all things at once. Beautiful. Graceful. And deliciously alive.

It was utterly insane.

When his lips drew away, she could only look up at him, disoriented and confused. Was she still on the planet Earth? Or had she, in one brief flash of lightning, reached heaven?

He felt like standing on top of his apartment complex and shouting, "I love Laura." He settled for holding her in his arms. "Yes."

"Yes?" she echoed, confused and trying to get her bearings.

"Just checking."

The impact of the kiss left her reeling. Slowly, reality began to take hold. What had she just done? "For what?"

He heard the confusion, the wariness in her voice. He could understand her feeling that way. This had happened so suddenly, it had all but knocked him out. "To see if you were the one."

She picked up her purse from the floor and brushed off the suede. Her heart was still hammering. Just what kind of power did this man possess to do this to her? "For what?"

Tim grinned. "You're repeating yourself."

Laura eyed the front door over his shoulder. It wasn't too late to make a break for it. Or was it? She had a nagging feeling that she couldn't outrun this no matter how hard she tried. He had unearthed something she didn't want to thrive. "And you're not making any sense."

He wanted to hold her again, to slowly cover every inch of her face with kisses. But he could see that she was going to need time to adjust to this, even if he didn't. "I just wanted to make sure that I wasn't wrong. And I wasn't. You are the one."

Laura stopped casting about for ways out and looked up at him. "For *what?*" she demanded again.

"For me."

The simple reply stunned her. "Excuse me?"

He had felt more confident swaddled in the red-and-white costume, he realized. Now there was nothing to hide behind. And all he had were his exposed emotions. They made for a clear target. "I guess I didn't put that very well."

Knowing it was foolish, she took a step into the living room. The bright sunlight made her feel safer. Almost. "No, I don't think you *could* put that any way and have it turn out right."

Maybe if he started more slowly. "I'm twenty-nine."

"Oh?" He *was* crazy.

"I thought you'd want to know that."

Growing nervous, Laura began to back away. He was moving too quickly, and she was reacting too fast. She knew where that sort of thing led and she didn't want to go there again. Once had been too painful. "Why would I want to know that?"

Words tumbled out. He was a lot better on paper, he thought, where there was room to compose and edit. "Women usually want to know the age of the man they're going to marry." That hadn't come out right, either.

She had thought he was about to try to talk her into his bed, not to the altar. Laura began to cough and then stared at him with eyes that were watery and totally shrouded in disbelief. *"What?"*

"Do you need some water?" He was already hurrying into his kitchen. She heard the faucet running. "I don't mean today." Returning, he handed the glass to her. "I just meant inevitably."

Laura debated pouring the contents of the glass over his head. Men didn't just propose after knowing you less than a day. She thought of Craig and her lips twisted slightly. Some men didn't propose at all. "Tim, are you crazy?"

Since she wasn't drinking, he took the glass from her and placed it on the coffee table. Then, before she could move away, he framed her face with his hands. "Just about you."

He was making her jittery, *very* jittery, especially since there was a tiny part of her that was inclined to—

No, it wasn't!

She pulled away. "How could you be crazy about me? You don't even *know* me."

Now that it was out in the open, he felt better. "Yes, I do. You're the one I always knew I'd meet."

No, she wasn't going to get sucked into this. She wasn't going to let him fill her head with impossible thoughts. "Tim, maybe some other girl would be very flattered." *And I would be, if I wasn't who I was and didn't know what I know.* "You sound like you belong on the inside of a Valentine card, but that's not for me."

Along with the momentary desire, he had seen fear flash in her eyes just before he had kissed her. Fear of what? "Why?"

Why did he have to probe? "Because I've done the young-and-innocent-palpitating bit." She tried to make herself sound hard. Remembering the past helped. "I've done 'starry eyed' and know that it just doesn't happen."

He lightly placed his hands on her shoulders. "People make things happen, Laura."

She wanted to get free, but it was the emotion he created within her that held her trapped far more cleverly than his hands did. "Maybe. Look, I don't have time to debate this with you." She blew out a ragged breath, hating herself for it. "Now do you have work for me or not?"

"I do." He nodded toward the room on the left, which served as his office at home. "But I'd like to talk first."

She raised her head. "I get paid by the hour," she reminded him.

He could afford this, even if it took every dime he owned. "Consider this a coffee break."

"Those usually happen after some work's been done."

Tim shrugged. "I'm not orthodox."

"You can say that again," she muttered loud enough for him to hear.

"Sit down?" He indicated the love seat.

"No."

He sat at one end. "There's nothing to be afraid of."

Laura sat on the other end of the love seat. There wasn't much space between them. Not nearly enough to make her feel secure. There wasn't that much space available in the universe, she realized. "I'm not afraid, because nothing's going to happen."

"That you don't want to happen," he concluded.

Her eyes narrowed. "Exactly."

Tim only smiled, and she had the impression that she had just snapped the trapdoor shut. Behind her.

"Laura." Tim tried to take her hand and she shifted away. He lifted an eyebrow, but he didn't attempt to move. "I don't want a starry-eyed innocent. I want the woman I see here today. The woman who made something of herself. The woman who loves her son and her mother."

It wasn't that he was getting to her, she thought, it was just that what he said wasn't what she had expected. Craig had seduced her with far different words, words of passion, not gentleness. "It's kind of hard not to love them." She relented for a second. "Look, you're very sweet, Tim—"

He could settle for that. For now. But not for long. "That sounds hopeful."

She wasn't trying to offer him false hope. Why did he keep twisting everything around? "But my life is very full just as it is."

"No room for someone to love?"

When he said it so softly, she had to fight to remember that she was happy with things just the way they were. His kiss had made her long for a world she had once believed was in her reach. A world that didn't exist. And she hated him for that, even as she felt herself yearning. "I've got someone to love. Two someones."

He had a feeling she'd say that. He was beginning to know how she thought, at least partially. "All right, a taller someone." The grin faded to a soft, promising smile. "Someone who could make you happy."

Looking at him, she could almost believe that he could. Almost. But almost wasn't good enough. "I'm not looking for that kind of happiness."

Did she really believe she meant that? He didn't think so, even if she did. "Why not?"

"Because I won't find it." There was no way to make him back off, except to tell him the truth. "Look, I was twenty—no, I was nineteen, *almost* twenty, when I met Robbie's father. Craig was all polish and charm in a three-piece suit." Her lips curved with bitterness as she remembered how mesmerized she had been. "He was gorgeous and everything I thought I wanted. Except honest. He forgot to tell me one little thing while he was busy sweeping me off my feet and into his bed." Even now, it hurt. "He forgot to tell me that he was married."

Tim saw the pain in her eyes and wanted to take her into his arms, to tell her not to go on. But he knew that he couldn't. She had to finish telling him this, and then they would bury it. Together.

"That little tidbit came up when I told him that I was pregnant." She laughed at her own stupidity. "I didn't even know enough to be frightened. I thought it was wonderful, a child of our making. What an idiot, right?" She looked at Tim, expecting to see pity or at the very least, agreement, and was surprised by the anger there.

"I wouldn't call you an idiot. I'd call him a few things, right before I strangled him, but not you."

She wasn't going to fall for it. She wasn't going to be duped into thinking of this man as a knight in shining armor. She knew that was what he was trying to make her believe. Still, her voice relaxed a little as she answered. "That's all right. I called myself all kinds of an idiot." She rose, signaling an end. "Now then, *Mr. Holt,* if you don't mind, I'd like to earn my salary." She looked around the room for effect. "Where's your computer?"

Again he pointed to the den right off the living room. "In there." He followed her there instead of leading the way. She seemed eager to put work between them, but then, she had shared a good deal of herself today, he thought. They had made progress.

The desk with its computer was perpendicular to the window. The sunlight that streamed in wouldn't bother her. It had been arranged that way on purpose. He seemed to conduct his life logically, all except for his so-called marriage proposals, she thought. Laura dropped her purse next to the computer and sat down in front of the screen. "I was wondering, what was a businessman doing in a Santa Claus suit?"

Since Laura seemed more inclined to talk when there was work to do, Tim gathered up the papers he had prepared and placed them next to her on the desk. "It's part of my job."

"What does that have to do with . . . ?" She gestured to the papers, not seeing the connection.

Tim sat on the edge of the desk, trying not to get lost in her eyes. But it was hard to concentrate. "The firm that's hired my company wants to know what children would really like for Christmas. What better way to find out than to—" He stopped. There was a look of angry disbelief on her face.

"Pose as someone they trust and pick their brains, all in the name of the almighty dollar."

The accusation took him by surprise. "No, that isn't what I do."

Laura rose and pushed her chair in so hard, she jolted him off the desk. "How could you?"

"Well, first I had to bribe someone at the last minute to take his place and—" He saw her open her mouth and then close it, speechless. "We're not talking about the mechanics of this, are we?"

And she had actually entertained feelings for him for a moment. How stupid could she get? Underhanded. They were all underhanded. "You betrayed them."

Maybe his hearing was going. "What?"

"You took those sweet, trusting little children and pumped them for information for your fat-cat client!"

Tim didn't understand how she could misconstrue all this. "You're getting a little carried away here."

"No, but you should be. On a rail, with tar and feathers all over you." She wished she could get her hands on something to throw, to really vent her anger—at him and her own stupidity for believing, even for one moment, that he was kind and decent and— Damn him! "I've had it with lies," she cried, "with deception. Childhood is the last threshold of innocence. And you've pushed greed into it!"

"We just want to give them what they want."

Did he think she was a complete idiot? That he could kiss her and reduce her to mush so that she couldn't think straight? "No. You want to *sell* them what they want." Laura grabbed her purse and raced from the room. "And that's a world of difference."

He stared at the door long after the sound of the slam had echoed away.

Chapter Six

"Would you like that gift wrapped, Santa?"

Though he clearly looked tired after an eight hour day, the young clerk couldn't stop grinning at the customer in front of him. The idea of wrapping a gift for Santa Claus seemed to tickle him tremendously.

"What? Oh, yes, please." His mind elsewhere, Tim was barely aware of watching the young man wrap the train set in shiny, bright green paper. He had hurried directly to the toy store in the mall, afraid that if he took the time to change into his own clothes first, the store would be closed. On Sunday, everything closed early. The longer hours didn't take effect until two weeks before Christmas, when people suddenly realized that they only had fourteen days to fill gift lists that were a mile long.

Try as he might, Tim couldn't stop thinking about the way Laura had looked at him yesterday before she'd fled. There had been something in her eyes that had made him feel guilty even when he knew he was blameless. After all, this was just a marketing survey he was conducting, one of many, and possibly, he thought with a touch of what he felt was justifiable pride, more astute than most.

But it had certainly gone over like a lead balloon with Laura.

He nodded his thanks as he accepted the huge box from the clerk and made his way out of the store. The clerk was right behind him and locked the door as soon as Tim went through it. Tim looked toward the far end of the mall, to the entrance of Mattingly's Department Store. It was dark. He sighed and looked down at his outfit, then smiled to himself. Maybe this was more appropriate after all. She hadn't shouted at Santa Claus, only him.

It didn't *really* have to do with him, either, he thought as he walked out into the parking lot, or with his ruse as Santa Claus. It had to do with Robbie's father and lies whispered to a trusting nineteen-year-old.

For the first time in his life, Tim felt a flash of white-hot anger, a desire to punch someone. Laura had been a trusting young woman, hopelessly in love, and she'd had all her ideals destroyed by some callous idiot who was too blind to realize what he had.

Fortunately for him, he added. Hefting the box to the side, he opened his trunk and deposited the gift inside, next to the jumper cables. He smiled and patted them, then snapped the trunk lid closed.

Despite everything that had happened to her, Tim could tell that she wasn't a bitter woman. There was no bitterness in her eyes. It was her eyes that had attracted him immediately. Her eyes and the relieved smile she had flashed when she had hugged Robbie to her the first time Tim had seen her.

The rest of Laura had only sustained his initial reaction.

Tim climbed into the driver's seat, pushing his bulky padding down as he maneuvered himself into place behind the steering wheel. And despite what she said she didn't want, the woman who had kissed him in his apartment hadn't forgotten what it was like to want to be needed. Or to need to be wanted.

Holding on to that thought, on to the warmth that flooded through him when he relived the touch of her parted lips against his, the feel of her body molding to his own, Tim set out to bring a peace offering.

He stroked his beard for luck, turned the key in the ignition and drove to Laura's house.

The melodic chimes of the doorbell surprised Laura. It was after seven o'clock. No one she knew would be coming over at this hour. And door-to-door salespeople usually were polite enough to call a moratorium on Sundays.

She rubbed the back of her neck and looked up from her book. Papers were spread all over the dining room table. Today, for some reason, she hadn't really wanted to be alone while she worked. She wanted to be in the midst of things, to see Robbie play, to listen to the sounds of her mother creating yet another holiday offering. She had taken her armload of papers from the den and deposited it on the dining room table, where she could work and still be a part of everything. The dining room, just off the kitchen, opened directly into the living room. She had a clear view of Robbie laying on his stomach, playing with his toy soldiers. If she wasn't mistaken, they were firing at the infamous, artificial tree.

The doorbell rang again.

"Are you expecting anyone?" she asked her mother.

Janka came out of the kitchen, wiping her wet hands on her apron. "Hoping, yes. Expecting? Maybe."

Laura shook her head. Once she made up her mind, the woman never gave up. "Mother, I already told you that after the chewing out I gave Tim Holt, he won't be showing up around here again."

Laura could only stare, speechless, as her mother opened the door.

Janka smiled as she stepped back to admit Tim. "Apparently—" she glanced at her daughter, then beamed at Tim "—you do not chew as well as you t'ink you do."

Tim felt as if he had stepped into Wonderland all over again. But that was one of the things he found most charming about coming to this house. One look at Janka's encouraging smile buoyed his confidence. It also helped balance out the frown he saw on Laura's face.

"Good evening. I hope you don't mind me stopping by." Mechanically, he pulled off the wig and beard, realizing that he had left them on again. He saw Robbie scrambling up, eyeing the large, shiny green package under Tim's arm.

Laura didn't see a package. All she saw was Tim. And her further undoing. "Why are you here?"

Janka shut the door and drew Tim into the living room. "Laura, t'at is not polite."

"No, she has a right to ask, Mrs. Lekawski." He wasn't going to give Laura a chance to summon her anger. "I brought Robbie something to maybe help make the tree less awful for him."

Robbie's eyes opened wide with anticipation.

Laura crossed the room quickly, some of her indignation from yesterday returning. "More market research?"

The touch of sarcasm only served to make her look that much more alive, that much more radiant. And desirable. "It's Sunday. And I'm off duty."

"You're off base," she retorted.

Robbie brought the argument to an abrupt close for them by taking the box from Tim. He buckled under the weight. "What is it?"

Tim grabbed an end to steady the boy. Together, they placed the box on the floor.

"It's a train." Tim pointed to the yet unadorned tree. He wondered what Laura was waiting for and if she'd let him help decorate. "To run around the tree."

"Can I open it now?" the boy asked breathlessly.

"That's the idea." Tim had hardly finished his statement before green wrapping paper started flying in all directions. Tim grinned. The display of enthusiasm had him reliving his childhood.

From the look of the box, the train set was an expensive one. Laura definitely couldn't have afforded it. "Are you using the train to get to me?" she hissed, stepping closer to him. Suspicions flared. He wasn't above using children. They had already established that. She wasn't about to let him use her son as a pawn. Besides, he had robbed her of the joy of giving a train to Robbie herself. Just who did he think he was?

Laura saw the look on Robbie's face and felt a twinge of guilt for being so petty. What did it matter who gave it to him? Robbie was happy, that was all that really mattered.

A feeling of gratitude began to push through the barriers of her heart and she fought hard against it. The man didn't play fair. It was a warning she was going to heed. She hoped.

"No." Tim bent over to gather together some of the discarded paper. "I'm using the train to get to Robbie. Maybe if I get to him, then you'll be willing to start over."

Janka deftly took the crumpled wrapping paper from him. "Of course, she will."

They were discussing her again like some kind of merchandise. "Mother, I—"

"Laura." Tim moved closer to her, trying to block out his impulses and the scent of her perfume. "Listen to your mother."

Outnumbered three to one, Laura threw up her hands in frustration. "I give up!"

Tim flashed a grin that Laura was finding harder and harder to resist. "I certainly hope so."

"I need help with this," Robbie declared, holding up a transformer. He was surrounded by several cars, an engine and countless pieces of track.

Tim tossed aside the beard and wig, then unbuttoned his jacket and yanked out some padding before he sank down tailor fashion on the rug. "I was counting on it." As Laura watched, Tim began to plan the track layout.

He was making himself at home, she thought, searching for the outrage that she knew had to be somewhere. She caught her mother's satisfied smile. Helpless, Laura turned back to the work she had abandoned on the table.

Tim fit two pieces together and joined them to another length of track. "I haven't put one of these things together since I was a kid. Actually—" he leaned in closer and confided to Robbie "—I just got to watch and throw the switch at the end. My dad and brothers got to have all the fun. They were all older than me."

"I don't have a big family," Robbie said matter-of-factly. "Just my mother and Nana." Robbie handed Tim another piece of track. "I'll let you put it together with me."

Tim suppressed a grin. "Thanks, champ." Tim pointed to another piece, and Robbie scrambled to reach it for him.

Handing him the track, Robbie picked up the caboose and discovered that the doors opened and closed. He grinned, delighted. "You know, you're pretty okay for a guy who pretends to be Santa Claus."

Tim paused and sat back on his heels. "What would it take to get you to believe in Santa Claus, Robbie?"

Robbie shrugged, brushing his hair out of his eyes. "A dad," he whispered, his eyes on his mother. Satisfied that she hadn't overheard him, he added, "And snow. Snow for Christmas Eve, all over the front of the house." He sighed, remembering. "Just like back home. It was really neat last Christmas. It snowed for two whole days."

Tim heard the hunger in the boy's voice, but there wasn't anything he could do about it. At least, not the request for snow. The other part he was definitely willing to work on. For both their sakes. "Getting snow around here is a pretty tall order, Robbie."

"Not for Santa Claus." The words had tumbled out. But they were words that belonged to a little child, Robbie thought, embarrassed. "*If* there was a Santa Claus," he added quickly, looking up at the man at his elbow. "But there isn't, so what's the point?" He pushed over another length of track toward Tim.

"I need a curved one now," Tim directed, pointing to a stack over on the side. Robbie obliged. "You don't talk like any little boy I know."

Robbie touched the tiny bell on top of the green-and-red engine. It swayed beneath his fingertip. "Is that good?"

"I'm not sure," Tim replied honestly. But there was something sad about being so young and excluded from the world of fantasy.

Robbie cocked his head, studying Tim. "You know a lot of little boys?"

Tim did a mental tally. "Seven."

"Your kids?"

"My nephews."

"You married?"

Tim could have sworn he heard a slight hopeful note in the boy's voice. He wondered if Robbie realized it. Tim looked up and glanced in Laura's direction. Though she was busy writing, he had a feeling she was listening to every word. "Not yet."

Laura let out a long breath and rose from the table, heading for the kitchen. This was getting to be too much to endure.

"Am I forgiven?" Tim called after her.

"I'll think about it," she said over her shoulder, disappearing.

Janka looked up from the simmering pot on the stove. A warm, pungent aroma wafted around her. "What did he do to ask for your forgiveness?"

"A hundred different things." Unconsciously, Laura ran her fingertips over her lips. Janka smiled and nodded to herself. "He's posing as Santa Claus to find out what children want for Christmas."

"Yes . . . ?" Janka looked at her daughter, still waiting to hear the first terrible crime Tim had committed.

There were times her mother was just too naive. She had a habit of overlooking obvious flaws. "Don't you see? He's picking their minds."

Janka's eyes narrowed as she tried to uncover the reason her daughter looked so annoyed. "Picking t'em up from where?"

An exasperated sigh escaped Laura's lips. "He is taking the information they unsuspectingly tell him and writing a report for a toy company."

Janka considered the statement. "Why is t'is bad? Shouldn't children get what t'ey want instead of a lot of junk t'ey will not play wit'?"

"You just don't understand," Laura cried helplessly, flopping down on the nearest kitchen chair.

"On the contrary," Tim put in as he walked into the kitchen. "She understands perfectly." He winked at Janka before dropping onto the chair next to Laura's. "That's the whole idea behind the report. To get rid of the waste, to produce the best possible, most desirable toys."

She couldn't think clearly with him being so close. His eyes were too green, too intense. Laura looked away. "You make it sound as if you're working on a cure for the world's diseases."

"No, just trying to alleviate some of the world's clutter. Everybody's got the right to get what they want most." As he said it, he placed his hand over hers, completely covering it. "Everyone."

She didn't like the fact that his hand felt as if it belonged there, didn't like feeling somehow safe and protected because of it. He had no business making her feel like that when it wasn't true.

For once, her mother unwittingly came to her rescue. "Let us drink to t'at," Janka proposed. She dipped a ladle into the pot on the stove and poured the red, steaming liquid into a mug. With an encouraging smile, she handed the mug to Tim.

Chapter Seven

Laura almost laughed out loud at the uncertain expression crossing Tim's face. "You don't have to drink that."

He saw the way Janka was watching him, waiting. The hell he didn't. "Sure I do." He took a sip. It was hot and bitter, but not altogether unpleasant. "Umm, what am I drinking?"

"Barcz," Janka informed him.

Well, that clears everything up. Tim lifted an eyebrow as he looked at Laura. "Which is?"

"Borscht." Laura didn't bother hiding her amusement. "Hot beet juice."

"Oh." His first urge was to place the mug on the table as far away from him as possible. But because Janka was still watching, he forced himself to take another sip. "It's not bad," he managed. He looked toward Janka. "Grows on you."

Janka pressed her hands together, pleased. "I like you, Timot'y. You are toy."

Now she had completely lost him.

Laura had given up trying to keep a straight face and was laughing. "I think she means that you're *game.*"

Janka didn't see the problem. "T'at was what I said." She poured a mug of borscht for Laura. "Toy, game, it is t'e same."

Tim couldn't let this opportunity slip by. He figured after the borscht, Janka owed him one. As did Laura.

"That's just the point. There *are* differences. That's what my marketing survey is all about."

Laura accepted the mug her mother handed her. As Tim watched, fascinated, she took a healthy swallow and apparently seemed to like it. Remarkable woman. But then, she was probably raised on the drink. Laura sighed. "I'll concede the point."

"'Yes, Virginia—'" Tim looked heavenward "'—there is a Santa Claus.'"

Why was he always so ready to make more of the situation than there was? Defiantly, Laura wrapped her hands around the warm mug. "I just conceded the point, Tim," she said stubbornly, "nothing more."

"It's a start." Pleased, he took another sip himself. This stuff *did* start to grow on you, he thought.

Laura shook her head as her mother went back to fussing over the pastries she was preparing. "Are you usually this optimistic?"

He grinned. There had always been optimism to draw on, in one form or another. "Incurably."

She'd been that way once. Until she had learned. "Hasn't anyone ever rained on your parade?"

"Sure." Tim eyed Laura pointedly. "An entire monsoon."

So he *was* receiving all the signals she was sending. Then why wasn't he backing off? Unless, of course, he was misreading the signals. It couldn't be... No, she refused to believe that she was sending out mixed signals to him. That would have been absurd.

He lifted a shoulder and let it drop casually. "But it has to dry up sometime."

Dry up. Used and dried up. That was the way she had felt inside after Craig had pressed money into her hand and disappeared completely from her life. He had never even bothered to find out if she had had the baby or opted for the abortion he had flippantly suggested.

She stared down into the mug. The dark liquid reflected the light overhead, playing with it. "Some things are never good as new once that happens."

Tim reached out to take her hand. Laura kept them firmly wrapped around the mug. She wasn't yielding yet. But she would. He firmly believed that. "Sometimes, they're even better."

"Tim," Robbie called urgently from the living room, "I need help."

"Don't we all," Tim murmured, looking directly into Laura's eyes. "Hang on, I'm coming."

What did he mean by that? *Don't we all?* Was he trying to tell her she needed help and he was ready to offer it? Well, she didn't need it. She was just fine the way she was.

Laura waited a moment before she rose from the table. There was still work waiting for her. Steeling herself, she walked into the dining room.

Tim was on the floor, working on the huge metal oval that was to run around the perimeter of the tree. Robbie hovered over him, his face puckered in concentration, eager to do Tim's bidding.

She sat down and looked at her papers. The words all ran together. Nothing seemed to make sense anymore. She'd lost the orderliness in her life.

The sound of his deep laughter filtered into her system, curling through it, soothing, stroking. Making her yearn for things she couldn't permit herself to want.

She didn't want to like him. Liking him would lead to letting her guard down, and that would inevitably lead to other things. Things she didn't want to happen again. Her judgment in men was flawed. She knew that. She knew she couldn't trust herself to make a wise choice. Even if she was willing to risk it, there was more than just her own feelings at stake now. There were Robbie's. She didn't want to see him get hurt, to see him become involved only to wind up rebuffed in the end for one reason or another. She and her son were a package deal.

It was too big a gamble to take, and she had already gambled once and lost. It could easily happen again.

"T'ey look happy toget'er," Janka whispered.

Laura looked up, startled. Engrossed in her thoughts, she hadn't heard her mother come up behind her. "Yes, they do, don't they?" There was no way she could have denied the way it looked. But was it genuine? And could it last?

At least she had admitted that much, Janka thought. The rest would come. "Time for bed, Robbie," Janka announced cheerfully, clapping her hands together.

A mournful, hangdog expression came over the small face. "Aw, do I have to?"

Laura noticed that he didn't address the question to her or to his grandmother. He was asking Tim for permission to stay up. This was getting out of hand. "School's tomorrow, honey."

"Just five more minutes, Mom," Robbie pleaded. "We've almost got the trans—the trans—" He looked at Tim for help.

"Transformer," Tim supplied.

"That thing," Robbie finally said, "together. I want to see it run. Please, Mama?"

Screwdriver in hand, Tim looked up at her from where he sat on the rug. "Five more minutes won't really matter, will they?"

It was a trend. Since he had appeared in her life two days ago, she seemed to be giving in when she wanted to remain firm. It wasn't a trend that was destined to continue, she promised herself. But there was no harm in saying yes this one last time. "As long as it's just five more minutes."

Tim saluted her with the screwdriver. "I do some of my best work under pressure."

Laura refused to ask him just what he meant by that.

Five minutes dragged into ten and ten dribbled into fifteen.

Janka sat on the sofa, watching the two work side by side. It warmed her heart. Finally, the setup was connected and ready. Tim let Robbie turn on the power switch and then slowly increase the speed. The old-fashioned train, complete with smoke, circled the track, pulling five cars and a caboose.

"Wow!"

"Yes, I guess that says it all," Tim agreed, more pleased than he thought he would be.

Laura tried to deny the surge of pleasure she felt, because its ultimate source was Tim.

It came anyway.

"All right, Mr. Engineer," Janka said as she rose from her seat, "now it is time to go." Taking him firmly by the hand, Janka escorted her grandson out of the room.

"Thank you!" Robbie called back to Tim.

"Don't mention it."

"Will you be here tomorrow?" he asked suddenly, stopping on the stairs.

Tim craned his neck to see Robbie. "I'm going to try my darnedest," he promised.

Oh, no, you're not, Laura vowed.

She kept her eyes on her work, purposely trying to ignore Tim. Why wasn't he leaving? He was just sitting there on her floor, tinkering with the tracks. After what had happened in his apartment, Laura didn't want to be alone with him, even with her mother and son upstairs. Knowing they were there did nothing to negate the nervousness that was now zipping up and down her body like energy building up to an explosion.

It increased as he crossed to her. Unable to ignore it or him any longer, she looked up. "Thank you for the train."

"I was making a point."

Her breath caught in her throat. "Oh?"

He nodded, taking the pen out of her hand. It slipped out of her fingers effortlessly. "The right present, the right child."

"Your marketing survey."

"My vindication." When he took her hands in his, he found that they were icy. Because he knew she was nervous, he found that he wasn't any longer. He smiled. They complemented each other. "I'm not the brain-cell-sucking monster you seemed to envision me to be yesterday."

Without realizing that he was doing it, she let him urge her to her feet. "I guess I did go off the deep end."

He smiled again, playing with a strand of her hair. "Just a little."

Her throat suddenly felt dry as dust. "But you have to understand, I hate deception of any kind." She wished her heart would stop lurching in her chest this way.

"I can understand that." Tim slowly trailed his fingers along her cheek.

Her eyes almost fluttered shut against her will. Everything was happening against her will. "Umm, don't you have to be home?"

"No." The word seemed to glide along her skin, soft, seductive.

"The report..." She began grasping at straws, fighting the sensation that she was drowning.

"Is coming along slowly. I'm typing it myself." It was a small lie, but in the grand scheme of things, considering the stakes, he could be forgiven it. "I type pretty well." He held up two fingers of each hand. "These can really fly when necessary."

A sting of guilt nettled her, especially after he had been so nice to Robbie. "If you'd like, I could input the report for you on the computer." Laura had had absolutely no intentions of volunteering to do that for him. More rebellion.

"I'd like." Rather than drop his hands to his side, he cupped her face, tilting it up toward him.

Laura felt her nerves begin doing high hurdles. "Tim, please."

He stroked his thumbs gently along her cheekbones, soothing, exciting. "Shh. Don't talk." He lowered his mouth to hers.

This time she was ready for it. This time, she knew what was coming. This time—

The world exploded.

On a scale of one to ten, the first kiss had been a twelve. This one was a fifty.

She hadn't felt the hunger before, not his, not hers. She felt it now. Hunger and passion too long denied. Her mouth was as desperate as his, seeking, giving, searching and finding. His hands left her face. She felt them roaming along the length of her back, felt her own reaching up into his hair, pulling him closer to her. The world, what was left of it after the explosion, had tilted completely out of focus as she plummeted into an abyss of heat and colors and impossible dreams.

The kiss went on forever.

It was over much too soon. Every inch of her body ached for more. For him.

It frightened her to death.

It was a long moment before her heart left her throat free enough for her to speak. "I really wish you wouldn't do that."

Tim said nothing. He only looked at her, his eyes serious, probing. Finally, she couldn't stand it any longer. "What?"

"Nothing, I just thought you said you hated deception of any kind."

Laura had the decency to blush. She hated him for that. Hated him for a lot of things. Mainly for making her feel again. She turned away from him. "I won't be ruled by hormones again. Or blindness."

"I'm not asking you to." He reached for his jacket, pulling it on. "I'm asking you to approach all this logically, with common sense."

She turned around and stared at him. What was he up to now? "What?"

"Sure." He buttoned the Santa Claus jacket. Without the padding, it hung around his midsection like a tent. "Your mother likes me. I think Robbie's definitely coming around." He tucked the beard, hat and wig together, placing them on top of the padding. He looked at her pointedly as he picked the bundle up. "That leaves you."

"Yes, that does." She cleared her throat, wishing that there was more conviction in her voice. "And I'm going to stay left, Tim. I've been hurt too much. I just can't, even if—" She realized her mistake as soon as the word came out.

"If?" he said encouragingly, stepping closer.

She sighed. "Even if I wanted to, I couldn't." There, it was out. Now maybe he'd leave her alone.

She should have known better.

Laura could tell by the look in his eyes that the siege was far from over. "We'll see." Lightly, he brushed another kiss on her lips, lingering only a moment. It was long enough to feel her sway into him. Soon, he promised himself. Soon. "Tell your mother good-night."

Laura raised her head, determined that he wouldn't see the effect he was having on her. "I'll tell her you said goodbye."

"No, not goodbye. Good-night," he corrected, his hand on the doorknob. "There's a difference." And with that, he left.

A difference. Yes, that was exactly what she was afraid of.

Laura pressed a hand to the flutter that was gathering in her stomach, telling herself that she was acting too much like an adolescent. Again.

Chapter Eight

As Laura sat adding yet another change into Tim's report, it occurred to her that she was seeing a great deal of someone she kept telling herself, as well as her mother, that she didn't want to see. A little more than three weeks had gone by since she had first looked up into that bearded face, seeing green eyes the color of a sparkling pool in the Florida Keys. Just three weeks.

And in that short amount of time, he had become part of almost every single day. Or, more specifically, every single evening. Because his days were busy, the report had to be done at night. Feeling uneasy with him at his apartment, Laura had suggested working on his report for Imagination Toys at her house.

He had gladly agreed. It gave him a built-in excuse to come over every evening. And Laura's mother seemed to instinctively know when to clear the room and leave them alone together.

Laura heard laughter coming from the living room, where Robbie and Tim were throwing tinsel on the tree they'd been decorating for the past two hours. It seemed, she thought suspiciously, that he always found "just one more thing" to add to the report. Another graph. Another variation on an interpretation.

Another reason to haunt the recesses of her mind and make her crazy.

"Laura," Tim called out with the familiarity of a man who had staked out his claim and was now comfortably settling in.

She stared at the bright colors on the screen and searched for patience. "Yes?"

"Come out here," he coaxed. "You're missing all the fun."

That's not all I'm missing.

"Doesn't this report have to be finished soon?" She knew she sounded like a shrew, but her defenses against him were definitely getting frayed. In their place panic was setting in.

Tim peeked into the room, tinsel dripping from his fingers. The strands caught the lamplight, winking and twinkling at her. He leaned a hip against the doorjamb, looking a lot more comfortable than she felt. He was wearing his own clothes for a change, and she found she almost missed the absurd red suit. He was far too athletic looking, far too dangerous to her peace of mind in his dark green pullover sweater and chinos.

"The report isn't due until the first of the year. Or, actually," he said, reconsidering, "the fifth of the year." He didn't add that he had given her a dummy disk. The real report had been finished, except for perhaps a footnote or two, in the wee hours of last night. He took his obligations seriously. Just the way he took his emotions. "A half an hour won't matter."

Yes, it will, she thought fiercely. *It will if I spend it in your company.*

She was already devoting much too much time thinking about him, looking forward to the sound of his knock on the door, his shy, quirky smile that seemed so right for him, so suited.

So suited for the Santa Claus character he played.

Though she hated malls in the height of the Christmas crunch, she had easily "allowed" both Robbie and her mother to talk her into making several trips to the mall containing Mattingly's Department Store. Each time they went, they just happened to wander into Mattingly's third-floor children's department. And watched Tim play Santa Claus.

He seemed born to that red suit, she thought, and seeing him with children gave her a glow. Just as seeing him with Robbie did.

She had to stop doing this to herself.

You're getting carried away. You know what happens when you get carried away, she warned herself. But she was slipping, and she knew it.

Robbie popped in, wiggling past Tim. Both his fists were filled with gleaming silver strands. Silver on the carpet marked his progress to her den. "C'mon, Mama, throw tinsel at the tree."

All right, what would a few minutes hurt? She'd be spending it with Robbie. It wasn't her fault that Tim just happened to be there as well.

"You don't throw," Laura told Robbie as she rose from her desk. Pressing a few keys, she saved her work. "You drape." With a twist of the wrist, she shut off the computer.

Tim looked at Robbie. The smile that passed between them was clearly condescending—as Tim meant it to be. Nothing got her going faster than her pride. "She doesn't know very much, does she?"

His loyalty momentarily torn, Robbie looked at Laura. "She's okay... for a mom."

Since she wasn't moving, Tim got behind Laura and, placing his tinsel-filled hand against her back, gently pushed her toward the doorway. "You need a lesson in proper Christmas decorating, Ms. Lekawski."

"Yeah!" Robbie's eyes were bright as he hopped about excitedly. He danced backward all the way to the Christmas tree, watching to make sure his mother didn't make a U-turn and escape.

It was hard to miss the pure joy shining in his face. He certainly did look a lot happier since this man had come into their lives, Laura thought ruefully.

Something small and cold tightened within her stomach. No, she had to keep her guard up. Day-dreams and hopes had made her lose sight of all the things she believed in before, and she had been made a fool of. That wasn't going to happen again.

"Now watch," Tim counseled her, aware that her expression had changed slightly. He wondered what was going on in her head. "Fire away, Robbie."

Robbie launched first one fistful of tinsel, then the other in the general direction of the tree. Some of the tinsel caught on the branches. Twinkling silver balls lodged themselves in various places. But more than half of the tinsel rained down on the carpet, forming little pools of silver.

Laura noticed that a good deal of tinsel had accu-mulated in a semicircle around the tree rather than *on* the tree.

"Are you decorating the tree or the carpet?" she asked Tim.

"Picky, picky, picky." He laughed, then draped one silver strand in her hair. "We're decorating anything that gets in the way."

She brushed the tinsel away. "Thanks for the warn-ing."

"You're welcome." He winked.

It was his smile that got to her, that always seemed to unglue her as easily as if she was an envelope being steamed open over one of her mother's kettles.

"*Chruschiki,* anyone?" Janka walked in with a tray brimming with twisted, white-powdered confection that had just emerged, hot, from her overworked stove.

"Excuse me?" Tim handed another collection of strands to Robbie.

"*Chruschiki,*" Janka repeated slowly. An impish smile played on her lips as she raised her tray in Tim's direction.

He was game to try anything, and these did look good. "This is the woman who can't pronounce th's?" he asked Laura. There was no way he could even begin to get his tongue around whatever it was she called the things on the tray.

Instead, he applied his tongue to the light pastry. After taking a bite, he grinned, a little powdered sugar outlining half his lower lip. "This is really terrific."

"But, of course." Janka beamed. "You were expecting not to enjoy t'em?" She cleared a place on the coffee table and set the tray down. Robbie momentarily abandoned the tinsel and attacked the offerings.

"Sorry, lost my head." Tim popped the rest of the delicacy into his mouth. Unable to resist, he picked up another piece, this one shaped like a bow tie. A tiny shower of white powder fell back onto the tray as he raised the pastry to his lips. "You know, I'm beginning not to need the padding on that Santa suit."

Janka patted his stomach. "Hard, like a rock. I would not worry." She smiled at him as she crossed to the kitchen again. "Save room for my cake."

"Cake, too?" He almost groaned. There was such a thing as too much of a good thing.

"Special cake," Janka said, her voice floating in from the kitchen.

It was hard to resist a man who pleased her mother so much, who made her son so happy. Without thinking her action through, Laura wiped the bit of sugar from the corner of Tim's mouth with her thumb. She hadn't anticipated the spark of electricity that shot through her. Or the desire that followed. But she should have.

She dropped her hand, aware that he was looking at her. "She's in her glory, you know, watching you eat everything she makes."

Janka returned, bearing a golden bundt cake she had just finished slicing. "Now this," she urged, setting the cake down on the table next to the *chruschiki*. She handed him a napkin just before a timer went off in the kitchen. Tim was afraid to ask if there was more coming.

Tim slid a piece of the cake onto a napkin. "As long as I make someone happy."

"I wouldn't have too many pieces of that cake if you expect to drive home," Laura warned just as he took his first bite.

A tingling feeling wound its way through Tim as he swallowed, not unlike the initial feeling he experienced each time he kissed Laura.

"I see what you mean." He widened his eyes slightly. "First time I ever ate cake with a kick to it." He shook his head. Mrs. Lekawski was amazing.

Laura nibbled on a small piece herself. "She likes to put rum in that."

"You two gonna talk or decorate?" Robbie asked impatiently. He wiped his mouth with the back of his hand, erasing less than half of the powdered sugar that still clung to his lips.

Laura picked up a napkin and wiped away the rest. "Decorate."

With deliberate care, Laura picked up a few strands of silver from the box Tim had opened and draped them over a high branch that had gone untouched, despite Robbie's enthusiastic pitching.

She turned around to look at Tim and Robbie, who were eyeing her in feigned disgust. "Now, that's how it's done. It looks pretty that way."

Obviously not to them.

Tim sighed and shook his head. He took one more bite of Janka's rum cake before he took a handful of silver from the box. As Laura watched uncertainly, he circled behind her.

"What are you doing?"

"Teaching you," he said, the words drifting into her hair as his breath caressed her cheek.

Yes, he was teaching her a lot of things, things she didn't want to learn about herself. Like how she had no control over her body whenever he was around her. It responded to him, no matter how much she tried not to let it.

He transferred the tinsel into her hand. "This way," Tim instructed. Snaking his hand over hers, he lifted it and went through the motions of tossing, though both of them were far more aware of the way her body fit against his, as if his was the haven that hers had been seeking for so long.

Except she knew that was impossible.

The tinsel just barely made contact with the closest branch. More tinsel fell on the rug.

"I think I get the general idea," Laura said, stepping back, her voice just the slightest bit shaky. As was the rest of her.

Tim smiled down into her face. When would she stop fighting this? "I sincerely hope so."

Chapter Nine

The next evening passed all too quickly. Tim stopped by, as usual, with an addition to the ever-expanding survey for Imagination Toys. This was to be the last of it. Tomorrow was Christmas Eve. There would be no more Santa Claus, no more survey after that. When he arrived, Laura took the data from him and efficiently changed the report for the last time. There was a wave of sadness hovering over her as she did so.

While it was printing, he and Laura sat down with Robbie and Janka and shared a late dinner like a real family. This was the way it could be all the time, Tim thought, if only Laura would come around.

He wondered if he was just chasing rainbows. Looking into Laura's eyes across the table told him that, sometimes, rainbows could be captured.

If you believed hard enough.

But now it was time to leave. He had promised his family that he would be with them for Christmas Eve. It was a tradition he had always looked forward to, especially after he moved away to start his business. This year, he wasn't so eager to go.

He had placed gifts under Laura's tree for all three of them. An intricately woven scarf for Janka. A space shuttle for Robbie. A gold charm in the shape of Santa Claus for Laura. There was nothing left to do but say goodbye and wish them all a Merry Christmas.

He moved as if there was glue in his veins. He didn't want the evening to end. Reluctantly, he made his way to the door, his neatly bound report in his hands.

"Oh, I almost forgot." He reached into his pocket and drew out Laura's check.

Laura looked at him in surprise. "This is too much." She tried to return it, but he shook his head.

"Overtime," he said simply.

There was too much of a note of finality about this. Janka needed to assure herself that this man who had been coming over every night would be here again tomorrow. "Of course, you will join us tomorrow night for Christmas Eve." She held out his sheepskin jacket for him. Her expression forbid him to refuse the invitation. "We have big party. Neighbors, friends. It is t'e time for celebrating for us."

It had become a habit with him to look to Laura for an explanation if he didn't completely understand what Janka was telling him.

"We celebrate Christmas Eve the way you do Christmas morning." Laura placed her hands on her son's shoulders, as if that would steady the sudden uneasiness she was experiencing. It didn't. "I used to tell Robbie that Santa came here first before he made his rounds. It made him feel special."

Robbie shrugged his mother off. The train was rumbling through the tunnel Tim had brought for him tonight and he wanted to go and watch. "That was before I found that there wasn't one," the boy said over his shoulder.

Tim shook his head. "Still don't believe, huh?"

Robbie looked up from the elaborate layout. Every evening Tim had brought more figures and buildings to place around the train. Robbie was now the proud owner of a complete village. "There's no snow."

And no daddy. The words echoed silently between them.

"So you will come, yes?" Janka tottered on her toes as she reached up to straighten the back of Tim's collar.

Tim faced her. He didn't like turning her down. "I'm afraid I can't."

The wide face puckered slightly, puzzled. "But why?"

"Mother, he has other plans." Laura kept her voice even, trying to deny the sudden slash of disappointment she felt. *See, it's happening already, the disappointment, the sadness. Better to cut it off now than later, when bigger things will be at stake than having him sitting next to you at midnight.*

Janka was not one to give up easily. She had managed to bring herself and her daughter over to America, to survive in a new world while learning a foreign language, stubbornly refusing to give in when everyone had advised her to stay in the old country and be content with her lot. She wasn't about to let Tim go and spend the holidays somewhere else without knowing why. "What plans?"

"I'm driving up tomorrow afternoon to see my family." Though he addressed the words to Janka, he was looking at Laura.

Did she care? Did it bother her the slightest bit that he wouldn't be here with her? "In Santa Barbara. They're all waiting. Well, maybe not all," he amended, thinking of his brother Sam. Sam was a newlywed and didn't seem to care who was around him, as long as he was with Eileen. That was what he wanted, Tim realized. The kind of love that blotted out everything else. And he knew he could have it with Laura. He had felt it in her kiss, had seen it in her eyes in those unguarded moments when she watched him playing with Robbie. All she had to do was let go.

Janka looked expectantly at Laura, but Laura merely nodded at the excuse. Janka sighed. Some things she could not do for her daughter. They had to come from her. "You will miss my pierogi."

Tim lifted an eyebrow. "Pierogi?" he repeated.

"Kind of like ravioli with fried sauerkraut in it." Laura answered automatically. She smiled. "It was always my favorite breakfast Christmas morning."

Tim took Janka's hands in his. "Would you save me some?"

Janka smiled as she nodded. "I do like t'is boy, Laura."

If he cared the way he claimed to, he would have found a way to be here, Laura thought. This just proved that she had been right in her initial feelings. You shouldn't get involved. It just wasn't worth it. "We already know that, Mother."

Janka turned to her daughter. "How about you?"

Laura's mouth dropped open as she stared at her mother. When she could finally speak, her breath whooshed out of her. "Mother!"

Tim made no effort to hide his amusement, but he knew it would be best if he spared Laura any further embarrassment. He had a feeling she delivered quite a wallop when she wanted to. "I'd better be going. I have packing to do."

"Will you stop by?" Laura heard herself asking. "Before you leave?"

He didn't know if that would be wise. If he stopped by, Janka would play on his inclinations to stay. And he really wanted to. "I'm not sure—"

How could she be so stupid as to actually ask for rejection? Laura shook her head quickly, interrupting any poor excuse he might feel obligated to offer. "Never mind. Pretend I didn't ask. I don't know what came over me."

He drew her into his arms. Out of the corner of his eye, he saw Janka move over to Robbie and begin an animated conversation about one of the figures at the train depot. The woman was a saint. "I'd like to think you said that because you're going to miss me."

She didn't want him to hold her, but she didn't have the strength to push him away. Her arms didn't seem to want to work. "You've been very good with Robbie."

"But not so good with you." He lifted her chin with the tip of his finger. "I'll have to work on that after Christmas."

He kissed her, shutting out the other two people in the room, shutting out everything except for the sensations created by this soft, desirable woman in his arms. Though he had to hold back the passion that pleaded to be set free within him, Laura's response when he kissed her told him everything he needed to know.

Well, he mused, slowly releasing her, that part didn't need working on. He grinned. Or at least it didn't need improvement.

"I'll see you after Christmas," he promised.

"Have a nice holiday." There was more enthusiasm in her voice when she spoke to the mailman or the grocery-store clerk. She shut the door behind Tim, wishing the emptiness would go away. Wishing she wasn't such a fool.

Janka abandoned the train station and rose heavily to her feet. She aimed a reproving look at Laura. "Why did you not try to talk him into coming tomorrow?"

Laura didn't think she was up to coping with this. She needed time to sort out her feelings and put them where they belonged. In the trash. "You heard him, he's spending it with his family."

"Yes, I heard him." Janka crossed her arms before her, the expression on her face dark. Though she was a good five inches shorter than her daughter, she cast a large shadow. "What I did not hear was you stopping him or asking his family to come join us."

"We could use the reprieve." Laura walked into the kitchen. She could use a little of her mother's eggnog right about now. "Mother, he's here all the time for one reason or another." She reached into the refrigerator to get one of the bottles her mother had prepared.

"For only one reason."

Laura swung around. There was a pleading look in her eyes. "Mother, it's better this way."

Janka's expression softened as her heart ached. "For whom?"

At the last minute, Laura kept herself from slamming the bottle down on the ceramic countertop. "For all of us." Her voice dropped as her tension abated. "For me. I can't go through what I did the last time."

Was Laura so blind that she couldn't see what was there before her? "Who is to say t'at you will?"

But Laura remained unconvinced. She had been so sure the last time, so in love. Just as, she realized, she was now. Oh, God, she *was* in love with Tim. But it didn't matter. It didn't change things. "I can't take that risk." Her hand shook as she began to pour the eggnog.

Janka took the bottle from her and finished pouring. She handed Laura the glass. "You have to risk your heart in order to find happiness."

Laura took a long sip and felt the thick liquid slide down her throat. "I've risked it once, thank you." She held the glass in both hands. "That's enough."

Janka frowned at the philosophy. "Once is never enough for anyt'ing, unless you are dying. Only t'en is it enough."

Laura closed her eyes. She couldn't recall ever winning an argument with her mother. "Mother, please, it's almost Christmas."

"I know t'is."

Laura placed her glass on the table and threaded her arms around her mother's shoulders. "I don't want to argue."

"T'en do not. Call him."

Laura pressed her lips together. There were times when her mother could be absolutely infuriating. "No. If he wanted to, he could have changed his plans for tomorrow on his own. I won't beg."

Janka sighed and patted the arms around her. "You are a stubborn girl."

Laura laughed and hugged her. "I wonder where I get it from."

"T'is I do not know. But I do know t'at you will be sorry if you push him away."

Laura dropped her hands and shoved them into her pockets. "Then it'll be my loss."

"Yes," Janka agreed sadly. "It will."

There was no resolving this. Laura nodded toward the stove and the large pot that was boiling madly. "Do you need any help with that?"

Janka liked to work alone in the kitchen. It was the only time she preferred her solitude. She didn't like anyone looking over her shoulder as she experimented. "No. If you want to do somet'ing, you could wrap Robbie's presents for me."

"You haven't wrapped them yet?" Why did that surprise her? Her mother always did things just before they were due.

Janka shook her head in reply and then let her shoulders rise and fall in a careless shrug.

Laura believed in efficiency, in being early. This was the biggest bone of contention that existed between mother and daughter. Up until now. "Why do you always wait until the last minute?"

Janka grinned broadly. "Because t'en I can ask you to do it. I hate to wrap things, you know t'at. I just like to buy them and watch faces light up when you and Robbie open t'em."

"Are mine wrapped?"

"Yes."

"Well, then you—"

Janka merely smiled, smoothing a wrinkle out on her apron. She knew what Laura was getting at. She couldn't take credit where none was due. "Robbie is getting very good at it."

Laura tried to picture her six-year-old wrapping gifts, and she shuddered at the image. "Mother—"

"I must get back to my work." Janka turned toward the stove. She looked over her shoulder just as Laura began to leave. "T'e telephone is right by t'e closet in t'e hallway."

Laura didn't bother turning around. "I know where the phone is, Mother."

Janka nodded as she stirred. "Just making sure," she said cheerfully.

Chapter Ten

Christmas Eve had never seemed lonelier to her. Her mother had invited everyone on the block, plus Robbie's teacher and the women who worked for Laura's company. People and gifts, good music, fine food and cheerful voices had filled the house from a little after six until almost eleven o'clock. Yet Laura couldn't remember when she had felt so alone, so lonely. It was as if something she had come to expect, to rely on, was missing.

He was missing.

She was a complete idiot.

Laura sat up in her bed and pulled her knees up to her. What was the *matter* with her? This was her very favorite time of year, a time when everything seemed a little brighter, a little better. Even in those very lean years, when there had been no money and she and her parents had nothing but love to share, she had never felt this deprived, this adrift inside.

Not even when Craig had abandoned her.

Laura sighed as she dragged her hand through her hair. It was ridiculous to feel this way about a man she hardly knew. All right, so his smile had wound its way into the hidden, darkened corners of her mind, and his kiss had brought sunshine into her soul...and a need so great, she could barely stand it. Was this any reason to be depressed because he wasn't here?

How could she feel as if she was sitting at the bottom of a dark abyss? She didn't know a damn thing about him except for a few scraps of information she had pretended not to listen to.

She knew enough to know.

The emptiness inside her made the bleakness larger. Darker. Laura pushed back a sob.

Damn him. Damn him for making her feel again. For making her want to be loved. For making her believe that it could really happen.

"Restless?"

The sound of her mother's gentle voice floated into the bedroom. Laura looked up and saw the short, well-rounded figure wrapped in a long, pink robe standing in the shadows of the doorway, the worn moccasins she loved on her feet. "What are you doing up?"

Janka came in, her robe brushing along the rug. "Listening to you sigh. T'e walls are only so t'ick, you know. T'ey probably hear you sighing back in Ohio. You miss him, huh?"

Janka sat down on the edge of the bed, ready to listen the way she used to when Laura was much younger and problems could be sorted out in the space of an hour or two. She covered her daughter's hand with her own.

"No." Oh, what was the use of lying? Especially to herself. "I don't know. Maybe." Laura shrugged, feeling hopeless. "I miss something." And then she looked up, her eyes growing defensive as her expression hardened. "I have everything. You, Robbie, a job I like, a home."

Janka nodded as she listened to the list Laura rattled off. It didn't fool her. "Yah. And your favorite television program is still on every week.'' An impish smile played on the older woman's lips.

Laura laughed. She had never been able to fool her mother, not even when she was younger. "What are you trying to say?''

Janka wanted to hold her daughter, to stroke her hair and assure her that everything would be all right. But Laura was not a child anymore. There were things she had to face on her own. Risks she had to take by herself. No one else could do it for her. "T'at you are using a lot of words to get away from what you know is true.''

Laura raised her chin in a movement that reminded Janka of Laura's father. There was such a thing, the older woman reasoned, as too much pride. "I don't need a man, Mother.''

That was something Janka didn't believe. Granted, Laura did not need *a* man. But she needed *the* man. The man who would love her for all time. "We all need someone to love in t'at special way.''

"All right,'' Laura relented, her bravado disappearing, "then I'm afraid to need a man.''

The smile was warm and comforting. "Everyone is afraid.'' Janka remembered her own youth, her own love. "And excited. Ot'erwise, it would not be so special when it is right. And I t'ink, wit' Timot'y, it is right.'' She squeezed Laura's hand. "Call him in t'e morning.''

She wanted to, oh, how she wanted to. If only she wasn't so afraid. "And say what?''

"Merry Christmas would be a good start.''

Laura laughed. "I guess it would.'' And then her expression sobered.

"What?''

"He's up with his family, remember?" Laura said. "I don't have his number."

A deep, thudding noise echoed in the stillness of the night air. "What was that?"

Janka shrugged. There were more important things on her mind than a faraway noise. "Maybe just a car firing back."

"Backfiring," Laura corrected. She cocked her head. The noise sounded as if it was close, perhaps coming from down the street. She pushed the covers aside and grabbed her robe. "That sounds as if Mr. Sinclair is bussing in his whole family for the holidays." She could have sworn she heard the grinding of gears. What *was* going on? "And dumping them on the front lawn."

She went out into the hall to investigate, her mother right behind her.

"You forget your slippers."

"This is California, Mother." Laura pulled her hair out from beneath the robe and tied the sash. "I don't need slippers."

Just as she entered the hallway, she heard Robbie yelling for her. "Mama, Mama, come quick!"

Her pulse jumping, she tried to tell herself what she heard in his voice was excitement, not fear. She hurried into his room, but he wasn't there. "Robbie? Robbie, where are you?"

"In the rec room!"

Instead of waiting for Laura to find him, Robbie rushed into the hall. Eagerly, he grabbed her arm, pulling her to the room he had just vacated. "Mama, you gotta see this! You, too, Nana! It's Santa Claus!"

The two women exchanged looks.

"Santa Claus is building a snowman on our lawn right now!" he insisted. "With real snow!"

"What?" Laura looked over her shoulder at her mother, but the older woman shrugged, as confused as Laura was.

"Maybe he had a dream or a fever." Janka automatically reached out to touch the boy's forehead.

"No! Come look!" Robbie dragged Laura to the bay windows. The full moon illuminated her front lawn perfectly. Laura looked out to see a man wearing a red suit. He had a flowing white beard and he was building what looked like a snowman. Out of snow.

Laura felt as if she *had* stumbled into a dream. "What the . . . ?"

"He's real, Mama," Robbie cried. "Tim was right. Santa Claus really does exist!"

His enthusiasm in a fever pitch, Robbie suddenly dashed past his mother and out of the room. He sailed down the stairs, barely holding on to the banister as he flew. He didn't bother closing the front door behind him as he ran out of the house.

"Robbie, wait for me!" Laura knew he didn't even hear her. She hurried after him with her mother huffing behind her.

It was snow.

Real snow.

Laura could tell as soon as her bare toes made contact with it. She would have shivered if she hadn't been so stunned. Snow covered her entire lawn, almost reaching the front step. Where had it come from?

Tim couldn't resist dramatically swinging around just as she reached him. "So what d'you think?"

Laura pulled at the beard hesitantly, afraid that she had happened upon a miracle in progress. But the beard slid off easily enough. Even then, she was afraid to hope, afraid to believe her eyes. "Tim?"

He nodded. The look in her eyes was worth all the trouble and expense he had gone through. Anything was worth the way she was looking at him. "The real one couldn't come. All those toys, you know." He turned to Robbie. "It's his busy night."

"This *is* snow!" Robbie threw handfuls of the white powder up in the air and laughed as it fell, hitting his face.

Tim tousled his hair. "You betcha."

Robbie couldn't believe it. It was too good to be true. "But where...?"

"Would you believe the North Pole?"

At this point, Laura had a feeling that Robbie would believe anything, but she shook her head. "No."

Tim drew her aside to the porch, not wanting the magic to be ruined for Robbie. When he was older, he'd explain it to him. That's what dads were for.

"I found someone who knows someone in the company that delivers snow to Knott's Berry Farm. I placed an order of my own."

Laura touched his face. She still couldn't believe he was here. "What about Santa Barbara? Your family?"

"That's the nice thing about families, they understand." They had more than understood, they had wished him luck. And he had needed it to arrange all this. It had taken Tim the better part of the day to get in contact with the right people and rent a Santa suit. The other one was now boxed away in the recesses of Mattingly's Department Store.

With Laura's hand in his, he turned back to Robbie. "How about our deal? You said you'd believe in Santa Claus if he brought you snow for Christmas Eve."

Laura felt her throat growing tight. Tim had done all this for Robbie. To make him believe in Santa Claus.

"I asked for a dad, too." Robbie cocked his head, looking from Tim to his mother. His expression was clearly expectant.

Tim spread his arms wide, indicating that it was out of his hands. "That's up to your mother."

Laura wasn't aware that she had started crying. But she was. Her cheeks felt damp, and they tingled in the cool night air. She threw her arms around Tim's neck and leaned her face against the warm beard that was now hanging down on his chest.

What was the use of denying it? Of denying herself. She *did* love him. And it was easy to see that Robbie approved of the match. He was crazy about Tim. As was her mother. Who was she to drag her feet? Especially when those feet no longer wanted to be dragged.

"I guess a man who can find a way to bring snow to a little boy in Southern California just to put the magic back in his life is someone I'm willing to take a chance on."

Tim folded his arms around her. This was where she belonged. "No. No chances, Laura. This is a very sure thing."

Beneath the star-filled sky, Tim kissed Laura on the front porch for all the world to see. There was a promise in his kiss, a promise of many more magical evenings to come. Laura felt it and hugged the promise to her.

"Looks like you got both your wishes, champ," Tim said to Robbie. "Now you *have* to believe in Santa."

Robbie rose, brushing the snow off his robe. "I guess if someone as big as you can believe in him, he must be real."

Tim smiled at Laura's upturned face. "He is that, Robbie. He is that." With one arm tucked around

Laura, Tim looked over toward Janka. "Any pierogi left over?"

Janka beamed and linked her arms through his for a moment. "For you, always." And if there weren't, she'd make more. "And Timot'y—"

"Yes?"

"If she changes her mind and does not marry you—" Janka nodded at her daughter "—I will."

Tim laughed. "It's a deal."

"Oh, no, you don't," Laura warned, peering at her mother. The emptiness that had been so all consuming only minutes ago had completely dissolved. "Find your own Santa Claus."

Janka turned and took Robbie's icy hand in hers. She rubbed it and smiled. "I t'ink we have all found San-ta Klauss tonight."

Laura looked up into Tim's face, her heart brimming. "I think you're right."

* * * * *

A Note from Marie Ferrarella

When Silhouette kindly asked me to write a Christmas story, I became very excited. I absolutely adore Christmas. Traditionally, I start shopping in July. Yes, I know I'm stretching the season out beyond reason, but it makes me happy—and I avoid the Christmas crunch.

To me, Christmas is memories, like the one from the time I was twelve. We—my parents and two younger brothers—were living in New York. I don't remember why, but there was a tree shortage that year. We were still treeless on Christmas Eve. My brothers and I were heartbroken...until my dad arrived home. He had found a tree and brought it home on the subway. The tree paid full fare.

Christmas is also mint-chip brownies, endless lists and bad wrapping—no matter how hard I try. But most of all, Christmas to me will always be Mama. She made Christmas special for us when we were growing up, even when there was no money for gifts. She brought laughter and love in her own unique way. She came to this country when she was twenty-eight—with me in tow—and though she learned English by doing crossword puzzles, hers was always a very special brand of English. I'd like to share her rendition of "The Twelve Days of Christmas" which she sang to us as we decorated the tree. The words are hers, the comments, mine.

"On t'e first day of Christmas my truly love gave to me a partree-gee in the forest (it isn't every day you can give a partree-gee, which was probably an Italian partridge). Two someti'ings (possibly also in the forest). T'ree or four French hens (who's counting?). Five GOLDEN RINGS (this was the only one she was sure of and she always drew it out). Six geesen (obviously they had to be German geese). Seven Swansons swimming (I always pictured TV dinners floating on a lake when she got to this part). Eight maids living (which she then changed to eight maids milking seven cows—times were rather hard in Christmas carols). Nine Scotchmen jumping. Seven gentlemen leaping (three must have broken their legs leaping over the jumping Scotchmen and couldn't come). Eleven trimmers trimming. And twelve drummers dreaming.''

Mama's been gone ten years now, but she's back with me each year at Christmas. From me and my full house to you and yours, I wish you only happiness and joy this holiday season. And always.

With love,

Marie Ferrarella

BASKET OF LOVE

Jeanne Stephens

A recipe from Jeanne Stephens:

STRAWBERRY-CREAM CHEESE PIE

½ to ¾ cup sugar (to taste)
3½ tpsp cornstarch
16 oz to 20 oz frozen, sweetened strawberries, thawed
3 oz cream cheese
2 tbsp milk
1 baked pie shell
sweetened whip cream or Cool Whip

Mix together sugar and cornstarch. Add to thawed, undrained strawberries. Cook in a medium-size saucepan over medium heat, stirring frequently, until mixture is clear. Let cool.

Soften cream cheese at room temperature. Spread over bottom of cooled pie shell. Add strawberry mixture. Refrigerate for several hours or overnight.

Just before serving, spread with sweetened whipped cream or Cool Whip.

Chapter One

Why had she let the support group talk her into this? Nina Duncan wondered as she climbed out of her car in the hospital parking lot. Tugging her coat collar up against the wind, she joined a group of employees who were gathering to deliver a Thanksgiving basket to a needy family.

Lynda Westin stood in the center of the small group, waving her arms and talking a mile a minute. Organizing everybody, as usual. Her co-workers joked that if God ever wanted a day off from running the world, Lynda was prepared to step in.

"Okay, you guys, Bob brought the basket. He decorated it himself. Isn't it great? Let's see now—we've got lots of veggies and fresh fruit, dressing mix, ham, turkey, pies, butter, candy—ah, look, chocolate turkeys—and... Who was supposed to bring milk?"

"Here," Nina called, hoisting a gallon jug.

The tall man standing in front of Nina reached for the jug and passed it to Lynda, who deposited it in the basket. Before returning to the business at hand, Lynda gave Nina a nod of approval. Clearly she had doubted Nina would show up.

"Dinner rolls," Lynda continued. "Who was assigned to bring the rolls?"

"I think it was Jeff Eberhart," said a woman named Sally, a secretary in the hospital's executive office.

"Jeff, where are you?" Lynda called.

"He had to work late," an older man replied, "but he said he'd be here." Jeff was one of the hospital's in-house attorneys. Nina had had lunch with him several times in the past three months, but she continued to turn down invitations to dinner and weekend outings. Lunching with Jeff in the hospital cafeteria, or even at one of the nearby restaurants, didn't feel threatening. Their lunch time was limited, and there were always plenty of other people around. But going out in the evening with tall, lean, handsome Jeff Eberhart, that was downright scary.

"He's got exactly five minutes," Lynda pronounced flatly. "If he doesn't show, we'll pick up rolls on the way to the Summerses' house."

Even though they could wait at least fifteen minutes and still make it to their destination on time, nobody contradicted Lynda because nobody else wanted the responsibility for Care and Share projects, which Lynda usually ramroded. If they criticized her, she might not volunteer next time. Lately Lynda had been feeling put-upon, anyway, complaining that she was tired of being the hospital martyr.

To give credit where it was due, Lynda, who worked with Nina in the hospital business office, was good at taking charge and getting other people involved. Eighteen months ago she had taken charge of Nina. Like a mother hen with a single chick under her wing, Lynda had made the transition a little smoother when Nina was new on the job, new in town, new at supporting herself. New at being alone.

Lynda had also coaxed her into enrolling in several craft classes and prodded and cajoled until she attended a grief recovery support group which met weekly at the hospital. Dan and Candi had been gone seven months when Nina entered the group, but she hadn't begun to deal with her grief. She had simply repressed it, "stuffed it," as the group leader said. The support group helped her see that. And for the next six months, the group was the anchor she clung to in a sea-gray world which seemed to hold nothing worth staying afloat for.

The previous February she had dropped back to one meeting a month, and in April she had stopped attending group meetings altogether, feeling she had recovered enough to face life on her own.

And she had been fine. She enjoyed her job and liked her co-workers. Her days took on a satisfyingly placid flow. She still noticed stocky, blond men and little girls with long blond hair, but the stabbing pain in her heart at the sight of them grew less and less severe. Maybe she hadn't reached the point where she could handle a turbulent disruption like sexy-eyed Jeff Eberhart, but, on the whole, she was coping.

Until the weekend before Thanksgiving, when Christmas decorations appeared in store windows and on homes and business buildings all over Tulsa. And the devastating memories of Christmas two years ago had deluged her, like a roiling, black sea, its undertow threatening to pull her to the bottom.

Innervated by depression, she had stayed in her apartment all day Sunday, unable to summon the desire or the energy to fix a meal or go out. Having slept poorly Sunday night, she'd come to work Monday morning, looking haggard and hollow-eyed.

Lynda had known right away what was wrong. "Tough weekend, huh?"

"I've had better."

"Are you going to Fort Worth for Thanksgiving?" Lynda had asked.

Nina shook her head. "Dad just retired and my folks are celebrating by going on a cruise."

Lynda went into her mother hen routine, clucking and patting Nina's shoulder sympathetically. "Holidays are rough for people without families to share them with. I know this time of year is especially hard on you, Nina. But you'll make it through Thanksgiving—*and* Christmas—trust me. And next year will be easier."

Nina had wanted to believe her. She dragged through the day, performing the duties required of her, feeling so heavy that merely walking across the office seemed overwhelming. Lynda had watched her like a hawk.

When Nina had declined lunch with her co-workers, saying she wasn't hungry, Lynda had ushered her into the records room and talked to her like a wayward child. "Okay, let's nip this in the bud, Nina. You have to go back to the Tuesday-night support group."

"I went there for more than six months," Nina protested. "What can anybody say that hasn't been said a hundred times?"

"You need to be with people who can empathize," Lynda insisted.

Nina picked up a ballpoint pen that was lying on a file cabinet and clenched it tensely. "I thought I was doing so well."

"You were, and you will again. But right now a few meetings with the group can help you get through the holidays."

Too weary to argue, Nina had agreed. It hadn't mattered to her, one way or the other; if she weren't with the group, she'd be moping at home. On Monday nothing in the world had seemed to matter.

But talking to the group last night made her face the fact that at least she wasn't the only person in town who was depressed by the holiday glitz and gaiety. When she'd told them she didn't think she could face Wednesday night's Care and Share activity, which she'd signed up for weeks ago, several group members urged her to reconsider.

"I'm too depressed," Nina countered. "I'd be a damper on the evening."

"I used to think I was depressed," said an elderly man, "but after the first few months, I was really only wallowing in self-pity."

"Why—why that's not what I'm doing."

"Oh, I didn't mean you, Nina," the man said with a gentle smile. But his shrewd gray eyes suggested she might want to think about it, anyway.

"Remember what we always say," a middle-aged woman put in hastily. "You have to fake it till you make it."

"You can't think of two things at the same time," said another, "and taking a basket to that family will give you something else to think about for a couple of hours."

"You might be surprised," said a third. "You may actually enjoy it. Isn't it worth a try?"

In the end Nina had decided to go. Already she regretted the decision. It would take all her determination to chat and smile and pretend that she was in the holiday spirit. She felt utterly exhausted already. Well, maybe she'd be tired enough to sleep tonight.

"Here comes the bread man," Bob announced.

They all turned to see Jeff Eberhart, in jeans and a windbreaker, loping across the parking lot carrying a brown grocery bag.

"Barely in the nick of time, Jeff-o," Lynda scolded. "We were about to leave without you."

Jeff gave Lynda that mischievous little-boy grin that always made Nina feel as though something inside her was melting. He set the bag on top of the food in the basket. "I bought three kinds of dinner rolls. I even got Danish pastries and donuts for breakfast Thanksgiving morning."

Lynda gave an exasperated shake of her head, but she couldn't repress a smile. "You did good, Eberhart. Okay, listen up. We're taking Bob's van. We should all be able to squeeze in."

Nina had planned to go in her car so she could leave when she wanted to but, as usual, Lynda had her own plans. If she didn't go with the others, Lynda would scold her for not making more of an effort to be part of the group. She could hear Lynda now: *I know it's hard, Nina, but you have to give it your best shot.*

"Right," Nina muttered to herself, "fake it till you make it."

Reluctantly she trailed behind the others as they clambered into the van. She lost sight of Jeff until he came up behind her and placed his hands on her shoulders. "I haven't seen you all week," he murmured close to her ear. "I called your office this morning to ask if we could have lunch. You didn't return my call."

The pressure of his hands on her shoulders and his warm breath fanning her cheek made her feel so ill at ease that she stammered. "Oh, uh, Jeff, I'm sorry. I was going to call, but—but the office was so hectic, it slipped my mind."

"You sure know how to flatter a guy."

"I'm really sorry. I couldn't have gone, anyway. I worked straight through my lunch hour." The truth was, though today had been much better than yesterday, she still hadn't had the courage to deal with Jeff Eberhart.

She stepped into the van, Jeff right behind her. Only one empty seat remained. She turned back with a feeling of relief. "There isn't room for both of us. I'll take my car and follow the van."

Jeff grabbed her arm before she could brush by him. "No problem." He maneuvered into the empty seat and, before she knew what was happening, pulled her down on his lap.

She sat very straight, breathless suddenly, gripping the back of the seat in front of her as though the van were a roller coaster. She couldn't have been more tense if it *had* been. "I'm too heavy," she said weakly.

"Nonsense. You hardly weigh anything." He settled her back against him. "There." Bob started the engine. The others talked and laughed as they drove off the parking lot. Sally, the secretary, launched into the latest joke making the rounds at the hospital.

Jeff's hand remained pressed against Nina's ribcage, just below her breast. He smelled of some musky male cologne, and she couldn't seem to get enough air in the sudden hum of sexual tension between them. "Comfortable?" he murmured.

She cleared her throat. "Fine," she said and pretended to study the scene passing outside the window. She felt the panicked flutter of her pulse and sought to calm it. She could feel him watching her and stifled an insane desire to turn, bury her face in his shoulder and weep.

"I guess you're driving to Texas tomorrow."

"No."

"Your parents are coming here?"

"No. They're on a cruise."

"Are you going out for Thanksgiving dinner, then—with friends?"

"I'm cooking." Let him think she was making turkey and all the trimmings for...whoever. It was none of his business that she would probably fix a minute steak and baked potato and eat them alone.

His hand moved against the side of her breast. "Nina—"

"Oh, look," she chirped before he could press her for more details. "Did you ever see such a beautiful Nativity scene?" She almost choked on the lump in her throat.

He craned for a look at the house they were passing. "Nice." He returned to perusing her profile. She was very aware of it, but feigned an indifference he knew she didn't feel. Her back touched his chest, even though she hadn't really relaxed against him, but remained tensely alert. He watched her as she continued to stare out the window.

She wasn't knock-out beautiful, he thought. Not in the sense of having the stunningly perfect features he'd seen on film stars, features that he suspected owed much to the expertise of a plastic surgeon. But her face was arresting. Her mouth, though soft and sensitive, was a little too wide, and her brown eyes too large for her oval face. When she smiled, they lit as though from an inner fire. Tonight, he realized, shades seemed to have been drawn behind her eyes, leaving them dull, cut off from the light.

He felt the outline of her ribs beneath his fingers. She was too thin. Fragile. That was the thing that had drawn him to her initially, her seeming fragility. Even though he'd known that it was the old macho instinct to shelter and protect, he had been drawn, anyway. Soon he had discovered other things about her that intrigued him. Those big, vulnerable eyes. And the way she laughed sometimes, like a tinkling bell surprised by a sudden puff of wind.

But if he had thought vulnerable eyes and an appearance of fragility indicated weakness or malleability, he'd been wrong. For three months he had tried to breach her solid defenses, and he was no nearer to finding a way in than the first time he spoke to her. Except for a couple of pecks, which she had deftly diverted, he hadn't even kissed her. He had been waiting for some indication that she wanted to be kissed.

And he was damned tired of waiting. Maybe he would have to *show* her. A little demonstration to prove to both of them that she wanted his kiss. He could be stubborn, too. It had been years since he'd been this moved by a woman, and he wasn't about to give up without a fight.

He removed his hand from her side, brushed it upward over her breasts, and curled it loosely around her throat. She sucked in her breath. Beneath his thumb, he could feel an erratically beating pulse. He smiled and rubbed his thumb idly along the side of her neck.

Nina sat very still, willing her mind away from the lazy stroke of his thumb. *Why did she always feel so confused in his presence?*

A few moments later the van stopped. "Here we are, gang," Lynda said.

Nina leapt off Jeff's lap and fell in behind the others as they left the van. Jeff watched her nervous exit with a contemplative expression as he hurried to catch up with her.

The house they approached sat in the center of a block of small, dilapidated houses in one of Tulsa's poorer neighborhoods. The porch light was on. Lynda had sent word to the family through the welfare agency, so they were expected.

Lynda, after consulting with several of her co-workers, including Nina, had chosen the family from a list provided by the agency. Jerry and Becky Summers, who were in their early thirties, had five children. Four boys, ranging in age from eleven to six, and a four-year-old daughter named Penny.

Jerry Summers had been laid off from his job at a machine shop eight months previously and had been unable to find other work. The family had lived on unemployment compensation until that ran out and now received a modest monthly check from a local welfare organization. The agency provided money for a maximum of six months to families who had no other source of income. According to Lynda, the Summerses would not be eligible for financial aid beyond that.

Nina found herself thanking God for her job as Becky Summers opened the door and they all crowded into the cramped living room. Becky, a small, pale woman, seemed both appreciative and embarrassed to be the recipient of charity.

In addition to a worn couch and chair, bunk beds were placed along one wall. Evidently two of the children slept in the living room. Adjoining the living room was a narrow kitchen with worn linoleum and scant cabinet space. Nina was sure there could be no more than two small bedrooms beyond that.

The pine floors were bare, and there were no curtains on the windows, only frayed, yellowed shades. The poverty of the Summerses' home gave Nina a guilty pang when she compared it with her attractive south-side apartment.

The Summerses' four boys, their eyes wide with excitement, crowded around Bob, who held the basket of food. "Is it okay if they eat a chocolate turkey?" Bob asked Becky Summers. She said yes, and Bob set the basket down and placed foil-wrapped turkeys in four eagerly outstretched hands. "There's one more here for your sister," Bob said.

"Penny fell asleep a few minutes ago," Becky Summers told him. "I put her to bed."

Jerry Summers, a gauntly thin man with a heavy beard, had been standing in the kitchen doorway, observing the scene in silence. He must have mixed emotions about all this, Nina thought. He had to be grateful for the food, because of his family, but, as the man of the house—the provider—he must also feel humiliated and inadequate. Nina's heart went out to him.

Jerry Summers appeared to brace himself, then stepped forward to accept the basket. "We sure do appreciate this," he said. "The kids'll have a good Thanksgiving because of y'all."

"I've been saving a jug of cider for a special occasion," Becky Summers said. "It's already hot." She looked around helplessly. "I don't know where all of you are going to sit, though."

"The floor's fine," Jeff said. He lowered himself to sit against the wall near the door, folding his long legs. His brown hair was mussed by the wind, which Nina found oddly endearing. Reaching for Nina's hand, he pulled her down beside him. He seemed to be jerking her around a lot tonight—in more ways than one. "There's plenty of room for you here," he said. "We'll let the old folks have the couch."

That elicited a couple of sarcastic remarks, as the others found seats. The Summers boys flopped down on the floor in front of the couch, still eating their chocolate turkeys. Beneath the buzz of conversation, Jeff leaned over and murmured, "Who are you cooking Thanksgiving dinner for?"

Fortunately Becky Summers appeared before them at that moment with two chipped, mismatched mugs. "Thank you," Nina said with a smile that she didn't even have to force. "This is exactly what I need." Curling her fingers around the warm mug, she felt a rush of emotions. Compassion. Admiration. Even envy of Becky's large family.

Jeff settled back to sip from his mug. "You didn't answer my question, Nina."

"About Thanksgiving dinner?" Her tone was wary. "Why do you want to know?"

He shifted his mug, then slipped his free hand, warm from the mug, up beneath her hair to her nape. "You're being evasive."

"Don't be silly. I really wish you wouldn't do that." His fingers gently massaged her neck, and she could feel her pulse beginning to hammer.

His blue eyes narrowed speculatively. It's a crime, Nina thought, for a man to possess such long, thick lashes. She quickly averted her eyes and gazed into her mug as she sipped the hot, spicy cider.

One of the men, who sang in the hospital choir, started "Shine on, Harvest Moon," and the others joined in. Then the Summers boys wanted to sing "To Grandmother's House We Go," which they'd learned at school.

Jeff watched Nina. She finished her cider and set the mug aside. She leaned forward with her blue-jeaned knees drawn up and her sweatered arms wrapped around her legs. Her hair fell in dark curls around her lovely face. She joined the others in singing songs of thanksgiving, but the sadness that had touched her all evening still clung to her. He understood that the holiday season must be difficult for her. Lynda had told him something of what Nina had been through before he knew her, that her husband and daughter had died a couple of years ago during the Christmas holidays.

He longed to hold her, comfort her, but he knew she wouldn't accept that from him. She was afraid to be vulnerable with him. He took encouragement from the thought. She must feel *something* for him, or she wouldn't be so threatened by his attempts to get closer to her. If she lowered some of the barriers around her emotions, he might see more than she wanted him to see.

His hand came up, as though it had a mind of its own, to touch her hair. But the instant before his fingers made contact with the silky strands, she stiffened. The small amount of color that had been in her face drained out of it, leaving her as pale as ashes. She stared fixedly across the room to where Becky Summers sat on the wide arm of the chair occupied by her husband.

Jeff darted a glance at Becky Summers as she extended her arms to the little girl who had come into the room. Penny must have been awakened by the singing. Becky lifted her daughter onto her knee. Dressed in a faded, too-large T-shirt with her blond hair streaming down her back, the child rubbed sleep-swollen eyes as she shyly buried her face between her mother's breasts.

Beside Jeff, Nina whispered a single, tortured word: "Candi." Then she struggled to her feet and pressed a hand to the wall for support.

He thought she was going to faint. Standing, he took her arm to steady her. "Nina?" He was staggered by the grief in her pain-glazed eyes. "Honey, what's wrong?"

"Don't . . ." She shook off his hand.

"You'd better sit down."

Wordlessly she shook her head.

"Nina—"

"I—I have to get out of here." Whirling, she fumbled for the doorknob, opened the door and stumbled out.

Chapter Two

He found her in the van, huddled in the corner of a seat. Her forehead rested on her drawn-up knees. He sat down beside her and stroked her hair. She didn't acknowledge him, didn't move. He pulled her into his arms. She didn't resist. She was trembling.

"I'm sorry," she murmured. "I couldn't help it. I made a fool of myself, didn't I?"

"I don't think the others even noticed." He placed a gentle kiss on top of her head. She smelled of soap. "Don't worry about it."

After a small silence, she said softly, "When I saw that little girl...she had her back to me...all that blond hair." Her voice shook and she paused to compose herself. "I thought it was my daughter."

"Your daughter's name was Candi?"

"Candice, yes. She was four years old when she—when I lost her. I saw that child and it just came over me—a flash of—of certainty that Candi had come back somehow. I—I can't explain it."

He combed his fingers gently through her hair. "Don't even try."

She lifted her head to look at him. Her stricken, tear-streaked face pierced his heart. "You must think I'm crazy."

"Not at all."

"I lost my daughter and husband in a house fire, two years ago."

He framed her face in his hands, wiped her tears with his thumbs. "I know. Lynda told me."

She swallowed convulsively. "It was three days before Christmas. We lived in the country... a big, old, drafty farmhouse. Everything needed updating or repairing, but we didn't care. We loved it." She faltered to a stop, but after clearing her throat, she went on, "I'd gone to town to finish Christmas shopping. Candi was napping. They said Dan, my husband, must have fallen asleep in front of the TV." She paused again to steady herself. "The—the investigator said the fire started in the electric wiring. We'd put off having it replaced until we could save enough money to pay for it." Her dark eyes, immense and luminous, filled with fresh tears.

He held her until she stopped weeping, murmuring, "It's going to be all right. I promise you."

Finally she said, "Everywhere I looked last weekend, they'd put up Christmas decorations. It just—just brought it back, you know? I've been a wreck ever since. I shouldn't have come tonight."

He shifted to frame her face with his hands and look into her tear-swollen eyes. "Yes, you should have."

"No—"

"You can't shut other people out," he interrupted. "You're not the one who died, Nina."

She blinked owlishly, then, brushing his hands aside, pulled away. His blunt words had angered her. "There's nothing as devastating as losing the people you love the most. It's like losing your own life—worse, because you wish you could have died with them." She raked shaking fingers through her hair and stared out the window. "You don't have the right to preach to me, Jeff. You can't possibly understand."

"Yes, I can." He touched her cheek.

"That's easy to say."

"Look at me, Nina." She pushed at her hair with both hands and turned back to him. He placed his hands on the curve of her shoulders. "Five and a half years ago I lost my wife. She had leukemia."

Her eyes searched his and found something she had not recognized before. She had been looking inward, too engulfed by self-pity to see that he had loved deeply, too. And he had lost the one he loved. Had he, also, cursed the fate that left him to live, after the center, the purpose, of his life had been torn away?

Her guard slipped. She reached out to touch his cheek. "I'm sorry."

He covered her hand with his. "We'd been married less than two years when we found out. She died three weeks after our second anniversary."

"Oh, Jeff."

For a long, still moment, they looked steadily into each other's eyes. He noted the slight quiver of her bottom lip. She saw the intensity in his eyes.

Then his mouth came to hers. It was not the gentle kiss he'd offered her before. There was nothing of comfort in it. It was hungry and possessive and demanding. For a moment, while she still had the capacity to think, she resisted. Her mind said that she must stop him. If she hadn't been in such emotional turmoil, so raw and vulnerable, things would not have reached this point in the first place.

But Nina's body betrayed her. Her flesh began to heat. She heard her own soft moan as her fingers slid inside his windbreaker to clutch handfuls of his sweater.

Jeff drew her closer. There was something desperate and wild in the way his mouth plundered hers. This was not the easygoing man with the mischievous grin, whom she had come to know. But those sexy eyes should have warned her there was much more to him. Depths that she had chosen to ignore. Depths that she was terrified of plumbing.

He sought her response, reveled in it, and wanted more. She lost her weak struggle to gain control of the situation. At the moment her own needs were too close to the surface. Unable to resist, she relaxed against him and gave.

A shudder ran through him and he lifted his mouth from hers for an instant. Her eyelids fluttered open. His passion-glazed eyes had darkened to the color of a stormy sky. Nina tried to clear her thoughts.

Before she could, Jeff pulled her tight against him and began kissing her again. Somehow her arms were around him. Groaning, he took the kiss deeper. She tasted the residue of her own tears and the wet heat of his mouth. He was demanding things from her that she was not ready to give. Yet she never wanted him to stop kissing her.

His hand was hot and sure when he slid it beneath her loose sweater to take her braless breast. His fingers were lean and hard and wherever they touched, her flesh burned. Her body vibrated with the thud of desire. It frightened her, made her ache, made her dig her fingernails into his back. Nina had experienced physical pleasure many times before. She had an intimate knowledge of passion. But this was more, something beyond her store of memories. God help her, she wanted to experience it.

He slipped both hands under her sweater to cup her breasts. Her skin was incredibly soft—as soft and warm as expensive silk exposed to the sun. Desire thundered in his blood as his thumbs brushed across her nipples. The temptation to pull her down on the seat and take her right there pushed at him.

Nina's breathing was quick, each exhalation a soft, helpless moan. In the instant when the last remnant of sanity was slipping away from her, something pierced the needs that clamored in her brain.

Voices. The other members of the group were coming out of the Summerses' house, calling goodbyes.

Nina wrenched her mouth free and stared up at him, utterly confused. Disjointed thoughts and emotions tumbled through her. The taste of his mouth still lingered on her lips. Her body still ached with unmet needs.

"Well." Jeff's voice was raspy. "It's taken long enough, but now we know." He caressed the back of her neck with his fingers. A fresh wave of desire washed through her.

"Know what?"

He cocked a brow. "You want me as much as I want you."

A shiver of apprehension ran through her. "You don't understand. I'm not myself tonight." She slid out of his grasp and scooted over until her shoulder pressed against the van window.

Nina stared at a white cat slinking across a yard and sought to blot out the unacceptable thoughts that still possessed her. Later, when she was alone, she would try to understand what had happened. Now she only wanted to make her mind a blank.

Jeff studied her. It was gratifying to know that he had finally penetrated her defenses and touched the passionate woman he had always sensed was there. But she had struck a chord deep in the core of him, as well. He hadn't been prepared for the shock he felt in the instant she gave up resisting and responded to him.

As the others entered the van, Jeff made no move to shift Nina to his lap. He knew she would resist. Let two of the others double up for the return trip.

He needed time to regain his balance. He put his head back against the seat, closed his eyes and tried to take a clear-eyed inventory.

He had wanted her from the first moment he saw her. It had been a long time since he'd had a woman, far too long. But it wasn't just a woman that he wanted. If that were the case, there were several at the hospital who had made it clear they were available. He wasn't interested.

It's you I want, Nina. More than I've ever wanted another woman.

Nor was that the end of it, he admitted to himself. He was in love with her.

Thanksgiving day was chilly, but fair and windless. The night before, after a restless few hours, Nina had finally read herself to sleep about 1:00 a.m. She had slept deeply, awaking at nine-thirty. She showered, donned sweats and went for a brisk walk through the neighborhood. She was determined to keep busy and not allow herself to sink into another depression like the one she'd suffered earlier in the week.

She usually encountered other walkers, but not today. Everybody was at home, already making preparations for a big family meal, or away, visiting relatives. From today until the first of the year, everybody would center on families. People who were alone were left on the outside, looking in.

Nina brought her thoughts up short. No more meandering in that direction, she told herself. *You can't think of two things at the same time.* She concentrated on admiring the yards she passed. As yet the weather hadn't dipped below freezing, and masses of flowers, yellow, bronze, white and lavender chrysanthemums, bordered shrubbery beds and walks. Pin oak trees were at the height of their autumn glory with brilliant red and orange leaves. One of the things Nina liked best about Oklahoma was the change of seasons. Each one had its own special beauty.

Sometimes she thought about moving into a house or duplex so that she could putter in the yard. On the farm, she had had a huge vegetable garden, and there had been flower beds all around the house. When she'd sold the farm and moved to Tulsa, she hadn't wanted anything that might remind her of what she'd lost. But she found that she missed digging with her hands in the earth, the springtime ritual of choosing bedding plants at the nursery, planting and tending them, watching them flourish and bloom.

In fact, there was nothing to prevent her covering her tiny apartment patio with boxes and pots. She could buy a chaise and relax on the patio, surrounded by flowers. All at once she couldn't wait until spring. The realization took her by surprise. It was the first time in two years that she could remember looking forward to something.

You aren't the one who died, Nina.

She hadn't wanted to hear that last night, but Jeff had known she needed to hear it. To face it and finally admit that, in spite of the pain, she was glad to be alive.

Jeff, it seemed, had made her face a number of things last night. She was a young woman, still capable of feeling deeply. A woman with appetites and needs. Emotional needs. Sexual needs. Perhaps the most horrifying realization was that it had required only a few minutes for Jeff to shove the truth into her face. She rather resented him for the ease with which he'd done it. But mostly, it scared the hell out of her.

Nina had known all along that she wasn't brave enough to give Jeff Eberhart free rein in her life. Last night had merely underscored that knowledge.

On the way back to the apartment, she stopped at a convenience store for a newspaper. It was after eleven by the time she set a waffle, bacon, maple syrup, orange juice and coffee on the kitchen table and sat down to enjoy a leisurely breakfast while she read the paper.

She worked the crossword puzzle and the cryptoquote, saving the entertainment section for last. Finally she perused the movie guide, thinking that she might take in a late-afternoon film and stop at the cafeteria in a neighborhood mall for dinner. The minute steak languishing in her freezer no longer appealed. The cafeteria would have roast turkey, dressing and pumpkin pie. She didn't have to miss all of the tradition simply because she was alone on the holiday.

After dinner, she decided, she would stroll through the mall and look at the window displays. She had to get used to portents of Christmas on every hand—harden herself to the inevitable—and she might as well begin today. None of the stores would be open, but perhaps she'd get some ideas for Christmas presents for her parents and a few friends at the hospital.

Nina chose a comedy film starring Whoopi Goldberg, guaranteed to lift her spirits. Dressed in a soft pink sweater with a navy skirt and pumps, she was ready to leave at four o'clock. As she transferred her wallet and key ring to her navy purse, the doorbell chimed.

She tossed the purse on a chair and opened the door to Jeff Eberhart's mischievous grin. His bulky, white, crewneck sweater featured a band with an argyle design across the front. The design was the same deep blue as his eyes.

At her startled look, he slapped a palm against his forehead and exclaimed, "Egad, it works!"

She struggled to keep a straight face. "What works?"

"ESP."

She crossed her arms and leaned against the door. "You're going to explain what you mean by that, right?"

"Hey, try to stop me. All day I've been sending out ESP messages." His gaze raked her up and down. "Obviously you were on my wavelength."

"I doubt it. What was the content of these messages?"

He closed his eyes and intoned in the monotone of a hypnotist, "You will be at home when Jeff Eberhart rings your doorbell. You will see how lonely he is and feel sorry for the poor schmuck. You will go to dinner with him because you have a generous heart and you can't bear to send him off to dine alone."

Nina shook her head, briefly speechless. But only briefly. "Sorry, but I'm afraid we got our wavelengths crossed. I'm going to a movie."

His grin faded. "Have you already eaten dinner?"

"No, I had a late breakfast."

"Let's see if I have this straight. You're coming back here, after the movie, and have dinner. You did say you were cooking today, didn't you?"

"Not exactly. I mean, I said it, but I changed my mind about cooking." She felt her cheeks flush and knew he noticed her rising color. "It's true. I simply changed my mind. It's a lot of trouble to cook Thanksgiving dinner for one person. I'll grab something at the cafeteria."

"My idea beats that one six ways from Sunday. *We'll* go to the movie. Later we'll have dinner at Greenleaf's on the Park."

Greenleaf's was a popular restaurant in one of the city's most elegant hotels. It would be jammed today. Nina snatched at the excuse. "We'd have to wait an hour for a table . . . at least. It's not worth it."

"I've already reserved a table for two at seven."

She eyed him uneasily. "Sure of yourself, aren't you?"

Jeff's gaze didn't waver. "I was hoping you'd invite me to eat with you—I thought you were cooking. The reservation was plan B. I believe in being prepared and hoping for the best."

What exactly did he mean by the best? she wondered. But she had to admit that the cafeteria couldn't hold a candle to Thanksgiving dinner at Greenleaf's. To accept Jeff's invitation was probably asking for trouble; still, she was tempted. Trouble and temptation. The man was a walking, talking bundle of both.

So why didn't she shut the door in his face?

Because she dreaded eating alone in a cafeteria on Thanksgiving Day. Because she was cheered by the mere sight of him, she admitted glumly. Because she wanted to accept his invitation to a movie and dinner.

"Do you like Whoopi Goldberg?" Nina finally asked.

"I'm crazy about her."

"Okay, a movie and dinner. But I have to be home early."

He gave her a wry smile. "If you say you have to wash your hair, I'll punch something."

She laughed. "Let me get a jacket."

Chapter Three

She had been relaxed during the movie, laughing and sharing his giant-size bag of popcorn. Jeff loved to hear her laugh like that, spontaneously without inhibitions. She hadn't pulled away when he stretched his arm along the back of her seat and rested his hand on her shoulder.

Now, sitting across from him at Greenleaf's, she was once more on guard. He could feel the barrier between them and tried to hide his disappointment.

The restaurant's Thanksgiving buffet was elaborate, more dishes than any one person could possibly sample, and the food was delicious.

At least she felt comfortable enough to eat heartily, he noted with approval.

Outside the restaurant's south wall of glass, beds of yellow chrysanthemums, interspersed with the final glory of white impatiens and bronze zinnias, decked the hotel's parklike grounds. On a park bench, ringed by the flower beds, sat a lifelike sculpture of a young woman, reading a book.

Nina's voice pulled his attention from the view. She was asking him about his family, his childhood in the Oklahoma panhandle.

"My dad was a wheat farmer," he told her, buttering a hot roll.

"What I know about wheat farming, you could put in a thimble."

"You haven't missed a thing. It's back-breaking work, from daylight to dark in the blistering sun, and the wind never stops blowing in the panhandle. If it ever does, people will go nuts from the silence. And the few bent trees that have managed to survive will snap right in two."

She chuckled. "Do your parents still live on the farm?"

He shook his head. "They died in a flash flood several years ago. They'd gone to town for groceries and a sudden rainstorm came up. A downpour. There's never enough rain in western Oklahoma, but when it comes, it comes all at once." He took a bite of turkey and dressing, lost in contemplation for a moment. Then he continued, "They started home. The dirt road to the farm was practically a lake by that time. Their car flipped over and they were both killed."

"I'm sorry," Nina murmured. She reached for her wineglass, took a sip. "You've had a lot of losses in your life."

He picked up his own glass. "Everybody does, I guess. Sooner or later."

"Do you still own the farm?"

He smiled wryly. "No. My brother, Kyle, and I sold it. Dad and Mom loved that godforsaken country, loved farming. But, after spending all our summers helping Dad, Kyle and I couldn't wait to leave for college. We didn't have any sentimental attachment to the land. Believe me, I could happily live the rest of my life without setting eyes on the Oklahoma panhandle again."

"I know what you mean. I've driven through there once or twice. All that space is kind of daunting. Eastern Oklahoma's trees and hills are much more appealing." She set her glass down. "Where's Kyle now?"

"San Diego. He's married and has two daughters. He manages a posh hotel in the old town." He reached for the wine bottle and replenished their glasses. "You said you and your husband lived on a farm," he added, taking the opportunity to find out more about her. "Where was that?"

She shifted restlessly, but answered readily enough. "About sixty miles from Fort Worth. Dan's grandparents left him their house and three hundred acres. The land was mostly pasture. Dan used to visit his grandparents there every summer, and he had always wanted to live in the country and raise beef cattle. So when he inherited the farm, we decided to take the plunge. We managed to make a living only because the land and the house were paid for."

"That's about the only way anyone makes a living on a farm these days." He fingered the stem of his wineglass. "So, how did you end up in Tulsa?"

She concentrated on her plate for a moment. "After I lost Dan and Candi, I couldn't run the cattle operation by myself. The house was a total loss, anyway. But I wouldn't have wanted to stay, even if I could have."

He nodded in mute understanding.

"I really didn't want to move back to Fort Worth, either. I get along with my parents just fine, as long as we aren't living in each other's pockets." She smiled. "My mother's intentions are good, but she's the bossy type. I never did take well to that. We had some rough times when I was a teenager." Sometimes she wondered whether, if she'd been happier at home, she might have waited until she was older to marry Dan. "Anyway, I'd been through Tulsa several times and I always thought it was a pretty city. So I sold the farm and used the money to relocate and pay the bills while I looked for a job.''

''Have you regretted it?''

''Never. Oh, I know it's not wise to make life-changing decisions so soon after—after you've lost a spouse. But my life was changed forever, anyway. I like Tulsa as much as I thought I would. And I love my job.''

''What about your personal life?''

She stared at him. Memories of last night hovered at the edge of conscious thought. Suddenly she could feel his mouth on hers. She cleared her throat. ''I've made some good friends at the hospital.''

''Is that enough for you? Work and friends?''

She had thought so until last night. ''For now.''

Jeff gave her a long, careful look. ''I don't believe you.'' He pushed his empty plate back and rested his elbows on the table, his hands clasped in front of him. ''You're a very desirable woman. You shouldn't be alone.''

Color washed into her face. ''Don't, Jeff,'' she whispered. ''Don't make me sorry I agreed to have dinner with you.''

''Sorry because you want to be alone, or sorry because, down deep, you know I speak the truth?''

She looked at him for a long time, and then she glanced away. ''I've finished eating. If you have, I think I'd like to go home now.'' Methodically she folded her napkin and placed it beside her plate. ''Thank you for a lovely dinner.''

''You can't ignore your feelings—your needs—forever, Nina.'' He reached out and captured her hand, turned it over in his and traced her lifeline with the tip of his finger. He felt her shiver.

She disengaged her hand from his and dropped both hands to her lap. "It's not that simple."

He sat back and considered her. His eyes made a slow, thorough survey of her tense face. She dropped her gaze. "It is if you'll let it be."

The hint of annoyance in his voice registered and she looked up. "I've tried to make my position clear from the start. I'm not ready for a—a relationship."

"Funny. Last night I thought you were quite ready."

She gave him a direct look. "That's not fair. I had a shock last night."

"Well, I had a revelation."

"What are you talking about? What revelation?"

I'm in love with you, Jeff thought. But what he said was, "We'll make love sooner or later."

Nina knew it would be foolish to deny that she was attracted to him—after last night. Equally foolish to allow that attraction to overrule her better judgment. She had loved once, created a child from that love. She had been fulfilled, going through her days blithely, her major concern being how to stretch a tight budget to cover gifts for everyone on her Christmas list.

Then, without any warning, her world had been destroyed. Husband, child, home...all gone, as if they had never been. She still carried the pain, although it wasn't as all-consuming as it had been in the beginning. Time, they had assured her in the support group, would buffer the hurt. And they had been right. If it hadn't gotten easier to bear, it would have killed her before now. She had known she was getting better when she no longer wanted to die just to stop the pain.

And, yes, she was incredibly attracted to Jeff. But she wasn't reckless enough to involve herself emotionally and physically with him. She could come to love him;

she knew that somehow. Love, as she had a reason to know, always brought with it the risk of loss, of more hurt than anyone could imagine. Love was a gamble she wasn't prepared to take.

She said dryly, "You must be very good in front of a jury. You just keep hammering your points home, over and over."

"Whatever works."

"I'll say this for you. When you reach a conclusion," Nina observed, "you don't beat about the bush."

"It seems to me that's what I have been doing for the past three months. Today is the first time we've really gone out together. Lunches in the hospital cafeteria don't count."

"Oh, I see." She tilted her head. "You've decided now is the time for a direct approach. You have it all worked out. Why don't you tell me exactly what you expect to happen next?"

Jeff gave her that irrepressibly impish grin. "A leading question, if I ever heard one."

"I'm merely trying to find out what's going on in your head."

He grew sober. "Whatever it is, I don't want it to take another three months. I'm willing to give you time to get used to the idea of you and me together, to get over your fear of letting another man into your life. But I want to spend time with you, Nina."

For an instant his blunt words made her want to throw up her hands and flee. But to let him know how much he frightened her would be another mistake to add to the one she'd made last night.

She marshaled her defenses and smiled. "I'll tell you what," she decided on impulse. "Lynda has been complaining to everybody in the office about being the only one who ever takes charge of the Care and Share activities. I've decided to volunteer to head the Christmas project. You can be my assistant.''

"That should be exciting," he said, one corner of his mouth tilting in a half smile, "but it wasn't exactly what I had in mind."

"You said you wanted to spend time with me," she told him. "If we work on the Christmas project, we'll have to spend lots of time together. Deal?"

He shot her a look that was both amused and patient. "Deal."

"Can we go now?"

At her door, he kissed her gently on the temple. "Let me come in, Nina."

She was tempted. Perhaps, just this once, she thought. She looked into Jeff's eyes and wondered, what would it be like to make love with him? Remembering his kiss of the night before, she knew that he would be a passionate, demanding lover. The thought sent her scurrying for her better judgment. "I don't think so, Jeff."

He sighed, then with a defeated expression he traced the curve of her eyebrow with one finger. "I won't bite, you know. Not unless you want me to, that is."

Keep it light, she told herself, trying not to respond to his touch. "Good night, Jeff." She fumbled in her purse for her key.

"Wait a minute." He took the key from her fingers and inserted it in the lock. Opening the door with one hand, he curved the other beneath her chin and lowered his mouth to taste hers.

The kiss surprised her as much as the one last night. This was very different from the hot demand of the other. His lips were still possessive, but this kiss was gentler, slower. She could taste the wine he had drunk, feel the twin pressures of the door against her back and his chest on her breasts. Her lips opened under the tender quest of his.

She was drifting, in danger of abandoning the firm moorings that kept her steady and safe. She could not deal with this loss of self. Very carefully she drew her mouth from his. "Jeff," she began, then paused to exhale the pent-up breath from her lungs. He was smiling down at her, his knowing eyes crinkling at the corners. His fingers dropped to the curve of her shoulder to caress it gently. "You enjoy unsettling me, don't you?"

"Yeah," he admitted, "I do."

She looked up at him for a long moment. "Jeff, I'm afraid asking you to assist me with the Christmas project gave you the wrong impression." She was getting her bearings again. Her tone was lighter, more at ease. "I don't envision having any consultations in my bedroom—or yours."

He didn't even skip a beat. "You prefer neutral ground? Good idea. When shall we have our first . . . consultation?"

She tossed back her hair. "I'll let you know Monday at the hospital."

"Terrific." He kissed the tip of her nose. "Sleep well, Nina."

Chapter Four

Lynda was surprised, but grateful, when Nina told her on Monday that she would organize the Christmas Care and Share project. Pleased as she was, however, Lynda looked a bit skeptical. "Are you sure?"

"Yes. I need to keep busy."

"Okay. Great. I have too much to do between now and Christmas. I didn't know how I was going to manage the Christmas project, too." She was a plump, sweet-faced woman full of nervous energy. She would always have "too much to do," regardless of the season. "Of course, if you need my input..." Though she was willing to let Nina head up the project, Lynda couldn't help feeling proprietary.

"I can manage. Jeff will help me."

Lynda's eyebrows shot up. "You've already discussed this with him?"

Nina nodded. "On Thursday." At Lynda's curious look, Nina added, "Since we were both alone on Thanksgiving, we had dinner together."

"I *see*. So you finally decided to give the guy a break. I'm glad. You could do a lot worse than Jeff Eberhart, Nina."

"Oh, please Lynda—" She had known people would jump to conclusions if she saw Jeff socially. "Jeff and I are merely friends."

"Uh-huh," said Lynda doubtfully.

"Honestly. It turns out we have a lot in common. Jeff was married once. His wife died. Did you know that?"

"Sure. Doesn't everybody?"

Nina hadn't, until last Wednesday night. Before then, during all the cafeteria lunches she and Jeff had shared, she hadn't been interested enough to ask him more than superficial questions about himself. She'd been too self-absorbed. Maybe the man in the support group was right; maybe she *had* been guilty of wallowing in self-pity.

"I thought we might choose the Summers family for the project," Nina said. "Even if Jerry finds a job before then, they won't be able to give the children much of a Christmas. What do you think?"

"I think it's a grand idea." Lynda pursed her lips worriedly. "Nina, are you sure you're up to this? You didn't handle Wednesday night all that well."

So Lynda had noticed her reaction to Penny Summers. Nina wondered how many others had. She tilted her head. "What is this? You're the one who's always after me to get out, do things. Now I've decided to take your advice, and you're waffling on me."

Lynda laughed. "I admit it. I have a problem with believing that anybody else can run things as well as I do."

"I've noticed," said Nina dryly. "My mother has the same problem."

Lynda lifted her shoulders. "Okay, you've got the project. Run with it. If I forget myself and try to horn in, tell me to butt out."

"Oh, I will," said Nina sweetly and reached for the telephone. "I'll call Jeff's office right now and set up a meeting."

* * *

The December days, which Nina had expected to drag on and on, seemed to have wings. Along with her own Christmas shopping, organizing the Care and Share project occupied Nina's thoughts and filled her spare hours. After a second meeting with the support group, she didn't have time for a third. But keeping busy made it unnecessary.

She spent several evenings decorating a bushel basket, covering and lining it with a bright red-and-green gingham Christmas print. She sewed a wide lace ruffle around the rim and added several huge red bows.

With Jeff's help she worked out a food assignment sheet and found people willing to supply the items on the list. A group of nurses signed up to buy a tree and decorations. Once the food and tree were taken care of, Nina concentrated on the Christmas present list for the Summers family. Lynda and another woman in the business office volunteered to buy gifts for Becky and Jerry.

For three weeks Nina had talked to Jeff almost daily, and she felt much more relaxed in his presence. He seemed to be trying to give her time to get used to the two of them together, as promised, even if, occasionally, she caught him studying her with such concentration that a shiver skipped up her spine. She wondered what he was thinking when he looked at her like that, then brushed the question aside. She was afraid she *knew* what he was thinking.

On December 20, Nina and Jeff made a date for dinner, to go over the project plans one more time. About an hour before Jeff was due to pick her up, he phoned.

"It's snowing," he said.

"I noticed," Nina told him, peering anxiously out a window at the white flakes swirling in the light of a yard lamp. "Maybe we should cancel dinner and meet tomorrow at the hospital."

"My car has four-wheel drive, so I'm not concerned about driving. But there's no need for both of us to be out in this. Why don't I stop for pizza on my way over."

For three weeks Jeff had allowed her to fend off his suggestions that they meet at her apartment or his townhouse. Though he managed to hide it pretty well, she knew he must have grown increasingly impatient with her. Not only that, she realized, her mind had grown progressively tired of overruling her heart. Besides, she had run out of excuses.

"Okay. I'll make coffee." She thought she heard a relieved expulsion of breath on the other end of the line. Clearly, he had expected her to argue.

She hung up and put the coffee on, then tossed a green salad and set it on the kitchen table with three kinds of dressing. She flipped on the television to catch the weather report. The temperature was dropping rapidly, which meant it would probably get too cold for the snowfall to continue all night.

She decided to light a fire in the living room fireplace. It was the first time she'd used the fireplace since the previous winter, but she was prepared. She loved a wood fire and had bought a rick of cured oak early in the fall. The wood was stacked on her patio, against a wall beneath a wide roof overhang.

She carried in several logs, shivering in the cold. A box beside the fireplace was filled with kindling. As an adolescent at camp she had learned the proper way to build a wood fire and took pride in doing it exactly right. Soon flames licked hungrily at the carefully laid logs.

The apartment was cozy and pleasantly scented with the aroma of burning wood by the time Jeff arrived. He stomped the snow off his boots on the mat outside the door and handed her a giant-sized pizza box. "I had them put everything on it except anchovies," he said.

"Perfect." She didn't like anchovies, either.

While she carried the pizza to the kitchen and poured coffee, Jeff removed his down jacket and gloves and warmed his hands at the fireplace. It was the first time he'd been inside Nina's apartment. Which had to be some kind of milestone, he told himself. He turned his back to the fire to study the room.

It was like Nina, he decided, warm and soft and appealing. There was warmth in the cracking fire, in the yellow and green floral print of the sofa and matching Roman shades and the framed print of a field of daffodils over the sofa. There was feminine softness in the velvety gray carpet, the plump violet and yellow pillows on the sofa and chairs and the Dresden figurines gracing a corner curio cabinet.

The overall effect was extremely appealing to a man who lived with tans and browns. He had never been interested enough to brighten up the color scheme he'd inherited when he leased the townhouse. Although he'd lived there for two years, he had never even gotten around to hanging anything on his walls to break the flat expanses of white.

His townhouse was a place to sleep and keep his clothes, but Nina had turned her apartment into a home. There was even a small pine tree in one corner, decorated with bright ornaments and flickering lights.

"Jeff." She was in the doorway, lovely in a mauve shirtwaist dress, calling him to dinner. He had the odd feeling she'd been standing there for several moments, watching him.

He followed her to the kitchen, which was light and airy with pale oak cabinets, cream-colored floor tiles and flashes of bright colors in canisters and the ceramic molds decorating the wall.

"I see you decided to put up a Christmas tree, after all," he said, sitting down. A few days ago she had still been debating whether it was worth the trouble. He was sure she hadn't had a tree the previous year. He wondered if she realized what a giant step away from the painful memories of her past the tree represented.

"I got it last Saturday," she said, reaching for a triangle of pizza, "after my mother called to tell me they would be in Hawaii for Christmas. She wanted me to go with them. They've become regular gadabouts since Dad retired. I'm happy they're able to do it. They always wanted to travel."

He helped himself to pizza. "Since you got the tree, I assume you turned down your parents' invitation."

"Uh-huh." He watched her take a bite of pizza, then deal with strings of melted cheese by capturing them with the tip of her tongue. He found the gesture peculiarly sensual and arousing. God, she was lovely tonight. The soft mauve of her dress was perfect with her ivory complexion and dark hair and eyes. High color flushed her cheeks, and her eyes held a sparkle he hadn't seen before.

She discovered him watching her and laughed self-consciously. "I always make a mess when I eat pizza."

He grinned. "Is there any other way?" They ate in silence for a moment before he said, "I'm surprised you could resist the chance to bask in the tropical sun for a few days.''

''It wasn't difficult. I'm sure Hawaii's beautiful, but I don't want to spend Christmas there. It wouldn't even seem like Christmas.''

He savored a sip of coffee. ''Can you hear yourself?''

''What?''

''You're really getting into the Christmas spirit, aren't you?''

He was looking at her in that deep, searching way that left her slightly disconcerted. ''I suppose I am. It must be because I've been spending so much time thinking about the Summerses' Christmas.'' And because she'd been spending time with him, she thought. Even though she'd worked at keeping their conversations over the past three weeks on the project, merely being with him had cheered her enormously. Why, the last time she'd driven home after dinner with Jeff, she'd actually caught herself humming a Christmas carol. It's okay to enjoy his company, she told herself, as long as she didn't let things get out of hand.

''Are you going to spend Christmas with your brother's family?'' she asked.

He shook his head. ''Kyle called, but it's not a good time for me to be away. Too many important cases pending at the hospital.'' And, now that he knew she would be in town, he hoped to spend Christmas with her. He would have to be careful how he approached it, though.

She was still too easily unnerved by him. Whenever he touched her or spoke of personal things, she had a difficult time keeping still. She always managed to put a little space between them and start chattering about something inconsequential. But she was finding it harder and harder to keep her defenses intact. He sensed it in the way her voice softened when she said his name and occasionally in the way she looked at him with a dreamy expression. He wondered if she was aware of the precarious grip she had on her self-control.

After they had stuffed themselves with pizza, she said, "Let's take our coffee into the living room. We need to go over the project plans once more."

She refilled both their cups, and he took his to stand in front of the fireplace and gaze into the fire. When he heard her coming, he sat down on the carpet, leaning back against the raised hearth, and set his cup on the nearest table.

She dropped a handful of papers and notes to the floor beside him. Then she set her coffee cup next to his and grabbed two large throw pillows, passing one of them to him. "You'll be more comfortable with this at your back."

She settled beside him, leaning back against the other pillow. She reached for the papers. "Let's see now. We're going in Bob's van again. He's got tire chains, in case we have ice or snow." She ran a pen down one of the pages. "The food's all taken care of." She shuffled through the papers. "And the tree and decorations." More shuffling. "Lynda and Lou are getting gifts for Becky and Jerry Summers. So the only thing left is to find people to buy gifts for the kids."

He reached over and twined a lock of her hair around his finger. "I'll do that."

She looked at him sharply. "All five of them?"

"Sure." He tucked the lock behind her ear.

"Well, uh—"

"Am I making you nervous?"

"No, of course not." She shifted imperceptibly away from him. A slow smile curved his lips. "Why are you smiling?"

"Because you're such a bad liar. Every time I touch you, you get tense and jumpy."

"Jeff—" She dropped her gaze to the papers in her hand. "Er—what was I going to say? Oh, yes, I'll help you."

"Help me make you tense and jumpy? That sounds intriguing."

She looked up quickly at the taunt in his words. "I'll help with the kids' Christmas presents. You know very well what I meant."

His hand went to her throat. Her pulse was beginning to hammer. The feel of it against his palm caused desire to stir in him. "That's good. I can find plenty of things for the boys, but I never know what to get for girls."

"What did you buy for your nieces?"

"I sent Kyle money," he murmured, "and told him to let them pick out something."

With a nervous laugh, she jumped to her feet. "That's terrible. Where's your Christmas spirit?" She crossed to the window and raised one of the Roman shades. In the stream of light from the window, snow-flakes fluttered down. "I think the snow's letting up."

He followed her to the window and wrapped one arm around her waist from behind. She went very still, but did not resist. He wanted her. Standing there he could vividly imagine her slim, sleek body moving under his. He wanted to undress her, to explore the feminine angles and curves and feel the silken softness of her skin. He could not remember ever wanting a woman as much before.

"You smell of gardenias," he murmured into her hair. His voice brushed her skin as gently as his fingers.

"It's—a new cologne." Her voice was unsteady, and that frightened her.

"You wore it for me?"

"No," she lied, "I always wear cologne."

Gently he turned her to face him. "Nina, how long are you going to keep me at arm's length?"

She dropped her eyes. "I told you from the start—"

He took her chin and tilted her face. She closed her eyes against the honesty in his. "I want you, Nina."

Reluctantly she met his gaze. "Yes, I know you do, Jeff."

"We've already discovered that you want me, too. How long are your going to fight it?"

Shaking her head, she pulled away from him. "I don't know. I just know that right now I can't—well—"

"Make love with me."

"Yes," she said quietly. "I really can't." Turning, she stared out the window.

"You feel guilty because you want me."

Her only response was a lift of her shoulders.

"Do you see it as some kind of betrayal of your husband, of his memory?"

"That's part of the problem, I guess," she whispered.

"Nina, that's totally irrational."

"I know."

"You said that's part of the problem. What's the other part?"

I will fall hopelessly in love with you, she thought. The knowledge terrified her. If she let herself love him, and then she lost him... She couldn't bear the pain. Not again. He touched her shoulder and her muscles tensed. How long, she wondered, would she have the strength to deny him? To deny herself? Maybe, she thought crazily, if she made love with him, she would get him out of her system. But she knew that was nonsense. On the contrary, if she made love with Jeff, he would be in her blood and her heart. She would never be free of him.

"I don't think you'd understand."

"Try me."

"Jeff," she said quietly, "I am still learning to make a life for myself, alone. It may not be exciting, but it's satisfying. Tranquil. I have learned to value tranquillity."

"You're afraid of being hurt again?"

She heard the surprise in his voice and laid her forehead against the cold windowpane. "Oh, God, yes."

He bent and brushed his lips across her cheek. "I will never let that happen."

Her body ached for him. "You can't promise that. No one can." Her voice thickened. "Life is capricious." Jeff turned her toward him and folded her in his arms. She could feel her will giving way. "Please, don't."

He held her a little away from him and studied her intently, frowning. "All right, life isn't fair. But what is the alternative? To stop living?"

Tears began trickling down her face, and she couldn't stop them. She was losing control. "Don't you see, Jeff, if I let you in, it wouldn't be enough. I would want more." Home. Children. Oh, God, she couldn't even let herself think about it.

"Please, don't cry." Tenderly he kissed away the salty tears that had spilled down her cheeks. Then he looked down at her and drew a long breath. "I love you, Nina."

She stared at him with dark, stunned eyes. No, oh, no... Being loved was a huge responsibility. She couldn't cope with it. "Don't say that," she whispered.

He muttered an oath. "I couldn't have picked a worse time to get into this, could I? I didn't say it to get you in bed. My love doesn't obligate you to give me anything in return."

The bleakness in his eyes was almost more than she could stand. "I never thought you had an ulterior motive, but I can't handle this right now." She took a shaky breath. With a reluctance he doubted she was aware of, she stepped away from him.

"Nina?"

"I don't think we should talk anymore tonight."

He wanted to touch her again, to hold her, but the pleading expression in her eyes stopped him. He didn't want to tear away her last defense before she was ready. He didn't want to cause her any more pain. He just didn't know how much longer he could stand keeping his hands off her.

"All right."

"Thank you, Jeff." It cost her a great deal to look into his eyes. It cost her even more to hold his unhappy gaze and not relent.

He picked up his coat and gloves, put them on. "We have to shop for Christmas toys. Will tomorrow evening be okay?"

"Yes, fine."

"Shall I pick you up about seven?"

She nodded and managed to hold a smile on her face until the door closed behind him.

Chapter Five

South Tulsa's Woodland Hills Mall, the next evening, was filled with a mad crush of shoppers, searching for the perfect gifts to complete their Christmas buying. Many of the shoppers looked harried, and their patience was definitely wearing thin.

Nina was watching the children, lined up to talk to Santa in the center court of the mall. Parents were coaxing several of the smaller ones, who were wary of the red-suited stranger with the white beard.

"Don't you want your picture taken with Santa?" a bedraggled young woman asked a chunky two-year-old.

The little boy stuck out his bottom lip and stomped his foot. "No!"

You might as well give up on it this year, Nina thought with amusement. Just then Jeff grabbed her arm and pulled her from the path of a large, determined-looking woman carrying so many packages she could barely see over them.

"She would have plowed right through you," Jeff explained as he steadied her.

Nina laughed. "Thanks for noticing. I was watching the children."

Jeff took her hand. "Let's see if we can get through this mob." He began weaving a zigzag path through the shoppers, pulling Nina along behind him.

She was breathless by the time they reached the crowded toy store. "We must have set some kind of record, getting here," she told him. "Have you always been so aggressive?"

He grinned. "I noticed early in life that those who hang back often get trampled on."

She tilted her head, returning his grin. "You would have made a great professional hockey player."

"I thought about it. Problem was I never got to practice. There were no teams in the panhandle."

"So you decided to work out your aggression in a courtroom."

"Yeah. You aren't nearly as apt to come out of a fight with broken bones."

An elderly gentleman, wearing a blue stocking cap pulled down to his eyebrows, stopped in front of them, scowled and cleared his throat portentously.

"Good evening, sir," Jeff said. The man stared at him expectantly. "Do I know you?" Jeff asked.

"Never saw you before in my life, young man. You're standing in front of the G.I. Joes."

"Oops, sorry."

Nina stifled a giggle as they moved down an aisle between floor-to-ceiling walls of toys.

"Trucks are always good," Jeff said, stopping in front of a display of miniature pickups, vans and dump trucks.

Nina stooped to examine the display on the bottom shelf. "Look at these fire engines. Aren't they wonderful?"

He squatted beside her and picked up a bright red engine to examine it. It sported a whistle, ladder and fire hose. "The tank really holds water, too. We could get these for the two younger boys. What do you think?"

"I think they'll be thrilled."

Jeff grabbed two boxed engines and tucked them under his arm. "Now for the older boys," he said.

"Let's look in the electronics section."

Fifteen minutes later they had chosen a portable radio with earphones and a space-ranger game for the two older boys. Adding the two boxes to the stack, Jeff asked, "Do you have any ideas for Penny?"

"I've got my eye on that doll over there," Nina told him. When they had worked their way to the near-life-size newborn baby doll, they discovered that a small trunk containing a layette came with it. "This is perfect," Nina exclaimed.

Excusing themselves again and again, they finally arrived at the line of people waiting to be checked out. When they reached the cash register, a young man rang up their purchases while a grandmotherly woman bagged them.

"How many are you buying for?" the woman asked.

"Five," Nina told her.

"It looks like your children are pretty close together in age," the woman said.

"Oh, no—" Nina started to explain.

Jeff interrupted her. "Yes, ma'am. The twins are four and the triplets are two."

The woman's wide eyes rested on Nina. "Oh, you poor thing. I hope he helps you." Indicating Jeff.

"My, yes, he's a big help," Nina said, smiling sweetly at Jeff and handing him money for half the bill. "Pay the man, dear."

Jeff took the sack full of toys. "The devil made me do it," he said as they left the store with their purchases.

"You're full of the devil, all right," Nina agreed, taking his arm.

When they reached her apartment, he insisted on coming in and helping wrap the presents. As it turned out, Jeff's help consisted of filling out the name tags and holding a finger against the ribbons while she secured the bows.

Nina set the wrapped packages beneath her tree. They would take the Summerses' tree, gifts and food to them on Christmas Eve. Sitting back on her heels, Nina admired their handiwork. "They look fabulous, if I do say so myself."

Jeff cleared his throat. "So do you."

She glanced around and flushed when she met his intrigued gaze. She hadn't realized he was so close. "Hmmmm?"

"You're beautiful."

The wind had been blowing all evening, and she hadn't combed her hair since they came inside. Aware of her mussed locks and the fact that she'd chewed off her lipstick hours ago, Nina chuckled. "How can you say that with a straight face?" She raked a hand through her tangled curls. "Look at me."

Her soft laughter sent ripples of heat through him. He reached for her, his hands cupping her face. "That's what I'm doing." When he lowered his head, she tilted hers, meeting him halfway. Her lips were soft and sweetly responsive. At first only their mouths touched, but after several moments, he grasped her shoulders. Soon her breath was as ragged as his. That and the way her body melted against his told him more than she realized.

For a while his mouth was enough to satisfy her slowly awakening hunger. His heart beat against hers, hard and fast, telling her that his own hunger was escalating. It would be so easy to draw him down on the floor, to feel his skin against hers, to know finally the release of making love with him. But no—she had already decided she couldn't let things go that far. Yet she couldn't stop herself from imagining.

His lips wandered to the curve of her cheek, then on to her temple. "I love touching you, Nina. I want to touch you everywhere." His mouth came back to hers, hot and possessive. Her heartbeat thundered in her ears.

When he lifted his head, she made a soft, protesting sound. Her eyelids fluttered open and she gazed at him with bemused eyes. His own eyes were glazed by desire. He ran a thumb over her kiss-swollen bottom lip. "Come to bed with me, love," he muttered.

It would have been so easy to say yes. For endless moments she teetered on the edge of saying it. She wanted him with shocking strength. It almost overwhelmed her. What was happening to her? She was thinking things, feeling things that a few weeks ago she would have said were impossible. Now, nothing seemed impossible.

Her gaze drifted slowly down to his mouth, then flashed back up. Alarm flared in her eyes. She moved her shoulders and said over the pounding of her heart, "I don't think . . . no, I'm not ready for this."

He brushed a knuckle over her cheek. "When?"

She stared at him. You can never go to bed with him, her mind insisted. You don't want him to make love to you, to possess your body the way he has begun to possess your mind. But the words that came were "I—I don't know."

His hands were firm on her shoulders. The stark need in his eyes frightened her because she knew it was mirrored in her own. "You want me this very minute."

It would have been absurd to deny it. Nina took a deep breath. "Yes, but I don't like wanting you. It scares me." She let her breath out again. "I think you'd better go."

She saw the flash of temper in his eyes. A muscle in his jaw clenched. "I won't wait indefinitely, Nina," he said quietly. He stood, stuck his hands in his pockets, as though it were the only way he could keep them off her, and looked down at her.

She didn't like ultimatums. "Maybe you should find someone else," she said flaring.

He reached for his jacket. "I don't want anyone else. But I'm not going to take much more of your games, either."

"Games!" Angrily she got to her feet and faced him. *"Games!"*

He shrugged on his jacket, zipped it up. "All this maneuvering, when we both know what's going to happen in the end."

Nina narrowed her eyes. "Oh, really—"

Unperturbed, he pulled on his gloves. "We'll settle this Friday night." Friday was Christmas Eve. "I'll pick you up at six-thirty to go to the Summerses' house."

The door swung shut behind him before she could think of a suitable reply. How dare he tell her what she would do and when she would do it. How dare he speak to her like that!

But hadn't she known that his patience wouldn't last forever? Hadn't she known that he would force her to face her feelings sooner or later?

She stared at the closed door, already fearful about Friday night. She couldn't allow herself to need anyone again. But could she go back to being totally alone, as she'd been before Thanksgiving?

Chapter Six

Jeff went shopping alone for Nina's gift. At the jewelry store he stood for a long time in front of a display of engagement rings. One large diamond solitaire in particular took his eyes. It would look wonderful on Nina's left hand.

But he'd already pushed his luck as far as he dared for now. Ever since he'd left Nina's apartment, after wrapping the toys for the Summers children, he'd been asking himself if he'd gone too far, telling her they'd settle everything on Christmas Eve. He thought then that he'd given her enough time to adjust to a new relationship, but now he wondered if he'd been a bit premature.

Since that night she had been slightly cool when they ran into each other at the hospital. There had been no hint of the passionate woman he'd held in his arms. She was intent on keeping him at a distance. While being frustrated by her reaction, he had given her the space she seemed to need. Forcing the issue was dangerous, he knew, but his patience had about reached its limit.

No matter how many masks she wore, he told himself as he turned away from the rings and moved on to the pendants, she wasn't indifferent. As chilly as she appeared, she couldn't change the way she responded to him. She wanted him, and no matter how many times she denied it, the want overcame every other emotion when she was in his arms. Perhaps he would have to settle for that for now. But she would have to deal with her feelings, too.

Tomorrow was Christmas Eve.

"May I help you, sir?"

"Yes," he said as he shook off his thoughts to concentrate on the present task. "Let me see that diamond pendant."

How am I going to get through this evening? Nina wondered. Today was Christmas Eve. As she pulled up the past-due accounts on her computer, she thought back to the time before she married Dan. They had known each other since junior high, had been high school sweethearts. She had never seriously dated anyone else. She was nineteen when she had married Dan, and the wedding had been merely the next logical step in their relationship. The most natural thing in the world.

Oh, she had had some misgivings about dropping out of college, but Dan had already left to take a job. He had never liked school as much as she. Not that he had been crazy about his job for the next five years, either. She had been as glad as he that he could leave the job when he inherited the farm. She had been pregnant by then, and both agreed the country was the perfect place to raise a family.

There had been a junior college in a nearby town, and she'd entertained thoughts of taking a few courses. But she had never got as far as mentioning it to Dan—there was never enough money. So she had buried the vague yearnings that had given rise to thoughts of returning to college and concentrated on Dan and Candi and the farm.

Funny, now that she lived in a city with several colleges and universities, she had no burning desire to enroll. Not now, anyway. At the moment she was fully occupied with the challenges of her job. And Jeff.

Face it, she told herself, as she typed the Print demand for past-due notices, Jeff was the real challenge. Rather, her feelings for Jeff were.

As the printer beside her desk began spitting out notices, she reached absently for a pencil and the To Do list she had made upon arriving in the office that morning. She began checking off the items on the list. When she came to "meet Jeff at apartment, six-thirty," she pressed down hard on the pencil and snapped off the point.

She had been tempted to phone Jeff's office and say she'd meet him in the hospital parking lot. She had spent the better part of the morning arguing back and forth with herself about it. Several of her co-workers had noticed and commented that she seemed distracted. Sure it was Christmas Eve, and they were all working frantically so they could leave work early, Lynda had said, but Nina acted worried. Was it the Care and Share project?

No, Nina assured her. Everything was on track. She had gone back to thinking about calling Jeff's office. Finally she had admitted that preventing Jeff's coming to her apartment to pick her up and take her home tonight would do nothing but postpone the inevitable. No matter what she did, Jeff would be there, confusing her, keeping her in a turmoil of desires and fears. Even when he wasn't physically present.

Yesterday, after much debating with herself, she had gone out and bought him a Christmas present. A soft leather wallet and matching zippered tie case for traveling. A nice, impersonal gift, she'd told herself.

But she couldn't stop thinking about Jeff in a way that was far from impersonal. She would catch sight of him in a hallway or the cafeteria or someone would mention his name. Then she would remember the first time he kissed her and the challenge he'd issued: *You want me as much as I want you.* Thanksgiving dinner, the meetings about the Christmas project, talking and laughing together, shopping for toys. The way he had kissed her afterward. *I love you, Nina.* How desperately she had wanted him.

She'd just been getting her life together, making it neat and orderly, with nobody to please but herself, she thought as she began tearing apart the perforated computer-generated past-due notices and stacking them on her desk.

Then Jeff had grown tired of hanging around the edges of her life and barged inside, past her defenses. Upsetting the order of her days. Issuing ultimatums. *We'll settle this Friday night.* Nina closed her eyes on a sigh of frustration. How had she ever allowed him to make himself so at home in all the nooks and crannies of her existence? In her thoughts?

She had even caught herself several times, thinking about marriage and children—when she had been sure such things could not be in her future. She had told him that in so many words. What sort of man refused to accept a woman's simple statement of fact and accused her of playing games? A stubborn one, Nina decided, then caught her bottom lip between her teeth. Or one who saw beneath her words to her confused and lonely heart.

Nina stared down at the stack of notices, seeing instead Jeff's blue eyes. Abruptly she rose and went to the records room for computer labels and envelopes. The solution to her dilemma was simple, she told herself. All she had to do when Jeff took her home tonight was send him away for good.

Then she would be alone, effectively protected from the risk of hurt and loss. And love. And children. Her heart contracted painfully. Clutching a box of computer labels, she leaned against a file cabinet to steady herself. She thought of Jerry and Becky Summers, deprived of many material things, but they had each other and their children.

How she envied the Summerses their children. Making a living on the farm had been so precarious that she and Dan had decided they couldn't afford a second child. But Jeff was a well-established attorney with a secure position as hospital counsel. If she and Jeff married, they could have several children.

Stop this, Nina, she told herself sternly. Stop this silly adolescent fantasizing. Jeff hadn't once said the word marriage. But she knew that Jeff never did anything halfway, and he had said he loved her.

Sighing, she touched her fingers to her lips, the lips that Jeff had kissed. Sometimes with exquisite tenderness, at other times with hunger and possession. Remembering, she felt a warm weakness in the pit of her stomach. She had convinced herself that, no matter what Jeff said or did, she was in control of the situation. As long as she didn't make love with Jeff, she was in no danger of falling in love with him.

Had she been deceiving herself?

Spits of snow peppered Nina as she hurried across the parking lot to her car in mid-afternoon. By the time she reached her apartment, the white specks had turned to big flakes that fell in earnest. Fortunately she had already bought the makings for Christmas dinner, including a small turkey. And tonight she wouldn't have to drive.

When she had planned Christmas dinner, she'd intended to invite Jeff; but as yet she hadn't spoken of it to him. She would wait and see how the evening went. After tonight he might never want to see her again. If she sent him away.

If?

Think about something else, she told herself as she turned up the furnace thermostat. Chilled, she rubbed her hands up and down her arms. A hot bath would warm her, she thought, and there was plenty of time.

In the bathroom she turned on the tap and added a generous amount of gardenia-scented bubbling bath oil. She undressed quickly. With a sigh of pleasure, she slid down in the tub until the bubbles caressed her shoulders. Resting her head against the rim of the tub, she closed her eyes. Warmth embraced and relaxed her.

She languished in the tub until the water cooled, then dressed warmly in boots, jeans and a bulky red sweater. There was still an hour before Jeff was due to pick her up, so she made coffee and took a mug and two shopping bags into the living room. Putting the Summers children's presents in one sack, she placed them beside the front door. She was grateful that she'd planned enough ahead to drop off the Christmas basket that she'd worked so hard on to the volunteers who were bringing the food.

Crossing to the fireplace, she contemplated the logs and kindling, laid and ready for a match. More logs rested on top of the kindling in the box beside the fireplace. Glad that she'd had the forethought to make the preparations, she imagined curling up in front of a fire tonight, after returning from the Summerses'. With Jeff?

She brushed the question aside and went to the closet for her thick down jacket. Taking it out, she tossed it on the couch. Then she paced restlessly through the apartment, carrying her coffee mug. After the way she'd avoided Jeff the past few days, things might be a bit awkward when he arrived. She wanted to get it over with.

To her vast relief, he made the first moments easy for her. When he stepped inside, he was grinning. "I love a white Christmas," he said, touching her lightly with his gloved hand. The contact was fleeting and unthreatening, but somehow it closed the gap that her recent coolness had opened between them.

She took a deep breath and let it out slowly. She was going to enjoy the evening, after all. "Me, too. I'm really glad I'm not in Hawaii, missing it."

"So am I." He had moved to the couch and, picking up her jacket, held it out for her. She slid her arms into the sleeves, and he pulled the jacket close around her neck. His hands lingered there for an instant before dropping away. "Ready?"

"Uh-huh." She picked up one of the shopping bags. "Grab the other sack, would you?"

He swung the bag up with one hand and reached around her to open the door with the other. They waded through already ankle-deep snow to Jeff's car. They set the bags in the back seat and got in. Jeff settled behind the wheel. Turning to her with a smile, he brushed gloved hands over her curls. "You have snow in your hair."

She laughed and shook her head to dislodge any lingering flakes. "Something tells me I'll have more before this evening is over. It doesn't show any signs of letting up, does it?"

"Nope," he said cheerfully and started the engine. He backed out of her driveway and headed slowly down the street. "I got another present for the Summers kids this afternoon. It's in the trunk."

"What is it?"

"A sled."

Nina clasped her hands in delight. "Oh, Jeff, how wonderful. They have a hill at the end of their block, too. They'll be so excited about sledding they probably won't sleep tonight."

"No kid sleeps much the night before Christmas."

She settled back and murmured contentedly, "Yeah, I remember. I used to lie awake and listen to every sound in the house, determined to get a glimpse of Santa. Somehow I always fell asleep before my folks got up to put out my presents."

"How old were you when you discovered it wasn't Santa who brought the loot?"

She smiled. "I can't remember exactly. But I knew Santa wasn't real for at least two years before I told my parents. I loved leaving cookies for him and getting up Christmas morning to find the plate empty and my presents beneath the tree. I didn't want to change the ritual. Later I still got the presents from Mom and Dad, of course, but it wasn't quite the same."

Jeff chuckled. "Kyle is four years older than I, and when we were kids he loved to torment me. Typical older brother. He took devilish delight in shattering my belief in Santa when I was four."

"Four is too young to be so disillusioned," Nina sympathized.

"I thought so, too. It was years before I forgave him."

"Well, at least you had a brother. I always regretted being an only child. I used to want four children."

He looked over at her, wondering if she was aware of the wistfulness in the words. "Don't you still?"

She glanced at him warily. "It's not something I think about anymore."

Jeff didn't believe her but, wisely, he kept it to himself. This wasn't the time to get into such a serious subject. "The only time I envy Kyle is when I'm around his family," he said offhandedly. "I'll have a house full of kids someday."

Nina studied him, searching for a hint of hidden meaning in his face. "You really believe that, don't you?"

"Yep." He reached for her hand. "At Christmastime, anything is possible."

Nina let the subject drop, thinking that the conversation was getting a bit unsettling. "Aren't we riding with the others?" she asked as they passed the entrance to the hospital parking lot.

"We can't all fit into the van. More people are going than last time. I told Bob I'd take my car. The nurses went in another vehicle, too. They planned to get there before the rest of us to set up the tree."

"I hope we can all squeeze into the Summerses' house."

"We'll manage."

The van and a four-wheel-drive vehicle were already parked beside the small house when they arrived. Nina carried one sack of presents. Jeff carried the other and the sled, which he left on the porch, propped against the house.

Warm greetings welcomed Nina and Jeff as Becky Summers ushered them inside. Lynda assessed them. "Another five minutes, and we'd have sent out a St. Bernard."

Nina laughed at Lynda's hands-on-hips stance. "Cluck, cluck, mother hen."

"I told you we'd make it by seven, and it's barely that now," Jeff said as he shrugged off his jacket. "Have you no faith, Mama Westin?"

"Lynda thinks everybody should be early for appointments," Bob said, "just because she is."

"It's called compulsive behavior, Bob," said one of the nurses.

"Thank you very much for the free psychological profile," Lynda sniffed. But after a moment she joined in the general laughter.

The five Summers children were hovering over a box containing tree decorations. Penny looked up at Nina with a shy smile that melted Nina's heart. She knelt beside the little girl. She was relieved to realize that, except for the long blond hair, Penny didn't really look anything like Candi. Nina had had a few misgivings about seeing Penny again, but it was going to be all right. "I'll bet you're eager to start decorating the tree."

Penny nodded, her eyes alight with excitement.

"Mom said we had to wait till everybody got here," one of Penny's brothers said.

"Well, everybody's here now. Why don't you start?" Nina suggested.

"Can we?" asked Penny of her mother, who had come up behind them.

Becky knelt next to Nina. "You bet. In a few minutes I'll go fix hot chocolate for everybody." Becky was much more animated than she had been on their earlier visit, Nina noted.

"How are you doing?" Nina asked her.

"Just fine," Becky said. "Jerry—wait, I'll let him tell it." She waved to her husband, who was returning from the kitchen after putting away the food from the Christmas basket. Becky raised her voice. "Listen, everybody. Jerry has an announcement to make. Go ahead, honey."

Jerry scratched his beard and a grin split his gaunt face. "Starting January second, I'll be gainfully employed again."

Spontaneous applause broke out. When it had died down, Becky said, "He's going to be working at Woodland Hills."

"The mall?" Bob asked.

Jerry nodded. "I'll be a security guard."

"He gets to wear a uniform and everything," said the oldest Summers boy proudly.

"And we get to visit him at the mall sometime," said another.

Nina gave Becky Summers a spontaneous hug. "I'm so happy for you."

Becky hugged her back. "Thank you." She pulled back and her eyes misted. "We'll never forget what you people have done for us while Jerry was out of work."

"We should thank you," Nina told her. "When you're able to give something to someone who needs it, you get as much joy from it as the recipient."

Becky nodded. "I never really thought about that before Jerry lost his job. But after this Christmas I'll never again be able to pass by that Salvation Army tree at the mall without taking down a card and buying a present for the one whose name is on it." She got to her feet. "I'd better go make that hot chocolate now."

The children were hanging ornaments on the tree. One of the boys paused to peer into the sacks Nina and Jeff had brought. "This package has my name on it."

"It sure does," Nina said. "There's one for each of you. We'll put them under the tree when you finish decorating it."

Penny lifted from the box a large silver star. A circular niche in the center of the star held a small angel complete with white gown and wings. Penny laughed in delight. "Look." She held the star for Nina to see.

"That goes on top. Shall I hold you up so you can reach it?"

"Oh, yes." Nina lifted the child. She smelled of floral-scented soap. Her long hair brushed Nina's face as she raised the star to set it on the topmost branch.

"It's beautiful," Nina said, oddly reluctant to set the little girl down.

Penny twisted around to face her and, with the quicksilver change of thought typical of four-year-olds, asked, "What's your name?"

"Nina."

"That's pretty," said Penny gravely.

Nina kissed the tip of her nose. "So's Penny." She set her down and Penny ran back to the box for another decoration. Over the child's head, Nina noticed Jeff, watching her. His eyes were full of some strong emotion as he smiled at her.

She responded with a smile of her own and bent to help Penny pull a sack of red satin balls from the box. From the corner of her eye she saw Jeff walk across the room and speak to Jerry Summers.

Finally the box that had held the decorations was empty, and presents had been arranged beneath the tree. "Get ready, everybody," Bob said. "I'm going to plug in the tree lights. Lynda, flip off the overhead light."

Soft oohs and ahhs filled the room as red, blue, green and gold lights flicked on all over the tree. Nina was standing next to Penny, and Jeff came up behind her, put his hands on her shoulders. She leaned back against him, and Penny reached for Nina's hand.

"Oooo, it's so bootiful," the little girl whispered.

"Yes, it is," Nina said, blinking back an errant tear. Jeff's arms came around her and tightened.

Chapter Seven

They sat wherever they could find a spot in the blinking multicolored light from the Christmas tree. They sipped hot chocolate and sang carols.

Nina and Jeff occupied the corner between the couch and chair. When the singing started, Penny wandered around the room peering at faces, until she found Nina. "I want to sit with you," she said.

Nina made room for the little girl on her lap. As her arms went around the small, warm body, a wave of longing strangely mixed with happiness engulfed Nina. A woman's arms were made for this, she thought. To shelter a sweet, trusting child. As though Jeff knew what she was feeling, he put his arm around her and settled her, Penny and all, against his shoulder.

Twisting on Nina's lap, Penny whispered in Nina's ear, "Do you know what's in my present?"

Nina hugged her. "Yes."

"What?"

"I can't tell you. It's against the rules."

"Oh." Penny sighed. "I guess I'll have to wait till tomorrow to find out."

"I guess you will."

Somebody started "Silent Night." Penny sighed and snuggled against Nina. "You know what?"

"What?" Nina asked.

"This is the bestest Christmas ever."

Jeff chuckled and bent to brush his lips across Nina's cheek. She smiled up at him, glad that the room was so dimly lighted, for her eyes had filled with tears.

Driving back to her apartment, Jeff said, "I told Jerry about the sled. After the kids are asleep, he's going to put it under the tree. As a gift from Santa."

"I wish I could see Penny's eyes when she sees that doll," Nina murmured.

Jeff reached for her hand. "Penny really took up with you tonight."

"And I loved every minute of it," Nina admitted.

"The maternal instinct," Jeff mused. "You'll be a wonderful mother."

For an instant, sadness dimmed the contentment she'd been feeling. She shrugged it off. "Was," she corrected.

He squeezed her hand. "Will be," he said.

Wordlessly she pulled her jacket more tightly around her. Deep inside she began to tremble.

They drove the rest of the way in silence. At her apartment Jeff's car crept into the driveway through a deepening drift of snow. By the time they reached the door, wet snow had spilled over the tops of Nina's boots.

"It's good to be home," she said, stepping inside. She went straight to the hearth and lit the fire. Then she sat on the carpet to pull off her boots and wet socks. Holding her feet near the fire, she shrugged off her jacket. "Ahh, that feels wonderful."

Watching her, Jeff drew a small red-and-gold-wrapped package from his pocket and removed his jacket. He went to sit on the floor beside her. "This is for you."

With a widening of her dark eyes, she accepted the package. "Oh, Jeff..."

"Open it."

"Wait. I have one for you, too." She rose, padded to the tree and came back with his gift. Simultaneously they tore into the wrappings.

Nina gasped as she lifted from the box an oval-shaped diamond pendant on a slender gold chain. "It's beautiful! Oh, Jeff, you shouldn't have. It's too much."

"Not as much as I wanted to give you," he said quietly as he examined his wallet and tie holder.

"But your gift is so much more than mine. I feel—" She faltered to a stop as his intense eyes caught hers and held.

"I don't care about the gift," he said gravely. "All that matters is that it's from you. Not that I don't like it. I do, very much. Thank you, Nina."

Suddenly flustered, she handed him the pendant and, turning around, lifted her hair. "Will you put it on for me?"

Gently he dealt with the chain's fastener. Then his hands cupped her shoulders, squeezed convulsively. "You're trembling," he murmured. Frowning, he turned her to face him. "Are you all right?"

"I'm afraid," she said simply, honestly.

"Of me?"

"Yes, and of myself. Of my feelings. They're so confused."

He caressed her flushed cheek. "I know I said we'd settle things tonight, but if you need more time..."

Her quick no surprised even Nina. "I don't think more time will help," she went on. Hesitantly, as though feeling her way through darkness down an unfamiliar, unmarked road, her arms crept around his neck. "It's just that I thought... I mean, after Dan and Candi died, I never—'' She drew a shaky breath. ''Well, I never expected to need anyone, ever again.''

''I felt that way for a while, too. Then I met you.'' Already his mouth was seeking hers. ''They're gone, honey, and I'm here. We're here. I love you. I—''

All Nina's doubts crumbled. She silenced him with a deep, desperate kiss. She could not fight him any longer, couldn't fight herself. She didn't know how or when it had happened, but in that moment she knew that she was in love with him.

Moments later he lifted his head to look at her with love-filled eyes. ''Nina, are you sure?''

''Shh.'' She pressed two fingers against his lips, then pulled his mouth back to hers. ''Just love me, Jeff. Please.''

Then there was nothing but the taste of his mouth. Wrapping her arms more tightly around him, she responded to the heightened demand of his kiss with long-denied hunger. Lips, teeth, tongues. Tastes and textures brought shuddering arousal so quickly that it stunned them both.

Jeff held tightly to his wildly escalating passion, wanting to move slowly, to savor every taste and touch, to make it last. *Finally,* she wasn't pushing him away, and he wanted to savor every second. For long moments he contented himself with her mouth. Her lips were softly yielding under his, even as her breathing speeded up and her fingers clutched his shirt. Desire pushed at him. God, how he wanted her, wanted... everything. But he touched only her lips, reveling in the sweet taste and mesmerizing texture of her mouth.

Moaning softly, Nina pulled her lips from his to roam his face. She had spent so many hours thinking about him, remembering the way his eyes crinkled at the corners, his smile, the line of his jaw. She had memorized each angle, crease and slope. His face was forever engraved in her memory. Years from now she would be able to close her eyes and call up every detail, exactly as it was tonight.

Her fingers slid inside his collar and undid a button, then moved down to loosen another and another. Parting his shirt, she kissed the damp skin of his neck and shoulders, savoring the faintly salty taste on the tip of her tongue.

Then she spread both palms against his hair-roughened chest and felt a deep shudder run through him. She brought her mouth hungrily back to his.

Her hands blazed a burning path over his naked skin. Her yielding mouth and exploring tongue made him feel drunk. His head swam and his labored breathing hurt his chest. Now her mouth was no longer enough. He wanted to touch her everywhere, to feel her naked flesh against his. Shifting, he drew her down onto the carpet, her body lying across his. Groaning, he cradled her head in his hands and buried his face against her neck. His lips tasted her throat and his nostrils drew in her scent.

Shifting her off him, he settled her on her back on the carpet and gazed down at her. Her eyes were huge and dark with emotion as she murmured his name. His fingers shook as he unbuttoned her sweater and slid it down over her shoulders. The tremor in his hands increased as he tried to loosen her bra.

She gave him a lazy smile and helped him dispose of the bra, then gasped as his fingers trailed over her exposed skin. His thumbs brushed her nipples, bringing them to instant erectness. She cried out, an incoherent sound of desperation, and pulled at the waistband of his jeans.

Somehow they rid themselves of the rest of their clothing. Nina reached out for him, dragging him closer. Her mouth, open and hungry, came to his while her hands roamed, restless and frantic, over his bare back and hips. His body covered hers and he crushed her mouth with his as he took her moan into his own body.

Nina moved beneath him, but he held her still with his body, trying to keep his passion in check. But her desperate hands on his skin were shattering his control. He couldn't hold back any longer. Rolling over, he lay on his side, facing her. He felt the heat from the wood fire on his back and the heat from his pounding blood in his veins. Her dazed eyes fluttered open. His mouth crushed hers as he slid his hand between her legs to find the warm, moist center of her desire.

Nina writhed against him, moaning, aroused beyond belief by the lazy movement of his fingers. With incredible swiftness, he brought her to a shuddering crest. And then he moved atop her, taking her higher.

He took her swiftly, with a passion so intense it threatened to tear him apart. She gave without restraint. She was his at long last. Totally his. Her body knew this, even if her mind hadn't yet accepted it.

A long time later she stirred and sat up. Smiling, she traced the arch of a dark brow with the tip of her finger. His hand captured hers. Without opening his eyes, he muttered, ''I guess it's time for me to go home.''

''I think we're snowed in.''

He smiled. "Good."

"We might as well be comfortable, don't you think? Come with me."

She led him to the bedroom. With the warm comforter all around them, he pulled her to him. This time the loving was quiet, slow, exquisitely tender.

Afterward, Nina lay awake. He slept, his body warm against hers. She kept very still, not wanting to disturb him. Remembering all the nights she had occupied the bed alone, she marveled at how right it felt to share it with him. And she hadn't even told him that she loved him.

Tomorrow, she thought, as she drifted slowly into sleep.

Chapter Eight

Outside the bedroom window, the trackless white landscape seemed to stretch on forever. Jeff shut his eyes against the blinding whiteness and, mumbling contentedly, reached for Nina. His arm closed on nothing but rumpled sheets. He turned over on his back, stretched and squinted another look out at the winter wonderland beyond the window. He smelled coffee and heard sounds from the kitchen.

He lay there for several moments, feeling a rare contentment and enjoying the domesticity of it all. But the scent of coffee was too tantalizing to stay there any longer. Climbing out of bed, he noticed his clothes, neatly folded, on a table beneath the window.

He showered and shaved, using a bar of soap and a disposable razor he found in the medicine cabinet. Then he dressed quickly and followed his nose to the coffee-pot.

Nina was maneuvering a plump, uncooked turkey into a brown paper grocery sack. In a white terry cloth robe, the tip of her tongue held between her teeth, she was so focused on her task she didn't hear him enter the kitchen.

"I know there has to be a logical explanation for that," he said.

She gave a startled laugh. "It's a trick my mother taught me. If you want a perfectly browned turkey, you bake it in a grocery bag."

Soft color suffused her face as she met his look. He took advantage of her upturned mouth to kiss it. "Merry Christmas."

"Merry Christmas to you, too."

He poured himself a cup of coffee and leaned against the cabinet. He didn't think he would ever grow tired of watching her. After putting the turkey in the oven, she took down a large bowl and began crumbling dried corn bread into it. He sipped the rich, aromatic coffee. "Turkey and dressing, hmm? I hope I'm invited for dinner."

"Of course. It may be a day or two before you can get your car out of my driveway."

"Nuts," he said with an impish grin. "I guess I'll have to bear it."

She chuckled, gazing at him with a glow of happiness. She rubbed her nose with the back of her hand. "Why does your nose always start itching as soon as you get your hands in something messy?"

His eyes were soft with love for her. "Beats me."

Slightly flustered by the frank emotion in his expression, she finished crumbling corn bread, then washed her hands. It was silly, but she felt self-conscious. They had spent the night together, but somehow this morning-after scene in her kitchen was even more intimate. He seemed to feel quite at home there, she noted. She could easily get used to seeing him there.

Picking up her half-full cup of coffee, she turned toward the kitchen window. "Oh, I love snow," she said dreamily.

He set his cup down and, from behind her, folded his arms around her. "I love you," he said.

Sighing, she turned in his arms to face him. "I love you, too," she whispered. There, she'd said it, and it didn't hurt at all. "For weeks I've been telling myself that as long as I kept you at arm's length, I was in no danger of falling in love with you. Last night at the Summerses' house, I realized I loved you already."

His blue eyes moved over her face and his expression grew tender. "Thank you, love. That's the best Christmas present you could ever have given me." He took her face between his hands and kissed her gently.

"I don't know how you put up with me all those weeks. But I'm very glad you did." She pulled away from him a little, smiling up at him. She fingered the diamond pendant at her throat. "Last night you said you wanted to give me more than this. What did you mean?"

"I almost bought an engagement ring," he murmured. "But I was afraid that would be pushing my luck too far." He sought her lips again, then rained warm kisses over her face before stopping to cup her head with his hands and peer deeply into her eyes. "Will you marry me, Nina?"

She gazed at him mistily. "Oh, Jeff."

His face grew solemn. "It doesn't have to be right away. I know it must seem to you that things are happening fast. Just say yes, and then you can take all the time you need to get used to the idea."

"Yes," she breathed. "Oh, yes."

His stunned look made her laugh. Then he drew her back and kissed her with fierce possession.

Sometime later they pulled apart, breathless. "Sweetheart," he murmured, "I don't want to pressure you, but when do you think we could shop for your ring?"

She gave him a radiant smile and traced the curve of his bottom lip with one finger. "How about tomorrow, provided we can get your car out of the driveway?"

Joy lit his eyes. "Tomorrow's great. And when you're ready, we'll talk about a wedding date."

Nina drew a deep breath of pure happiness. "Valentine's Day has a romantic ring to it, don't you think?"

He threw back his head and laughed from pure joy. "Valentine's Day sounds perfect." Then he held her tightly, as though afraid she might get away if he didn't.

She pressed a soft kiss against the side of his neck, then nestled her head in the crook of his shoulder. Her arms tightened around his shoulders. "Penny Summers was right."

His hand smoothed her dark, silken curls. "About what?"

"This," she said, tilting her head back to look at him with adoring eyes, "is the bestest Christmas ever."

*   *   *   *   *

A Note from Jeanne Stephens

I love Christmas! It's my favorite time of year, and I start celebrating early to make this season of love last as long as possible. First, there's shopping for that special gift for each person on my list, which I usually start in October.

As soon as Thanksgiving is past, I decorate the house with cherished items collected over the years—two ceramic elves that belonged to my mother; a quilted wall hanging, which I made myself, for the front door; a ceramic tree with multicolored lights for the dining room buffet; a red basket centerpiece for the table; a giant wreath with red ornaments for over the fireplace.

During the month of December, whenever I have a free hour, I wander through the mall just to savor the sights, sounds and smells of Christmas.

Then, on an early December evening, I put a Christmas music tape on the stereo and my husband hauls down the tree lights and ornaments from the attic. Decorating the tree takes a long time because we're continually stopping to reminisce. So many of the ornaments bring back special memories of the Christmases when our three children were growing up.

Usually a week or two before the big day, we take a trolley tour of the most beautifully decorated homes in our city.

A few days before Christmas, our children begin arriving—our older son from another part of Oklahoma; our younger son and his wife from a Denver suburb; our daughter, son-in-law and two grandchildren from Indiana. Since in-laws have a claim on our children's time, too, we have our big family dinner on Christmas Eve one year and on Christmas Day the next. My sister and her family usually join us.

With several small children involved, opening presents—which we do before dinner—is joyful chaos.

Then we sit down to turkey with all the trimmings.

Every family member has a favorite dessert that he or she always requests for holidays. The strawberry pie, for which I have included the recipe, is my daughter's choice.

From my family to yours, may this season truly be one of joy and love and warm, shared memories of Christmases past and happy anticipation of many more to come.

Jeanne Stephens

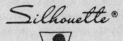

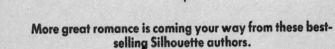

AMERICAN HERO

Every month in Silhouette Intimate Moments, one fabulous, irresistible man is featured as an American Hero. You won't want to miss a single one. Look for them wherever you buy books, or follow the instructions below and have these fantastic men mailed straight to your door!

In September:
MACKENZIE'S MISSION by Linda Howard, IM #445

In October:
BLACK TREE MOON by Kathleen Eagle, IM #451

In November:
A WALK ON THE WILD SIDE by Kathleen Korbel, IM #457

In December:
CHEROKEE THUNDER by Rachel Lee, IM #463

AMERICAN HEROES—men you'll adore, from authors you won't want to miss. Only from Silhouette Intimate Moments.

INTIMATE MOMENTS®
Silhouette®

Silhouette

SPECIAL EDITION

™

It takes a very special man to win

That **SPECIAL** *Woman!*

She's friend, wife, mother—she's you! And beside each Special
Woman stands a wonderfully *special* man. It's a celebration of
our heroines—and the men who become part of their lives.

Look for these exciting titles from Silhouette Special Edition:

January   BUILDING DREAMS by Ginna Gray
Heroine: Tess Benson—a woman faced with single motherhood
who meets her better half.

February   HASTY WEDDING by Debbie Macomber
Heroine: Clare Gilroy—a woman whose one spontaneous act
gives her more than she'd ever bargained for.

March   THE AWAKENING by Patricia Coughlin
Heroine: Sara McAllister—a woman of reserved nature who
winds up in adventure with the man of her dreams.

April   FALLING FOR RACHEL by Nora Roberts
Heroine: Rachel Stanislaski—a woman dedicated to her career
who finds that romance adds spice to life.

Don't miss THAT SPECIAL WOMAN! each month—from some
of your special authors! Only from Silhouette Special Edition!

TSW

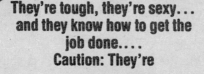

NORA ROBERTS

Love has a language all its own, and for centuries flowers have symbolized love's finest expression. Discover the language of flowers—and love—in this romantic collection of 48 favorite books by bestselling author Nora Roberts.

Two titles are available each month at your favorite retail outlet.

In December, look for:

Partners, **Volume #21**
Sullivan's Woman, **Volume #22**

In January, look for:

Summer Desserts, **Volume #23**
This Magic Moment, **Volume #24**

Collect all 48 titles and become fluent in

THE **LANGUAGE** of **LOVE**

Silhouette ®